Fertility and Other Stories

Sources and Translations Series of The Harriman Institute, Columbia University

The Harriman Institute, Columbia University, sponsors the Sources and Translations Series in the belief that important works of Russian and Soviet history, literature, and criticism, as well as memoirs and other source materials not readily available before (or available only in incomplete or inadequate form), should be made accessible to specialists and a general reading audience—either in skillful English translations or, when the occasions warrant, in the original languages. It is hoped that such publications will contribute to a knowledge and understanding of Russian and Soviet history and culture, as well as to an enhanced respect for the craft of translation.

》》》》》》》》》》 《《《《《《《《《《《《

Vsevolod Ivanov

Fertility
and Other
Stories

TRANSLATED BY VALENTINA G. BROUGHER

AND FRANK J. MILLER

WITH AN INTRODUCTION BY VALENTINA G. BROUGHER

NORTHWESTERN UNIVERSITY PRESS
EVANSTON, ILLINOIS

》》》》》》》》》》》 《《《《《《《《《《《

Northwestern University Press
Evanston, Illinois 60208-4210

Printed in the United States of America

ISBN 0-8101-1547-6

Library of Congress Cataloging-in-Publication Data

Ivanov, Vsevolod Viācheslavovich, 1895–1963.
    [Short stories. English. Selections]
    Fertility and other stories / Vsevolod Ivanov ; translated by Valentina G.
Brougher and Frank J. Miller ; with an introduction by Valentina G. Brougher.
    p. cm. — (Sources and translations series of the Harriman Institute,
Columbia University) (European classics)
    ISBN 0-8101-1547-6
    1. Ivanov, Vsevolod Viācheslavovich, 1895–1963—Translations into English.
I. Brougher, Valentina G. II. Miller, Frank J. III. Title. IV. Series. V.
Series: European classics (Evanston, Ill.)
PG3476.I9A23 1998
891.73'42—dc21   98-9292
                                                         CIP

For Adrienne Rich and Charles E. Merrill

»»» CONTENTS «««

»»» ACKNOWLEDGMENTS «««

In recognizing everyone who played a role in this volume, we must begin by thanking Professor Robert A. Maguire, Columbia University, for sparking Valentina's interest in Ivanov; Professors Joseph L. Conrad and Stephen J. Parker, Department of Slavic Languages and Literatures, the University of Kansas, for encouraging her to research Ivanov and move beyond his official image; and the late Professor Carl R. Proffer, for giving Frank the opportunity to translate *Bronepoezd 14-69* for the *Russian Literature Triquarterly* and to become acquainted with Ivanov's art.

It is with deep respect and affection that we thank the two people who became the volume's "godparents." Professor Elena A. Krasnostchekova shared her knowledge of Ivanov's life and art with unfailing generosity, and constantly encouraged our belief that more of Ivanov's prose deserved to be translated. David P. Harris, emeritus professor of linguistics, Georgetown University, spent long hours examining each story and typing out pages of comments. Many of his suggestions not only improved upon our version but made us more sensitive to the translator's task.

Valentina would like to express her gratitude to Professor Viacheslav Ivanov, University of California at Los Angeles and Moscow University, for clearing up a number of facts about his father's life and for offering his interpretations of a number of stories. The International Conference on the Serapion Brothers (Saint Petersburg, 1995) chaired by Professor Ivanov helped her to place Ivanov's writing in a clearer perspective. Professor Maria Cherniak deserves much credit for bringing together Ivanov scholars at this conference and for providing them with a unique opportunity to learn from each other.

We are particularly grateful to the staff at the Slavic Research Lab at the University of Illinois, especially Helen Sullivan, for helping us find the original versions of Ivanov's stories as well as relevant critical literature; and Jaroslava Zelinsky and Michael Miller of the Library of Congress, for assisting us with a variety of questions, bibliographical as well as linguistic.

We want to acknowledge the contribution of Professor Richard Sheldon, Dartmouth College, who made many helpful suggestions, and of the reviewer for Northwestern University Press, whose input contributed to a number of changes in the volume. We also want to recognize the efforts of our editors, Susan Harris and Ellen Feldman, whose guidance and patience ensured the publication of this volume.

Last, we both would like to thank Jack Brougher for providing many a dinner while we argued about the fine points of translation, and John Lee Brougher for allowing "that man Ivanov" to become part of his childhood.

»»» TRANSLATORS' NOTE «««

In the introduction, literary texts, and notes to the texts we use a system of transliteration which, we hope, will make personal names, place names, and special vocabulary more accessible to the average reader. In the notes to the introduction, the chronology of Ivanov's life, and the bibliography, we adhere to the Library of Congress system, with the specialist in mind.

»»» INTRODUCTION «««

The name of Vsevolod Ivanov is usually automatically associated with a work published in the first years of Soviet rule, *Armored Train 14-69* (Bronepoezd 14-69), which belongs to a cycle of short stories, novellas, and tales (*povesti*) about the Red struggle for power in Siberia, the Steppe (today's Kazakhstan), and Altai regions. Ivanov was one of the first young writers to come out of the Revolution and to use his generous raw talent to capture recent events of immediate relevance in a style resonating with the revolutionary spirit of the times.

Praised in 1922–23 as one of the most talented and promising young writers to come out of the Revolution, by the end of the decade, Ivanov, like many talented fellow writers, found himself increasingly under attack for being out of step with his society, both artistically and ideologically, and for not living up to his potential. He was subjected to barrages of criticism in the late 1920s and early 1930s but managed to remain a Soviet author. His short stories, plays, and novels continued to be published and republished in the Soviet Union—often after being subjected to "editorial" changes as well as rewriting by Ivanov himself—until his death from cancer in 1963. The eight-volume edition of Ivanov's work published in 1973–77 shows he was a prolific writer, and does not even include two major novels and some intriguing unfinished work. However, it was generally the partisan cycle of stories and novellas, especially

Armored Train 14-69 (as well as a 1927 play based on that novella), that continued to be cited by Soviet and Western critics in legitimizing Ivanov's place in the development of postrevolutionary Russian literature. The fact that *Armored Train 14-69, The Adventures of a Fakir* (Pokhozhdeniya fakira, 1934–35),[1] and five of his short stories from the early 1920s were the only works available in English translation[2] may have contributed to the somewhat limited, impoverished perception in the West of Ivanov's abilities and range as a writer.

The recent publication of Ivanov's two novels, *Y* and *The Kremlin* (Kreml),[3] and the republication of some of his best stories from the 1920s in several different editions[4] suggests that a reevaluation of Ivanov's contribution to Soviet literature is long overdue.[5]

This volume brings together some of Ivanov's finest prose from the 1920s and early 1930s, prose that contributed to his reputation as a talented promising writer, but also brought him a large measure of infamy. All but two of the stories appear in English translation for the first time. "The Child" (Dityo) and "Empty Arapia" (Polaya Arapiya), prime examples of Ivanov's talent at the beginning of the 1920s, are included in the present volume for the convenience of the reader. The exclusion of another well-known story, "How Burial Mounds Are Made" (Kak sozdayutsya kurgany), also available in translation, was dictated by our feeling that both "Empty Arapia" and *The Return of the Buddha* (Vozvrashchenie Buddy) also treat the themes of death and famine during the Civil War, but perhaps with greater artistry. Considerations of space led to the exclusion of other stories from the 1920s that deserve to be translated, for example, "The Gardener of the Emir of Bukhara" (Sadovnik emira Bukharskogo).

Not without some hesitation and regret, a decision was also made not to include any short stories from the "fantastic cycle," which Ivanov began writing during World War II and which appeared (with one exception) only posthumously. They are not without literary merit, particularly given the time in which they were written, but they do not match the artistic power and complexity of his best prose in the 1920s.

Ivanov's Life and Art

Ivanov was born in 1895[6] in the village of Lebiazhe in the Semipalatinsk oblast in what is today Kazakhstan, the son of a self-educated village schoolteacher and a Kazakh woman. He had very little formal schooling, and like Maksim Gorky—who would become an early supporter as well as a lifelong friend—he considered his wanderings through the countless towns and villages of Siberia as his school and "universities." He often joked that he inherited his wanderlust from his father, who never could stay in any one place too long. In his various jobs as an apprentice to a tradesman, sword swallower, magician, fakir, poet, and playwright, he crisscrossed prerevolutionary Siberia in search of adventure, the exotic, and the mysterious.

Twice he attempted to reach India, the mystical land of fakirs and yoga masters that often occupied a central place in his voracious reading on things occult. He also witnessed the Revolution and the Civil War in his native Siberia from a "double" vantage point: he worked as a typesetter for the White general Kolchak and served in the Red Guard (Krasnaya Gvardiya), finding himself in one camp or the other more as the result of chance and circumstance than conscious choice.[7] He even came close to being shot by the Reds, who evidently confused him with Vsevolod N. Ivanov, a well-known White journalist.[8]

Ivanov came to Petrograd in 1921 at the invitation of Gorky, who had included Ivanov's short stories in a volume of prose he edited, *Anthology of Proletarian Writers* (Sbornik proletarskikh pisatelei, 1918). After several months of working for the Proletcult—an organization devoted to fostering a distinct proletarian literature and culture—Ivanov, with help from Gorky and Viktor Shklovsky, settled in the House of the Arts (Dom iskusstv). There he became identified with the Serapion Brothers, a small circle of writers and critics who believed in the nonregimentation of literature and in its enduring "organic" quality. The evenings of literary readings spent with such fellow Serapions as Mikhail Zoshchenko, Konstantin Fedin, Mikhail Slonimsky, Lev Lunts, Yelena Polonskaya, Nikolay Nikitin, and the mentors they attracted, such as Shklovsky and Yevgeni Zamyatin, exposed the young Ivanov to others' ideas about the craft of writing and stimulated a less slapdash attitude toward his own writing.

But Ivanov brought his own measure of uniqueness to those gatherings as well. From descriptions in a number of reminiscences by his contemporaries, Ivanov's very appearance had something of the unexpected and exotic. For Slonimsky, the writer's eyes, round face, and stockiness, even the way he listened and smiled, suggested a resemblance to an "Asiatic idol, perhaps even Buddha."[9] Yelizaveta Polonskaya recalled the striking, unusual impression Ivanov made in the knee-length coat he fashioned for himself out of white bearskin.[10]

Tellingly, for the Serapions Ivanov became "our Siberian mammoth," a descriptive phrase first applied by Zoshchenko and quickly adopted by others because it seemed so appropriate: it evoked the unknown, distant lands from which Ivanov had arrived in the capital, and the element of the exotic and the unexpected that Ivanov brought to the Saint Petersburg literary scene. It also suggested the tremendous, almost primal, talent that was Ivanov's. Slonimsky reported how one evening Ivanov absolutely captivated those present when he started to read one of his stories, which opened with the simple yet powerful first sentence: "Palm trees don't grow in Siberia" (Palma v Sibiri ne voditsya).[11]

Ivanov's personal experiences in Siberia and Central Asia during the Revolution and the Civil War, refracted against a childhood and youth spent wandering through that vast expanse and nourishing his imagination on such Romantic writers as Edgar Allan Poe and Jules Verne, found a reflection in his writing. Critics singled out various aspects of his art for praise in the first half of the 1920s: the characterization of peasants-turned-partisans as strong, energetic men, fighting for the land they believed others to be taking away from them, land to which they were mystically bound with an elemental need; the great attention to ethnographic detail and the striking palette of colors employed to evoke the wild, mystical beauty of the steppes and forests, of distant and exotic Siberia; the expressive power of his prose, be it in capturing the particular flavor of peasant speech or evoking the mood in man and landscape; and the use of lyricism and unusual metaphors and imagery.

If some perceived a sense of measure sometimes lacking in his search for new narrative strategies and fresh figures of speech as well as in the use of dialectical turns of speech, Ivanov was universally acclaimed as a talent to be watched and nurtured. Aleksandr Voronsky, the moderate Marxist critic and influential editor of the "thick" journal *Red Virgin Soil* (Krasnaya nov)—who was among the first to draw the attention of the critical world to Ivanov's special talents both by publishing his work in his journal and writing a number of enthusiastic articles about his prose—pointed to Ivanov's stories as the kind of literature that responded to the call for immediacy and relevance and reflected "the spirit of the times."

In the second half of the 1920s Ivanov began to worry his supporters and to distress the growing number of critics who expected literature to educate the masses in the spirit of socialism and reflect the utilitarian rhetoric of the Soviet age of reason. When Ivanov took some stories, which had already appeared separately—"The Field" (Pole, 1925), "Night" (Noch, 1926), "The Life of Smokotinin" (Zhizn Smokotinina, 1926), and "Fertility" (Plodorodie, 1926)—and, with several other prose works, republished them under the intriguing title of *Mystery of Mysteries* (Tainoe tainykh, 1927), he became a center of controversy and polemics. Scattered in different publications, these stories had not drawn as much attention to Ivanov's "dangerous tendencies" as they did now concentrated in one volume. The more moderate critics who valued the talents of the "fellow travelers" saw much to praise, although they did express reservations about certain aspects of Ivanov's prose; the critics of the Russian Association of Proletarian Writers (RAPP) and the journal *On Literary Guard* (Na literaturnom postu) found, in general, only major flaws and "shortcomings."

Placing Ivanov's work in a positive perspective, A. Z. Lezhnev viewed *Mystery of Mysteries* as evidence that Ivanov was becoming a "new and different" writer by trying to describe his characters "from within" rather than "from without," and by moving away from the "ornamental splendor" and excesses of his earlier prose.[12] Voronsky shared Lezhnev's belief that Ivanov's talent was reaching a new level of maturity and that his prose now had a new deceptive simplicity; he felt, however, that as powerful as Ivanov's depiction of the instinctive, biological life of his heroes was, the necessary link between "the individual and the social" was missing.[13] Vladislav Yevgenev-Maksimov emphasized the "deep, eternal questions" that Ivanov's prose tackled as the writer explored the "mysteries" of human behavior, although the critic voiced regret that the "the stream of optimism and joy of life" that marked Ivanov's earlier prose was now significantly weaker.[14] And Solomon Pakentreiger drew attention to Ivanov as a writer endowed with a philosophical understanding and feeling for life.[15]

In great contrast, Leopold Averbakh, the critic and theorist who played a leading role in defining the position of the RAPP on major issues, argued that Ivanov's heroes were "asocial" and "antisocial," making his work "less and less in keeping with the times." He called for an outright fight against the direction Ivanov's prose had taken.[16] Another RAPP critic, I. S. Grossman-Roshchin, derisively dismissed Ivanov's new volume, writing that if in the eyes of some critics the writer was contemplating "cosmic problems" from artistic heights, in his judgment Ivanov's vantage point was that of a "sepulchral mound." The "substratum" of Ivanov's creativity, according to Grossman-Roshchin, was "mania and delirium."[17]

In general, the RAPP critics accused Ivanov of being a blind follower of Bergson and Freud, and of ignoring the new Soviet reality by choosing the backdrop of the "eternal" Russian village, with only an occasional seeding of detail from Soviet political and social life, ironically illuminated at that. They vehemently objected to Ivanov's shift in focus from strong peasant figures of the Civil War years—his heroes in the *Partisan Tales,* for whom the "holy of holies" was the land—to peasant figures held in the grip of "dark" forces and elemental, biological needs they were powerless to resist. Moreover, they found the dark violence that played a key part in the lives of these "creatures" deeply disturbing.

It is important to bear in mind the criticism that greeted the publication of *Mystery of Mysteries* in 1927 because it marked a watershed in Ivanov's development as a Soviet writer. Those who felt that Ivanov brought a new measure of artistic maturity, philosophical depth, and psychological complexity to Soviet literature soon found their voices drowned out by the often primitive pronouncements of the RAPP camp. Of particular relevance to Ivanov's standing as a Soviet writer is that the volume drew the attention of the increasingly more powerful and vocal critics of the RAPP to Ivanov's creativity and artistic vision ten years after the Revolution, and they found it deeply flawed. The "bard and poet of the Red partisan movement" in Siberia and Central Asia was now perceived as a writer with a "dangerously anti-Soviet" and "neo-bourgeois" vision of life. He was put on notice to change his ways. As a result, Ivanov's writing, beginning in 1927, was subjected to greater scrutiny than ever.

For a variety of reasons, the negative comments and reproaches could not but have some influence on Ivanov's development as a writer. Writing was a calling for Ivanov; it satisfied an innate need, and he could not imagine his life without it. Recognized by 1927 as a prominent member of the Moscow literary establishment (he had moved to Moscow in 1924), he also enjoyed the possibilities his writing gave him, and his family, to lead a more normal life and to indulge in his never-ending passion for travel. Moreover, as he would admit later in life, the partisan cycle of stories and tales had brought him a taste of fame, which, once experienced, he would continue to crave the rest of his life.

Like many of his fellow writers, Ivanov learned to exercise a degree of self-censorship and to search for themes and a style that were less controversial. He accepted the cuts and changes his "editors" demanded for publication—whether they involved a new work or a new edition of his earlier stories and novellas—with a mixture of bitter anger and resignation. According to his widow, Tamara Ivanova, he took the philosophical view that later generations would figure out "what was what" by examining his original versions.[18]

If a work was rejected, as was the case with his two "cherished creations," *The Kremlin* and *Y*, he put it away in "the drawer," returning to it as the spirit moved him. In moments of extreme unhappiness and despair, he even destroyed some "offending" manuscripts. Needless to say, we can only speculate about the kind of writing Ivanov could have produced had his talent been allowed to develop and mature without the constraints of publishing in the Soviet Union in the late 1920s and subsequent decades. That there existed real tension between his desire "to be in tune with the times" (byt sozvuchnym epokhe)[19] as a Soviet writer and the demands his own talent and vision placed on his writing is evident in the prose Ivanov wrote after *Mystery of Mysteries,* in such stories as "The Service" (Serviz, 1927), "The Mansion" (Osobnyak, 1928), and "Tannery Owner M. D. Lobanov" (Kozhevenny zavodchik M. D. Lobanov, 1929).

In the first half of the 1930s Ivanov's long semi-autobiographical novel of his youth in prerevolutionary Siberia, *The Adventures of a Fakir,* Part 1, brought him praise from various quarters. The newspaper *Pravda* (4 November 1934) judged it an "artistic success"; Gorky wrote to Ivanov that he read it "ravenously" and felt that every page "burned with . . . genuine sincerity . . . spiritual boldness and clarity."[20] N. N. Aseev's opinion—that this was a work which would move Russian literature into European or world literature[21]—proved correct, to some extent; a major portion appeared in English translation in 1935. But Parts 2 and 3 evoked generally negative criticism, and Ivanov found himself accused of following "the canons of formalism"—of lavishing too much attention on the structural and stylistic aspects of the work and failing to provide socialist realist illumination for the social aspect.

Perhaps in response to this latest stream of criticism and his innate need to be relevant to his society by continuing to write, he produced *Parkhomenko* (1938), about a Civil War hero by the same name. The novel assured the critics that Ivanov had heeded the advice offered to him with increasing frequency and insistence from

1927 on. Needless to say, that he was so willing to subscribe to the socialist realist standards of the day and to buttress Stalin's cult of personality—one much-respected scholar of Soviet literature characterized *Parkhomenko* as a work "conventional in form and neatly tailored to the Party line"[22]—had a negative impact on his reputation in the West.

But if Ivanov did not become "a master of the genre of silence," as Babel jokingly referred to his inability to get his own work published, or if he did not emigrate to the West as Yevgeni Zamyatin had done, he also did not abandon writing prose that was often satirical and in the style of fantastic realism, and continued to experiment with form and structure. Unfortunately, he was forced to relegate that writing to "the drawer." We know today, particularly with the publication of *Y* and *The Kremlin* in the 1980s, that his interest in philosophy, religion, history, mythology, psychology, and the occult in general continued to nourish his artistic imagination (his personal library included some twelve thousand books, representing various fields of learning; unfortunately, part of this vast library was lost in a fire at his dacha in Peredelkino during World War II).

Writing for a well-read audience who could accept his intellectual challenge to decode the multitude of allusions and references to human cultural heritage seeded throughout the novels, Ivanov attempted to write long prose works that captured the essence of the era in which he lived. As *Y* shows, he experimented with narrative planes and shifting tonality on a much more complex scale than is evident in his early short stories and novellas, and he sought to redefine linguistically—through word, image, and reference—the shape of time and space. *Y*, as well as *The Kremlin*, permitted him to continue his philosophical dialogue with the reader about the nature of human reality and to explore the illusional and irrational components of that reality. The central episode from *Y*, included in this volume, is offered as a small measure of the "private," as opposed to the "public," Ivanov at the end of the 1920s and beginning of the 1930s.

Commentary on Stories in This Volume

The opening pages of "Empty Arapia" provide good evidence why in the early 1920s Ivanov was sometimes described as a "literaturny risovalshchik," a phrase that can be translated approximately as "an artist who draws pictures by using the medium of literature." As Ivanov selects details and colors to convey the devastating effects of a drought on the world of nature and man within it, he looks to traditional impressionistic art and yet seeks to be modern by injecting something of the fantastic and the surrealistic. Man and the world of nature are inextricably bound, as the terms normally used to describe human activities and the human condition are now applied to the world of nature, and vice versa.

This angle on reality, captured in a rhythmic and terse style that also contributes to the poetic richness of such stories as "The Child," produces powerfully evocative writing. Preferring to work with suggestion and associative imagery, a method that would underlie his best stories in the first half of the 1920s, Ivanov allows ambiguity to veil a number of key moments in the story. He also shows an appreciation for the power of naturalistic details to assault the reader's sensibilities but manages to evoke the horror of famine without succumbing to the melodramatic, much like fellow writer and critic Shklovsky, in his sketch of the Civil War famine ("The Knight's Move" [Khod konya]).

"The Child," published in 1922, was singled out for praise by such diverse personalities as the poet Sergei Esenin and the writer-critic Shklovsky. It contributed to Ivanov's early reputation as "the bard of the partisan movement." The story evidences Ivanov's search for a prose style that reflects the ferment, energy, and uncertainty of the revolutionary years. His extensive use of ornamentalism and lyricism, and his skill in exploiting shifts in tone, register, and point of view, impart a poetic dynamic quality to his writing.

The unique talent Ivanov brings to his story about peasants–turned–Red partisans is evident from the artistic originality of the brief opening paragraph. Although an exploration of the relationship between man and nature is not a new theme, Ivanov's choice of perspective and imagery to establish a hostile, adversarial quality to the interconnectedness between the human and natural domains is bold and fresh. Mongolia is a land where "the rock is a beast, the water is a beast," and "even a butterfly . . . schemes to sting."

But the first paragraph also encapsulates metaphorically the basic "truths" on which the architectonics of Ivanov's narrative rest. The peasants, who hide in a gully and shoot two White officers, become a "rock" that kills like a "beast." And Afanasy Petrovich, the lachrymose childlike paymaster of the partisan detachment, turns out to be a "butterfly" that "stings." It is he who carries out Sergey Selivanov's reluctant order: he puts "the Kirghiz creature" into a sack and takes it out into the steppe to die.

It is noteworthy that Ivanov roots the motivation for the peasants' behavior in the environment, in the alien landscape of Mongolia, "a wild and joyless beast." The world of nature and of man become closely bound through associative imagery. Thus the coarse, sparse grasses, scorched by the sun, have their parallel in the human world: the hearts and souls of the peasants have also become "scorched" and changed. Descriptions of Mongolia—with its rocks, sands, and yurts of the Kirghiz tribesmen whose hearts are "worthless"—heighten and bring into relief the peasants' own feelings of weariness, boredom, and displacement. They yearn for what they have been forced to leave behind: the Irtysh River area, their fields, cattle, women, and children.

The elemental bond the peasants-turned-partisans feel with their native land—suggested briefly by a question or two they raise about hay-making and droughts back home—will form a recurring theme in many of Ivanov's stories in the 1920s. And the biological need for sex—which the peasants are powerless to resist and which they satisfy by "taking" Kirghiz women—will constitute an important part of Ivanov's portrayal of peasant life and psychology in subsequent years.

The Return of the Buddha (Vozvrashchenie Buddy) is a novella which appeared first in Berlin in 1923. It was republished several times in the Soviet Union in the second half of the 1920s, at a time when the Soviet Union was still courting the non-Orthodox nationalities of Mongolia, Tibet, and Central Asia.[23] This work received little critical attention, although those who noted its publication praised its focus on human psychology. Ivanov himself felt that the work represented a transitional stage in his development from the partisan cycle of works to the prose he would select for *Mystery of Mysteries*. Like "Empty Arapia," *The Return of the Buddha* conveys the dehumanizing effects of famine, although famine is presented not from a peasant perspective but from that of an intellectual, a professor and specialist in world literature. The work also shows Ivanov's serious interest in Eastern mysticism and his ability to interweave, with great subtlety, the basic premises of Buddhism into an artistic evocation of "a slice" of Civil War life.[24]

The work opens with the rituals Professor Safonov has established for himself in trying to meet his elemental physical needs for food and warmth. The rest of the story traces the roles which both the *gyghen*[25] Dava-Dorchzhi and the statue of the Buddha play in forcing the professor to reorder his life. It is, in fact, the story of the evolution of Professor Safonov from a being who treats the self as the center of life to a man who slowly, under various influences, refocuses his energy and redirects it outward toward others.

Underlying the philosophical thrust of the story—that the tension between man's physical and spiritual needs shapes his understanding of the nature of reality and, consequently, his responses to it—is the whole question of the role of individual human will. The latter is, of course, central to Eastern mysticism and to the philosophy of such men as Nietszche, whose ideas may have reached Ivanov not only through his interest in philosophy but through such writers as Dostoevsky. *The Return of the Buddha* represents an intricate study of motivation and human will as well as a cautious exploration of the existence of occult forces that may affect human behavior but are not immediately accessible to human reason.

The sociopolitical dimension to Ivanov's evocation of the Civil War years in *The Return of the Buddha* is especially noteworthy because it is here that we get glimpses of the deft touch with irony and satire that will mark—in much stronger tones and hues—a number of works written several years later, such as "The Mansion." There are a number of politically colored moments in the novella edged in irony and mocking humor—sketches of various Party men and Red Army soldiers, and references to Lenin and Lunacharsky.

One scene in particular deserves a few words. It involves the Deputy Commissar for Nationalities, a Georgian named Tsviladze. He speaks in a "guttural voice," stands erect, and is "wise for his years." As he delivers a monologue marking the beginning of the "Buddha mission," he touches upon relations between different nationalities, the issue of religion and the masses, and the Red-White struggle. However, his monologue quickly grows in absurdity on various levels the more he speaks and the more he tries to incorporate the rhetoric, and catch phrases, of the day. Thus what we get is a sketch of a man puffed up with self-importance and the power his position affords him.

It may well be the first satiric portrait of Stalin in Russian literature, predating Pilnyak's Number One in "Tale of the Unextinguished Moon" (Povest nepogashennoi luny, 1926). That possibility is buttressed by the fact that the two novels which never appeared during Ivanov's lifetime, *The Kremlin* and *Y*, contain, respectively, allusions to Stalin as the Antichrist of the coming apocalypse and as an arrogant rooster with hypnotic occult powers over the masses.[26]

As noted earlier, "The Field," "The Life of Smokotinin," "Night," and "Fertility" appeared in Ivanov's 1927 "slim volume of prose," *Mystery of Mysteries*. The latter was one of the two books (the other being *The Adventures of a Fakir*) in which he took great pride and which he felt would endure the judgment of time.[27] The focus these stories have in common is suggested by the very title under which they, and a number of other works, were brought together. Inspiration for this mystically loaded title may have come from one of the Old Russian magic books, *Tainaya tainykh*, republished by M. N. Speransky in Saint Petersburg in 1908.[28] Interestingly enough, this is the book the semi-autobiographical narrator in *The Adventures of a Fakir* tries to find in his search for books on the occult.

It can be argued that the prose Ivanov selected for this volume represented his own mystical "alchemical" manuscript, except that instead of "the magical and medical properties of precious stones" or the "divinatory practices of physiognomy" found in the "Old Russian version of the pseudo-Aristotelian Secretum secretorum,"[29] the stories in *Mystery of Mysteries* represented literary studies of the peasant mind and soul, of the "mysteries" that lie hidden within. Voronsky observed that the volume contained what was largely absent from contemporary Soviet literature: "philosophy translated into a language of images."[30] Indeed, at an international conference devoted to the Serapion Brothers (Saint Petersburg, 1995), there was general agreement that no other work in Ivanov's oeuvre matches the originality, artistic power, and psychological depth he brought to his stories in *Mystery of Mysteries*.

A strong appreciation for the intuitive, the irrational, and the subconscious in people's response to the world around them informs the philosophical core of each of these stories. It may be that Ivanov's interest in Freud, such philosophers as Bergson, and such writers as Gogol, Dostoevsky, and Khlebnikov, influenced his own artistic vision. But the particular quality of life in prerevolutionary Siberia, where Ivanov spent his formative years, also played a vital part in molding his attitude toward human reality.

Siberia at the turn of the century was a land where Orthodoxy and shamanism existed side by side; this was a land where folk beliefs in witches, spirits, and various occult forces—both malevolent and beneficent—were further nourished by the interest in spiritualism and all things occult that swept through Europe in the nineteenth century and seized the imagination of the Russians with particular force at the beginning of the twentieth century.[31] As *The Adventures of a Fakir* reveals, young Ivanov became intrigued with the power of hypnosis and suggestion, from its role in folk beliefs and superstitions to the art of a fakir and the practices of a yoga master. It is this power that Ivanov explores with uncommon artistic sensibility and complexity in the four stories from *Mystery of Mysteries* included in this anthology.

In "The Field" and "Fertility," hypnotism is an occult component of the shamanistic power of nature over man. Ivanov takes the pantheistic view that man is a creature whose responses are subject to universal elemental forces he is powerless to resist, once they have been released. "The Field" portrays Milekhin's physical and emotional withdrawal from the army barracks and his ever stronger closeness to the land, an affection charged with almost sexual overtones. The story culminates in a powerful image of a peasant and army deserter who heeds the more powerful call of the land in springtime and finds bliss standing in his tilled fields.

In "Fertility," Martyn's responses to the world around him also reveal an emotional, affectionate, and sensuous bond with nature, reminding us of the lyrical power of a number of Ivanov's earlier stories and tales from the "partisan" cycle. Ivanov captures the look, feel, smell, sound, and even taste of the landscape (the grasses, grains) by showing Martyn responding to the natural world with all of his senses. And it is Martyn's bond with nature that makes him seem a better and nobler being, something more than the idle good-for-nothing his wife and fellow villagers believe him to be.

But just like the partisans in "The Child," whose hearts become as "scorched" as the scorched Mongolian sands around them, so Martyn, too, pays a price for his mystical bond with the world of nature. He rapes the wife of a fellow villager, whose round figure and thick braids have "bewitched" him at a time when he has found himself "bewitched" by the atmosphere of fertility that rules the world of nature at harvest time. Although the motivation for the rape can also be traced to a complex web of feelings of inadequacy on Martyn's part, particularly his failure to receive the recognition he believed was due him for identifying the source of the floodwaters, it is the hypnotic effect of nature that is at the root of his problems and dooms him to end his life violently.

"The Life of Smokotinin" also reflects Ivanov's interest in the power of hypnosis and suggestion, but from the perspective of folk beliefs and superstitions and the role the latter play in village mentality. Constructing his story on an intricate system of associative images and moments—a technique that in the 1920s the critic A. Z. Lezhnev particularly valued and understood—Ivanov traces the course of the life of one young villager, Timofey, from his silent infatuation with the widow Katerina to his violent death at the hands of the man he had contracted to kill. The kindling that Timofey had forced Katerina to drop at his work site, the kindling that figures in the curse he attributes to Katerina, and the kindling that is scattered in the hut as his coffin is being prepared for him resonate against one another, suggesting that both the spoken word and the unspoken word (a mere gesture, a thought) wield incredible power over the course of human life. Once Timofey's subconscious has accepted the idea that Katerina has "given him an illness," releasing a love curse against him, he moves through life like a somnambulist, without a will of his own.

"Night," a psychological portrait of a village fellow, focuses on the interplay between the conscious and the subconscious, the rational and the irrational, to reveal the complexity of human motivation and behavior. The tension between Afonka's low self-esteem and his reactions to his brother's death, particularly his self-suggestion that Glafira has closed herself off to happiness with any other man, are refracted against his parents' insistence that he marry his brother's widow for the dowry.

The sexually nuanced atmosphere of the wedding celebration and night, the "emptiness" that Afonka notes in Glafira's eyes, and the presence of an old beggar woman on the coal car next to him—whose gesture of holding on to his coat pocket as they struggle for space resurrects an association with a sexual encounter that had lain buried deep within his memory—all intersect in his subconscious. As the irony of his situation, of what fate has put in his path, begins to surface from his subconscious to the conscious, Afonka responds to this bitter realization by hitting the old beggar woman and killing her.

In "Night" the narrator's tone, cadence, and phrasing suggest a man who understands Afonka's world well because he is no stranger to village life himself. This particular aspect of Ivanov's writing provides an excellent example of the *skaz* technique[32] that Ivanov—like his contemporaries Babel and Zoshchenko—often employed in his prose of the 1920s to great effect. The *skaz,* combined with descriptions of village wedding traditions and peasant life in general, makes Ivanov's perspective on village family life seem particularly honest, truthful, and perceptive. That this peasant life continues in the "darker" tradition of nineteenth-century literature—bringing to mind both Chekhov and Bunin—helps to explain why many critics of the day felt that Ivanov was out of step philosophically with a society touting positive change on all fronts.

Written in 1927–29, "The Dinner Service," "The Mansion," and "Tannery Owner M. D. Lobanov" reveal a shift in Ivanov's choice of heroes, thematics, and style. These stories suggest that Ivanov was making efforts to evolve into the more socially conscious and responsible Soviet writer that the RAPP critics kept insisting he become. That he was not always "successful" is clear from the outrage that "The Mansion" provoked.

"The Dinner Service" focuses on the life of a woman who had spent some seventy years serving others. Seconds before her death, Katerina Alekseevna smashes two plates from an old dinner service that it had been her duty to guard against breakage, even as the world around her "broke" ("wars, bank failures, and even revolutions"), a gesture powerful in its symbolism and finality. "Tannery Owner M. D. Lobanov" is a story about a rich but unhappy man who loses his wealth, finds a new, more meaningful life under Soviet rule, and dies during a business trip to Paris for the Soviet state, after discovering, ironically, that a prerevolutionary investment has made him a rich man again.

Stylistically, the portraits of both Katerina Alekseevna and M. D. Lobanov reveal Ivanov moving away from anchoring his stories on a complex system of associative images, as in "The Life of Smokotinin" and "Night," and relying instead on the telling detail, a device favored by such writers as Tolstoy, Chekhov, and Bunin. The tummies on the cherubs carved into the heavy dark oak sideboard shine with dark layers of oil, suggesting the long years of care that Katerina Alekseevna lavished on them; and the roses on the dinner service are now old and faded with age, as is the woman who looked after the dishes for decades. Similarly, Lobanov's negative psychological state in Paris is captured in a series of telling details, from his reduction of the Arc de Triomphe to nothing more than a "horseshoe" to all Parisian neckties being "tasteless rags."

Ivanov's ability to offer convincing psychological portraits of his characters does not rest on telling details alone. In the case of Katerina Alekseevna, Ivanov skillfully delineates her portrait by keeping the tension between her inner world and the world in which she moves constantly in the reader's field of vision. Katerina Alekseevna's old age, frailty, and irritability stand in striking juxtaposition to the young girl assigned to help her, and to the outdoor summer market that beckons to the latter, a place filled with sun, human voices, bold colors, and intoxicating smells. In the case of M. D. Lobanov, Ivanov uses a black-white palette to capture his initial reactions to Parisian life, and then adds illusive gray colors to the portrait after Lobanov's newfound fortune makes the world no longer seem "so clear and simple as it had been recently." The result is a convincing portrayal of a man who finds himself confronted with unexpected new choices.

Ivanov's psychological portrait of Lobanov was not necessarily appreciated. The journal *On Literary Guard* called the publication of "Tannery Owner M. D. Lobanov" in the pages of the newspaper *Izvestiya* a "mistake," referring to it as an "artistic work which represented a sermon on a class world."[33]

In "The Mansion," life for Ye. S. Chizhov consists of opportunities to be seized, profits to be made, and desires to be satisfied.

There is something reptilian about the moral vacuum in which he operates and the purposeful, unyielding way he seeks to satisfy his instinctive, elemental needs, be they for sex, food, or material goods. Above all, he is a survivor, a Darwinian creature able to adapt to whatever regime is in power. From exploiting his customers and those around him, like the bookbinder's wife, before the Revolution, Chizhov turns to exploiting the Soviet system for his own gain. Within a few years of Soviet rule, he learns that "it [is] possible to dupe this power just as easily as he had previously duped state institutions or merchants." He becomes adept at writing denunciations, be it in an attempt to eliminate the grand duke, whose mansion he covets, or a fellow he perceives as a rival for the affections of his intended, Manichka Yepich. Ironically, he postures as one of the poor, shedding a tear about his childhood while working on one of his denunciations.

The end of the story depicts Chizhov living his dream: he has a view of the square from the house he had coveted, upholstered silk furniture, raspberry preserves with tea, and "faithful" Manichka by his side. Chizhov's acquisitive nature, philistine tastes, vacuous moral nature, and even his illusions about Manichka Yepich suggest a Gogolian ancestry. Gogol's heroes, however, are forced to confront and dispel their illusions, but Chizhov is allowed to keep his version of reality. Even the "dark rust [of the road] resembled silk, so essential for furniture and for happiness!"

It is not surprising that "The Mansion" was perceived as a literary work hostile to the regime, and evoked cries that Ivanov was dangerously cynical and negative about the kind of society the Bolshevik Revolution was engendering. One critic wrote that in Chizhov, Ivanov had provided a portrait of "a little man with a thrifty soul, making a mockery of the Revolution."[34] Obviously, for the RAPP critics, Ivanov's ironic, satirical portrait of a bourgeois, the new Soviet model or version, was a damning comment on the foundations of a system that laid claim to having eliminated injustice and the exploitation of one human being by another.

The short story "The Drummers and the Magician Mattsukami" (Barabanshchiki i fokusnik Mattsukami, 1929) provides a window on the experimentation with form and content that was part of Ivanov's life even as he continued to produce stories, such as "The Dinner Service," in a more traditional realist mode reminiscent of Chekhov and Bunin. Ivanov taps into his broad knowledge of fakirism, shamanism, and folk-story art to produce his own modern fairy tale. Like a number of his contemporaries—Bulgakov, Platonov, and Zoshchenko, to name only three—Ivanov also exploits irony and satire to illuminate and expose some fundamental features of contemporary Soviet life.

Ivanov's interest in shamanism and the art of fakirs and dervishes is reflected in the image of the beggar—who tells the story of the old man and his daughter—and in the beggar's hypnotic effect on the first-person narrator. The beggar's story of Varvara and her father involves such folk elements as a beautiful, talented, and obedient daughter whose hand in marriage is sought by different suitors, magic and bewitchment as various transformations and changes take place, and the travels of a father in search of his lost daughter.

The text incorporates a number of features that can be read as encapsulations of the directions in which Soviet life and society was evolving. The bandits worry not only about their own "happiness" but about everyone else's (the fundamental philosophical thrust of Soviet ideology). In his wanderings through the various towns and villages, the father finds three Varvaras: one Varvara is "galloping around the meadow" with "her skirt pulled up around her waist, her eyes crazed, her mane trimmed" (new mores and changed fashions); another Varvara has "gotten obese and big breasted," and has swollen eyes—she beats her husband and has turned back into a sow (family life has not gotten better but more primitive and dark);

and the third Varvara, like the second one, lives in a filthy house and has a record for writing denunciations (the moral decay of society and the perversion of social conscience). The end impression is that Ivanov uses the vehicle of a modern fairy tale—colored with irony and laughter—not only to question the quality of the new life but to deride, and lament, some of its already visible results. As might be expected, Ivanov was accused of "serious ideological errors" in "The Drummers and the Magician Mattsukami," thereby joining the ranks of such writers as Fedin, Bulgakov, Zamyatin, and Pilnyak, who were also under attack for their writing in 1929.

The last piece of prose included in this anthology is an excerpt from Ivanov's experimental satirical novel *Y*, written in 1929–32. Only several excerpts appeared in print in the early 1930s. The intriguingly minimalist title should be read both as a letter of the Russian alphabet and as the Russian interjection "y" (that is to say as "u" in English transliteration and as "oo" in phonetic transcription), as well as the letter *y* in the Latin alphabet (as in *x, y, z*). A close examination of the novel reveals that Ivanov intended both the visual and aural power of "y" to generate a whole web of emotions, allusions, and suggestions at different levels of the text. Although the novel was published in the Soviet Union in 1988, it evoked little critical interest, perhaps because Ivanov was perceived as an orthodox writer, the author of the Soviet classic *Armored Train 14-69*.

Y suggests that Ivanov, living in the Soviet age of reason, when various strategies were being touted for changing and ordering life along rational lines, nonetheless never abandoned his interest in world mythology and in the role of illusion, suggestion, and hypnotism in human perception of reality. Drawn to the writings of Gogol and Dostoevsky, and intrigued by the linguistic-literary theories of such contemporaries as Khlebnikov, Ivanov continued to search for that newness and freshness of artistic vision that marked his early attempts to capture Civil War reality.

The work taxes a reader who is not acquainted with Soviet reality of the 1920s—the housing shortage, various theories about human psychology, labor productivity and the work ethic, the underground economy with the end of NEP in 1928, trials of "saboteurs," new mass holidays and celebrations, and the political power in place, Stalin. There are numerous references to nineteenth- and twentieth-century writers, whole pages imitating the style of Gogol and Dostoevsky, polemics with Ivanov's fellow writers (Viktor Shklovsky, Leonid Leonov) and with the RAPP critics.

This multifaceted novel is seeded with references not only to members of the literary establishment but to major philosophers (Plato, Aristotle, Pythagoras, Descartes, Nietzsche, Schopenhauer, Kierkegaard, Marx, Bergson, et al.), mathematicians (Newton, Euclid), psychiatrists (Bekhterev), and the Soviet Union's two political leaders—Lenin and Stalin. In the latter case, the references are particularly oblique, through allusion and associative imagery. The novel, which can be called philosophical and historical, taps into the rogue tradition in literature. Its structure and approach to mirroring reality are complex and experimental (in the positive sense of the word), although, admittedly, Ivanov's bold and noble attempt to capture the "spirit of the times" is not entirely successful. Ivanov can be accused not only of lacking a sense of measure in his use of allusions and veiled satirical jabs at almost every facet of Soviet life, but also of attempting to pack so much into the work that the density of time and space overwhelms the reader.

The excerpt included in this anthology is a dream of one of the major characters, Yegor Yegorych, which occupies a central place in the novel. The subconscious of Yegor Yegorych serves as the repository of various impressions and truths about contemporary life, locked in the imagery of a dream about a very special rooster. The imagery can be traced to various moments in the work itself, particularly to references to Leon Leontych Cherpanov, a rogue and master at deception. The prophetic nature of the dream, and its sociopolitical context, brings to mind the role of dreams in the Bible.

Yegor Yegorych, through what lies hidden in his subconscious, is the mediator to whom a particular wisdom about life, hidden from others, is imparted. He sees in his dream an arrogant rooster with striking eyes, a fiery tail, and incredible power over the proletarian masses. People run after the rooster through a Moscow seething with the activity of the first Five-Year Plan, with the intention of killing it. When they finally encircle it, the rooster generates his own transformation, striking a Napoleonic pose and sporting a suit, vest, and cocked hat. The seemingly hypnotized people fall at its feet in awe and veneration.

That transformed rooster, coded with signs that suggest Napoleon, Lenin, and the heir of Lenin's legacy—that is to say, Stalin, Lenin's self-styled "best pupil"—represents the role and image of Stalin from 1929 on. It was in that fateful year that myth-making, begun during Stalin's fiftieth-birthday celebrations, reached hyperbolic proportions, hypnotizing people into accepting the illusion that Stalin was the incarnation of Lenin, or Lenin II of the Revolution. Had Stalin been aware of this portrait of himself, rather than the fatherly one in *Parkhomenko*, he would not have been amused, and Ivanov would not have survived to write and publish until 1963.

Valentina G. Brougher

»»» BIBLIOGRAPHY «««

Ivanov, Vsevolod. *Kreml'; Y: romany*. Moscow: Sovetskii pisatel', 1990.

―――. *Perepiska s Gor'kim. Iz dnevnikov i zapisnykh knizhek*. Ed. T. V. Ivanova and K. G. Paustovskii. Moscow: Sovetskii pisatel', 1969.

―――. *Povesti i rasskazy*. Moscow: Khudozhestvennaia literatura, 1987.

―――. *Sobranie sochinenii v vos'mi tomakh*, Moscow: Khudozhestvennaia literatura, 1973–77.

―――. *Tainoe tainykh*. Moscow: Gosizdat, 1927.

―――. *Vozvrashchenie Buddy*. Berlin: Knigoizdatel'stvo pisatelei v Berline, 1923.

―――. *Y*. Lausanne: Editions l'Age d'Homme, 1982.

Critical Literature

Averbakh, Leopol'd. *Kul'turnaia revoliutsiia i voprosy sovetskoi literatury*. Moscow: Gosizdat, 1928.

Brainina, B. "Na perevale. Vsevolod Ivanov za 1930 god." *Literatura i iskusstvo* 2–3 (1931): 118–27.

Brougher, V.G. "Ivanov's *Y* and the Rooster Metaphor." *Slavic Review* 53, no.1 (Spring 1994): 159–72.

―――. "Myth in Vsevolod Ivanov's *The Kremlin*." *Canadian Slavonic Papers* 35, no.3–4 (1993): 221–34.

―――. "The Occult in the Prose of V. S. Ivanov." In *The Occult in Russian and Soviet Culture*, ed. Bernice G. Rosenthal. Ithaca, N.Y.: Cornell University Press, 1997.

Brown, E. J. *Russian Literature since the Revolution*. Rev. and enl. ed. Cambridge, Mass.: Harvard University Press, 1982.

El'sberg, Ia. E. *Krizis poputchikov i nastroenie intelligentsii*. Moscow: Priboi, 1930. 146–75.

Evgen'ev-Maksimov, Vladislav. *Ocherk istorii noveishei russkoi literatury*. Moscow: Gosizdat, 1927.

Friche, V. M. "V zashchitu 'ratsionalisticheskogo' izobrazheniia cheloveka." *Krasnaia nov'* 1 (1928): 242–44.

Gel'fand, M. "Ot 'Partizan' k 'Osobniaku.'" *Revoliutsiia i kul'tura* 22 (1928): 70–76.

Gladkovskaia, L. *Zhizneliubivyi talant*. Leningrad: Khudozhestvennaia literatura, 1988.

Gorbachev, Georgii. *Sovremennaia russkaia literatura. Obzor literaturnoideologicheskikh techenii sovremennosti i kriticheskie portrety sovremennykh pisatelei*. Moscow: Priboi, 1928. 220–37.

Grossman-Roshchin, I. S. "Napostovskii dnevnik. O svoem i chuzhom." *Na literaturnom postu* 20–21 (1928): 43–48.

Iakubovskii, Georgii. "Literaturnye bluzhdaniia. Psikhologicheskie prikliucheniia trekh pisatelei." *Zhurnal dlia vsekh* 3 (1929): 118–26.

Ivanov, Viacheslav. "Goluboi zver'. Vospominaniia" (Part 1). *Zvezda* 1 (1991): 173–99.

———. "Pochemu Stalin ubil Gor'kogo?" *Voprosy literatury* 1 (1993): 91–134.

Ivanova, T. V. *Moi sovremenniki, kakimi ia ikh znala*. Moscow: Sovetskii pisatel', 1984.

———, ed. *Vsevolod Ivanov—pisatel' i chelovek*. 2d ed., enl. Moscow: Sovetskii pisatel', 1975.

Kogan, P. S. "Poputchiki." *Literatura velikogo desiatiletiia*. Moscow: Moskovskii rabochii, 1927. 116–60.

Krasnoshchekova, E. A. *Khudozhestvennyi mir Vsevoloda Ivanova*. Moscow, Sovetskii pisatel', 1980.

Lezhnev, A. Z. "Chelovek i ego goresti." *Pechat' i revoliutsiia* 2 (1927): 104–6.

———. "Khudozhestvennaia literatura," *Pechat' i revoliutsiia* 7 (1927): 97–98.

————. "Russkaia literatura za desiat' let." *Literatura revoliutsionnogo de-siatiletiia*. Moscow: Proletarii, 1929. 5–117.

L'vov-Rogachevskii, Vasilii. "Belletristika revoliutsionnoi epokhi." *Noveishaia russkaia literatura*. Moscow: Izdat. L. D. Frankel, 1924. 346–53.

Maguire, R. A. "The Pioneers: Pil'nyak and Ivanov." In *Major Soviet Writers*, ed. Edward J. Brown. Oxford: Oxford University Press, 1973. 221–53.

————. *Red Virgin Soil: Soviet Literature in the 1920's*. Princeton, N.J.: Princeton University Press, 1968.

Maliutin, Z. "Novyi povorot Vs. Ivanova." *Na literaturnom postu* 20 (1930): 54–59.

Messer, Raisa. "Poputchiki vtorogo prizyva." *Zvezda* 4 (1930): 203–11.

Minokin, M. V. *Put' Vsevoloda Ivanova k romanu (20-e gody)*. Orel: Orlovskii gospedinstitut, 1966.

Nosich, N. "Vs. Ivanov. *Tainoe tainykh*." *Molodaia gvardiia* 4 (1927): 206–8.

Ognev, Nikolai. "Otkrytoe pis'mo Vsevolodu Ivanovu." *Literaturnaia gazeta*, 30 December 1929.

Pakentreiger, Solomon. "Po sledam zveria." *Pechat' i revoliutsiia* 3 (1927): 65–70.

Pereverzev, V. F. "Na frontakh tekushchei belletristiki." *Pechat' i revoliutsiia* 4 (1923): 127–33.

Polonskii, Viacheslav. "Ocherki sovremennoi literatury. O tvorchestve Vsevoloda Ivanova." *Novyi mir* 1 (1929): 216–35.

Pravdukhin, V. P. "Pafos sovremennosti i molodye pisateli." *Literaturnaia sovremennost' 1920–1924*. Moscow: Gosizdat, 1924. 57–78.

Ryzhikov, K. "Optimizm i pessimizm Vs. Ivanova." *Na literaturnom postu* 16 (1929): 49–60.

Selivanovskii, A. P. "Na otshybe." *Molodaia gvardiia* 12 (1929): 75–76.

Shcheglov, Mark. *Istoriia russkoi sovetskoi literatury*. Vol. 1. Moscow: Nauka, 1967. 301–23.

Shklovskii, V. "Druz'ia i vstrechi. Vsevolod Ivanov." *Zhili-byli*. Moscow: Sovetskii pisatel', 1966. 415–36.

————. *Sentimental'noe puteshestvie*. Berlin: Gelikon, 1923.

Slonimskii, M. L. "V Sibiri pal'my ne rastut . . ." *Kniga vospominanii.* Leningrad: Sovetskii pisatel', 1966. 119–26.

Struve, Gleb. *Soviet Russian Literature: 1917–1950.* Norman: University of Oklahoma Press, 1971.

Voronskii, Aleksandr. "Literaturnye otkliki." *Krasnaia nov'* 2 (1922): 270–72.

————. "Literaturnye siluety. Vsevolod Ivanov," *Krasnaia nov'* 5 (1922): 254–75.

————. "O knige Vsevoloda Ivanova 'Tainoe tainykh'." *Mister Britling p'et chashu do dna.* Moscow: Artel' pisatelei "Krug," 1927. 157–60.

————. "Vsevolod Ivanov." *Literaturnye tipy.* 2d ed., enl. Moscow: Artel' pisatelei "Krug," 1927. 81–107.

»)» CHRONOLOGY «(«

1895 (1892?)	Born February 24 (12) in Lebiazh'e, Semipalatinsk oblast', Stepnoi Krai (today Kazakhstan).
1912–17	Attends village schools, including half a year at Nizshee Sel'skokhoziaistvennoe uchilishche. Various jobs, from fakir to typesetter. Periods of wandering, particularly summers, through Siberia, Central Asia, and the Urals.
1915	First story, "V sviatuiu noch'," published in Kurgan, Siberia, where he works as typesetter.
1917	Typesetter in Omsk, which falls under White control, 1917–18. Moves between both political camps.
1918	"Po Irtyshu" published in *Sbornik proletarskikh pisatelei,* ed. Maksim Gorkii.
1919	*Rogul'ki.* First volume of stories, typeset by Ivanov himself and published under pseudonym V. Tarakanov.
1921	Leaves Siberia and moves to Petrograd with Mariia Nikolaevna Sinitsyna. Begins working for the Proletkul't, but soon becomes associated with the Serapion Brothers. "Partizany" appears in the very first volume of *Krasnaia nov'.*
1922? 23?	Anna Pavlovna Vesnina becomes second wife.
1922	*Bronepoezd 14–69* appears in *Krasnaia nov'.*
1923	*Sed'moi bereg. Rasskazy. Sopki. Partizanskie povesti*

(includes *Bronepoezd 14–69, Partizany,* and *Tsvetnye vetra*). *Golubye peski,* novel, appears.

Vozvrashchenie Buddy published in Berlin.

1923   At end of year moves to Moscow.

1924   *Chudesnye pokhozhdeniia portnogo Fokina.*

1925   *Nikitinskie subbotniki. Rasskazy.*

With Viktor Shklovsky, writes adventure novel, *Iprit.*

Ekzoticheskie rasskazy.

1926   *Gafir i Miriam. Rasskazy i povesti. Pustynia Tuub-Koia. Rasskazy.*

1927   Dramatizes *Bronepoezd 14-69* for Moscow Art Theater (MKhAT) in honor of the tenth anniversary of the Revolution. Trip to Germany and France.

Tainoe tainykh published. Becomes center of controversy and polemics. On new editorial board of *Krasnaia nov';* Voronskii hurt and angry.

1928   "Osobniak" published; comes under harsh attack by the RAPP critics.

1929   Marries Tamara Vladimirovna Kashirina, actress and student of Meyerhold; birth of son Viacheslav; first variant of *Kreml';* writes *Blokada,* a play about Kronshtadt in 1921.

1929–32   Works on *Y.*

1930   Trip to Turkmenia and Central Asia as member of writers' brigade.

Writes *Puteshesvie v stranu, kotoroi eshche net.*

1930–31   *Povesti brigadira M. N. Sinitsyna, rasskazannye im v dni pervoi piatiletki.*

1932–33   Among the writers who travel to the construction site of the White Sea Canal and produce a collective volume about their visit.

	Travels to Berlin, Paris, and Florence; visits Maksim Gor'kii in Sorrento.
1934	Speaks at the First All-Union Congress of Soviet Writers: "My za Bolshevistskuiu tendentsioznost' v literature."
1934–35	*Pokhozhdeniia fakira* (Parts 1 and 2 appear in English translation in 1935).
1938–39	*Parkhomenko*
1941	Play, *Parkhomenko*, staged. Begins working as special correspondent for *Izvestiia* (also for *Gudok*, a year later). Resides in Peredelkino, where his friends include Leonid Leonov, Konstantin Fedin, Boris Pasternak, and others.
1942	Spends ten months in Tashkent where film "Parkhomenko," based on his script, is being shot. Writes *Prospekt Il'icha* (novel rejected in 1943 by *Novyi mir*).
1943	Reporting from the Western front.
1944	*Na Borodinskom pole. Rasskazy 1939–43.*
1945	As special correspondent for *Izvestiia* and *Gudok*, witnesses the German capitulation ceremony in Berlin; present at the Nuremberg trials. *Pri vziatii Berlina* published in *Novyi mir*.
1946–47	*Vstrechi s Maksimom Gor'kim.*
1950	*Lomonosov* staged in Moscow Art Theater.
1955–63	On the Admissions Committee, Union of Soviet Writers, and on examination panels of the Moscow Literary Institute; awarded title of professor.
1957	*Istoriia moikh knig.*
1958–61	Trips to India, France, Japan, England, Scotland.
1960	*My idem v Indiiu* (serialized in 1956–59)
1962	*Khmel' ili Navstrechu osennim ptitsam.*
1963	Death from cancer.

Published posthumously:

1965	*Edesskaia sviatynia* (completed in 1946).
1968	*Vulkan* (written in 1940).
1975	Stories from the "fantastic cycle," written during World War II, included in vol. 5 of *Sobranie sochinenii v vos'mi tomakh.*
1976	*Sokrovishcha Aleksandra Makedonskogo* included in vol. 6 of *Sobranie sochinenii.*
1981	*Kreml'* published in a censored version under the title *Uzhginskii Kreml'.*
1982	*Y* published in Switzerland.
1988	*Y* published in the USSR.
1990	Uncensored version of *Kreml'* published in the USSR.

⟫⟫⟫ GLOSSARY ⟪⟪⟪

The list below includes words that appear in a number of stories. For quick reference, they have been grouped under three subject areas. Additional vocabulary items, which are specific to a particular story, are provided in the notes.

Political Terms and Administrative Units

gubérniya	province, administrative district in tsarist Russia and the USSR until the advent of the *raión* system
ispolkóm	*ispolnítelny komitét* = executive council
ókrug	small administrative district
óblast	large administrative region
raión	small administrative unit within an administrative region (*óblast*) or within a large large city
uyézd	an administrative region in tsarist Russia and the USSR until the advent of the *raión* system
vólost	small rural district, a subdivision of the *uyézd* in tsarist Russia and the USSR until the advent of the *raión* system

Glossary

Units of Measurement

arshín	about 28 inches
pud	36 pounds
sázhen	2.13 meters
vershók	1.5 inches
verst	(Russian *verstá*) 3500 feet

Peasant Reality

izbá	peasant hut, log cabin. There is also a *pyatisténnaya izbá*, a hut with five walls, larger and more impressive than the common one with four walls.
górnitsa	a second room in an *izbá*, for sleeping or for company
zaválinka	(plural: *zaválinki*) a mound of earth around a peasant hut serving as protection from the weather; often used for sitting on
mir	peasant community

Fertility and Other Stories

Empty Arapia

I

At first they saw the rats.

They ran in leaps and jumps, their squeals resembling the thin, high-pitched sounds grass makes. From the rose-colored shroud where the sun began to the end of the fields they streamed in a soft grayish sheet.

The contorted branches didn't grasp as before the earth sucked dry by the heat. Shreds of crows' nests moved mutely among the branches.

The trees grew out of rats. The sun began out of rats, and the wind blowing above the rats was a thin-ribbed hungry dog.

Then birds with hungry scarlet beaks flew out from behind the sky. Carts began to squeak. Horses seized and tore the rat meat with their long protuberant teeth. In the distance dogs ran like shepherds after the gray shroud.

The peasants beat the rats with sticks; they scooped them up with shovels and filled their carts. Half-dead rats, resembling huge cucumbers, crawled back down to the ground.

Carts approached from the neighboring *izbas;* those who didn't have horses pulled the carts themselves. Pots began to smell of meat. They said you should add birch bark to the mixture for the taste.

The sun, fat from overeating, settled on the trees. The clouds stuck out their fat protruding stomachs.

Lands gnawed bare. From the sky to the earth—a thin-ribbed wind. From the sky to the earth—thin hungry dust.

The rats kept running and running south.

Then Yefimia from Yesterday's Eye[1] appeared.

II

In the morning Faddey was the first in the village to notice the rats.

In a hoarse, broken-down voice he woke his family: his son Miron, his younger son, Senka, and his daughter, Nadka. His old wife, Lukeria, was gnawing at her sheepskin coat for the fourth day in a row without getting up. Sheep's wool quivered on her lips. She drank water often, then vomited thick, bluish pieces of skin.

"Let's go! Let's go! If the peasants see, they'll come running. The animals will get scared and run away. Come on!"

Nadka, putting down the child wrapped in rags, said to Lukeria, "I'll go, Mom. . . . And you, if the little fellow begins singing, stick a *zhamka*[2] in his mouth."

"Fine, if . . . "

"As soon as he starts howling, stick it right in."

"Go, go! I will."

There is wet wool between Lukeria's lips. The old woman smells sour from the sheepskin. Her cheeks have sunk under her cheekbones. Her cheekbones are like a worn-out piece of canvas under her eyes.

There is no strength left in people's bones. The body is as flexible as a rag. With its eyes bulging, a horse was gnawing on rats, striking the squealing solid mass with its hard hoof, dry like the sky.

And people's hands were like dust. With four working, they had barely gathered half a cart by evening time.

"We'll have to start," Faddey said. "It's time to eat."

Nadka cooked up some warm little pieces of meat. Miron was about to close his eyes. Waving his spoon, Faddey shook the pot.

"So you're squeamish! Eat it or I'll pour it out. Look at me."

And he hastily dipped his spoon, scraping up a piece of meat from the bottom.

Having gotten her fill, Nadka cooked another pot and sent it back with Senka to their mother in the village.

Right there, without leaving the campfire, they fell asleep. Senka walked a verst and fell asleep, too.

He returned in the morning. Handing over the pot, he said, "Mom asked for more."

Poking a stick into the mass of sharp rats' heads, he said, "Mom wanted to feed your little boy but dropped him on the floor. And she couldn't pick him up. The animals ate his nose and hand."

Nadka grabbed her stomach, threw down her stick, and headed for the village.

Her mouth, narrow and dry, stretched like a whip across her dust-covered face. Her weeping couldn't be heard over the squeaking of the running rats.

"Get to work! Where the hell are you going?" Faddey shouted. "He won't die! He'll live!"

Timokhin, the chairman of the *ispolkom*, came to their *izba*. He felt the child's gnawed-off hand. He covered the child with a rag and, seating himself on a bench, said, "Got to make a report. Maybe you ate him yourselves. The '*spolkom* has been told to report all such incidents to the proper channels."

He took a good look at the tall Miron, who wasn't losing any weight.

"Just look how well fed he is. Maybe he's the one who ate him. My responsibility is not to believe. Then again, why should a rat eat a person?"

Lukeria, covered with a sheepskin coat, was sleeping. She hiccuped once in her sleep. The chairman got up, poked the weeping Nadka, and started to go.

"And you, Nadka, don't howl. You'll make another one. It's very simple. As for the report, I'll send the secretary. Once I write the report, bury him. I'll have dinner and send him over. Just look, you even had meat to break your fast with."

The smell of cooked meat wafted from the table. No one could find the strength to wash the child's blood from the floor.

It was then in the evening that Yefimia from Yesterday's Eye appeared.

III

Miron was sleeping by the hayloft, under a canopy on an old wood-sledge. Nadka came and sank to the ground near the wood-sledge.

"We can't help with tears," Miron said. "He's dead and gone."

The rosy-violet darkness hid Nadka. The earth blazed in dust-filled shaggy stuffiness. Nadka's speech was somewhat hoarse, with gasps for air from hunger. She didn't have enough saliva for words.

"I thought I'd be able to bring the child up all the way. . . . But now the rats have eaten him. Oh, Lord! . . . Why couldn't they have eaten the old woman? In the village, they say, the Fadeevs have eaten it themselves, they say that about us."

"Let them tell lies. They eat pretty good themselves."

Something began to crawl lightly across the sackcloth covering his chest. He felt around and discovered his sister's bones, dry like sandpaper.

"What are you up to?"

Nadka began to whisper: "Eat . . . I left it for you. A crust. Bread. The old man's hidden everything. 'Miron,' he says, 'is full even without it. He's got his own reserves. Hasn't lost any body weight,' he says. Eat!"

"So if I have bones like these, is it my fault? If I can't lose any weight. . . . I even eat less so they don't reproach me."

"I have to take some to Yegorka. . . . Have you seen him?"

"To hell with him! You want to marry him, is that it?"

"Don't yell. The old man will hear. Yefimia has come. They brought her. Yefimia. . . . "

"So?"

"They say that beyond Syr-Daria[3] a certain land has been opened up, the unsettled land of Arapia. If you sow, it rains for three weeks in a row. And everyone is let in free, you just have to go. There's lots of land. Yefimia tells a story that makes sense, Miron."

"She's probably lying. Where's she from?"

"They've brought her. If she feels like it, she'll take the folks to that very Arapia. Dad's not going. But in some villages people have gotten ready and left. The rats are also heading that way. And the birds are flying there. Our parts have been cursed for thirty-seven years: neither rain nor grass. . . . Then they'll return if they survive that long. . . . They've opened Arapia for thirty-seven years, and then they'll close it again."

IV

The village men gathered and readied the carts. Whoever's horse had not been eaten was fed a bit of haydust and dry manure. Those without horses made handcarts as best as they could.

The rats were gone.

The lands were running, turning into sand. They ran in shaggy silent whirlwinds. They ran south.

The bark on the trees dried out like the skin on the people. The trees made a knocking sound with their dry white bones. The land made a knocking sound with its dry bones.

Miron hid his large body from the people. From people's eyes, eyes nakedly greedy for meat. Miron ate little: pounded and cooked bark; skin cut off carrion, rose-colored slop. Nevertheless, flabby meat hung from his bones like wet sand, and his bones, as if suspended in sand, were dying away.

Nadka was before his eyes constantly—flat, with greenish skin and flared eyelashes covered with pus. Pressing a rag to her chest, she'd say: "Don't show yourself, Miron. The peasants have gone mad, especially at night. They'll sin, they'll kill you. . . . You'd better lose some weight. Lose some weight."

"I can't lose weight!" Miron wheezed. "I suffer but can't lose weight!"

He shook his head overgrown with dusty hair. He hid under the canopy.

"It's an illusion. Water is not body meat. Feel!"

Nadka timidly felt his legs.

"Yes, it's an illusion. Was this how bodies used to be? I remember. But you know they're not going to believe you, they'll kill you. Better not show yourself to the peasants, Miron."

Nadka fed Yegorka furtively, for love. In the evening, hiding from view, Yegorka would come to the barn and eat, wheezing. Miron would steal up and listen to Yegorka's wheezing as he ate, and then the dry heavy breathing of love by both, breaking loose. . . . Breathing quickly through a mouth as wide as a well, Nadka would disappear into the hut.

Miron slept with his eyes open. The nights were long. And at night, like during the day, there was the sun. The night was dry like the day. He would string ropes by the canopy so that he could hear a stranger's thievish arrival.

Dry like the day was the voice of Yefimia from the spring at Yesterday's Eye. There was such a holy new spring in the Four Birches. The old woman Yefimia sat constantly, day and night, in a cart in the yard of the *ispolkom* chairman, Timokhin. Her small white-haired face hid in a dark kerchief. Her ancient voice was wrinkled and barely audible. In a singsong way she would say bombastically: "Gather together, Orthodox people, from all ends of the earth! . . . The gates to the unsettled land of Arapia have been opened for a short time. Go, all of you. Some will reach it through the sands, through the Sarta,[4] and from there along the Indian mountains. The gates have been thrown open for thirty-seven years. Whoever gets there first will get a piece of land closer to home. The grass there is perfect for bees and honey. Grain ripens in three weeks. Besides that, the Arapian people are giving everything you need, including pants with green buttons. . . . "

She'd sigh with a sleepy sigh. Her eyes, thin and silent, sleep. Her voice is sleepy, strange, and frightening.

Miron had wanted to see her but was afraid to show himself. Someone brought her by in a cart for a few fleeting minutes to persuade the people on the Anisimov farmsteads. The people on the farms were waiting for grain from Moscow and refused to go. Later the farms caught on fire and blazed for one night.

And when the woods caught on fire, smoke wrapped the birdless sky in an orange shroud. Dust began to crawl along above the bed of the dried-up river. All of a sudden the wells ran dry.

The peasants took off from the village and went to empty Arapia. Miron went too.

V

The whole earth is sand. Blue sands. And the sky is blue sand.

Distant lands, empty, uncultivated fields of Arapia! Which paths to take, which roads?

Lame beggars huddle in fear, the birch with dried-up arms; aspens without bark. Rabbits have run off to the lands of Arapia, leaving the bark for people to gnaw on. It's a sly animal. People do their gnawing with crumbling gray and yellow teeth.

Gnaw! Gnaw! You'll be gnawing on rocks! You're far away, lands of Arapia. Far away! I don't know where.

Or perhaps someone knows?

Or perhaps someone will find a road, point the way?

The soul freezes over, freezes over in blue ice, which doesn't melt.

You're far away, lands of Arapia!

VI

Little children covered with swollen sores turned off the road and dug in the earth, breaking off small roots. They fought often, scratching each other with their long black nails. Their thin yellowish blood resembled dust.

They ate the leather off the horses' harnesses. Bare bones, gauged out by a knife, were all that remained from the horses that died. The wind whistled into reed pipes abandoned by the people.

The second week Faddey's horse fell. The village ate it in one day. The marrow left on the bones was given to Yefimia.

Then all the horses fell, one by one.

Yefimia was hauled by peasants in groups of four taking turns.

Pointing with her crooked finger shaped like a beak, she would look to the south and repeat the same words about empty Arapia:

"Gather, Orthodox people, from all ends of the earth! For a short time they've opened . . . "

Old Lukeria died. Faddey took her from the cart, put her on the ground, and covered her with sand. The sand kept rolling off. Lukeria's nose and feet stuck out of it sharply.

Once Nadka turned off the road and found a half-dry pile of horse dung under the sand. She scratched the dried crust with her fingernail and called Yegorka: "It's got oats. . . . Come here!"

She rested her chest on the ground and chewed the softish smelly gruel with grains of undigested oats. . . . Yegorka walked up and began to pick out the oat grains. . . .

At night Miron had a dream about a harvest. A thick yellow spike of grain was passing under his hand, but he couldn't grasp it with his fingers. But suddenly the ear began to bristle with rose-colored whiskers and headed for his throat.

At this point Miron woke up and felt someone feeling his legs: from his calves to the groin and back again. He jerked his leg and shouted: "Who's there?"

The sand made a ringing sound. Someone moved away. Nadka woke up.

"I have a heavy feeling in my stomach."

Pulling on his sackcloth, Miron, stumbling over his words, uttered, "They're feeling . . . they're feeling the meat on my body!"

"Then come lie next to me. I don't sleep well. I hear everything."

And pulling his trembling body toward her, she stroked the upper part of his back with her gentle inaudible hand. She muttered in a wilting whisper, "They say they'll get there soon. Soon the land of the Sarts will begin, and although they don't have grain, Yefimia says they'll fatten us up a bit with milk. May the Lord grant that. At least you'll get there. . . . But I'll probably die tomorrow, Miron."

"You'll make it."

"I'll die. I'm choking . . . on the horse. . . . My belly feels like it's got red-hot bricks from the stove in it. . . . And I'm sick to my stomach. I can't throw up but I feel sick to my stomach, like there's a lump in my throat. There's no one to dig me a grave."

"They'll dig one."

"No one has the hands. The land is for walking and people."

"Ashes!"

"Ashes, Mirosha! . . . I was thinking, in the winter when we get there, I'd marry Yegorka. There, in Arapia, the people, so says Yefimia, are black and without priests. But the priests probably ran off there earlier with the rats."

"Doesn't Daddy have any kind of grub?"

"He thinks you eat on the sly. . . . Give me a piece, Mirosha. . . . "

"Don't have none."

She pulled at his beard, combed the hair on his head with her finger, and barely audibly whispered in his ear, "Give me, Mirosha, a tiny piece . . . to suck on. A little piece of bread. . . . The warm bread sticks to your teeth and the tongue. . . . Give me, Mirosha, honest to God I won't tell. Just enough for one tooth . . . hmm . . . hm . . . a tiny piece. . . . And then I'll die, I won't tell anyway. . . . "

She pushed her head under his elbow. She nibbled at his sleeve with her teeth. By morning she was vomiting. A sticky bluish liquid darkened on the ground next to her face. She licked her vomit. . . .

All contorted, she died.

The village got up. Set out. The peasants, pushing with their shoulders, were moving the cart with Yefimia.

"You'll bury her?" Faddey asked as he was leaving.

A small distance away on the ground sat Yegorka, narrow-headed, his thin lip sticking out below a hard yellow tooth.

"Go on," Miron said to him. "I'll bury her."

Yegorka shook his shoulders, moved the stake under his knee with his hand. He said panting, "I'll . . . myself. . . . Don't touch. . . . Myself, I say. . . . I wanted to marry her. . . . I'll bury her. . . . Off with you. Go."

Kids were sitting around the fire, like hungry dogs. Yegorka waved his stake above his head and shouted, "Beat it . . . gnashing your teeth . . . beat it!"

While he was turning around, Miron put his hand on Nadka's bosom, felt around and found on her a small piece of something hard, pulled it out, and was about to hide it in his pocket. Yegorka saw this and, stamping his stake, drew nearer.

"Drop it, Miron, I'm telling you. . . . Drop it! . . . It's mine . . . my piece, my bride. . . . "

Yegorka waved his stake over Miron's head. The latter walked away and dropped a small darkened cross. . . .

Yegorka flipped it with the stake toward his feet. . . .

"Go away . . . it's mine. . . . I'll bury. . . . "

He didn't look him in the face. His fingers rested strongly on the gnarled stake. . . .

Miron left without turning around. . . .

The little boys, running off, shouted, "He'll eat that bride of his. . . . "

VII

While trying to catch up with the peasants who were already far away from him, Miron noticed a flock of kids fighting by the side of the road. Stuck deep into the ruts in the road, the abandoned carts became fixed in the earth at an odd angle. Rotten bits of rags hung from the boards and wood chests. Almost all the carts had the sickening smell of corpses.

Faddey and Senka weren't with the peasants.

"Didn't see them?" Miron asked.

Somebody swore hoarsely and for a long time. One said in a squeaky voice, "They're well fed. . . . They hide to eat."

A tight cutting pain moved through Miron's stomach. His tongue shifted back and forth along his gums, trying to find some saliva. Something cutting his temples and making itself felt in his nose and palate was settling on his head from above. . . .

Miron wandered off, stumbling. He spotted a piece of leather lying by the cart. Miron stuck it between his teeth.

A hunchbacked woman with disheveled hair tugged at his sleeve.

"There's none," said Miron. "I want to eat myself."

The woman, getting down on her crooked knees, motioned with her head.

"I know. . . . Let's go under the cart. . . . How much you give me?"

She opened her mouth and sticking out her chest, evilly shook her bones. She bared her teeth.

"Let's go? . . . You'll give me a little piece? You're fat."

Miron ran away from her, his elbows making a jerking motion. When he turned around, the woman and three more strange peasants were walking behind him.

Miron staggered to the side. The lilac wormwood stung his leg. A small animal appeared for a second from behind the bush. Miron rushed after it, wanted to catch it, but fell. The small animal slipped into its hole.

Miron was about to dig it up but then remembered: he must not remain alone. The four were walking behind him, looking back now and then. He must catch up with his village.

He pushed his body up with his hands and raised himself up a bit.

A narrow hungry pain twisted his stomach. His ribs were breaking away and pressing against his skin. It was as if the ribs had lost their way inside. He began to walk.

His legs were walking across the whole earth, across all the sands without picking themselves up in the air. And his body seemed to be crawling along the sand . . . across the sand . . . a bit more, a bit. . . .

Miron couldn't catch up with the peasants.

He raised his eyes toward the sun. It moved a bit, yellow and fat, like a mare in foal.

"You're eating!" Miron said to himself. "Putting it away? But why must I wait? Why me?"

He didn't feel like walking. Groping, he felt a cart lying nearby: warm wood and hot nails.

At this point he again remembered the four catching up with him. They were walking, holding each other's hands, a few steps away and looking at the villagers disappearing in the dust.

Miron began to hurry.

"They'll put an end to me. I have to be with the peasants. They'll put an end . . . to me."

He remembered Nadka, who had taken pity on him. He began to weep. He wanted to wipe away his tears; his eyelids were dry, like the road, like the fields. The dust rolled off his eyelids and eyebrows.

His tears were retreating inside of him, into his stomach, torturing his whole body. . . . The earth was torturing his body with dry and prolonged torture.

The villagers came to a stop.

Miron caught up with them.

"What?" he said hurriedly to one of the peasants who came stumbling toward him.

"We have to feed Yefimia. There's nothing to feed Yefimia with."

The peasant for some reason took off his long coat and shirt. And then he hastily put them back on. Dragging one foot, he moved away.

"They'll feed her," Miron said wearily, lowering himself to the ground.

As soon as he lay down, the pains moved from his stomach to his legs. He put his legs under him.

Above him: the boards of the cart, smelling of corpses and dust. He searched for some tar in the wheel spokes. He picked off a little ball with wood in it and began to chew, his teeth sticking together.

The four were already lying opposite him, under another cart: one woman and three men. The men, covering their beards with the palms of their hands, were looking at a field, and the woman, at him. Miron thought he even saw her wink at him.

The tar rolled out of his mouth: a dry, black little ball.

Miron crawled further, under the front of the cart. He wanted shade. The red-hot sun lay beyond the carts, on the sand, on the road.

A large metal spoke scratched his backbone. Then after his backbone it ripped off his pants, baring his flesh. And only the sun, which had jumped between the carts, warmed his flesh.

He crawled to the back portion of the next cart, stretched out his body, and peered out. Under the cart where he had lain before were those four. . . . The woman winked again.

Miron shoved his head toward the wheel spokes and closed his eyes. A field of grain—crimson red, green, and brown—spread out before him, waving and quivering. Throwing around the spikes of grain with its horns, a dull and fat cow's face appeared and glanced at him. And suddenly its eyes faded, settled, and above him there surfaced the pointed face of a wolf.

Miron opened his eyes. Next to him behind the wheel squatted the woman, and the peasant behind her was shoving a hammer into her hand. "They're gonna eat me," Miron thought. He pressed his head against the spokes and, grabbing the sand with his mouth, screwed up his eyes.

1922

>>>> <<<<

The Child

I

Mongolia is a wild and joyless beast! The rock is a beast, the water is a beast; even a butterfly, even it schemes to sting.

One knows not what kind of heart a Mongolian has—he wears animal skins, looks like a Chinese, and has taken to living far away from the Russians, across the Nor-Koy Desert. And, it is also said, he'll migrate beyond China to India, to the unexplored blue lands on seven shores. . . .

More and more Kirghiz from the Irtysh River[1] area, who had migrated into Mongolia because of the Russian war, kept appearing where the Russians were. One knows what kind of a heart they have—mica-like, worthless, transparent through and through. They made their way here without hurrying—and they brought their cattle, and children, and even their sick.

The Russians had been driven here mercilessly—that's why they were healthy and strong peasants. They left their excess weakness on the rocks and mountains—some had died off, others were killed off. Their families and clothing and cattle were abandoned to the Whites. The peasants are vicious, like wolves in the spring. In ravines they lay in their tents and thought about the steppes and the Irtysh. . . .

There were about fifty of them, with Sergey Selivanov presiding, and the detachment was named the Red Guard Partisan Detachment of Comrade Selivanov.

They were bored, homesick.

While they were being pursued through the mountains—the rocks, huge and dark, terrified their hearts. When they got to the steppe, there was weariness, homesickness. Because the steppe here resembles the steppe around the Irtysh: sand, coarse grasses, and strongly forged sky. Everything is different, not your own, unplowed, and wild.

And it was also hard without women.

At night they told off-color soldiers' stories about women and, when it became unbearable, they'd saddle their horses and catch Kirghiz women in the steppe.

And the Kirghiz women, sighting the Russians, would lie down submissively on their backs.

It wasn't right, it was repulsive to take them—motionless with tightly closed eyes. Like sinning with cattle.

The Kirghiz—afraid of the peasants—kept moving deeper into the steppe. When they saw a Russian, they'd threaten with their rifles and bows, whoop but not shoot. Maybe they didn't know how?

II

The paymaster of the detachment, Afanasy Petrovich, was given to crying, like a child. And his face was like a child's: small, hairless, and rosy-cheeked. Only his legs were long and strong like a camel's.

But whenever he mounted a horse, he'd become stern. His face would recede somewhere deep within, and he'd sit: gray, angry, and frightening.

On Whitsunday[2] three men—Selivanov, paymaster Afanasy Petrovich, and secretary Drevesinin—were sent out on detail: to look for good grasslands in the steppe.

The sands smoked under the sun.

The wind blew from above, from the sky. The warmth from the earth rose into the quivering sky. The bodies of people and animals were hard and heavy like rocks. Yearning.

And Selivanov said hoarsely, "And how's the hay-making back there?"

They all knew: he was speaking about the Irtysh. But the thinly bearded faces kept silent. As if the hair of their beards had been burned by the sun like the grasses in the steppe. Their narrow eyes shone crimson, like a wound from a fishhook. Heat.

Only Afanasy Petrovich responded plaintively, "Do you think there could really be a drought there, too, men?"

His small voice was whining, but his face wasn't crying, and only the big, long eyes of the tired and breathless horse under him shed aching tears.

Thus one after another, treading the paths beaten by wild goats, the partisans left for the steppe.

The sands smoldered drearily. The sultry wind clung to their shoulders and to their heads. Their sweat burned in their bodies and could not escape through their dry skin.

Toward evening, as they were already moving out of a hollow, Selivanov pointed toward the west and said, "Some travelers moving fast."

And so it was: the very horizon swayed with the rosy dust of the sands.

"Must be the Kirghiz."

They started arguing: Drevesinin said that the Kirghiz lived far away and didn't come near Selivanov's gullies; Afanasy Petrovich said it was definitely the Kirghiz; it was Kirghiz dust, thick.

But when the dust had come rolling closer, everyone decided, "People we don't know."

From their masters' voices the horses sensed that something foreign was being carried in the wind. They pricked up their ears and fell to the ground long before the order was given. Gray and yellow horse carcasses lay in the gully. They looked helpless and absurd with their thin polelike legs. Was it from shame they shut their large frightened eyes and breathed by fits and starts?

Selivanov and paymaster Afanasy Petrovich lay at the edge of the gully. The paymaster cried and sniveled. So as not to be frightened, Selivanov always placed him beside himself, and his heavy peasant's heart would almost grow cheerful and mischievous from this childish crying.

The trail began to churn up dust. There was the intermittent clatter of wheels. And, like dust, black manes swirled in their collars.

Selivanov said confidently, "Russians . . . officers."

And he called to Drevesinin from the gully.

Two persons wearing caps with red bands sat in a new wicker cart. You couldn't see their faces for the dust. It was as if the red-banded ones were swimming in a yellow cloud. There was a rifle—its barrel protruded when the hand with the whip emerged from the dust.

Drevesinin thought a minute and said, "Officers . . . probably on business. An ixpitition[3] . . . Of course."

His eye and mouth took on a mischievous look.

"We'll give 'em what they need, dear Selivanchik."

The cart was carrying the people, carrying them firmly. The horses. They were having a fine time, and behind them, like a fox with its tail, the cart was covering up its tracks with Mongolian dust.

Afanasy Petrovich drawled out tearfully, "No need, guys. . . . Better take 'em prisoner. . . . Hold off on killing."

"You're not worried about your own head . . . is that it?"

Selivanov got angry and, noiselessly, like someone undoing a button, silently uncocked the gun.

"This isn't the place to cry, paymaster."

What angered them most of all was that the officers appeared in the steppe alone, without an escort. As if there were a host of them, as if they meant death for the peasants. There, for example, an officer was standing up straight, scanning the steppe, but he couldn't see well: dust; wind evening-red on burnt grasses; on two rocks by the gully, resembling horses' carcasses. . . . What rocks? . . . Carcasses? . . .

In the red dust, the cart, wheels, people, and their thoughts. . . . Rushing along.

They fired. . . . Whooped. Fired again.

All at once, brushing against each other, the caps fell into the cart.

The reins became slack, as if they had snapped.

The horses gave a sudden start . . . almost bolted. But suddenly their withers foamed a milky white. . . . With their mighty tense muscles trembling, they lowered their heads and stood still.

Afanasy Petrovich said, "They're dead. . . . "

The men approached and gave a look.

The red-bands were dead. They sat, shoulder to shoulder, with their heads thrown back, and one of the dead was a woman. Her hair had become undone and was covered with dust—it was half blond and half black—and the soldier's high-collared tunic was raised high by the woman's breasts.

"Strange thing," said Drevesinin, "it's her fault—shouldn't put on a cap. Who wants to kill a woman? . . . Society needs women."

Afanasy Petrovich spat.

"You're a monster and a bourgeois. . . . You have no feelings, you bastard."

"Now just a minute," Selevinov broke in. "We're no bandits. We have to inventory the people's property. Give me some paper."

Under the front part of the cart, in a Chinese wicker basket among the other "people's property," lay a white-eyed and white-haired baby. Grasped in his little hand was the corner of a brown blanket. A tiny babe in arms, it squealed lightly.

Afanasy Petrovich said tenderly, "He, too, you see . . . probably telling us in his own way what and how."

Again they felt sorry for the woman and didn't remove her clothing, but they buried the man naked in the sand.

III

Afanasy Petrovich rode back in the confiscated cart and held the baby in his arms and, rocking it, sang softly:

> Nightingale, nightingale, sweet little bird
> Little canary
> Mournfully sings. . . .

He remembered the village of Lebiazhe[4]—his home, driving home the cattle, his family, the kids—and he cried in a thin voice.

The baby cried, too.

The shifting, flowing, and scorched sands raced along and cried in a thin voice. The partisans raced along on short, stocky Mongolian horses. The partisans were scorched-faced and scorched-hearted.

Spread along the trails was wormwood, strangled by the sun and resembling sand—fine and imperceptible to the eye.

And the sands are wormwood, fine and bitter.

Oh, you trails, goat trails! Oh, you sands, bitter sands! Mongolia is a wild and joyless beast!

They examined the officers' property. Books, a suitcase with tobacco, shiny steel instruments. One of them, on three long legs, was a four-cornered copper packing case with compartments.

The partisans came closer; they examined, felt, and weighed the property in their hands.

They smelled of sheep fat—out of boredom they'd been eating a lot, and their clothes had become covered with grease.

The high-cheekboned ones with soft thin lips were from the Don *stanitsas;*[5] the dark-complexioned ones with long black hair, from the lime pits. And they all had legs curved like shaft-bows and guttural steppe voices.

Afanasy Petrovich picked up the copper-headed tripod and said, "Tiliscope."[6] And narrowed his eyes. "A good tiliscope, it's worth more than a million. People looked at the moon through it and found gold deposits on it, boys. No need to pan it, it's real clean gold, like flour. Just pour it into a sack. . . . "

One of the young city fellows burst out laughing: "The lies he's telling—you've got to laugh. . . . "

Afanasy Petrovich got angry: "So I'm lying, you two-bit bastard? You just wait. . . . "

"Who 'just wait'?"

Afanasy Petrovich grabbed his revolver.

"Shush," said Selivanov.

The tobacco was divided up, and the instruments handed over to Afanasy Petrovich—as paymaster he can exchange them with the Kirghiz for something else when the opportunity arises.

He piled up the instruments in front of the baby.

"Go on and play. . . . "

The baby doesn't see them: it keeps squealing. Afanasy tried this way and that way (even got sweaty), but the baby keeps on squealing and won't play.

The cooks brought dinner. There came a thick smell of butter, kasha, and cabbage soup. They pulled out their big Semipalatinsk[7] spoons from their boottops. All the grass has been trampled down by the camp. On the cliffs above, a sentry shouts: "Can I . . . soon? I want some grub. . . . Replacement . . . come on!"

They finished dinner and remembered: got to feed the baby. The child is squealing incessantly.

Afanasy Petrovich chewed up some bread. He shoved the moist chewed-up lump into the wet, wide-open tiny mouth and made some smacking sounds with his lips. "Mm . . . mm . . . it's good . . . eat, little wood-goblin. . . . So tasty."

But the baby shut its little mouth and turned its head away—wouldn't take it. It cried through its nose, a thin and piercing cry.

The peasants came nearer and stood around the baby. They looked over each other's heads at the child. They didn't say anything.

It was hot. Cheekbones and lips glistened from the mutton. Shirts were undone. Feet were bare, yellow like the Mongolian earth.

One of them suggested: "Some cabbage soup for him. . . . "

They cooled some cabbage soup. Afanasy Petrovich wet his finger in the soup and stuck it into the baby's mouth. Good greasy cabbage soup runs down its little lips onto the pink little shirt and the flannel blanket.

It doesn't want it. It squeals.

"A puppy's smarter—it'll eat from a finger. . . . "

"A dog's one thing, but this is a human being. . . . "

"What a know-it-all!"

They didn't have any cow's milk in the detachment. They thought of giving it mare's milk—they did have some mares. But you couldn't—koumiss would get it drunk. It could get sick.

They left to stand among the *telegas*[8] and, worried, they exchanged comments in small groups. And among the *telegas* there was Afanasy Petrovich rushing about, a tattered *beshmet*[9] on his shoulders, his small eyes also tattered. His voice was thin, troubled, childlike, as if the child itself were running around complaining.

"So what do we have here? . . . It won't eat, men! . . . But it's gotta, doesn't it? . . . Think of something, you bastards. . . . "

The big, powerful-bodied men just stood there with a helpless look.

"It's a woman's job."

"Of course."

"From a woman he'd eat a whole ram."

"That's just it."

Selivanov called a meeting and declared, "A Christian lad shouldn't die like an animal. Let's say the father's a bourgeois, but what about the child? It's innocent."

The peasants agreed. "It's not the child's fault. It's innocent."

Drevesinin burst into laughter: "Grow, boy. Our boy'll grow up, fly off to the moon. . . . To the gold deposits."

The peasants didn't laugh.

Afanasy Petrovich raised his fist and shouted, "You're a hopeless bastard. The only one in this detachment who likes to ridicule!"

He shuffled his feet, wrung his hands, and suddenly started shouting in his shrill voice: "A cow. . . . We need a cow for him!"

In one voice they responded, "It'll be death without a cow. . . . "

"We really need a cow. . . . "

"Without a cow he'll starve to death."

Afanasy Petrovich said decisively, "I'll go after some cows, boys."

Drevesinin interrupted mischievously, "Back to the Irtysh, to Lebiazhe?"

"There's no reason, you ignorant fool, for me to go back to the Irtysh. I'll go to the Kirghiz."

"And trade for a tiliscope? Go to hell, benefactor. . . ."

Afanasy Petrovich rushed up to him and shouted in anger, "You son of a bitch. Want one right across your ugly face?"

And since they started cursing and got disorderly, Selivanov, the chairman of the meeting, cut them off: "That's enough."

And this is how they voted: Drevesinin, Afanasy Petrovich, and three others were to ride out into the steppe, to the Kirghiz *auls*,[10] and bring back a cow. If possible, they were to bring back two to five cows, because the cooks were running out of meat.

They strapped their rifles onto their saddles and put on Kirghiz fox-fur caps so they'd look like Kirghiz from a distance.

"Good-bye."

They wrapped the baby up in a small blanket and put him in the shade under a *telega*. A young fellow sat beside him, and for his and the baby's pleasure, he'd take potshots at a wormwood bush with his revolver.

IV

Oh, you joyless Mongolian sands! Oh, you poor blue rocks, you wicked deep-earth hands!

Russians cross the sands. Night.

The sands smell of heat, of wormwood.

The dogs in the *auls* bark at the wolf, at the darkness.

The wolves howl in the darkness at hunger, at death.

The Kirghiz fled from death.

Can you drive your flocks away from death?

The *aul* smells of dung and *airan*—sour milk. Thin and hungry Kirghiz children sit around yellow campfires. Bare-ribbed, sharp-faced dogs lie next to the boys. The yurts are like haystacks. . . .

There's a lake and reeds behind the yurts, and from the reeds gun-shots suddenly ring out into the yellow campfires: "O-o-o-at!"

The Kirghiz sprang out of their felt yurts in an instant. They began to shout in fright: "*Ui-boi . . . Ui-boi, . . . ak-kyzyl-uruss*[11] *. . . Ui-boi!*"

They jumped on their horses. Their horses, you can be sure, were bridled day and night. The yurts resounded with hooves. The steppe resounded with hooves. The reeds screeched like a wild duck: "Ai, ai, Red Russian—White Russian, ai, ai."

One graybeard fell off his horse into a *kazan*—a copper caul-dron—and knocked the cauldron over. Scalded, he let out a deep howl. And right beside him, a shaggy dog, its tail between its legs, timidly poked its hungry snout into the hot milk.

The mares neighed faintly. The sheep, as if frightened by wolves, thrashed about in their pen. The cows breathed heavily, as if out of breath.

And when they saw the Russians, the submissive Kirghiz women lay down submissively on their felt blankets.

Drevesinin laughed lasciviously: "Are we a bunch of stallions? . . . We don't always need to. . . . "

He quickly strained some milk into a flat Austrian flask and, snap-ping his whip, rounded up the cows and calves by the yurt. Freed from their tethers, the calves quickly poked the soft udders with their heads and joyfully grabbed the teats with their large soft lips.

"See, they're hungry, poor things. . . . "

And Drevesinin discharged his rifle into the calves.

Afanasy Petrovich ran through the whole village and was on the point of following Drevesinin, when he suddenly remembered: "We need a nipple. Hell, we forgot a nipple!"

He rushed through the yurts in search of a nipple. The fires in the yurts had gone out. Afanasy Petrovich grabbed a glowing log and, scattering sparks and coughing from the smoke, searched for a nipple. In his one hand the log crackled; in the other was his revolver. There wasn't a nipple to be found. The submissive Kirghiz women, their bodies covered with *chuvluks*,[12] lay sprawled out on felt mats. Children were howling.

Afanasy Petrovich got angry, and in one of the yurts he shouted at a young Kirghiz woman: "Get me a nipple, you heathen bitch, a nipple!"

The Kirghiz woman started to cry and quickly began undoing her faille caftan and then pulling off her blouse.

"*Ni kirek . . . Al . . . Al . . .* Take." And next to her on the mat cried a baby wrapped in rags. The Kirghiz woman was already raising her knees. "*Al . . . Al . . .* Take."

But now Afanasy Petrovich grabbed one of her breasts, squeezed it, and whistled with joy: "Here we go . . . A nipple. Ah! A firm one!"

"*Ni kirek . . . Ni . . .* What?"

"All right, don't quack. Let's go! A firm one!"

And he dragged the Kirghiz woman by the arm after him.

In the darkness, he put the Kirghiz woman on the saddle and, feeling her breasts from time to time, raced back to Selivanov's gullies, to the detachment.

"I've got it, men," he said joyfully, and he had tears in his eyes. "I can find it, brother. I can dig it up from the ground."

V

But in the camp it turned out—Afanasy Petrovich hadn't noticed in the darkness—that the Kirghiz woman had taken her child with her.

"Let her," said the peasants, "there'll be enough milk even for two. We've got cows, and she's a healthy broad."

The Kirghiz woman was quiet, stern, and she nursed the babies out of sight from everyone. They lay next to her on the felt mat in the tent—one white, the other yellow—and they squealed as one.

A week later at the general meeting Afanasy Petrovich complained, "Why hide it, comrades? That foul Kirghiz woman, she's feeding us a lie—she gives her kid her whole breast, and ours whatever's left. I watched her on the sly, brothers. You just go and take a look."

The men went, and they see: the children are like all children, one white, the other yellow like a ripe melon. But it looks like the Russian one is thinner than the Kirghiz.

Afanasy Petrovich threw up his hands. "I gave him a name, Vaska, . . . and now just imagine . . . the unexpected. Trickery."

Drevesinin said without so much as a grin on his face, "And you, Vaska, are puny, near death . . . "

They found a pole and fixed it on the wagon shaft so that one side wouldn't outbalance the other.

They put a baby on each end to see which one would outweigh the other.

The babies, who were suspended in lassos of hair, were squealing in their little rags. They had the light smell that babies have. The Kirghiz woman stood near the *telega*, and not understanding a thing, she cried.

The peasants are silent, they're watching.

"Go on," said Selivanov, "let the scale go."

Afanasy Petrovich let go of the pole, and the Russian boy immediately went upward.

"See, the yellow-mouthed bastard," said Afanasy Petrovich irately, "he's put on the weight."

He picked up a dried-out sheep's skull that was lying on the ground and put it on the Russian child. Then the babies evened out.

The men started fussing and shouting.

"She's fed him so much so that he's a whole head heavier, hasn't she, men?"

"You can't watch her all the time."

"What a beast . . . how's she's fed him."

"Who watched? . . . "

"We've got our own work to do—are we to watch over the children?"

Several of the older men agreed: "How can you watch all the time? After all, she's his mother."

Afanasy Petrovich started stomping his feet and screaming, "So you think a Russian person should die because of some heathen. . . . He should die? My Vaska?"

They looked at Vaska; there he lay, white and skinny.

The peasants became somber.

Selivanov said to Afanasy Petrovich, "And you . . . him . . . that one . . . God be with him, let him die . . . the Kirghiz creature. We've killed enough of them . . . you answer . . . once. . . . "

The peasants looked at Vaska and went their ways quietly.

Afanasy Petrovich took the Kirghiz creature and wrapped him in a torn sack.

His mother started to howl. Afanasy Petrovich struck her lightly on the teeth and went from the village out into the steppe.

VI

A couple of days later the peasants stood on tiptoe by the tent and, over each other's shoulder, peered inside where the Kirghiz woman was nursing the white child on the felt mat.

The Kirghiz woman's face, with eyes narrow like oat grains, looked submissive; she was wearing a purple faille caftan and soft kidskin boots.

The child was poking her breast with his face and moving his hands on her caftan, and his legs kicked in a funny and clumsy way, as if he were jumping.

The peasants looked on and laughed heartily.

And Afanasy Petrovich was the most tender. Sniveling, he said weepily, "See, he's gobbling it down."

And beyond the canvas tent, no one knew where, ran the gullies, the cliffs, the steppe, alien Mongolia.

No one knew where Mongolia ran—the wild and joyless beast.

1922

```
»»» «««
```

The Return of the Buddha

Chapter I

*The Story of the Washing of the Dishes and
the Tale of Dava-Dorchzhi about the Three-Hundredth Awakening
of Siddhartha Gautama, Named the Buddha*

> One Buddha appeared in countless forms, and in each
> of these countless forms is one Buddha.
> —*A rock placed near Peking (the year 1325, the 16th
> day of the third Moon)*

The pot should be moved closer to the stovepipe, the hot coals
away from the stove walls; then the flames leap upward, and the top
of the stove gets hot faster—the potatoes cook in sixteen and a half
minutes. You should eat them immediately, with the skins if possible, and use the hot water first to wash your hands and later the
dishes.

Today the professor isn't able to do the dishes. He was about to
put his fingers and even his whole hand into the pot, but he barely
got his fingernails wet when the doorbell rang.

"Wait!" shouts the professor. He sticks his hand in deeper, takes
a pinch of sand, and rubs the plate vigorously. Again the doorbell.

Professor Safonov raises his thin eyebrows: "But I'm not a doctor. I have to wash my dishes so as not to light the stove again. Just wait a minute, citizen."

The professor feels a nice warmth in his stomach from the potatoes; his hands have soft warm sand on them. He puts some sand in his hand and rubs the sides and the inside of the blue bowl. There's a hard knock at the door. It's a strong knock, not a hungry one. The professor is worried.

He puts on his fur cap and takes his coat from the sofa. In front of the door latch he speaks into the darkness, to the floor. "They were here with a search the day before yesterday . . . and yesterday, too—sorry, I forgot. Do you have a warrant?"

There's an unhurried but loud answer from the other side of the door.

"I have to see Professor Vitaly Vitalevich Safonov on a personal matter."

"Just a minute."

The professor puts on his coat and, holding the collar around his throat, he opens the latch.

"The doctor's a floor higher, I . . . "

"It's you I must see!"

A man in a soldier's overcoat and cap (in 1918 all of Russia wore soldiers' clothing—Russia was at war) quickly passes through the entrance hall into the professor's study.

The professor, catching up with him, says hastily, "I can hear, and I get the point immediately. I'm used to it. If you have any potatoes or flour to offer, say so. Feel free to take off your overcoat, the stove stays warm for forty minutes. In these minutes I speak to no one. I take off my coat and read or write. Have a seat."

The professor takes his bowl. The soldier also walks over to the bowl.

"I'm listening, citizen."

Suddenly the man in the overcoat gently pushes the professor aside and sticks his hand in the pot.

"There aren't any more potatoes. I've eaten them all. Now the dishes are being washed, citizen soldier."

"Permit me, I'm more experienced."

The man opens the lower part of his overcoat, evidently to let in more warmth. He takes the bowl quickly.

"My name, citizen professor, is Dava-Dorchzhi. I'm from the Tushutu-Khan *aymak* . . . "[1]

"You're a Mongolian?"

"I'll be as brief as possible! Don't interrupt me."

"I repeat, citizen soldier, you must take off your overcoat for forty minutes."

"Thanks. By the way, I haven't taken off my overcoat for two weeks."

The citizen professor and the citizen soldier take off their coats. The citizen soldier washes the professor's dishes. Professor Safonov sits in the armchair opposite him. The soldier has dirty cheeks, an unusually thin, scraggly beard, and very black eyes, as if they had been lacquered. The professor also notices that the soldier has a guttural and sharp way of speaking.

The bowls clatter. The professor closes the damper of the stove carefully.

"The hermit Tsagan-lama Rashi-chzhamcho came to Khu-Khu-khoto from God knows where. Having accomplished a moderate number of miracles in town, he left for the mountains. In the mountains, citizen professor . . . "

"Vitaly Vitalevich, if you please."

" . . . in the mountains, dear Vitaly Vitalevich, he settled for an ascetic life near the Dunu-khoda cliffs and spent time here, constantly reading the laws, helping people study the rules of Buddhism, and fervently perfecting his spirit. Soon he unclasped his hands, which had been folded in a praying position, and in the year of the Fire Rabbit . . . "

"Approximately 1620?"

"In 1627, Vitaly Vitalevich, in that year he built a heathen temple five *styazns*[2] high in a valley of the Tushutu-Khan *aymak* near the mountain Baubay-bada-rakhu, at the sources of the Usutu-Golo stream. And in order to secure blessings for the lamas, *uvari-ki*,[3] and all living creatures, he walled himself off from the world in the Dungu cliffs and lived there for seven years, enduring his difficult feat and helping people master the laws and teachings of Buddha. He died in the twentieth year of the rule of Shuno-chzhi after spending about thirty years in meditation. His principal students—Tsagay-daychi, Chakhar-daychi, and Erdeni-daychi—opened the wall to his cell with the appropriate reverence and discovered not the bones of Tsagan-lama Rashi-chzhamcho, but a gilded bronze statue, a *burkhan*[4] of Siddhartha Gautama named Buddha. . . . Thus came to be the three-hundredth earthly awakening of the exalted lama Sak-ya, the eternal savior of all living creatures and the giver of all virtues."

"Wonderful!" exclaims the professor. "I haven't ever read that legend. Wonderful. Let me write it down. That was, you say, citizen soldier . . . in the year of the Fire Rabbit. . . . "

Dava-Dorchzhi carries the bowls over to the cupboard. The professor is about to pull the little table closer to the iron stove. The ink on his pen sticks like pitch. The professor does not write; touching the bookshelf, he says suddenly to the Mongolian, "Lavis and Rambo, *History of the Nineteenth Century in Eight Volumes*, The Granat Publishing House. I also have *The Court of the Empress Catherine II, Her Attendants and Confidants*, an almost brand-new edition! I could get half a *pud* of potatoes for it. Please note, someone else with a more extensive circle of acquaintances than I would hardly sell it to you for such a price, especially since interest in history always intensifies in revolutionary times."

"From time immemorial, the landowners of the Tushutu-Khan *aymak*," drawls the soldier without looking at the professor, "from time immemorial, they have cared for the statue of the Buddha with the proper respect. The edges of his clothing are trimmed with gold filigree, and his fingernails are also trimmed with it."

The professor put his pencil down and pushed aside his pen. He looks at the bookshelf. "What can I offer you if you don't want books? Look for yourself. How much are potatoes in real money?"

The soldier shakes his head with its badly trimmed hair. Then the professor asks about flour. The soldier doesn't have any bread or flour. The professor's jaw trembles slightly. They both put on their overcoats because the forty minutes are about gone. Professor Safonov stares at the floor and waits for the soldier to give him his hand and say good-bye. The soldier Dava-Dorchzhi's hand is rough, strong, and narrow. In the entrance hall, he announces boastfully, "In the Tushutu-Khan *aymak*, Vitaly Vitalevich, I have three thousand head of cattle. . . . Then, in the year that the *burkhan* of the Buddha appeared, there appeared in the sands . . . "

The professor looks at the torn collar of Dava-Dorchzhi's overcoat, at the patches under his arms, and angrily thinks about the three thousand head of cattle. He remembers the warm shearling overcoats he saw some time ago in Siberia. And unlatching the door, he mutters indistinctly, "Yes . . . yes . . . citizen, I'll definitely write down your kind offer, . . . that's to say, your legend. Although I'm not a specialist on Mongolia, I certainly have an interest in it. I can't write it down today, it's too cold. I'll write it down tomorrow or tonight, if I light the stove."

The flap of an overcoat flashes by in the staircase. Down below a log scrapes on the stone staircase; someone's dragging fuel to his apartment. For some reason the professor starts to feel sorry for the Mongolian, and he shouts, "Good-bye!"

The professor wraps the blanket over his overcoat around his legs and thinks about fuel, potatoes, and money. Again he remembers the three thousand head of cattle, and he realizes what he should have said to the Mongolian. He wants to pull his finger out from under the blanket and shake it at him, but the Mongolian is gone. Then his chin starts moving as he begins to lecture: "During a revolution the goal of self-preservation makes it essential to stay home. But if there's mobilization, then it's essential to go home immediately and not visit busy people, taking their time and warmth, and spend forty minutes telling legends about Buddha statues. There are so many statues in the world. And if you have three thousand head of cattle, then you should have at least a shabby sheepskin coat."

The professor recalls the Mongolian's words, "His fingernails are trimmed with gold."

The professor says, "It would've been better if he'd brought some potatoes!"

Instead of using these daily forty minutes to write down those thoughts that accumulate in a day and penetrate the brain like cold threads, the next day, just like the night before, the professor finds himself thinking about Dava-Dorchzhi.

"It must be," the professor decides, "because no one has ever come to see me with such strange stories. Now if someone would have come to buy or bargain for something like my brains, my nerves, or the day gone by, I would have forgotten about it just as soon as the buyer had left."

He jokes like that as he lights the stove and puts the potatoes into the pot. Today's portion of potatoes is smaller. Every other day the professor eats half a portion and then goes to bed with the lights on.

There's a knock on the door: Bang! Bang! Bam!

The professor, coatless and hatless, shaking his hands angrily, runs to the door and throws back the hook, shouting, "I don't have time to write down your stupid tales. I'm not your doctor and not your Mongolian specialist either. Why do you bother me every day?"

On the threshold there's a narrow-bearded man in a leather jacket and a brown cap with a visor (split in three places). He asks softly, "Does Professor Safonov live here?"

"I'm Professor Safonov."

"Vitaly Vitalevich?"

"I'm Vitaly Vitalevich."

Spitting on his fingers for some reason, the man reaches into the side pocket of his jacket and looking at one corner of the jacket, says softly, "To Professor Safonov from the People's Commissar for Enlightenment, to be delivered to him personally."

Safonov forgets to latch the door. The man in the leather jacket lowers the hook carefully, as if it were the packet, covering the cold metal with his jacket. Rubbing his hands over the stove, he asks, "Have you noticed? It's fifteen degrees below on the Reamur scale."[5]

"Take off your jacket."

"Thanks, comrade professor, but a car is waiting for us."

Then the professor quickly tears open the packet and reads: "The All-Russian Union of Cities, in addition to its memorandum, for the second time reminds . . . "

"The devils!" the man in the jacket shouts in irritation. "Those devils! Again they've used the memorandum paper of the Union of Cities to type on. How many times have I ordered them not to type important papers on . . . Turn it over, comrade professor. It's the typists who are sabotaging . . . "

The professor reads what is typed on the reverse side:

> The People's Commissar for Enlightenment of the North-
> ern Communes, 16 November 1918. To Prof. Vit. Vit. Safonov.
> The People's Commissar requests the immediate presence of cit-
> izen Safonov at a meeting of specialists in the mansion of the for-
> mer Count Stroganov.
>
> > The People's Commissar (signature)
> > Secretary (signature)

"There's no signature," said the professor. "What specialists?"

The man in the leather jacket takes the paper: "I'm the secretary," he says. "They forgot to give it to me for my signature; well,
I'll . . . right now."

"No, why bother?"

"No, I must, it's protocol."

The jacket takes out an indelible pencil. The professor notices
that the red star on his cap is drawn with the same kind of pencil.
The jacket signs his name. The professor rolls up the paper and
puts it into his desk.

He remembers his stove only as they are crossing the Troitsky
Bridge.

Chapter II

Knitted Articles, Some Discourse about Archeological
Research, and about the Russian Red Army

> The more tedious the procession through secluded
> places, the longer the important roads.
> —*Sykun-Tu*

The carpets of the Stroganov Palace are covered with burlap.
The soldier at the entrance is smoking a pipe. The soldier's boots
are wrapped up in burlap so that his feet don't freeze. He asks for a

pass, but doesn't get up from the stool so that his feet don't get cold.

Catching up with the secretary on the staircase, Professor Safonov queries, "And if the People's Commissar comes in, will he get up?"

"I doubt it. But that's really not important. Over here, comrade professor."

So as not to dirty the carpets, there's burlap on the floor in between the pieces of gilded furniture. Life in 1918—trying to stay alive, you eat dogs and cats. You barter so there'll be potatoes. Such are the professor's thoughts. He's thinking of explanations for the reasons.

The jacket pulls back his hat. His forehead is full of dirty wrinkles.

"Is Comrade Lunacharsky here?"[6]

Another person answers. He's in a black overcoat and has a thick briefcase, round like a log. He's wearing unusually large gray felt boots and a long, multicolored scarf that reaches to the floor.

"He's not going to come."

"Why are you trying to deceive me, Comrade Anisimov? He said, 'I'll be there in half an hour.' I went chasing off to the Vyborg side after the professor."

In his excitement the soldier with the briefcase gets his fingers all entangled as he shakes the professor's hand. Jumping back and moving the briefcase under his arm, he says in a rush, "Comrade Divel, you never get things coordinated! I just got a call here. This, they say, is not the business of the People's Commissariat of Enlightenment but of the Commissariat of Nationality Matters. What the hell do I need Lunacharsky for! The Commissar of Nationalities must speak. That won't do, comrade, making the leaders of the Revolution run around like that."

"Before uttering such words, Comrade Anisimov . . . "

"No, you're the one who's saying them, Comrade Divel."

"Then I'm not responsible for the meeting in any way. I . . . Pardon me, professor, you may go home."

Comrade Anisimov indignantly raises his briefcase above his head. Comrade Anisimov has a huge mouth. He shouts out words as thick as his briefcase: "What do you mean, Comrade Divel, 'You may go home'? Why must you create friction between departments? Stay, professor . . . "

The jacket makes a sharp, leathery gesture: "Allow me to repeat: the offer to you, professor, was from the People's Commissariat of Enlightenment. Now the offer is rescinded. Let them find their own expert. I'm not an errand boy to go and find professors for the Commissariat of Nationalities. I have my own urgent work."

They pull the professor by his sleeves: the briefcase toward the hall and the jacket toward the exit. The briefcase gets in the short one's way; he gets tired fast. The jacket takes the professor quickly. Anisimov jiggles the telephone: "Hello! Is this the commandant's office? This is Anisimov, the palace commandant. Are you there? . . . What? Yes! Yes! Me, me! Detain Professor Safonov on his way out, and let the other one, Divel, pass. What? Arrest? Yes, yes!"

The professor stumbles on the burlap and, embarrassed, says to the shoulder of the leather jacket, "No, I'd better stay, citizen . . . "

The jacket raises his thin finger and, pointing with it, shouts, "I shall report all this to Comrade Lunacharsky."

"Report it to Lenin if you want to. The schemers, they've latched onto us. Go, go, before he stops you . . . "

And picking up his briefcase, Comrade Anisimov—sweaty, with his scarf catching in his felt boots—runs further into the hall.

"You wait here, citizen professor, I'll be right back. I'll call the Nationalities to hurry them up. Hello, hello? Are you snoozing again? Hello-o-o!"

The professor waits in a chair. He looks in confusion at the furniture and wardrobe cabinets; everything has new numbers on it, and the heavy door curtains are marked with chalk. Anisimov is on the phone, swearing at a driver. A typewriter is crackling coldly in the next room.

"Did you write that down, Vitaly Vitalevich?"

The professor turns around. Behind the armchair in a filthy soldier's overcoat and shaggy sheepskin cap stands Dava-Dorchzhi.

"I forgot to mention to you the history of the Temple of Emanating Peace. Although it has to do with later times, it relates directly to the events surrounding the *burkhan* of the Buddha. The Tushutu-Khan *aymak* during the dynasty of . . . "

The professor rips off his hat in exasperation and wants to hit his knee with it, but instead pulls it tightly on his head again. He says with indignation, "You, citizen, perhaps are a civilized person and are above all this revolutionary fervor . . . "

Dava-Dorchzhi nods.

"In . . . in that case allow me to ask you to help me get out of here. I have precious little time, and don't have enough of it at my disposal to go around examining all the palaces seized by the revolutionaries."

The professor lies courageously, "I have written down your legend and am extremely . . . "

Here, tripping on the burlap and dropping his briefcase, Comrade Anisimov runs by, choking and shouting, "Comrade delegates . . . Comrade professor. Please come in, Comrade Tsviladze has arrived."

Dava-Dorchzhi follows the professor and mutters under his breath, "All this will be over fast. Tsviladze is the Deputy Commissar of Nationalities, hot-tempered like a Georgian should be, but wise for his years. Here, Vitaly Vitalevich, over here . . . "

The burlap is gathered up into a heap. A crowd of dark men with broad cheekbones, in soldiers' overcoats and quilted jackets. There is a heavy smell of barracks—or is it sour bread and cabbage?

And also the slight smell of sheepskin, perhaps, or water. "The steppes," thinks the professor and looks attentively into their faces with narrow eyes. And their eyes rest not on the professor, and perhaps not on the tall commissar Tsviladze, but on the one whom the professor sees with surprise in back of the commissar.

On a high marble pedestal about nine feet high stands a gilded cast object in a tall crown. There are lotus flowers in his palms and on his soles, and fanlike decorations near his temples.

The professor remembers: *The edges of his clothing are trimmed with gold filigree, and his fingernails are also trimmed with it.*

And with his small round chin raised high, Dava-Dorchzhi looks over the head of the People's Commissar directly into the eyes, dark and narrow like steppe grass, of the statue of Siddhartha Gautama called the Buddha.

And it's possible that the guttural voice of the People's Commissar Tsviladze reminds them—those with the broad cheekbones— of the evening sounds of horses, or, better yet, of the morning sounds . . .

The People's Commissar, his chest thrust high, a wears a gray jacket and gray lambskin hat. There are newspapers sticking out of his pocket. "Comrades and citizens, toilers of the East! I greet you in the name of the Council of People's Commissars of the Northern Communes. In our group, comrades and citizens, we see representatives from distant Mongolia and even, it would seem, from China. Behind me [the People's Commissar waves his hand and glances at his notes] is a statue of the Buddha, seized and removed from the Mongolian Lamaistic monastery of the Tushutu-Khan *aymak* by the tsarist general Kaufman. . . . This statue is a religious fetish, an object of worship for monks and the ignorant masses deceived by them. However, comrades . . . we, the proletariat, are capable of respecting not only principles of nationalism, but also sincere religious feeling. At the time that the tsarist general Kaufman lost the statue of the Buddha at cards to General Stroganov, we, the communists, respecting national unity and acknowledging that there, where national barriers and isolation from other nations shatter and destroy the obsolete framework of the patriarchal-patrimonial and feudal-patriarchal world, shatter the reactionary bonds of family, clan, tribe, and neighborhood societies . . . create the essential historical basis for the class struggle—there communism offers national unity in counterbalance to the patriarchal-feudal anarchy and external foreign oppression, such as now are the attitudes of the Chinese imperialists toward you. . . . It's impossible to go from khanish feudalism to organized socialism all of a sudden, just like that. We wish that out of this ignorance and darkness, out of this spiritual poverty, will emerge national types—Kirghiz, Turkmen, Mongolian. . . . However, comrades, aid to the emergence of national types does not mean aid to the clergy, lamas, and monks, and, therefore, citizens and comrades, the resolution of the Little Council of People's Commissars about the edict regarding the transfer of the . . . object located here in these rooms into the hands of the representatives of the Mongolian nation."

The People's Commissar raised his fist high, poking angrily at the Japanese tapestries, Tibetan weapons, and at all the small idols of tiny Buddhas made of dark strong-smelling wood.

"That is, the statue of the Buddha from the Tushutu-Khan *aymak* in the chambers of the Stroganov counts does not mean that the Bolsheviks are protecting the lamas. No, the statue of the Buddha is being given back as a museum rarity, as a national artistic treasure. For the observance of the precise execution of the instructions of the Narkomnats,[7] the representatives of Soviet power in place at the Mongolian border will be allowed to cross into Mongolia, and from the center Political Instructor Comrade Anisimov and the representative of the experts, Professor Safonov, are being dispatched to accompany the transport."

"Permit me!" shouts the professor indignantly. "I haven't agreed!"

The People's Commissar glances at him in passing, wipes his forehead, and leaves, shaking the hands of the people in soldiers' overcoats on his way out.

Dava-Dorchzhi gives the People's Commissar the newspapers that have fallen out of his pocket and says quietly, "Mr. Professor, evidently, wishes to object."

And then, squeezing the papers in his fist, People's Commissar Tsviladze, with a sudden Caucasian accent, says quickly to the professor's face, "Citizen professor . . . when there's a revolution going on, it's not an opportune time to drag your feet. Tomorrow at 11 A.M. you will be so kind as to appear in my office in the Narkomnats for instructions and mandates. . . . Yes, indeed!"

Throwing the papers on the burlap on the floors, he shouts to the Mongolians, "Long live the international revolution and the emancipation of the workers!"

"Hurra-a-ah!"

Professor Safonov returns home on foot. Five little boys are sledding down from the Palace Bridge.[8] A woman in a soldier's hat walks past carrying a horse's head. Thinking about something else entirely, the professor asks out of habit, "Are you selling it?" Glancing at her hand, the woman, probably out of habit, too, answers, "No." Then the professor feels hunger, and he's overjoyed that he didn't get to eat his potatoes for lunch. On official trips you get food provisions, and for accompanying the Buddha, he should get an even bigger ration. Therefore, at home he makes a full pot of potatoes and uses more firewood than usual. His books and papers look like brown piles of snow; they always look like that when the professor, warming himself, wonders to whom he should leave his books and manuscripts.

Professor Safonov lectures on the history of world literature in the Central Pedagogical Institute, and his current work is "Reflections of the Scandinavian Saga in the Russian Byliny."[9] He ties up his manuscripts with twine and writes on each one with a red grease pencil, "Manuscript of Prof. V. V. Safonov, who left on official busi . . . " But he thinks a bit and corrects it to "who left for the Mongolian border on a research trip. Please handle with care." There are a lot of manuscripts, and he adds more firewood; it's warm. He takes off his knitted sweater; one of the sleeves is coming apart. He puts aside an encyclopedia so that he can acquire some warm knitted clothing. On a scrap of paper he writes, "2 sweaters, 1 shearling coat, 4 pair of socks," and adds some more books to the encyclopedia. Nonetheless, he is reluctant to burn the wood for some reason, and he stokes his stove with manuscripts and unneeded books. It turns out that he has a lot of books he doesn't need. Ashes rise and spread throughout the whole room; there are gray pleasant-smelling ashes on the professor's cheeks. Flicking them off, the professor thinks about the flocks in Mongolia and about eating mutton. That's how the political instructor Anisimov found him when he entered.

"You've got to tie a kerchief around your head, or else your hair will fall out from the ashes from the paper. And it will be hard to wash your hair with this soap crisis. . . . "

It's always as if Anisimov has been running uphill: he's sweaty, his unwound scarf is fluttering, and his felt boots are wide and cheerful like a spring roof. Happy with his energy and the thick briefcase that takes the place of his stomach, he helps the professor rake his papers into the stove. In order to make him feel good, Safonov asks, "Did he complain?"

"Who?"

"Divel."

"No, he did some shouting and that was that. Last night he came over to play checkers. We live in the same commune. . . . Strength, or as I like to say, dynamics. . . . But Divel?"

The professor sees a person from a commune for the first time. He asks about his children. Anisimov has three children, and the smallest, who's five years old, loves cars. He cuts them out of paper and colors them with ink. Anisimov has been in the party since 1916, and by profession he's a lathe operator.

"Is there going to be a commune[10] in Russia?" the professor asks carefully, as if stung.

"A commune? And where else should it be if not here? Absolutely!"

Feeling warm, he suggests that the professor go see how the Buddha is being moved. Professor Safonov says he has to pack. Anisimov looks around at the shelves and the desk.

"Yes, you must. Have you been a professor long?"

"Twelve years."

"And you haven't been a member of any party?"

"No."

"So, and you're close to fifty."

"Forty-eight."

"That's not unusual. Well, I'm going. We'll go together to the commissariat for the mandates. Tomorrow. Although they ordered us to come today, tomorrow's better, and, what's more, they probably won't have them ready."

Shaking his briefcase and waving his hands as if he's at a rally, he rushes down the staircase.

And that's just the way it was: the next day they had to wait two hours for the mandates to be prepared, and then they ran around half a day getting orders for the *teplushka*.[11] Walking from the train station, they saw on Nevsky[12] a black truck loaded with wood and smelling of gas from afar, pulling a large *telega* with thick iron wheels. Several soldiers in the *telega* were holding onto a plank crate held together by a rope around its sides. The crate was fresh and bright, and the letters of the words "This side up" and "Fragile," scrawled in red lead paint, bobbed up and down gaily.

"They're ours! That's dynamics for you. Along with the Buddha, they're taking firewood to the station," said Anisimov. "Let's go help . . . "

Dava-Dorchzhi quickly and respectfully pulled off his shaggy sheepskin cap.

But Professor Safonov walked past.

The professor has a sled. He takes it to the institute once a month to get his ration. But more often than not, he usually carries his ration home in his hands; they give very little. The professor lets a student he knows, Lazar Neitz, move into his apartment. When the professor gets back from the station, Neitz—with his legs pulled up to his chin and his arms around his knees—is playing his balalaika. He has a long nose, thin like a balalaika, and there's always some kind of sound coming from it.

"I have malaria in my nose!" says Neitz.

The professor packs his baggage into the sled, and Neitz helps.

"Will you return in half a year, or are you going to stay there forever? Mongolia is famous for its cattle-breeding, citizen professor. . . . "

The professor takes his sled to the Nikolaevsky station. The streetcars have stopped; the tracks are covered with snow, and the snow has frozen hard, like ice. Soldiers, in bast shoes and overcoats drawn tight with leather belts, walk with a red banner and overtake him. For a moment he thinks they're going to occupy his spot in the *teplushka*. He hurries, his boots slipping on the ice.

"The bourgeois is going to sell stuff!" shout the soldiers.

"We should search him!"

And very close to them the professor hears the clanging of rifles.

Taking the cold rope in his other hand, the professor remembers about the mittens. He forgot to get some, and there are still books left back there. "They'll move in people like those walking next to me. . . ."

Dava-Dorchzhi is waiting for him by the entrance. Pushing away an old woman who had run up to him ("Will you sell or trade something?"), the Mongolian leads him through bodies lying side by side. "Move to the right, to the right, citizen professor! If I had the time, I would make every effort to help you. But the snow is hard, and your sled has iron blades. . . . It's easy, I assume."

The professor breathes heavily; he feels a sharp pain in his chest. "Has Anisimov arrived? When does the train leave?"

"Don't worry, we have an endless amount of time before departure. Comrade Anisimov won't be late."

"But he has the mandates and all the papers . . . "

"Don't worry, he'll get here."

The walls of the *teplushka* are covered with strips of felt taken from mattresses, and the soldiers sleep on straw. There is a small iron stove in the corner; on a log next to it stands a bottle of kerosene with a long smoking wick. A woman is fixing this lamp. The professor cannot see her face; outside there is dusk and snow. Somebody runs past under the floor, banging on the wheels with a hammer. . . . Behind the stove, running the whole length of the car, is the plank crate. It smells of resin, and its new nails sparkle in the light of the lamp. The narrow space between the walls of the car and the crate is filled with bricks. Snow is melting off the bricks, and there's a strong smell of water. The Buddha is sailing in his new boat. There's a sign in red paint on the boat: "This side up . . . fragile."

Dava-Dorchzhi is splitting firewood with his small hatchet. "We have orders for twelve persons, not counting you, professor. You and Comrade Anisimov have a different travel warrant. But the twelfth person refused to go back to his homeland, and I've taken a woman. . . . "

"Is she Mongolian?"

"Yes. I've taken a woman and acted wisely."

"Is she someone's wife?"

"I don't know, it's possible. But she's a woman, and a Mongolian woman doesn't know how to say no. The Europeans and Russians explain their behavior by saying that the Chinese have corrupted them because, according to the laws of their country, they cannot take their own women with them into Mongolia. Don't you find that I've acted wisely, professor?"

"Wisdom is relative."

"And that's why I've chosen you as my traveling companion, professor."

"Chosen?"

The log won't split. Dava-Dorchzhi opens the door and jumps down with the log. The buffers clank icily; the locomotive has been connected to the train. Shaking his briefcase, Anisimov comes into the car.

"But where's your baggage?" asks the professor.

Anisimov points to his briefcase, and putting aside a felt boot as long and wide as an executioner's block, he sermonizes in response, "What baggage does a commune need? That's backward indifferentism. Yes-s. . . . "

He bangs on the crate, snorts, and then jumps down and runs toward the station. The professor calls to him, "At least leave us that mandate!"

Anisimov laughs loudly, but nevertheless pulls out the envelope with the mandates. "Hold on to them, comrade professor! Over there in third class they've called a meeting about the Red Army. . . . We've uncovered a little Menshevik. I . . . It's all right, all right, I won't get left. I'll tell them to hold the train for half an hour. It's all right. . . . "

The professor warms his hands over the stove.

"I would like to hear you explain your strange words, or, more precisely, one word. What do you mean by you 'chose' me, Dava-Dorchzhi?"

The Mongolians are spreading out the straw, and the woman goes off to a corner. The soldiers gather in a group and listen to something. The professor begins to make out their faces—they're covered with something blue. Dava-Dorchzhi shakes his finger at them; they squat down, all in a row.

"We have a lot of time in front of us, citizen professor, both for explanations and for reflections, devout or otherwise . . . May the dragons weave nets over your thoughts, Vitaly Vitalevich."

The speaker before Comrade Anisimov took about fifteen minutes. In the fifteen minutes remaining to him, Comrade Anisimov could not explain the role of the Communist Party in the international revolution, the role of the Red Army in the Russian Revolution and the unusual principles of its organization. If you're going to delay the train, you can't cut short your speech; you have to destroy the Menshevik argument to the core. It won't occur to the station commandant to hold the train. And Comrade Anisimov fulminated against the Mensheviks and the Right S–R's[13] and the White Guards for forty-five minutes.

Meanwhile, the train left. . . .

The Mongolians in the *teplushka* were praying by the pine crate with the Buddha. Dava-Dorchzhi, with his arms spread wide, was reading the eulogy:

"I bend my knee and express my special homage, based on the three principles, before the highest lama, whose authority knows no boundaries, and even the specks of dust raised by his feet are adornments for the foreheads of many wise men. . . . I bring my hands together in prayer, scatter flowers of praise before the one possessing the might of ten forces, before the great worth of the delicate fingernails of the one whose crowns are adored with a hundred *Tengyurs*."[14]

Covered with a blanket, the professor lies near the stove. His neck aches; he must have caught a draft as he was dragging his baggage. "I'll have to barter for a scarf at the next station," he thinks. But he doesn't have any books. What is he going to barter with? The straw under his hands is soft and pleasant like butter.

Chapter III

Uniforms of Italians and Frenchmen, Peacock Tails, and Also a Conversation about the Water Closet of the Grand Duke Sergey Mikhailovich

> Earlier lives the thought. Enchantment resides outside the picture. Like a sound nesting in a string—like a haze becoming a fog.
> —*Khu-An-Yue*, The Category of Pictures

Outside, on the door, the professor has written in large letters in chalk, "No entry. Office of the People's Commissar of Enlightenment." Nevertheless, soldiers kept looking in and asking, "Is it possible, comrade, to get a ride?" Dava-Dorchzhi would answer, "We're accompanying cargo, move on!"

The Mongolians in the *teplushka* drink tea all day long. At the stations they grab boiling water by the bucket, and the woman warms up teapots, one after the other. While drinking tea, they talk about cattle, medicines, and religion. Sometimes Dava-Dorchzhi lies on his back yawning, and slowly, as if threading a needle, translates the soldiers' conversations for the professor. Often they sell something, bargain, criticize, and praise what's being sold and strike a bargain by the squeezing of fingers, and, in doing so, one of them lowers his sleeve while the other sticks his hand into it. After striking a bargain by squeezing their fingers secretly, the Mongolians resume their tea drinking.

At first the professor writes down their conversations, his thoughts, and meetings, but he loses the paper and, covering his feet with the blanket, sits for days on end in front of the stove. During the night, the soldiers steal firewood, boards, and railroad ties at the stations. The stations are packed with trains. The rails strain and ring. The *teplushkas* are packed with soldiers, women, and people with bags of goods for sale. All of this flashes past—ringing, squealing, and rumbling. Sometimes they put the *teplushka* onto a siding, and it stays there for days, until it gets connected during the night.

Suddenly, while the train is stopped on a siding, Comrade Anisimov comes running into the *teplushka*. His scarf is even dirtier, and his felt boots are covered with soot. Banging his fist on the crate, he shouts dumbfounded, "Here you are. On your way? I barely found you. All right, I memorized the number. Do you have anyone with typhus? Right now there's a battle with epidemics. The Whites are pressing down on us. I'll be right back!"

Again he runs. His briefcase has become thinner, and hairs, the color of old bread, grow here and there on his nose. Grabbing his head, he jumps on the locomotive of a passing train and disappears again.

The professor is irritated by idleness, the incessant tea drinking, the bartering, his unexpected trip, his inability to get comfortable, and the cold and wind outside. Going to sleep, he says to Dava-Dorchzhi, "I'll be forced to warn the political instructor, citizen, that in your person there hardly resides a representative of the working people of Mongolia."

Dava-Dorchzhi rustles the straw.

"Does Vitaly Vitalevich really know the working people of Mongolia? The People's Commissar himself reported to you that 50 percent of our population are lamas."

"The *politruk*[15] doesn't know your relationship to the statue of the Buddha . . . when, insofar as I understand, you are a *gyghen*.[16]

"Am I really to blame that the most holy and most blessed Buddha in his current reincarnation has chosen my sinful body?"

"You didn't mention this to the People's Commissar."

"He wouldn't believe it. You're the only one who believes it."

"I believe it?"

"Then why laugh at the religious prejudices and beliefs of others? We can talk about something else; for example, about the uniforms of Italians and Frenchmen. By the way, I know a joke about uniforms having to do with a peacock's tail. . . . First I'll tell you a few words about how I landed on the German front, and then I'll . . . "

The professor, coughing and for some reason sensing a trembling in his thighs, says, "If I were more base, I'd tell the *politruk* about your officer's rank . . . It's possible . . . "

Professor Safonov chokes suddenly; his mouth is stuffed with hard straw. Something is painfully pricking his nostril, and a slippery warmth covers the roof of his mouth. Dava-Dorchzhi pokes him in the ribs with his fist, and spitting in disgust mumbles quickly, "Lucky for you, you bastard, that you're less base! . . . Ah, I'll show you what an officer's rank means. What's the matter, don't you have enough bread, or have you gotten a desire for meat? *Naran.* Hey!"

The woman lights the lamp. Dava-Dorchzhi jumps up. The professor spits out the straw and in fright mumbles his apologies. Dava-Dorchzhi quickly buttons up his overcoat; he looks in the corner and says, "If your portion of bread isn't enough, we can increase it. If you need a woman, I'll tell her to lie with you. She doesn't understand Russian."

"Leave me alone!" the professor says quietly.

Then Dava-Dorchzhi opens the doors and looks down at the wheels.

The soldier covers himself with the sheepskin coat and shouts, "Hey, close them!"

The woman puts out the lamp; there's not much kerosene. It needs to be saved. Dava-Dorchzhi says to him out of the darkness, "Or perhaps you're interested in more frivolous anecdotes? Then I could tell you a wonderful anecdote about the life of the grand duke Sergey Mikhailovich. The grand duke's water closet, as you know, often served as his study. He had a library there, mainly of classics, a light musical instrument, and views of Palestine. . . . "

The professor sticks his face in the straw. The smell of cold iron wafts from the stove. The soldiers are snoring.

"You should be ashamed of yourself!"

"I also wonder, professor, why it is that two intelligent people can't find a common topic of conversation. . . . I keep trying to talk about your Russian culture, without touching upon our steppe truths. I, you know, assumed something entirely different . . . although you'll be able to settle down in Siberia quite comfortably. . . . There's bread there and everything necessary for our existence. I don't insist on Mongolia."

The professor remembers angrily that Dava-Dorchzhi walks with his legs slightly bent. Evidently he got some pleasure from feeling like a man of the steppes. He spoke about the Russians with contempt. And again, angrily, his heart growing numb, the professor thought: "He became like that after the Revolution. It's after the Revolution that he began to speak like that about Russia." In order to convince himself, he says into the darkness, "Where did you go to school?"

"In the Omsk Cadet. . . . Alas, they felt it was even necessary to teach a reincarnated Buddha. Anyway, I wanted to myself. I've no one to blame. I wasn't wounded in the war and, moreover, I was a volunteer. . . . "

"Did you have your own division?"

"Yes, on the Caucasian front."

"Why are you transporting the Buddha?"

He guffaws, "I'm going to open an ethnographic museum in the Tushutu-Khan *aymak*. . . . You're going to be the director, professor. We've signed an agreement—to pay the Bolsheviks five hundred head of cattle for the Buddha. . . . Do you think the People's Commissar was speaking for nothing? We'll hand over five hundred head of cattle to them at the border. They'll receive five hundred head. . . . A museum nowadays is very expensive for unenlightened barbarians. . . . Just look, the Russians have taken and confiscated the palaces of counts and turned them into museums, and with property they don't need, they make national policy for the East. It's both cheap and noble."

In the morning, as the professor is going for boiling water, he notices a Mongolian soldier behind him. The Mongolian looks at his hands and laughs. The Mongolian has lips that are wide and long, like a sword. His teeth against his lips are like geese in a river.

The professor asks why he's following him. Winking, the Mongolian asks for the ring on his finger. The professor returns without getting any boiling water. Rocking his shoulders, Dava-Dorchzhi listens to the professor. Then he asks the professor to show him the ring and is surprised that the professor, during such a famine, hasn't exchanged the ring for something. The Mongolian, he explains, will kill the professor if the latter takes it into his head to go for a stroll, for example, to the Cheka.[17] He's stupid, understands Russian poorly, but we're so used to denunciations that during a denunciation a person puts his lips like this: "Show us, San-Da-Gou."

And San-Da-Gou twists his lips. The professor has a sweetly gnawing pain in his chest. The woman leaves to get some boiling water. As she is jumping down, the professor notices the thick firm muscles of her calves.

That same day a Mongolian soldier escapes from the *teplushka*. There was a political meeting at the Vologda station, and the Mongolian remained behind. At first, Dava-Dorchzhi looks at the professor's finger and his coat. He turns away.

"He understood too much Russian, professor. I'm afraid that could be bad for you. Knowledge. . . . The soldier, of course, won't return. Either he got frightened or he'll make a denunciation . . . even though the Bolsheviks don't pay for denunciations."

The lamp burns the whole night; they're expecting arrest or they're afraid that the professor will escape.

A sentry sits on a log by the doors.

The professor is bored; they've given him more bread than usual, and at first he didn't want to eat it, but then he ate it. The sentry has blocked all the light from the lamp with his overcoat; inside the *teplushka* it's just as dark as it always is at night. But the professor can't sleep anyway.

Professor Safonov is thinking about his study and about his dacha near Peterhof. He remembers his late wife—her image is flat and unclear, like a photograph, but he lived with her for six years. After her death he couldn't make up his mind to remarry, and every Saturday a girl would come to see him. Sometimes, most often when he was working more intensely, he would order the girl to come over twice a week. Today is Saturday. He catches himself: Did he think about the girl before thinking about his wife?

His legs are getting warm. The warmth moves higher. He glances around at the sentry. The latter throws his cigarette butt toward the stove and dozes off. Whose business is it what he's thinking about! He pulls the blanket over his head, but it's hard to breathe; he's sweating under his arms.

He gets up to throw a log in the stove but, without forethought, he starts crawling. Halfway, he stops and looks at the sentry. He's dozing. He looks in the corner with the Buddha. The professor's eyelids have begun to sweat; he wipes them with his warm palm. His lips are sweating and drooling. Bending close to the floor, he spits.

The woman is sleeping next to the crate with the Buddha. The professor doesn't add any wood; he crawls up to the reddish sheepskin coat and touches the round corpulent body. The body raises its head, evidently not recognizing him, and with a habitual motion pulls back its leg. Then he gets under the coat with the woman.

In the morning while drinking tea, Dava-Dorchzhi tells the professor about his horses. The professor wonders whether she recognized him or not. He looks at her on the sly and suddenly he senses on his lips her gaze, slow—like the lakes of the steppe—and evanescent. He feels his cheeks flushing.

"What's her name?" he asks.

Dava-Dorchzhi pours tea into a saucer. "Whose?"

"That woman's."

"I don't know."

He asks the soldier her name and, sighing loudly, he sips his tea and says, "Tsin-Chzhun-Chan. . . . It's very long, professor. But Russians have even longer ones. What was your wife's name, Vitaly Vitalevich?"

Chapter IV

*High-flown Discussions about the Mandates of Our Souls,
the Downfall of Civilization, and Pine Crates of Various Sizes.
Careless Stokers Who Are to Blame for Wolves Being Seen
in the Steppes. The* Gyghen *Is Worried.*

> On the evening of his dwelling on this thought, the
> Buddha flew like an apparition through the air, dis-
> playing his golden body.
> —*Tale of the Female Builder Pu-A.*

Vitaly Vitalevich pretends he has forgotten what transpired during the night; he smiles and jokes. As he smiles, his grayish mustache tickles his cheeks, and the more he smiles, the more unpleasant his cheeks feel. It's as though someone else's mustache and
someone else's smile are tickling his cheeks. But the *gyghen* Dava-
Dorchzhi doesn't look at him; he's trimming a strip of wood with
his long pocketknife, and Shurkha the Mongolian is looking over
the *gyghen*'s shoulder. At first the strip of wood turns into a sword,
then a fish, and in the shape of a bird it disappears in the stove.
Shurkha laughs shrilly; his skull is covered with tufts of hair that
hang loose and resemble rags.

Vitaly Vitalevich sees some sort of an omen in the strip of wood,
and he makes a cross out of another strip of wood. He ties it together with thread. He doesn't have a knife, which means that he's
completely unarmed. He tosses the cross into the stove, but even at
this moment the *gyghen* does not turn around. Shurkha the Mongolian follows the professor everywhere. "Perhaps I should write a
note and toss it out," the professor laughs to himself.

At the stations there are more and more posters. On each one the
same red-cheeked general is sticking a bayonet into a worker and a

peasant. Everywhere there are arguments next to the posters. In the station snack bars, soldiers on leave cast their votes: should they let this train pass or detain it?

No one will take his note. Who needs his call for help? People are reading slogans, posters, leaflets, brochures, and, in gray newspapers, reports about the various fronts.

The train moves with long stops in between. Conductors in black sheepskin coats walk around, both day and night, with lighted lanterns; the cars are long and dark, like coffins. The tracks whine and strain; they speak of explosions. There are security forces on the trains—every night there are shoot-outs with bandits. If the Greens[18] detain the train, they make the communists stand to the left, the non-Party travelers to the right. Those on the left get shot right on the railroad embankment.

"Where will they make me stand?" Vitaly Vitalevich wonders.

"You'll find out in due time," says Dava-Dorchzhi.

After Vyatka the fogs begin. Shurkha walks right next to the professor and, coughing, looks at his hat; he must be scared of the fog. Sometimes the pine trees along the embankment jump out like huge frightened birds. The floors of the car shake unsteadily, and the shaking reverberates in people's knees and leads to nausea.

Also because of the fog, faces lengthen and darken; the switchmen, people in long overcoats are—like the whole station—just gray, limp folds of overcoats. They accompany the trains with a hungry, jaw-clenched stare. Bending their necks, the locomotives tear into the fog, and the fog tears into them. The passengers cut down pine trees along the embankment and saw them up and split them—that's when the locomotives stop. The iron womb heats up again—and the steam engine tugs at the cars for a long time, freeing them from the frozen tracks. Sometimes they need water (the water towers at the stations have been emptied by other trains), and then they throw snow into the tenders. The soldiers, women, and conductors stretch out in a long chain far into the fog and pass buckets of snow.

Once during the night they were passing water to the tender from a river next to the bridge. From far off in the bushes the train came under fire (it's possible that the crunching sound came not from the bushes but from the snow), and someone shouted, "Surrender or we'll wipe you out!"

Throwing down their buckets, people began to crawl, falling (the incline suddenly turned to ice), and then ran toward the cars; and a woman, her voice catching—as if she were being beaten—was calling her child. The engineer—he was taking the water and pouring it in the tender—also threw down his bucket and from somewhere, where there was a crate with wrenches and screws, he pulled out a machine gun and climbed onto the tender. The soldiers, clapping their mittens, lay down with rifles between the wheels of the car, asking the passengers to get into the cars.

The professor can't get to sleep for a long time.

In the morning (again, can you really explain these days?) he looks into the hungry darkened faces. Of course, you keep seeing them every minute, every hour, every day. There aren't enough tears and howls for these freezing fogs, blizzards, and snowstorms—their faces are like posters.

"Argonauts!" says Dava-Dorchzhi at the professor's words.

And the *gyghen* intentionally talks about the excavations near the cliffs of the town of Kalgan, called "The Camel's Heel." He tells the legend about Khasar, the brother of Genghis Khan; he speaks, after remembering the fog. "It's clear, Genghis Khan didn't attack Russia from here. . . . There wouldn't have been such fogs then. He cleaned all the damp places with human blood. . . . Remember Turkestan, professor."

Sometimes people in sheepskin coats over their leather jackets come into the *teplushka*. They're checking mandates. They don't examine the papers closely; they look over the heads as if they know by smell if the right people are going to the right places. During migration, birds probably do the same thing. And their eyes have gotten dark red from the winds, and their nostrils have become unusually distended.

The professor saw just such nostrils on the Mongolian Chzhi; Dava-Dorchzhi was trying to get permission from the station commandant to link onto the next train. The professor asked for a mug of warm water. When giving him the mug, Chzhi used its broken handle to draw an irregular five-pointed star on the filthy spit-covered floor and then, spitting, he quickly poked his chest with his finger.

The professor should have learned Mongolian. He's sorry that he didn't, and maybe that's why the water seems unusually sweet to him.

That night the Greens shell the train again. The commandant mobilizes all the soldiers on the train. The woman, Shurkha, and Professor Safonov are guarding the *teplushka*. Chzhi and three others don't return.

The professor asks, "Did they get killed?"

Dava-Dorchzhi points the revolver at the crate. "They went off! With the Red Army men! I'd shoot those dogs myself, if it weren't . . . What are they going to do there? How am I supposed to understand that here?"

Vitaly Vitalevich recalls the star that Chzhi drew on the floor and understands.

At this station (did the Mongolians understand Russian?) the equipment catches up with the *teplushka*. The blue-gray coverings on the vehicles arch up and glitter with hoarfrost. Dark mounds of armored cars. A yellow wing of an airplane. (Or, most likely, those who ran off smelled war?)

All night long station platforms hurl past with a heavy rumble, seemingly obliterating the ringing tracks as they vanish into clouds of dust. *Teplushkas* filled with people respectfully make way. Steel machines throw into the *teplushka* posters and bundles of newspapers on which the bold words "War! Comrades . . . " are like splashes of hardened steel.

And right behind the vehicles there are people in leather jackets. To the professor they also look like parts of the vehicles, only without covering. He notices only their chests, just as he would notice those of women in the days of his youth. These chests are breathing strangely; even, slightly protruding glistening squares, they are probably very warm, as they exhale such strong and pungent air.

The fog is settling behind the pine trees. The professor goes back pensively to the *teplushka*.

Soon Dava-Dorchzhi comes running there, and after him the sweaty Anisimov. He doesn't have his briefcase, but surprisingly enough his leather jacket resembles a briefcase. He shakes the professor's hand ardently and looks around.

"You're going? Go on, go on! I'll stay and fight here a bit. I've joined our Petersburg division, a division of communists. The generals are attacking, there's general mobilization. The slick-haired bastards!"

He shakes the professor's hand once again.

"I'm really counting on you, Comrade Safonov. Although you're a professor, I liked you the moment I saw you. Sitting and heating the stove with paper, just like we do. And I even tell him to wrap his head. . . . We began right then and there to talk about the universal revolution . . . the whole night long. Let's go to our *teplushka*, I'll treat you to some tea, and we'll play a game of checkers. Divel's with me. Let's go . . . "

He looks around and feels the crate. "Are you going to stay here?"

Dava-Dorchzhi touches the professor's shoulders affectionately.

"I doubt the professor will go with you, Comrade Anisimov. Even though we find ourselves in the most disgusting conditions, in spite of all that, we've decided, like enlightened Europeans . . . rather, I mean the professor . . . we've reached a decision and use our daily free time for a series of scientific investigations in the area of Mongolian studies. Even though I'm just a humble representative . . . "

Anisimov straightens out his jacket, strokes his snub nose, and quickly walks toward the exit. "In a word, you have no time! Everyone's doing his own thing, the same old story. . . . I'm not going lecture you, if you can't, you can't! It's very simple!"

He jumps down. The station bell rings. The train is leaving. Onward.

The train is standing in some pines. Maybe the Greens are somewhere around. The pines are rustling, touching each other; it's cold and windy, and the pines feel melancholy. The soldiers, up to their waists in snow, are gathering twigs. The *teplushka* smells of resin, but not from the Buddha's crate. The woman Tsin-Chzhun-Chan is asleep. The *gyghen* himself visited her recently, before the train had to stop. She's happy; the *gyghen* is a living reincarnation of the Buddha; she's happy.

Professor Safonov heard this visit. And it was not at all because of this that he spoke in an angry voice.

"I can do as I wish. If I have the desire to go see Anisimov, can't I go? And then I'm outraged by your constant lying. I don't have any trust in you!"

"Vitaly Vitalevich! First of all, cover up better; the soldiers are constantly coming in, and it's easy enough for us to catch colds. How can you say that you can't do as you wish? . . . Yes, oh lord Sakia-Muni! Everything is done in your interests, every step you take is my constant worry, and it's not my fault if you reject it. I'm used to traveling. Why should you subject yourself to unnecessary dangers? Should you go over to the Bolshevik invaders and eat and drink their food?! After all, they've sent you on a journey filled with death, wars, and hunger! But all I do is worry. You've got food, warmth, stimulating conversation, and a woman who is young and skillful in love . . . and it's not my fault . . . "

The professor looks at the ceiling. "That's a poor theatrical declamation."

"It would sound much better in Mongolian, Vitaly Vitalevich . . . almost like a song. We have a wise saying: never get angry at your traveling companion."

The professor taps his fingers on the stove. The Mongolians are getting ready for bed; they want tea, but the damp wood doesn't burn well. It emits long gobs of spit with a hissing sound.

"As a result of the Revolution foreigners are going to despise Russia just as much as they were afraid of it before. This is a vile trait, Dava-Dorchzhi. Moreover, you've been deeply spoiled by civilization, and the East is not for you."

"Irritation heightens the power of observation."

"A tendency toward cheap maxims! Your love for wisdom. . . . Ha! . . . You'll leave by yourself, Dava-Dorchzhi, without me."

"They'll call only me a thief. Anisimov won't come back. What does he have to do with us? He's been ordered to destroy, but we're creating and strengthening, if it so please you to understand.

"I'm sick and tired of you, Dava-Dorchzhi, and although it's painful for me to speak like this . . . "

Professor Safonov sits down. Probably from the shaking of the train his lips are quivering. He reproaches the *gyghen* for a long time, enumerating all the insults to his person. Dava-Dorchzhi is lying on his back, one leg under the other. Stroking his overgrown hair that's brittle like reeds, he listens very carefully. The Mongolians are asleep. It smells of damp smoke.

When he finishes speaking, the professor, just like Dava-Dorchzhi, lies down on his back. They don't say anything for a long time. The *gyghen* gets up to add some wood to the stove. He sits down in front of the stove, his legs in a lotus position.

"If my people. . . . Do you know what they say to me? You must go to Mongolia and make Bolsheviks. . . . They've left me my herds for the time being, because I helped them to get out of here. They don't know Russian well, but they're making significant progress . . . just like you in Mongolian, professor . . . but they decided to divide up the herds belonging to other *gyghens* and lamas just as they've divided them in Russia. If my people don't believe me, how can I convince you, professor?"

His lips are the color of ashes, like a charred log that's almost burned out. His soldier's shirt is unbuttoned, and his bulging veins are visible; he's extremely thin. He wants to apologize to the professor, but he doesn't say anything.

"I can get to the Tushutu-Khan *aymak* without people and without the *burkhan* of the Buddha. . . . I could be there already. But I can't go without this pine crate. . . . While I was fighting against the Germans, they seized my herds and tents."

"Who?"

"There . . . different people. . . . They'll return them to the Buddha. Those who are lying next to us don't believe it; they say that Bolsheviks with a red star can get more herds and tents."

"So the three thousand head aren't yours?"

"They're mine, but their milk is being drunk by people I don't know, by people who aren't even relatives."

"So which five hundred head will you pay the Bolsheviks?"

"After the Buddha's arrival, you'll go with me and also . . . you'll say that the Buddha's at the border."

Suddenly opening his mouth, he shouts, "They'll return the herds, or else! Or else!"

The woman jumps up in fright. He waves his hand, and she lies back down.

"She's used to changing my opium pipe when I shout, that's why she jumped up. . . . You could call it the curse of the Buddha in your language, professor; he'll never reincarnate in those families that don't return my herds. We call it *Hoshun-turuin-erdeni-beyle.*"

"That's the first time I've heard that."

"Write it down, or better yet, remember it. . . . With all due respect, no one will lend you a pencil. I don't have any money. I spent it all in Petersburg. . . . That is, if you're interested in the financial aspects of the expedition."

"I don't have any money either."

Dava-Dorchzhi pokes his finger in the fire. He says dreamily, "They're selling *kalaches*[19] at the stations."

"I also saw cottage cheese and even a goose. They trade meat only for salt."

"Yes . . . we don't have much salt."

Calmed down, the professor falls asleep.

Later he tries to understand what calmed him down. With a bit of pity he looks at the little dark man. Dava-Dorchzhi's right boot has split, and he's mending it. The rotten leather crumbles into pieces, falls apart at the seams, like mud; the narrow awl gleams, like the eyes of the Buddha.

The soldiers have guttural voices, and Vitaly Vitalevich seems to understand their shouts and even why they drink so much tea. Only he doesn't understand where they get the tea; there's no tea at all in Russia right now. He dips a thin piece of dry bread in water and spends a long time telling Dava-Dorchzhi his thoughts about the downfall of European civilization and about how Europe will soon be a huge dead museum.

Dava-Dorchzhi has his own thoughts. Later, when the professor falls silent, he shows him with his fingers how the Tibetans catch yaks. Dava-Dorchzhi was in Tibet and presented the Dalai Lama with a musical clock; that was a long time ago, when he was a little boy. The soldiers, shouting approvingly, watch his fingers.

Now Professor Safonov wants to understand himself, what it is he wants. Near a large poster attached to the toilet door with the sign, "Civilians keep out," the professor says to the *gyghen*, "I'm going to have a conversation with you."

He talks like this so that he can decide more quickly what he wants. Knocking off the hard bluish snow that sticks to his boots, he walks back and forth from the toilet to the station bell. Shurkha the Mongolian keeps an eye on him.

All the stations resemble each other, only in some of the them the ringing is done by striking on a car buffer instead of ringing a bell; that means the station had been taken by the Greens; for some reason they take away all the bells. But the Buddha has already passed through Vyatka.

The professor thinks about the bells, the stations, about how the dead are buried now without coffins, the dead have their hands closed into a tight fist, clenching at the ground, the ground freezes harder and harder and won't let corpses in, and there are a lot of them—epidemics, high mortality, famine. When they went into a village to barter a blanket for bread, an old woman said angrily, "Ask those over there, they'll give you . . . !"

Three huge log barns were packed from top to bottom with corpses. Why do the dead need a barn? It's the living beings who need warmth. However, no one gives either bread or wood.

Isn't it all the same, whether you to go to Siberia, Turkestan, or Mongolia? You won't reach any destination. Let Dava-Dorchzhi dream on about his herds and heathen temples with a thousand Buddhas cast in Dalae-Nore. Some Red Army soldier is using the professor's library to heat his cast-iron stove, and there'll come a time when they will heat the buildings on the corner of Nevsky and Sadovy Streets with manuscripts and the Ostromir Gospel.[20] Dark hordes dressed in leather and fur are rushing all across Russia on the remains of trains. They burn, starve people, and kill. They're also going to go through devastated Europe and feed the lords of England and the billionaires of America with rations of spoiled horsemeat.

The station bells jingle frostily. The station bells are ringing the funeral service for Russia. Professor Safonov is sitting in the *teplushka* next to the living reincarnation of the Buddha, the *gyghen* Dava-Dorchzhi. The *gyghen* eats frozen rutabaga and listens, nodding approval.

"Is anything going to be done to counter this disorganized darkness, this gloom and storm? Is it just going to be blood and death? Is it just going to be murder the way they do it? Are the generals going to hang, shoot, and rob the communists? The communists are going to rebel and shoot the generals, and the bells are going ring less and less, and snow will cover the buffers of the wagons . . . Dava-Dorchzhi?"

The fresh wood wouldn't burn well. The woman took refuge in the crate; she closed her eyes tight, somewhere inside her, pale blue lashes, pale from the snow. The professor gave her a blanket; the *gyghen* turned away. Because of the cold or something else, four more Mongolians left the *teplushka* and stayed behind, and only Shurkha was left.

Dava-Dorchzhi and Professor Safonov are standing by the doors. It's an oppressive dark blue night. There are sparks in the hills beyond the snowdrifts and pines.

"Wolves, professor!"

Vitaly Vitalevich is thinking about firewood. But there are guards by all the fences. They are fed punctually and haven't yet forgotten how to bolt the gates. The peasants don't need louse-filled dirty military clothing; they chase away the "pests." If they do allow them in, it's only to warm themselves in the cattle sheds.

Who will keep guard over them? They might drink the milk or cut off the leg of a live cow, and so they rarely let them into the cattle sheds.

Dava-Dorchzhi takes a jagged ax that is slipping off its handle and chops at the top part, where "BEWARE" is written in red lead.

The yellow, slant-eyed face emerges from the burlap and wood shavings, and smiles benevolently an eternal smile at the eternally warm fire.

The professor takes off his boots, and, wringing out his foot cloths, he says, "I've made up my mind, Dava-Dorchzhi. In counterbalance to this wild darkness, we shall let this blessed, persistent procession, washed by European inquisitiveness . . . go forward, I still don't know where . . . but at least we could get the Buddha past the waterfall . . . death and hunger. . . . I don't know what your motives for movement forward are, but I have mine: culture and civilization, a thought that's eternal and always intoxicating with its free will . . . I'm with you!"

Dava-Dorchzhi indicates to the woman with his finger: to return to the professor his blanket, it's warm now. Moving the teapot to a warmer place on the stove top, he answers, "I thought so, Vitaly Vitalevich!"

For a week they heat the stove with the boards that encase the Buddha. Seven days later his feet are visible.

Chapter V

Metal, Spreading and Smelling Sweetly of Tranquillity

> Confucius said at the river: that which is passing is similar, for it will not cease either during the day or during the night.
> —*Lun-Yuy*, IX, 16

A thick bell inevitably does not ring clearly. A blocked
ear inevitably does not hear.
— *Yuan-Mey*

The events described in the present chapter should begin as follows: a *teplushka* rushes forward in darkness, cold, and wind. The
gyghen, angrily brandishing his ax, is hacking open the crate. The
ax (I've written about it already) is jagged: fragrant shaggy chips go
flying. A short, gray-bearded man with slightly bowed shoulders
and a deliberately meek smile on his face is throwing the chips into
the stove. The woman and Shurkha feel intimidated: the golden
body of the bared Buddha frightens them. And he who has just
emerged from out of the pine boards greets the snow and winds
with his lotus smile.

Shurkha leaves the car. The *gyghen* turns away when the Mongolian collects his rags.

"Now there's no one to guard you, professor."

"I'm my own guard."

"Recently I've had to lower my head or turn away frequently,
professor. This is the most terrifying of my wars. Will you be able
to keep guard over yourself? They're drawn by the star and I don't
know what else. . . . "

The Buddha sits. They placed him in that position when they were
taking out the bottom boards. Fanlike decorations are visible near his
temples. Is this not why Dava-Dorchzhi is feeling his hand?

"It means, professor, that it's really difficult, if Shurkha has
made up his mind to leave. . . . There are some kind of spirits here
besides hunger and frost. He was more loyal than me."

"What do you want to say, Dava-Dorchzhi?"

"What is there for me to say? What kind of herds does he have?
None. Nevertheless, he was the most loyal of all. More loyal than
me."

Dava-Dorchzhi strokes the hand of the Buddha. Of course, the Buddha's body is more radiant than the body of the *gyghen* (is that why a smile emerges through his narrow tiger eyes?).

But the chapter begins not like that, but as follows:

Vitaly Vitalevich suddenly feels light perspiration along the inner part of his arms at the elbows, as if his empty bones were filling with water warm as milk fresh from the cow. Or it's possible that the taste of fresh milk precedes this feeling. He can barely remember it. The perspiration rises to his veins somewhere (it's difficult to pinpoint) with a sharp piercing pain and suddenly wrenches at his stomach, making his body shake. He is totally sure that Dava-Dorchzhi, who is in back of the Buddha, is eating bread and butter with the woman. The food was brought to him by Shurkha the Mongolian, who deserted as payment for his departure. He, Dava-Dorchzhi, eats greedily and doesn't even chew the pieces well at a time when Vitaly Vitalevich has been learning, from spring of this year, to chew his food as slowly as possible. (You have to close your teeth as tightly as possible—the taste of the food lingers a long time on the palate and on the gums.)

But on the other hand, Dava-Dorchzhi promises to feed Vitaly Vitalevich very well in Mongolia: mutton, milk fresh from the cow, and soft bread from spring grain. Vitaly Vitalevich walks past the Buddha hastily (the yellow metal is really very warm). Dava-Dorchzhi has managed to hide it; he is really scraping the wall of the car with his knife. He's cunning.

The professor pretends that he doesn't understand. He spreads his arms, and it's difficult for him to bring them back together again: he drops them. Man has unusually long arms.

"Are you planning to look for food today, Dava-Dorchzhi?"

"Yes, yes . . . I'm going!"

He's full. Where does he need to hurry? But to please the professor, he does hurry; he doesn't even wrap a towel around his neck.

It's clear why the professor should be suspicious—he had sniffed the towel: it smelled of warm rye bread. The professor smirks, and he shakes his finger at the woman.

"Cheaters, cheaters! Trying to fool an old man . . . a hungry old man!"

The woman is also smirking cunningly, and she wipes her lips with her hand: they are blood-red and thick. When a person eats well, will his lips be pale? She's apparently showing off. And Dava-Dorchzhi dares to complain about the lack of food!

Consequently, Vitaly Vitalevich has to save himself. Holding the lapel of his overcoat in his hand (he had exchanged his coat for an army overcoat long ago. Coats are now being buried in the ground by everyone: all of Russia is now wearing an army overcoat: she is rushing and waging war), he wanders quickly between the Buddha, the iron stove, and the piles of wet straw. The woman is sitting at the feet of the *burkhan;* her eyes are closed, and her face is moon-shaped.

In times past, if he had wanted to eat . . . he would have bought some food. He often talks with Dava-Dorchzi about what he had been able to buy earlier.

Still, Dava-Dorchzhi is deceiving him.

He feels sorry for himself, and he weeps. He's hungry, bare-foot, and all alone.

At this point he walks over to the Buddha. He believes that he has given long thought to the action he is about to take. It had begun forming in his head in the Stroganov Palace when he saw the Buddha for the first time. Or perhaps not then, but when Dava-Dorchzhi was washing dishes and telling him about the legend. "Dava-Dorchzhi is stupid and is allowing his people go for food; he's full and can't worry about the statue."

Leaping up, letting himself go, for which he stands on one foot, he jumps around the Buddha. His nails slip and break—they are repellingly soft. But the golden wire is tightly set into the hard copper, and there is no end he can grab and pull. He bolts the door, as he did during the night, and lights a sliver of wood that smells strongly of kerosene. With the *gyghen*'s knife he picks at and exposes the wire's end, and then pulls it. The wire in the recesses of the metal is secured with tiny copper nails; he cuts them, and the gold falls in a fine dust.

His palms are wet, and he loses his grip; he wraps the *gyghen*'s towel around his hand. As for the woman, he's forgotten about her; suddenly she's howling in the corner. He turns around and sees an inordinately large mouth and a dirty piece of a multicolored dress on her bony knees. He threatens her with his knife. He touches her lips with the hand wrapped in the towel and jumps back toward the Buddha again. It's as difficult to grasp her mouth under the towel as it was the wire. She quiets down; she has learned to understand orders in her lifetime.

The result is less than a fistful of a badly wound ball of wire. He loosens a board of the paneling in the corner, sticks the wire in there, and nails it shut again. Using his knife, he scrapes bits of gold off the floor—there are so few you can count them; he puts them in his pants pocket.

The woman will tell Dava-Dorchzhi what happened, and when the *gyghen* sells more wire, he no longer will hide the food and milk from Vitaly Vitalevich.

Cut by the wire, the skin between his fingers is very sore. Why did he try so hard? And Dava-Dorchzhi can do the same; moreover, he's younger and more experienced in all kinds of work. In vain.

But Vitaly Vitalevich finds it pleasurable to feel tired. Moreover, according to pagan beliefs, he has committed a sacrilege; Dava-Dorchzhi would hardly have done such a thing . . .

Dava-Dorchzhi returns late; the train is standing on a siding, and the village is far out in the steppe. He brings half a *kalach* and a board ripped out of a fence. And joyfully Vitaly Vitalevich thinks that the *gyghen* has eaten the other half of the loaf on the way here. The half is divided among the three. The woman pours the tea silently.

Vitaly Vitalevich's heart beats uneasily, and he waits for the *gyghen* to pull aside the splintered board and scream. But the woman is silent. Again that feeling of perspiration passing through his bones, and there's a sour smell under his arms. He finishes eating his share of the *kalach*.

"Will you have plain tea?" Dava-Dorchzhi asks.

The professor strokes his knee guiltily with his hand.

"I'm terribly hungry."

"That's your problem."

A button from the *gyghen's* soldier's shirt comes off and falls to the floor. He picks up a sliver of wood. The resiny sliver catches fire right away; he raises it above his head so that it will burn longer. He looks for the button on the floor. The resin falls in drops on his sleeve; he straightens up.

Hundreds of wood slivers speak in the Buddha; his eyebrows are soft and round.

Suddenly Dava-Dorchzhi cries out, "A-a-ah!"

He sticks another wood sliver into the stove, and with sparks crackling, runs to the statue. He grabs the Buddha's face with his fingers. He pulls on his hat and, with the burning wood slivers in his hands, jumps out of the car.

"Aha!" resounds from the fluffy blue and rose snow.

The evening sticks to the hard birch branches, and in them a bell rings with a black ringing sound to a passing train.

Vitaly Vitalevich waits. He has buttoned his coat and wrapped something tightly around his neck. He is ready for questioning and arrest. Things never turn out the way you expect. If Dava-Dorchzhi found it necessary to report him, like a thief, then is it worth keeping silent about his officer's rank? If they shoot him, then let them shoot the both of them.

Suddenly Vitaly Vitalevich feels grateful to the woman Tsin-Chzhun-Chan; she's kept quiet and will tell about the wire only if interrogated. He takes her limp hand and presses it. She smiles; she has a very young face and thin round eyebrows. She touches his forehead lightly with her short fingers and says, "*Lyarin!*"

"This probably means 'I love you' or something like that," the professor thinks.

He's waiting for the loud crunching sound of snow: people hunting down others walk with a quick heavy step. His shoulders ache badly, and his hands really feel cold. He never did manage to get some mittens.

Much later, Dava-Dorchzhi brings three peasants. One of them has a red beard and is wearing a sheep *beshmet*[21] with gathers; he points at the statue and says to the other, "That one?"

The one asking has the pink face of a child and a hoarse, completely masculine voice.

"It's a lot of work, my man."

They walk around the Buddha, tap it with their fingers, and praise the good copper. Dava-Dorchzhi runs his hands over the Buddha's face and the folds of his robe, and suddenly jumps back. His lips are twisted in rage; his spit sprays the professor's ears, and he pushes his fists into the professor's liver.

"They've ripped it out, the bastards, all the wire, to the very last bit. Now I understand why they've deserted me!"

"Who?"

"The soldiers, that's who! They constantly had me leave the car, but they themselves broke the crate open and ripped out. . . . As for you, you, what is it you were watching?"

"Me! Me! Me?"

"You! You! You're accompanying it, you'll answer for this, too.

There are three hundred rubles in gold here! I'd wondered why the crate had broken apart so easily. If I get my hands on them. . . . "

He swung with his fist, and turning around to face the peasants, he shouted, "Well, are you going to start?"

The red-bearded peasant took off his hat. He also had a red bald spot and a broad good-looking nose. The professor gave him a smile. The peasant looked at him, smiled, and gave him his hand.

"Hello, have you been traveling long?"

Dava-Dorchzhi interrupted impatiently. "Well, are you going to get started?"

The peasants exchanged glances carefully, and the red-haired one answered softly, "I dare say you can't even scrape off enough for one gold ruble. What do you think, Mitsha?"

Mitsha, wearing a knit ski cap and a sheepskin coat full of holes, answered evasively, "God only knows . . . the main thing is that it's not Russian . . . haven't even heard of it. Is that thing there, that statue, from the Chinese?"

The red-haired peasant pulled on his mittens decisively.

"We'll pay you depending on the work. We're not out to get you. Whatever we scrape off, you'll get. You can get into trouble with such gold. Today, you know, it's one, two, and up against the wall!"

Dava-Dorchzhi leans sluggishly against the stove.

"Hurry up and . . . start scraping. If you delay, they'll couple the car to the train. How will I be able to go with you? You'll have to remain with us."

The peasants went to get a tool.

The youngest one remains. Kicking around the straw with his boots, he walks around the *teplushka* and peers into every corner. Nodding his head toward the woman, he asks, "Is she your wife?"

Dava-Dorchzhi shoves his hand deep in his pocket. "No."

The peasant laughs loudly.

"Is she also for sale?"

"No, I loan her out."

Slapping his sheepskin coat, the peasant leans toward the *gyghen*'s ear and whispers. Vitaly Vitalevich suddenly finds his pink light-mustached face repulsive. Dava-Dorchzhi pushes the peasant away with his elbow: "You just try."

"Does she understand Russian?"

"Were you in the war?"

"No-o. . . . "

"Then she doesn't understand."

The peasant walks by the woman several times indecisively. Snapping his fingers, he touches her sleeve and returns to the stove. "To hell with her . . . could even catch something. . . . I have a wife."

The professor sleeps badly. The peasants have brought some wood; the warmth from the stove smells of fumes, and the drying clothing smells of man. The professor is ashamed of himself; he tosses and turns. Dava-Dorchzhi, full and sleepy, mutters, "Fleas won't let you sleep; we've got them now."

In the middle of the night Vitaly Vitalevich is awakened by the rustle of straw. He thinks the fumes have gotten to him—his mouth is dry. From the small window half-covered with snow, there are blue patches of light on the straw. A man is crawling on the straw. It's Dava-Dorchzhi moving toward the woman. The professor covers his head. But the *gyghen* returns quickly from the woman. The professor feels his hand touching him. His fingers move lightly over his body and feel his clothing and boots. The *gyghen* searches even in his pillow and in the straw under the bedding. Then he goes back. He's looking for the wire.

In the morning Dava-Dorchzhi says, "It's the Russians who've stripped the Buddha. I'm taking it home honestly. The Russians have ripped out the wire, and they are scraping off the gilding. But the sacredness of the deity increases with each desecration."

For three days the peasants scraped the gilding off the Buddha. The gilding was thicker on his face and on his round cheeks than anywhere else. And behold, his red, angry copper face emerges from under the gold. His lips look dark, and his eyes are all sunken; a wool scarf has been placed around the statue, and the gold falls there.

"We'll get every last bit," the red-bearded one says.

Bits of gilding remain here and there on the body: yellow spots, like pimples. They can't get the gilding to come off the Buddha's fingers.

The peasants bring a sack of frozen white bread, a measure of potatoes, and some wood in exchange for the gold from the Buddha. They carefully fold up the scarf onto which the grains of gold have fallen and wrap the leaves of gold from the face in a newspaper. Then the red-haired peasant, sighing, wrings his hands: "We've let it go for too little, but it's too late. . . . "

The *gyghen* managed to get a torn *koshma*[22] out of them as well. He made a bed for himself out of the wood. He constantly forces the woman to throw logs into the fire.

"If I had thought of it earlier . . . we would have traveled peacefully for the price of the wire. Now I've caught a cold and have the shivers. They've run off with it . . . "

He wraps himself in his overcoat. He purposely laughs in a loud manner. "I saw you at night. You were going to the woman, Vitaly Vitalevich. Should I tell her that she's not to resist you?"

"I don't care for your soldier's jokes very much, Dava-Dorchzhi."

"Then I can tell you an instructive Mongolian legend. Now I will permit you to write it down because I believe you. You've explained in detail what you want . . . for example, the story of the *ku-tukht*[23] Muniya, and his indecent and lecherous life."

"When will we reach our destination?"

"If we're good and economical, we'll have enough food for a month and a half. By that time we'll be in Siberia. Over there, there are many worshippers of my reincarnation, and I am inclined to believe that we'll have food, drink, and pious conversations worthy of me."

The professor, with his hands behind his back and slightly stooping, is walking back and forth in the car, from one end to the other. He's made a decision about the wire: he's tired of the arguments and the reproaches. He asks a lot of questions about the *aymak* of Tushutu-Khan. The *gyghen* is talkative, a bit flowery in his speech, and he often laughs with a sort of slurping sound. He gives the history of his lineage; there are a lot of names, revenge, and remarkable battles. The professor understands vaguely, but he listens willingly.

In the morning Dava-Dorchzhi shivers even more. He drinks even more tea and lies in bed, pressing his temples with his fingers.

The professor brings a doctor from the Red Army field hospital at the station. He feels the *gyghen's* head, bares his chest, and asks without waiting for an answer, "Does your head hurt? Do your feet hurt? Do you have the chills?"

The doctor has wide, long and thin, tonglike fingers. He runs his fingers along the professor's arm. "We have no medicine. Sometimes they take patients at the Omsk field hospital. . . . Everywhere it's overloaded. He has typhus. Coffee, clean linen, and compresses."

He looks at the Buddha, taps it with his nail and says "copper," and leaves.

The *gyghen* begins asking in a whining voice for his revolver. The revolver is under the professor's pillow; nevertheless, he takes it and hides it among his things. The *gyghen* threatens to shoot himself. He reproaches the professor for being lazy, because of which he, the *gyghen,* must die. It would be better for him to die right away if they can't get any medicine for him. He scolds the woman in Mongolian, and she falls on her knees, with her head pressed against the floor.

"What kind of home remedies are there? Where am I to get coffee?"

"Go and get something for the revolver!"

The professor goes.

Delirium sets in within a day. The professor is ashamed of his thoughts—that the *gyghen* is only pretending. He has no reason to think so, but it seems to him that Dava-Dorchzhi throws off the compresses and spills the coffee on purpose. The *gyghen* often sits up in bed after first arranging his overcoat behind his back (the wall is cold). Using the same words repeatedly, he utters sluggishly, "Into you alone passes the spirit of the Buddha. . . . You alone are the incarnation of the *gyghen,* Dava-Dorchzhi. . . . Give me from the side pocket. . . . I'll write to the *aymak.*"

He thrusts some papers at him with Mongolian inscriptions and complains, "Everyone has abandoned me. Only you are left before my death. I've already died . . . I am again the spirit of the Buddha."

The professor brings boiling water and applies the compresses.

Dava-Dorchzhi lay depressed and dehydrated. It was necessary to pour water into him all the time—to give him water to drink. His hair grew longer and unusually thick, and, somehow, all at once: it was eerie to look at the clumps of hair sticking out of his nose. His pillow became all sticky with his saliva. When turning Dava-Dorchzhi's head from one side to the other, Vitaly Vitalevich had to force himself not to shrink back. Cotton stuck out of his ears (the *gyghen* was afraid to catch cold in his ears), and now it resembled black cockroaches.

He often gives a guttural, protracted cry, and raising his emaciated arms, he greets the People's Commissar for Nationality Affairs in the name of the Mongolian people. Then he makes a speech about the oppressors, Chinese imperialists, and immediately, almost word for word (as far as the professor can remember), he tells the legend about the Buddha statue from the *aymak* of Tushutu-Khan. It begins with the words: "In the year of the Fire Rabbit," and Vitaly Vitalevich imagines a large reddish hare about the size of a dog, in an endless snow-covered field. Then he opens the door.

More often than not, this happens while the train is moving. Biting snow, hard like rocks, hits the professor's teeth. The cars cast off gray smoke.

"There is some kind of retribution for our actions," the professor thinks, returning to the stove.

The woman—the professor calls her "Tsin" for short—is washing the *gyghen*'s underwear in boiling water. He only has one pair and, once, when the woman was washing it, the professor had wanted to find out just how strong it was. He walked up to the large pot (there is no soap—the bunched-up rags simply stew); in chunks of dirt some gray specks floated on top. The professor bent closer: they were cooked lice.

For this reason or perhaps for another, that evening Vitaly Vitalevich feels a strange pain in his legs; he's cold although he's had enough to eat, and the stove burns brightly in the *teplushka*. He sits by the bed of Dava-Dorchzhi less than usual, and the surprised woman sees him putting out the oil lamp earlier than usual.

He kicks off his boots and lets them drop loudly to the floor, but he doesn't get under the blanket; instead, he sits, listening to something intently; his hands tremble, and he has to wet his gums.

Rubbing his hands, he says, "It's cold!"

And he walks over to the woman. She has already turned back

the fur coat, and her round breasts (she has stretched her hands along her body) are warm.

In the morning the professor told himself that he acted that way because it was unbearably cold to lie alone. His chills passed, and he ran happily for the usual hot water.

But the next night, too, he slept with the woman Tsin. And from then on, he no longer tried to find an excuse, and he no longer put out the oil lamp.

One morning Tsin goes to find some dry kindling wood. The *gyghen* is very delirious—he keeps jumping up and trying to run. The Bolsheviks are trying to catch him during an uprising. The professor's eyes hurt from the damp smoke, and that's why the *gyghen* shouts, "Why are your eyes bulging?" His thin, slippery hands irritate the *gyghen,* and his voice becomes squeaky.

Much later Tsin appears with the kindling. Near the door Vitaly Vitalevich sees a tall, hook-nosed man in a black coat made of dog fur reaching to his heels. A wide red band is visible on his hat.

The professor sticks out his head. "What do you need?"

"Oh, nothing," the man says, opening his fur coat wide.

The professor angrily pounds on the door handle, "Move on, there's a sick man in here. . . . Move on, we're telling you—there's government cargo in here! Get out of here!"

The fur coat, moving away to a pile of junk, drones, "Just don't squeal so much . . . government!"

Vitaly Vitalevich threatens Tsin with his fist. With a confused look she weighs the kindling she has brought in her hands—it's completely dry. She doesn't understand. Then Dava-Dorchzhi's words occur to him: "Our woman does not say no to anyone."

He walks up to her and shouts in her face, "Trollop! Trash!"

At dawn there's a scratching noise at the door. The woman Tsin takes down the bar and, slightly bending her head, looks into the darkness. Someone's shaggy-furred hand reaches in and pulls her by her dress. She leaves without even turning around.

The professor angrily grabs the *gyghen* by his outstretched hand. The latter sits down; his eyes run along the ceiling, and there is blissful joy in his face. The professor lowers his hands for him, and the latter shudders.

"Atte-e-e-e-en-tion!" Dava-Dorchzhi shouts. "Hello, fello-ows!"

Vitaly Vitalevich moves his shoulder, takes mincing steps around the bed, and, trying to outshout the *gyghen*, pokes him in the shoulder:

"Listen, she's gone, you know, gone! It's imperative to shout 'come back'! I don't know that word in Mongolian. Listen, her presence is in your interest—who will wash your underwear? I can't do half a dozen things at once! Listen to me, Dava-Dorchzhi!"

"Silence! What bastard is breaking formation? Don't move! Atte-e-en-tio-on!"

The professor opens the door wide and shouts into the night in a thin breaking voice, "Listen, you-ou!"

The snow makes a rustling sound as it rolls down the piece of kindling lying by the car's steps. The rustling sound is dry, and the kindling is dry, too. Tsin had dropped it.

Chapter VI

More about the Same Metal,
Exuding the Sweet Smell of Tranquillity

> The life of man is a continuation of his childhood.
> —*From Professor Safonov's notebook*

Thundering and ringing days let the trains pass. Boards, iron, and people are hurling forward. By the blue ice fields lonely wolves, their young muzzles tautly lifted, are howling at the singing steel. There should be one song in the steppe—that of the wolves. People's songs are human and iron. The wolf is frightened.

Dava-Dorchzhi has feeling in his fingers. This first feeling is anxious and joyful. To raise and to lower a finger, then to move it along the blanket just an inch or two. His whole body is wet and weak; his ears are burning. Flowers must bloom like that. A drunken flowering weakness.

By the stove, as always, there sits a stooped frail old man in his overcoat, girded with a peeling belt.

"Professor!"

The frail old man, one foot wobbling, moves toward the bed with a familiar step. Dava-Dorchzhi beckons to him with his finger and, choking for breath, whispers in his ear, "You see, haven't croaked yet!"

And he smiles. He thinks his whole face is smiling, but only his eyebrows and the muscles around his mouth have moved, ever so slightly.

The professor doesn't know what to do now. He can't get excited. He chews, squints, and sighs pensively.

"Ye-es . . . now you need nourishment."

"Go on and give me something!"

Dava-Dorchzhi eats.

The professor feeds him white bread soaked in water; Dava-Dorchzhi pulls the water toward himself greedily and sticks his fingers in the mug.

"More!"

In order to distract him, Vitaly Vitalevich says carefully, "Tsin has been hiding for three weeks already, and I haven't heard anything about her."

"More!"

"You were delirious and, in my opinion, it would have been

enough to shout just one word for her to return immediately. Some Georgian or Circassian took her away."

"More!"

The next day Dava-Dorchzhi is already making a fist and rubbing it on the blanket.

"Give me more, you old crone!"

"You cannot eat a lot, Dava-Dorchzhi. Your intestines have shrunk."

"Give me! Give me more, I want to eat! I've eaten everything . . . want some meat!"

Then the professor barters away his wedding ring in a settlement near the station. When he returns with meat and milk, the *gyghen* is lying on the floor: he's attempting to crawl.

"Give it to me!"

He grabs the milk with his teeth, spills it on his neck and sweeps it with his hand into his mouth.

"More! More! . . . "

The professor moves the bottle away from him:

"It's Omsk already, Dava-Dorchzhi. Where do you have friends here?"

The *gyghen* is full; he's sleeping.

The *teplushka* is on a siding, at the marshaling yard. Thousands of empty cars. Dogs roam between the trains. Vitaly Vitalevich collects logs and boards left behind in the cars.

In the commandant's office he is told: "There are White uprisings in the Far East and in Manchuria, comrade. We don't have any time to send expeditions with Buddhas . . . and what if you have in those Buddhas S-R appeals? Don't you think that's possible?

"Take a look."

"I have, comrade, seventy trains every day—I don't have the time to look under every skirt."

Nevertheless Professor Safonov takes off the burlap covering the

Buddha and wipes him off with a rag. During all the shaking a piece of the high crown has broken off; the copper glistens blood-red. The piece is not to be found; Tsin either swept it away or took it.

The professor examines all his mandates: there's an endless number of seals, corrections, and resolutions on them.

"Will we do better, Dava-Dorchzhi, if we head through Semipalatinsk, through the mountains? There's an uprising near Irkutsk. And trains are being allowed through to Semipalatinsk. . . . It's more difficult to travel from there."

"I don't care!"

Dava-Dorchzhi closes his eyes and presses his palms together so that you can hear the skin of one hand rubbing against the other.

"There are sheep in the *aymak* . . . the fat around the tail weighs fifteen pounds. Just press—fat comes out of it."

"You might not see any sheep, Dava-Dorchzhi, if you don't listen to me."

The *gyghen's* eyebrow twitches. "I'll see. I'm clever. Give me something to eat, I don't care."

The professor, his hands behind his back, is walking around the car. The floor has been swept up. Boards and logs lie in front of the Buddha and all around. In his hands, folded in lotus position on his knees, is birch bark for starting the fire; it's easy to get it from there.

"Undoubtedly, this is the most sensible solution, but before taking this decisive step, I'll wait till you're completely well, Dava-Dorchzhi. In the meantime, I'll make out a detailed itinerary, and I could make a detailed estimate if there were money."

"I don't care!"

"Eat!"

He sees the round knots of muscle in the *gyghen's* jaw, and it seems that during Dava-Dorchzhi's illness the professor has acquired an incomprehensible power over him. He says sharply, "Don't eat! Don't touch!"

Dava-Dorchzhi timidly moves the cup away.

"But I want to!"

"Don't eat!"

"Just a bit!"

"I forbid you!"

And the *gyghen* says obediently, "All right."

The professor moves slowly around the car. "You may eat!"

He shakes off, for some reason, small pieces of kindling and some feathers clinging to him.

"And the stations we have covered in our journey, right up to this place, have not dissuaded me from those thoughts which I had expressed to you at some point, Dava-Dorchzhi. Moreover, they have become ever clearer. Your heroic attempts with the statue, with your native sacred object—it is more than likely your blood calling, the mysterious incomprehensible call to the East. Your disorganized idea, forgive me, has unconsciously accomplished a great feat: it has awakened within me and has forced me to want what I had considered an unimportant and dilettante aspiration . . . to put aside the materials for a promised lecture on 'The Comical Novel in the Time of Alain-René Lesage,' and instead to read the stanzas of wisdom of Sykun-Tu and his students or to find out about the research of the narrator in 'Tales on the Southern Shore of the Lake.'"

"Water!"

The professor splashed out the dust floating on the surface and handed him the mug.

"You, intoxicated with the explosions of sixty-ton shells and tanks destroying towns. . . . There are no such tanks yet, they will exist or you think that they already exist . . . in your delirium we saw them. Intoxicated with thirty-story houses and radio, you rushed there where Europe beckoned you. But the spirit of the ages began to speak before you when Europe threw off her cover and let out her wolves—for the time being only at Russia. You remembered that you are a reincarnation of the Buddha, a *gyghen*. You began the trip, through the fire and darkness, suffering torments yourself, cleansing yourself. . . . "

"Help me get up!"

Dava-Dorchzhi, pulling off the dried skin on his lips with his long dirty nails, was breathing quickly. And his neck was stretched forward, just like when running. His eyes had a sleepy look, like a cobweb.

"To study the peaceful movement of herds in my office? No! To experience them in freedom, where they resemble the flowing water in a lake. Their soft backs smell of reeds and earth, warmed by the bright rays of the sun. Meek women in love that knows no jealousy, heathen temples with the Buddhas, smiling like the heavens. . . . You were aspiring to this and to something else as well, Dava-Dorchzhi. . . . I am carrying the something else, the thing of more value. I cover large expanses, my way is blocked with huge rocks. Civilization, science, breaking open the earth with a roar . . . from the idle thought that I am one of the owners of the earth. This is perhaps a proud, foolish thought; the main thing is that it's hardest to tear yourself away. . . . This is a marvelous frivolous fool's cap on your head. The strengthening—there, near the herds and heathen temples—the strengthening of my soul alone will be the greatest victory, performed over the thunder and darkness that hurls past us—and we with it, forging our own way. The tranquillity that I feel more and more . . . so that my heart can descend into the warm and fragrant waters of the spirit. . . . "

"I want to eat!"

Through the rapidly chewing mouth and the greed-moistened eyes of the *gyghen*, the professor seems to see Dava-Dorchzhi joyfully agreeing. The latter is still silent; the words about food, thrown out by him, are garbled, babbled; but even if the *gyghen* had not uttered them, they would have been comprehensible nonetheless.

In his notebook (he had received it in Yekaterinburg, at a meeting in honor of the Third International: a young woman in a torn sweater, winking shamefully with her small whitish eyes, passed them out—"from the printers, to remember them by") he records: "It's snowing. Dava-Dorchzhi is trying to sit—it's difficult for him. It's necessary to give some thought to the extent that Eastern culture has influenced Siberia. The connection—between uprisings and Eastern culture. Here the struggle with darkness continues the longest. The influence is weak—they'll crush it." And further down: "The life of man is the continuation of his childhood."

Dava-Dorchzhi gets up. Using the wall for support, he staggers. The snow in the space between the cars is high and fluffy. The cars are being covered over, and without wheels they are happier looking; they resemble candy boxes.

"Our men are in town," the *gyghen* says. "They'll provide food."

The professor dresses obediently.

"You'll tell me their addresses?"

The *gyghen* smiles. Suddenly the professor notices what unusually large cheekbones he has, as if his ears had been pushed under his eyes. The skin on his cheekbones is dark and, most likely, very thick and hard, like a callus.

"I remember . . . but . . . I've completely forgotten."

Continuing to smile (now his smile covers his whole face and that way, perhaps, it's worse), he moves his fingers back and forth in front of his mouth.

"I've forgotten . . . forgotten . . . this was no illness . . . but my new reincarnation . . . yes. . . . Please bring me something to eat."

The professor is in town. He heads for the local branch of the Geographical Society. Soldiers are sleeping side by side in hooded deerskin coats in the museums. At the entrance to the library, on the staircase, there is a man in deerskin boots and a Samoyed[24] coat. There is a museum tag on the collar.

The professor must talk to the chairman of the society. The governing body and the director have been arrested for participating in the Cadet uprising. The Samoyed coat complains: "Who do you need?"

"They've drunk the alcohol in the specimen jars, they've used the crocodile to heat up the stove, and little boys are using the turtle to slide down a hill."

Who can tell the professor about the Mongolians—there aren't any on the shelves; the coat is guarding the library lest they plunder it clean.

"Go to the *ispolkom*."

The young woman at the *ispolkom* sends him to the *Kirsection*.[25] There a young Moslem is translating the Communist Manifesto into Kirghiz. In reply to the professor's question, he asks, "Comrade, are you familiar with the typewriter system? It is absolutely necessary in the most urgent way to change the Russian text to the Kirghiz-Arabic alphabet. There are no Mongolians in town, they have hidden, no one knows where, and, incidentally, if the comrade has a command of Mongolian, he can be offered a translation job."

Omsk is far behind the *teplushka*.

Dava-Dorchzhi leaves the *teplushka* with an uncertain light step as if his feet were made of paper. Vitaly Vitalevich supports him under the arm.

"In Novonikolaevsk I'll direct my efforts at getting us permission to follow the southern route to Semipalatinsk."

"I don't care."

Dava-Dorchzhi barely manages to muster enough strength to put on his boots when he takes a pot.

"Where are you going?"

"Through the cars . . . to beg for kasha from the soldiers."

"I can do that! You'll catch it again, Dava-Dorchzhi."

"I wasn't ill . . . how can I catch it again? They won't give you any kasha. You're an old man and look like a Chinese."

"Dava-Dorchzhi, I have my duty."

"Why are you starving me? You're finishing off everything by yourself on the sly."

The professor is ashamed to be thinking about the gold wire. Let it lie there in the corner, tightly nailed shut, and let it perish with the car. He hasn't used it for himself and won't use it—he's no thief. Thinking such thoughts, he feels calmer. The whole Buddha is covered with dust, only for some reason dust is not settling as much on the arches of his eyebrows. His back is covered with a greenish patina; the professor wipes it with oil, which he gets with a rag from the car's wheels.

One day, in a train taking communists to the Far Eastern front, he notices Comrade Anisimov among the leather jackets. But he doesn't take a really good look: he runs to the commandant's office and waits. If Anisimov comes inquiring, he'll catch him and tell him that the Buddha was thrown out at one of the stations and that he, the professor, is returning to Petersburg.

He waits in vain: Anisimov doesn't come.

Dava-Dorchzhi keeps bringing small kettles with kasha and cabbage soup. He eats greedily, putting his fingers in the food as if he wants to impregnate his fingers with the fat. His spoon is bitten all over, and the metal bears the round traces of teeth. And his teeth really seem to have grown bigger and sharper: it pains the professor to look at them. The kasha is thick and dark like earth, and its vile smell spreads along the floor.

The *gyghen* almost never talks to the professor and almost never asks about the journey. His movements are becoming quicker, and his back is getting straighter.

In Novonikolaevsk he disappears for a whole day.

In the distribution center a commissar somehow unexpectedly makes a notation on Professor Safonov's statement: "Comply, keeping to the requested itinerary."

Evening. The professor gets lost for a long time among the trains as he looks for his *teplushka*. The sign on the door has been scraped off: he sees this in the bright light of the arc lamp. "Have to make another one," he thinks.

Dava-Dorchzhi is sitting on the bed. He is opening wide a new goatskin coat and straightening the collar of his soldier's blouse.

The professor asks casually, "Did you get it as a gift?"

He wants to joke with the *gyghen*, and he wants to say, "Permission for the southern road has been denied."

"Got it!"

Thinking his own thoughts, he says with his head turned away, "Oh, so that's it. . . . Where do they issue sheepskin coats to pilgrims?"

The *gyghen* makes a gesture that is unusual for him: he places his hands on his hips. His face gets longer, and the professor sees his eyes, white as paper. Dava-Dorchzhi's voice rises, he's almost shouting.

"In the regiment, in the regiment, in the regiment. . . . What a bastard you are . . . leave me alone! I have to croak here with you! To die of hunger. . . . I won't go, I'm staying! I have to be here—I here . . . I . . . "

He tries to throw up his hands, which have suddenly become weak; the professor is scared that he'll do it. He undoes his overcoat, forgets, and once again feels for the hooks that have long disappeared from the eyelet.

"Of course, of course, that's your business."

He suddenly finds to his joy the one remaining hook, but there is no cloth beside the hook. There should be gray cloth wet with snow.

And so Dava-Dorchzhi will never raise his hands.

"I was thinking something else entirely, Dava-Dorchzhi. . . . I assume that we can reach an understanding. . . . I can, at last, get the money. Permission has been granted. In such cases, you know. . . ."

"You're going to go and denounce me—go on, denounce! I wrote on the form myself—officer. . . . "

The professor looks at his peeling face and his swollen eyelids (covered unevenly with scarlet bumps). Dava-Dorchzhi is shouting about his new reincarnation: from today on he is not the Buddha, and he is not a *gyghen*. He had not been ill—he had been dying, leaving the spirit of the one who was here, next to him, in gold spots; is that supposed to be illness? The professor says quietly, "Stop joking, Dava-Dorchzhi. . . . You're an officer, you're almost Russian, and should you go serve the Bolsheviks? You have your duty, you're a local person. . . . I don't believe you."

Dava-Dorchzhi gets the papers in his pocket. They're wrapped in the professor's handkerchief. He throws them on the bed.

With the erect gait of a military man, Dava-Dorchzhi walks over to the door. His legs are slightly twisted; he opens the door with a kick of his boot.

Dava-Dorchzhi, the *gyghen* and lama, leaves.

Crawling under the train to shorten the trip, he says, "I'm sick of you, you old bugger! Now take me!"

Chapter VII

*What Khirzet-Naghim-Bey Thought and What the Red
Guard Savoska Could Think, the Steppe in Spring,
Gophers, and (as Everywhere in My Writing) Brightly
Colored Grasses and Winds*

> In a puff of smoke, in the puff of smoke of a village of
> far-away people there is your own puff of smoke in
> the wilderness. There is no worldly dust on the doors
> and there is no worldly dust outside; in an empty
> shelter freedom lives in contentment. I was in a cage
> for a long time.
> —*Gao, "Your Own Garden"*

A man is trying the bolt. The iron in the hook holds tight. The
hand in the overcoat shakes a long time on the iron. The bolt can't
understand why.

Because the man is listening. After his illness it's difficult to recognize footsteps. But the foot of the expected one does not glide
along the steps.

The spaces between the cars are quiet. As everywhere, the railway men are in sheepskin coats and carry lanterns, whose oily light
has never had the power to stop anything. A car is hooked on, a
sheepskin coat rustles on the buffers and wall.

The man bends his entire body from right to left, and from left
to right. That's how a brush full of India ink bends on paper, and
the incomprehensible marks signify the incomprehensible. The
Buddha does not understand why the man is creating these marks.

That's not true!

"The Buddha understands everything. And his face is covered
with copper rage. And the lotuses of his hands are like blocks of ice

in finely broken drift ice, and his gold fingers break the blueness like the sun breaks mountain peaks in the morning. His spirituality is like an overturned *patra*."[26]

A man is lying in the *teplushka*. A pillow is pressing against the back of his head; he tears his head away and speaks in a tremulous angry voice. "What did you take? What? You thought of getting free, thought of getting free, thought of leaving alone! I'll leave!"

The man has no reason to raise his head: he is alone, and he hears himself well. His thin lips are sharply defined, almost hostile.

"You'll be horrified, and you'll bow to the one who brings you the sacred object. You'll open your clay monasteries so that tranquillity will shine upon him from there. He is passing through the last stages of darkness himself. He. . . . "

You have to talk to yourself in a high voice and roughly. And that's the way he speaks. He repeats to himself many times:

"One *suburgan*[27] passed—having peacefully made it here with the Buddha, a bouquet of opened *padm*[28]. . . . Dava-Dorchzhi has covered only one *suburgan*. Another *suburgan*—penetrating the great wisdom, *mama-bodiin*,[29] the transformation into the Buddha—Dava-Dorchzhi did not reach. . . . Dava-Dorchzhi turned away from the second *suburgan*. . . . "

The Buddha does not think that way. The Buddha's eyes are covered over with dust. . . . That's not true!

"The face of the one who has left blessed burns with the copper of all-perfect victory. The greatness of unusually long life settles in his round chin soaring like a bird over a desert. . . . His eyelashes see the creation of a million *suburgans* in the space of one hour. His eyelashes, like a dream, have renounced suffering. His power is written in the metal because he is the Buddha."

Professor Safonov is a European. He knows: in order not to

think, you have to occupy the mind and body with movement. Moving all the time, not reflecting about the point of the movement, Europe entered darkness. The East is motionless, and it is no accident that its symbol is the lotuslike Buddha.

Vitaly Vitalevich moves about and performs his usual chores in the car. At night, under the influence of darkness and despair (it's bitter to be left alone), he could perform any number of stupid cries and gestures. Now what's he to do? He is a European, he must fulfill his duty, and, moreover, for a civilized European a day, even several hours, is enough for victory over his spiritual concerns. He has been entrusted with taking the Buddha to the Mongolian border and handing it over to the representatives of the Mongolian people. In Petersburg he has an apartment, books, furniture, and manuscripts—the labors of his whole life. He will return after completing his mission. What if the Mongolian lamas, in gratitude for his service, will want to have him as a guest in their country? Why can't he stay and live out the end of the Revolution there, or simply rest and collect his strength? Both his and other people's opinion would be: it's his duty to get where he's going. He will deliver the Buddha to its destination.

Professor Safonov tears the boards away and puts a piece of gold wire in his pocket. Where grain grows, there gold flourishes. In the nearest village (the train is traveling as if the engineer is giving birth at each stop—water keeps pouring continuously into the tender, and the station managers are as quick as midwives) Professor Safonov offers the peasants a very short piece of the wire, the length of a match, for bread and butter. A peasant, fat and short like a cart and wearing a gray flannel shirt, takes the wire carefully, as if it were a worm. He rolls the piece in the palm of his hand, tests it with his teeth, makes it ring against a pan, and gives it back. Then he takes it again, feels and bites it, and again returns it. He brings a *kalach* and says, "It, so it would seem, is really gold, but you'd better take it back. It's gold, all right, it's gold. What if it's taken from some relics? Today, you know, all kinds of people come here. If it were only a ring or perhaps even a cross. . . . "

The professor takes the *kalach* and leaves. In other peasant huts he is given either *shangi*[30] or potatoes; nevertheless, everywhere the gold is given back to him.

At night he lies by the door bar, and when people knock, he presses his lips tightly to the crack (so that the sound does not resound in the empty car): "occupied . . . official business." The boards creak, hoarse hoary voices use foul language until the train leaves.

People with sacks are rushing into the grain-producing villages of the Altai region—like a louse out in the frost, they freeze, roll, crunch under the wheels, use foul language and blasphemy. With four-letter words, too, the peasants (they drove them in carts and wore them out with public service) scrape out shallow, waist-deep graves and throw corpses in them, stomping down the ground so that more will fit in. In the spring the corpses thaw, swell up, burst and stick out of the graves. And the land smells foul for long distances. And it may be for this reason that the plowman does not go out in the meadow.

Yellow sand blows into Semipalatinsk day and night; it blows particularly strong toward morning. In the steppe it exposes whole rocks shaped like houses. The Irtysh is protected by poplars, otherwise the sand would blow over it, and the water and the grasses, and even the sky, would grow dark like an extinguished candle. The sky is reflected in the Irtysh and lives only because of this.

Professor Safonov is at the commandant's office at the station in Semipalatinsk. On the breast of the commandant's double-breasted jacket is a red bow, but his face is gray and straightforward like a list. The commandant is used to writing on papers from corner to corner, and his fingers are holding the pen also somehow by the corner. He reads the professor's bills of lading, mandates, travel warrants, and the like. He reads a long time, as if he's stepping on each letter with his boot. The clock in the commandant's office squeaks out of boredom. He looks at the professor with a bored expression as if he's reading "the law code." Moreover, the professor is badly covered: he's ashamed of his suit.

"Sit down, Comrade . . . "—the commandant searches for his name a long time, as if his name is scattered in the mandates—"Comrade Safonov. Wait a minute"—he again searches—"Comrade Safonov."

Finally he folds the mandates and bends them as if he wants to read them once more. He puts one sleeve into the other and looks at him. "So you've arrived?"

"I have a request of you, comrade commandant."

The commandant's brains seem to have been covered over with sand. He twists his head furiously and opens his eyes with effort as if for the first time.

"What request?" he asks suspiciously. His eyes narrow, and he covers his cheeks and forehead. "What request, comrade?"

"The statue of the Buddha, which I was entrusted to accompany, has been unloaded from the *teplushka*, and it is lying outside without anyone keeping an eye on it. I'm afraid it might get damaged since the statue is valuable not only from an archeological or religious point of view but also because of its high artistic and social significance. The *Sovnarkom* of the Northern Communes, in entrusting me . . . "

With regret the commandant lowers his sleeves, which had been tucked in the sleeves of his coat, feels his chest, and blows air through his nose on his mustache as if he wants to blow it away.

"So-o. Unloaded it, that's good. Why should it stay for a year in a *teplushka?* Everything's expensive in Peter[31] now. What's bread?"

"I beg you, comrade commandant. . . . "

As the commandant is getting up, he turns the chair slowly and with a heavy gesture, as if it were a cow, feels the seat, and then pulls the chair along slowly, like a rope, into the next room:

"Sergey Nikolaevich . . . yes?"

And just as drawn out, thickly, just like a log rolling from the next room.

"Bu-u-ut. . . . "

"Well, go on!"

Finally, a short man with an unbelievably long black mustache appears from the other room. And his bass voice seems to have been especially made for such a mustache. They read the mandates together, and suddenly Sergey Nikolaevich laughs loudly, producing thick long peals of laughter as if he were coating them with tar: "Bu-u-ud-dha! God! The devils! We-e need Perun![32] Ha-ha-ha!"

The commandant looks into the latter's mouth, restrains himself for a long time, and then suddenly, as if he had caught it in his hand, starts guffawing. They roll on the table, and chairs fall over. Young girls come running, take a look, and, suddenly squealing and pinching each other in excitement, laugh and jump about with light, tiny leaps. Sleepy soldiers push against the backs of the young girls, and the corridor shakes with laughter. On the platform, with her elbow resting against a short ladder, an old decrepit woman is dying of laughter.

But at this point the commandant grabs a revolver and shouts into the crowd, "Clear out! You're interfering with work!"

He wipes the tears off his mustache and asks Sergey Nikolaevich anxiously, "Are those the correct signatures?"

"It would seem so."

"But it must be determined if they're really the correct ones."

"But how can you determine that they're the correct ones?"

"We have to compare them."

"Do we have any certified signatures from Petersburg?"

And the commandant drags out a new thought slowly, as if he were pulling a bucket of water from a well, "If there are no certified signatures from Peter on file, that means they're forgeries. If these were the correct signatures. . . . "

The professor wants to spit or shout or do something even worse.

"Allow me to note, comrade commandant, I've come from Petersburg with these signatures."

"Petersburg is one thing . . . but you're here. You couldn't have gotten here from Semipalatinsk. If only you had the correct signatures. . . . "

Sergey Nikolaevich gives a deep sigh that sounds like a brick thrown into an empty building. "The right signature means that everything's in order, that's the way I see it."

The commandant sits down in a chair and again brings his sleeves together. Again a bucket is being pulled, and saliva splashes on his lips.

"Maybe we should telegraph for certified signatures in the city center?"

He again moves his sleeves apart, like they separate train cars, and wonders out loud, "Strange, why did they send us a Buddha? They want to turn us into Chinese or something? And we could have forged ten fresh Buddhas for them from any bell here. Strange!"

"It is strange!" Sergey Nikolaevich's bass butts in.

"Should we take a look, Sergey Nikolaevich?"

"Yes, take a look!"

The three go to the freight yard. A young girl follows and catches up with them, carrying a piece of paper for a signature. She sticks the paper into the flying, shifting sand—she's drying the ink. The commandant lowers his foot on the *burkhan* gracefully, as if he were dancing. Sergey Nikolaevich moves his finger along the broken crown: "A little damage." The commandant again brings his sleeves together.

"The fingers are gold."

"Gilded."

"That's right, that's exactly what I think. How would they allow gold fingers out of Petersburg?"

He nods his head: "But it's harmless. Let it lie there."

The professor puts the mandates in his pocket. "I will take it away!"

"Go on and take it. So what is it you really need from us?"

"Place a guard!"

"A guard?"

The commandant looks at Sergey Nikolaevich. The latter turns the thought over somewhere deep within him. "You can place a guard."

The commandant nods his head quickly as if his neck is being cut off: "That's possible. Put Savoska there—he likes to sleep. Let him sleep."

Savoska has short legs, and he walks so slowly that you might think his feet are under the ground and that he's continually looking for them; his eyes are fixed on the floor and his eyelashes are curly. He carries his overcoat on a bayonet, spreads it out next to the statue, and suddenly his legs appear. He lights up and taps the Buddha's side with his finger. "Copper," he says loudly with respect.

"And you, uncle, do you know any folktales?" he asks the professor. And while Vitaly Vitalevich was trying to answer him, he fell asleep.

Professor Safonov swallows dust: it has a strange taste, which he senses as cold in his temples. The piles of snow are melting, but the hats of all the people he meets are pushed down over their heads even more than in winter. Could they be protecting their temples from the dust?

Beyond the station the professor's overcoat gets caught on the fence; he wants to free it from the nail. But this is not a nail but a man's finger, and beyond the finger is a man in a *beshmet* that resembles a rotted wood fence. The *beshmet* seizes the professor's pocket and says in words that roll and reverberate like a handful of loose change that's been thrown down, "Watch out for your munny. . . . No end to swindlas. . . . Whatcha bring?"

It's difficult for the professor to move and, moreover, the man is holding him by the belt on the back of his coat.

"Show me where the soviet is!"

"*Sovit?* Here lot *sovits* . . . There's *sovit*—has houses, my house also this *sovit* have. There's *sovit* in jails puts, Bilizhman sit for fifth month. . . . No *sovit* for trade, gives everything free."

"I need the *ispolkom* of the soviet."

"Lots of people there. No need to fear, let me take you."

The Tartar waddles, complains as they walk, and tries to find out what goods are being allowed through. In the entryway of the soviet he stays and waits. After finishing his business, the professor will go to his place to have some tea and sleep. The Tartar pokes the professor in the nape of the neck and makes smacking sounds with his lips. "I have such a soft bed!" With what will the professor pay him? Then the Tartar points his finger to the professor's temple, "Ask, in *sovit* give ever'one . . . wave hands more. Oh *purmay*, what kind things *chaman!*"[33]

The secretary of the *ispolkom* reads the mandate quickly. The secretary is long and round, his shoulders are almost even with his head, and above the table he resembles a package wrapped in cloth.

"You should have gone in the direction of Irkutsk."

"We didn't want to hinder the movement of the army. I will travel from Semipalatinsk to Lepsinsk, across Lake Chulak-Perek, and from there along the border area to Sergiopol, and then through the villages to the border itself."

"But that's a whole expedition . . . And the Buddha, what does the Buddha have to do with it? And where are your comrades?"

"They joined the army."

"So much the better. Are you by yourself?"

They go into the chairman's office. The secretary points to the mandate derisively. "The Buddha has come! He's asking for horses?"

The chairman's eyes bulge fiercely (he is unbelievably kind, and that's why he has to shout all the time). "Send him packing to the devil! We are forced to transport political agitators on camels, but he needs horses. You just send him to me, to me. . . . I'll fix him!"

The secretary again turns into a package wrapped in cloth:

"If you like, I'll raise your question at a meeting of the plenum of the soviet. Leave your mandates and stop by in the middle of the week. Do you have a card for the cafeteria? Since you're here on official business, see Comrade Nikitin in the *Gubprodkom*.[34]

The professor takes back his mandates. "Then allow me to leave."

"Go ahead. Please, comrade, only I warn you . . . "

The secretary writes out a pass: "Permission to Professor Safonov, as the escort of a statue of the Buddha, to go to the boundary of the Semipalatinsk Province."

The Tartar Khizret-Naghim-Bey is waiting for him at the entrance.

"Did you get it?"

The professor has to go to the *Gubprodkom* to get his rations card. Then Khizret-Naghim-Bey will feed him and do it very cheaply. In a month there'll be *kurmysh*.[35] Is he a Mohammedan?

Solai.[36] What Tartar is a Christian, and as for Mongolians, he knows nothing about them—they have gone into the steppe with the Kirghiz. Is the man in the overcoat going with him? He is? Very good. *Solai.*

The professor follows the Tartar obediently. His stooping back is all stripes, oily and deep, as if pieces of dirty suet had been sewn into the Tartar's back. The sandy town is phantomlike: Professor Safonov had imagined it just like this. Yellow sand keeps moving in sleepy streams; they are unusually hot, and the professor finds it pleasant to remember that it was only a week ago that he saw snow-covered pine trees and the white tops of mountains. The *teplushka* had rushed a whole week through the snowdrifts. People are sleepy in the streams of sand and, as in a dream, the professor forgets the faces he's seen. The Tartar turns around often; he is very pleased with something, and each time the professor sees a new face. So it should be: at the threshold of another culture wander other people, drunk with sleep, who are foreign to this culture. They are sleepy, unchanging, and they assimilate thoughts with difficulty, like a rock assimilates water. They cannot move forward into the desert. Only with courage and a clear mind, feeling your tightening muscles—from their tightness the professor experiences a pleasure he can taste—can you create. The desert understands his creativity—and for this reason he's so clear and simple. He looks happily at the Tartar's face, and the latter nods his head: "good."

Suddenly the professor wants to be open and to tell the Tartar something pleasant and cheerful. He steps with pleasure on the *koshmy* in the Tartar's *izba* and, although the Tartar does not bring him into the clean half (he's afraid of disease), the professor is pleased. He feels the log wall and says, "It's a strong hut," and listens attentively to the Tartar's story about the confiscation of a brick house.

Here, on the *koshmy*, Khizret-Naghim-Bey seems to fracture

the language less; he is more understandable or that's the way it seems. Nonetheless, the *koshmy* are too puffy and soft, and the walls are unusually strong. A woman brings herb tea; she is lightly made up and resembles Tsin. The professor bows to her cordially. Low tables, a quarter *arshin* high, bent (as if by wind) teapots, doors curtained with a clear curtain. There's golden pale blue light (it smells of milk), and a cat that raises the curtain with its paw and goes somewhere through the wall.

The professor takes a piece of gold wire, the same one that he had tried to sell to the peasants. He feels that this is a different world, and that they will appreciate his wire. Exactly so: the Tartar barely touches the wire and hangs it on the nail of his little finger. The professor looks lovingly at his sharp nail, long like a sliver of wood.

"Is there a lot more?" Naghim-Bey asks.

The professor, in handing him the wire, had wanted to buy food, but he quickly says, "A lot."

At this point the Tartar gets to his feet and straightens up. His dirty *beshmet*, it turns out, had hidden clean velvet *sharovary*[37] and a yellow shirt. Naghim-Bey takes the professor to the clean part of the hut. More Tartars gather. Naghim-Bey bustles and disappears; the professor understands: he is trying to find out from a Russian whether the wire is really made of gold. "Everything's great," thinks the professor and drinks a lot of tea. He's in the desert; here they drink a lot of tea.

The Tartars surround him: the Russian jeweler said the wire is made of Chinese gold, and that it's the most expensive and ancient gold. The Tartars stand around Vitaly Vitalevich; with respect in their eyes they look at his poorly patched overcoat, at his hair the color of a molting toad, and at his gold false tooth. Judging by his false tooth they decide, "not a thief," and Khizret-Bey asks, "How much are you asking?"

The professor needs a strong cart, four camels, two drivers, and as much food as the journey calls for. He's taking the statue of the Buddha past Lake Chulak-Perek to Sergiopol and from there through the villages to Chuguchak. He has mandates and an official pass. The professor explains what the statue of the Buddha is.

"*Burkhan . . . burkhan . . .* ," the shaved heads nod.

They want to see the *burkhan* for themselves. Professor Safonov takes them to the freight yard.

With his head tucked in the Buddha's side, Savoska is sleeping. Next to him are cigarette butts: the wind is trying to carry them off and yet can't—just as Savoska, lost in his thoughts, had puffed on his cigarettes for a long time.

"Four camels won't be able to carry it," the Tartars say, and straining intentionally, they try to roll the statue over on its other side. "It's eight hundred versts to Chuguchak. It's spring in the steppe—it's difficult for the camels to move. There's no way you can do it with fewer than eight camels."

They return, drink tea, and agree to transport the Buddha to Sergiopol for the wire.

"I'll find others," the professor says.

The Tartars argue: the war is going on, Whites are beyond Sergiopol, they'll drive off the camels. They're killing people. Will you be able to buy a lot for the wire? Finally, they agree to give four camels and to go beyond Sergiopol to the village of Ak-Chuliysk.

Vitaly Vitalevich rolls a fatty piece of meat around in his fingers delightedly and puts it to his lips.

The fences are warm and happy; the professor runs the palm of his hand over them. Making a sound against his boots, the sand blows, tears his hand from the fence and, joyful and fluffy, forces its way into his hand. The professor walks around the yard for a long time. The camels are taking long and noisy breaths; the smells coming from them are also endless and steppelike: wormwood and young spring grasses.

It's nice to see Savoska, too. He gets up and taps the statue with the butt of his rifle.

"And what if they had stolen it from you?" the professor jokes.

Savoska again does not have any legs; he has a four-cornered shape and he's brown like a piece of carton, and his weapon is like a piece of kindling stuck in.

"Stea-eal it? Who needs it? People are like a bell, it would be heard everywhere! Wood is a different matter—they swipe it . . . that's for sure. You're transporting a god, aren't you, uncle?"

"I am."

"And people pray to such things?"

"They do."

"That's strange."

A sandy, yellow-ribbed town. White houses like rocks that become exposed by the wind. A fellow with chairs on his shoulders, a small boy in tight-fitting pants, and dogs making shallow, sandy, barking sounds accompany the Buddha. He is lying on the cart, covered with *koshmy* and tied tightly with rope. His face is peaceful and coppery, with his ears tightly pressed together like a sleeping animal's.

A dreamlike, sandy town. Foggy dark brown eyes coming toward you, no lips—even the sand-covered shroud begins at the eyes.

The cart is moving silently through the sands; the camels take wide steps with their plump feet; the drivers are silent and gloomy—the Buddha is leaving town.

Khizret-Naghim-Bey looks out the window and thinks about the funny man taking a piece of copper to Mongolia. Khizret-Naghim-Bey tried to persuade him to stay in town: he could sleep well in exchange for the wire, and the *koshmy* are long—you won't roll off and wake up like when you roll off a bed. Khizret-Naghim-Bey is thinking about the four camels given to the man with the gold tooth. They won't get the right care; the man is a total drunk.

Khizret-Naghim-Bey regrets giving the camels and cart. Khizret-Naghim-Bey saddles his horse.

Simple and clear is life, like the grasses, like the wind.

The steppe stretches before Professor Safonov.

"Ho!" the drivers shout.

Professor Safonov repeats, "Ho!"

The camels have their own thoughts. Roan fur hangs in large pieces on their necks. The cart is squeaking—the road is long and dry—and helping itself with its own noise. Whether from one's own or someone else's shouts, it's merrier in the steppe.

The professor senses a merry shiver that sends sparks through his veins. His shoulders seem to be growing; he throws off his greatcoat and merrily looks at gophers darting into their burrows.

"Ho-o!"

Poor small animal. It hides in its dark burrow, and then again jumps out into the world. And the professor rejoices at this simple and sentimental thought. The journey frightened the empty and stupid Dava-Dorchzhi, and food lured him on; he darted into a burrow. But he will make it. Now Dava-Dorchzhi sits in an office and issues papers: he's teaching the young to kill the old and those like him.

The Buddha rocks in the cart. The Buddha, with his eyes covered over with a piece of felt, will pass through sands and steppes in a state of sleepiness.

Under the professor's boots is new grass that still smells of earth. He picks a handful, and his hands also begin to smell of growing things.

"Ho-o!" shout the drivers.

Do the camels need all this shouting? They're moving and will go like that a year, and two, and even three, as long as there are sands and villages. It's man who needs the shouting.

The professor joins in the shouting in a thin voice, "Ho! Ho! Ho!"

On the morning of the third day of the journey horsemen come galloping toward the caravan out of the sand hills overgrown with haloxylon bushes. One of them has a black rag on a long pole. The rawhide reins slip out of their hands (they're inexperienced, apparently) and they howl in fright: "Aiiiii! Aiiiii!"

The drivers, covering the backs of their heads with their hands, fall to the ground. The camels move on. Then one of the horsemen cries, "*Chokh!*"

The camels lie down.

Professor Safonov is calm. For some reason he thrusts his hand in the pocket of his overcoat. While he is walking from the road to the horsemen, he manages only the thought: "absolutely should have demanded a guard." Feeling somewhat guilty, Professor Safonov slows his step. At this point the horseman with the black rag rides right up to him. The horse's leg is rubbing against the professor's side and there's a noticeable smell of wet hide. The Kirghiz—he has an almost Russian large-nosed face and marvelous strong teeth—bends in the saddle, and throwing the reins on the pommel of his saddle, asks, "Where are you going?"

The professor feels even more sharply his incomprehensible guilt, and for this reason answers a bit hastily, "To Sergiopol. . . . And where are you heading, fellow citizens?"

But here the Kirghiz makes a waving motion and strikes his head with something dull and warm. The professor grabs the saddle with one hand, and the other he stretches to his neck. Everything around him is slippery, yellow, and binding—with a faint smell. The Kirghiz hits him in the shoulder, letting out whoops.

The professor falls.

Then the horsemen, whooping, circle around the cart, whip the horses, and tired of chasing after each other, ride up to the Buddha. The drivers get up and expectantly look to the hills. One more horseman comes galloping from there; he has a small soldier's cap on his head; it sits badly on his head, and his hand is bouncing on his head. It's Naghim-Bey. He had been waiting for them behind a hill. The Kirghiz are in a hurry; they hack off the twine and roll the Buddha off into the sand. "Here," Naghim-Bey says, and they hit the Buddha's chest with axes. Lamas often hide precious stones in the Buddha's chest cavity, but the chest is empty. Then one of the Kirghiz chops off the gilded fingers and puts them in his trouser pocket. Khizret-Naghim-Bey walks up to the prostrate man. Naghim-Bey is sorry for him, but the camels are even more valuable. The Kirghiz who had hit the man with his stick wants to have his gold tooth, but Khizret-Naghim-Bey says sternly, "*Kiter.*[38] Let him die with his tooth!"

This path is to the side of the high road (the man had been stupid: a wise one understands roads). The Kirghiz slowly turn the camels around.

And later, in the evening, before his death, Professor Safonov tears his shoulders from the ground and grabs with his hand: forward, backward, to the right. . . . Under his fingers the water is thick and sticky. . . .

But this is not water—it's sand.

Sand.

The chest which has been split open is filled with dark, crimson wounded copper. His nipples are cracked from the axes. His high chin is humiliated by the exposed iron. His gold fingers rush on, feeling the smelly skin of the Kirghiz. And his eyes are turned upward; they are looking somewhere past and higher than the sands streaming by. But why and who can they ask there: "Where should the Buddha now direct his path?"

Because. . . .

There is only the taut, stony, silent sky filled with the smells of earth above the Buddha.

Only. . . .

1923

The Field

Milekhin got a four-hour leave.

"Get back late, and I'll send you off with a detachment before your turn comes," said the company commander, stamping his passport with a bang.

But even an hour was enough for Milekhin. He told the commander that relatives had come from the village, and, in saying that, he had lied. He felt like getting some fresh air. The March sun, the dirty cigarette butts on the floor, and the walls, gray with filth, made the barracks seem especially gloomy. Someone had used white clay to write a bad word on the blackboard (there used to be a school here), and on the board next to it, stuck on with the soft inside of a loaf of bread, was a poster saying: "Kolchak is bringing sausage, the Soviets—freedom." And so, when Milekhin slammed the burlap-covered door and set out across the wide yard to the square, he felt warm, satiated, and joyful.

The railroad station was about four versts from town, and a local train went into town every four hours. Milekhin didn't feel like waiting for the local, and he set out on foot across the huge square to the station.

The sun baked from above, but from below it was freezing. The square had already thawed, and only the raised portion of the road lay like a dirty yellow ribbon on the black swollen earth. Beyond the white willows, straight to the west, the Irtysh looked blue and frozen; the broken-up patches of road, which could be seen on it, resembled scraps of paper.

"It must have broken during the night," Milekhin said.

But the cracking sound of the ice, which had begun to break up, couldn't be heard yet.

"It'll start moving soon."

Milekhin smiled and felt good, as if the ice belonged to him. Loudly stomping with his English boots, he walked along the edge of the road, and the crust of the snow broke up under his feet. And this crunching sound gave him pleasure. His greenish English greatcoat, which looked like an ordinary overcoat, and the blue French puttees on his calves somehow didn't go at all with his huge rabbit hat and its earflaps and with his thin reddish beard.

The white wing of a gull flashed above a willow.

"It'll start moving soon." Milekhin thought again.

The station was crowded with people, mostly women with sacks, and soldiers with tin stars on their hats; three Chinese were selling cigarettes and sunflower seeds. Water dripped from the roof, and frequently long glistening icicles fell with a quiet ring.

Milekhin stood a while by the door to the third-class waiting room. A commissar with a yellow briefcase under his arm ran into him while walking by and muttered quietly, "Excuse me."

So as not to get in anyone's way, Milekhin moved to the side and sat down on the windowsill. Trainmen kept running by with lanterns and black boxes; locomotives whistled in different voices, and the buffers of the train cars banged against each other. From above, quietly and in no hurry, the large clear sun warmed both the station and the dirty train cars as well as the earth, swelling with moisture.

An icicle dropped beside him. Milekhin bent down and picked it up; it was solid inside. A second one fell, a third, and they were all like that.

"It's going to be a good harvest," thought Milekhin, "every kernel of grain will get nice and full and there'll be a rich yield. Gr-e-a-t!"

And he remembered that the snow melts not from the sun so much as from the temperature of the earth at night. And it melts at a steady pace.

"It's going to be a good harvest," Milekhin said aloud, and in saying so he thought of his village.

He guessed that everything was fine with his cattle, the roan one and the brown one, and that all was well on his farm. Last year's harvest was bad, but this year's ought to be good. All of March was dry, and now, if April is wet, it'll be heaven. But now, at such a sacred time, it's either clean your rifle or stand guard at some depot or other. He began to feel uneasy inside; he got up and paced up and down the platform three times and then decided to return to his company. At that moment someone called his name.

"Kolsha!"

Milekhin turned around and recognized one of his comrades from the company, Fedka Nikitin. A month ago he had come down with typhus and was taken to a hospital. Milekhin went up to him, and they grabbed each other's hands.

"Well, how are you?" Milekhin asked.

"Not bad. They're letting me go back to the village for two months to recuperate. I'm about to leave."

"What *uyezd* are you from?"

"Tatarsky," Nikitin answered with pleasure. "In half a day, brother, I'll be home. And you?"

Milekhin answered reluctantly.

"Novo-Nikolaevsk. A two-day trip. Nowadays the trains run terribly, and with a Maksim locomotive,[1] it's a whole week.

"For sure if it's a Maksim," agreed Nikitin, and in a ringing voice said, "Come over to my car for some tea."

Milekhin agreed. As they were walking, Milekhin noticed that Nikitin was weaving from weakness, but to look at him, you'd think he was about to get married. Milekhin envied him.

While they were having their tea, Nikitin, like all people who have just had a bout with typhus, ate a lot and kept offering Milekhin food. But Milekhin kept thinking about his own village and didn't hear what Nikitin was telling him about the hospital and doctors.

And when he said good-bye to his friend and left the car, he decided to go home on that very same train. Three cars went by—he wanted to sit in the rear of the train—but he couldn't hold out and got in the next car, went past one compartment and crawled under the bench in the next one.

Five soldiers were sitting in the compartment. One of them, with his nose smashed open, asked, "Where're you going?"

"Home," Milekhin answered.

"Uh-huh," said the soldier, and another one, dunking a piece of dried bread in a glass of tea, asked, "Do you have far to go?"

"Novo-Nikolaevsk. The next to the last station."

"That's pretty far. You don't have any papers."

"No."

"And no bread either?"

Milekhin answered angrily, "Well, no, but what's it to you?"

"Just lie there quietly," said the soldier. "You'll get there one way or another."

Milekhin spent two days under the bench without crawling out, and on the third day during the night he got off at Grachevo. It was only fifteen versts from Grachevo to Krutoy, and in the morning, Milekhin was home.

Milka started squealing and threw herself at his legs. The goose took off in fright under the overturned sled; just like a year ago, a sparrow was sitting on the skull of a horse stuck on the fence post and preening its wings. Senka stuck his head through the door and shouted into the hut, "Mommy, daddy's home."

His wife got the samovar ready, brought in some milk, cut some bread, and, standing behind the stove and wiping her eyes with her skirt, asked, "Have they let you go for long?"

"Two months," Milekhin said gravely, and even he himself seemed to believe what he had said.

"Is the war over, maybe?"

"Far from it. They let me go because I was sick."

"Sick with what?"

"Who the hell knows? The doctors know."

"Of course the doctors know," Marya said with sobs in her voice. "They wear out a person's health and then they don't even say what he's got."

In the village people would ask him, "Have you joined the commonune?"[2]

Milekhin replied, "They say I'm not good enough."

"You don't say," the peasants said with surprise. "And people here, they say in Omsk they're signing up everyone for the commonune, and whoever doesn't want to gets his head shaved and sent to the Germans. You haven't seen any of them, have you?"

"Haven't run across any," Milekhin answered.

"It's stupid to get the people stirred up; don't expect any good to come of it."

Milekhin agreed, "Don't expect any good."

But all these questions soon ceased. The plowing season had begun and everyone went off to the fields. A quiet spring was approaching; April was wet. Brief but heavy rains fell.

"What a blessing," Milekhin said in a quiet voice so the evil spirits wouldn't hear him. "The shaft for the horse will be overgrown with grass in one night."

"What wonders!" sighed his wife.

The plow bounced briskly as it cut through the black earth. Burko sweated, and a sharp and sweet smell wafted from the harness. The plowshare sparkled, Burko's damp hide also sparkled, and it seemed to Milekhin that the earth was parting by itself—it was tired of lying fallow. The air smelled of reeds in the lakes, the trees were coming out, and unopened buds that looked like large beetles shone damply here and there on them.

And for some reason it never occurred to Milekhin that in Omsk, in the second platoon, rifle No. 45.728 lay by his bunk, and that he was not Uncle Kolya at all but Nikolay Milekhin, a soldier of the Red Army.

The chickens would leave the roost late. During the night Milekhin's wife would smile and whisper into his ear, "It's going to be a good harvest."

"Fine," Milekhin would answer in a sleepy voice, and he would feel a slight pang in his heart. He would press his wife to himself and fall asleep.

When the bird-cherry tree was in full bloom, they began to sow. In the morning, a light breeze was blowing from the east—that was good, the seed grain would fall to the west, to peace; then, toward midday, the wind ceased completely—even better. The sun remained a warm red circle; it watched the large yellow grains fall evenly and heavily to the earth.

Then Milekhin went into the field and saw the dense green slope. From the top, the observation spot where he was standing, the plowed field resembled a green Kolomensk tablecloth. All around it were burnt black tree stumps that looked like glasses of brick tea.

"Would you just look . . . ," Milekhin said to himself with awe in his voice, and, remembering that the cattle had not been watered, he headed back home.

Senka met him before he got to the gate.

"Daddy, there's a police constable there."

"Where?"

"In the front room. He's wearing a b-i-g hat. I'm scared."

"He won't bite," said Milekhin, climbing the front steps.

The policeman took Milekhin to the *volost,* and from there to the *uyezd* military commissariat. From there they sent him to the *guberniya,* where the Provmiltrib[3] decreed: for absence without leave from the Red Army in a time of intense battle with the enemies of the Socialist Fatherland, one-half of his real and personal property is to be confiscated on behalf of the state.

1926

The Life of Smokotinin

When, for the first time after the long wars, carpenters came to the village to build a new *izba* for the rich peasant Anfinogenov in place of the one that had burned down, people laughed and joked a lot. Some shouted that the axes had gotten dull during the Revolution—they'd chopped off too many heads; others said that since people had forgotten how to chop down trees, they couldn't tell an aspen from a birch; others simply used inexplicable soldiers' curses. But still, it was nice to know that the new times, when you could get paid for your work and build an *izba* for yourself, were worth it. And everyone walked around for a long time beside the mound of yellow logs and felt the blades of their Zlatoust[1] axes.

The contractor who was building the *izba* was their own Yevgraf Smokotinin, from the village, a short, broad-footed old man. Yevgraf had become frightened by the war, the famine, and the incomprehensible taxes, and he became even more intimidated when he started accepting orders again after a long break. Without a down payment, he had built a store for a cooperative in the *volost;* he was told he would get his money the next day, and then the cooperative went broke. And the way the courts work, it was impossible to understand who was at fault and whom to sue. After this he never trusted anyone again, and he himself paid in advance and demanded payment in advance for any work to be done. On the eve of the raising of the new *izba,* he fell ill or feigned illness in order to train his children to do the work, and sent his youngest son Timofey to act as supervisor.

Calm Timofey, with his rosy cheeks and ringing voice, was bored supervising the work and urging on the carpenters. He grabbed his ax, chose one of the heavier logs, and struck it. The ax clanged, the wood groaned. . . . It was a cool morning; the dew on the underside of the leaves hadn't disappeared yet. Next to the barn, doves were cooing—and their voices were businesslike, like everything that morning. Seeing how hard their boss was working, the carpenters also grabbed their heavy axes. They were not from here; they didn't like this "well-fed" village, and they wanted to demonstrate how one should really work. And it looked like the boss wanted to compete with them.

At this point, Katerina Shepelova, a widow, emerged from behind the barn; her husband had been killed in the war, and she was left with one child. Who knows how she managed to live? Rumor had it that the *volost* cooperative ordered knitted mittens from her, which it then resold. But how much of a profit can there be in knitting mittens? Often, during the night, an unknown hand would reach out of the darkness into her open window and leave a small bundle of food—secret alms. She was tall and healthy, the silent type; she held her head to one side, and her chestnut-colored eyelashes seemed to sweep the earth. . . . Going around the pile of scrapwood, which smelled strongly of resin, she walked up to the carpenters, and slowly, as if ashamed, took a large strip of wood, about one and a half *arshins* in length. She bowed low to them. The carpenters looked at their boss. He was working feverishly on a log. He had intended to hew a ceiling beam out of it, but he hit a large knot, which made him look foolish; ceiling beams can't have knots in them.

"That woman's like a window, she needs a good frame. Then

it'll be bright and warm for you," said one of the carpenters following Katerina with his eyes.

Timofey raised his head, and only then did he notice Katerina.

"Who gave her that strip of wood?"

"She took it herself," the same carpenter answered with displeasure. The boss, young and stupid, evidently didn't know it was customary for carpenters to give scrapwood to whomever they wanted.

Timofey got angry because of the ceiling beam that didn't turn out right and because he could tell from the voices of the carpenters that he had said something really stupid. He ran after Katerina, who had already disappeared behind the barn, grabbed her by the sleeve of her jacket, and shouted in anger, "Who said you could take the scrapwood?"

Katerina shrugged her shoulders gracefully; her jacket was old, patched, and not buttoned up right, and she must have been naked underneath it—that's why she held the wood tight to her chest, like a child; and because of this Timofey was completely bedazzled. He reached out—he wasn't bashful with women—and instead of the piece of wood, he grabbed her breast through the unbuttoned slit in her jacket. Unlike other women, Katerina didn't shriek, and she didn't squirm; her feet rooted to the spot, she didn't seem to be in any particular hurry to push him away. She merely said, "Enough," and let go of the wood.

The wood slid down slowly and hit the ground with one end, and before falling over, it swayed lightly as if sighing. Katerina put her hands under her shawl and turned around, and suddenly it seemed to Timofey that his heart had also slipped out with that piece of wood, with one end pointing up the same way and swaying the same way. . . .

"Go on, you stuck-up . . . ," he shouted and, striking his boot with the piece of wood he had taken away from her, went back to his work. And that piece of wood was heavy, and it felt as if he were hitting himself with a log.

"Money for profit and scrapwood for kindling," the same carpenter laughingly teased him.

But Timofey didn't snap back.

He was about to try a new log for the beam, but suddenly it turned out that all the wood was swamp pine, knotty and green; that the spot chosen for the *izba* sloped and had to be leveled and evened out. Moreover, the carpenters wasted a lot of time smoking and laughing. He felt like going home for some tea; perhaps he should go to the river and take a dip.

"He'll be more of a dawdler than his father," the sarcastic carpenter said after him, "one more scoundrel in our ranks."

And all the carpenters agreed with his words.

The father was lying on the ledge above the stove, and when the son came in, he began to sigh and groan. Timofey was disgusted to see this pretense. His father began asking questions about how the *izba* was coming along. The boiling samovar was on the table, and Timofey's sister poured him a cup of tea and passed him the glass sugar bowl, which resembled a milking pail. Timofey didn't answer his father and bawled out his sister, "All you know how do is drink tea, and it costs two rubles a brick."[2]

He left the house and went to the river. Women, gathering black currants, were shouting back and forth to each other in the thickets on the other side of the river. He even got angry at that. He was about to pull off his boot—he wanted to take a swim. The cloths[3] wound around his feet were hot and had gotten all twisted and only vaguely resembled the form of his foot. He struck one of them with his fist.

The summer was quiet, good for plowing. Toward evening it usually rained lightly, and the raindrops would make a netlike pattern in the dust; the dew was warm and heavy. The May beetles—

sweet-smelling beetles—would fly around in the evenings and hit people's hair as in play; they were wishing people a good harvest. To work, to hew timber this summer, to plow all the fields, to build all over the place, to cover the entire *okrug* with *izbas!*

But since that morning, Timofey had never once checked on the building of the *izba*. His father cursed a bit and cursed some more and then came and took the job over himself. Timofey didn't want to go out to the fields either, and since everyone would come back tired, there was no one to drink with, and even the distilling of moonshine had decreased. Timofey decided to walk along the river with his dragnet, but when he stuck his foot into the water, he almost threw up.

"I guess I've been given some kind of illness," he said bewildered and dropped his net on the warm sand.

In the evening a woman practicing sorcery sprinkled holy water on him and gave him some holy water to drink, but even this didn't help him feel better. He even began to sleep badly. He promised the same woman a wool skirt if she would bring Katerina to the hayloft at night. The old woman got alarmed.

"Why don't I bring you Lizaveta? She isn't so skinny and she'll agree. Katerina will never get into bed. 'I'm faithful to my husband,' she says, 'and I'm not going to get married or sleep with another man.' Maybe if you promised her a real present, like shoes. . . . "

But Katerina answered the old woman, too, with the same vague word, "Enough," and the old woman, looking intently at her lashes, suddenly shushed her and began waving her hands.

The summer heat had begun in the heavens, and there was heat in man's soul. The ears of grain were maturing, and both dusk and dawn were drunk with their abundance and merriment like the fields.

Then Timofey talked his father into fixing up a cart for him and left for the city to work as a cabby. But he turned out to be an uncommonly bad cabby. Although he stood at the busiest intersections, like the one near the green church resembling a bast basket filled with mushrooms; although his horse was well fed and his cart new, painted blue; although he was a lad who seemed full of spirit, when a fare would approach—a drunk, a fool—he'd take a look at the coachman and head for the next one. Timofey never invited anyone anywhere; when he'd accumulate a bit of money, he'd head for the beer hall and, with his elbows on the table, he'd drink his beer; silently, like at the crossroads—seeing no one—he'd gaze at the tables. Once, on a holiday, he happened to get seven rubles; he went with his fellow boarders to a tavern. One of them, who had pimples and spoke through his nose, described how he had taken a young girl the day before and how she yelled and scratched at the wall. Those who listened laughed at each word for a long time.

"I'll sleep with her a couple more times, and then to hell with her . . . too much of a whiner," finished the one who spoke through his nose.

"You won't feel sorry for her?" Timofey asked suddenly.

"What for?" the one who spoke through his nose asked in surprise.

Timofey shook his head and demanded a glass of vodka. . . . His friends also drank a glass to keep him company. Then Timofey said, "And I was the ruin . . . of one widow. Just didn't want to get married, and she says to me, 'May the one after whom I sigh into kindling wood dry. . . .'"

They only had half a glass of vodka left. They began to discuss what to drink next—beer or vodka. Everyone had long forgotten Timofey's words, but he still wanted to finish telling why he didn't marry her and how her words turned out to be nonsense, and that his real luck started only after her words: he's earning piles of money, soon he'll buy himself a carriage with real rubber tires. There was a lot he wanted to tell them, but he never got the chance.

In the morning, at the same tavern, he had some hair of the dog that bit him. His head cleared up right away, which was amazing, and he felt happy like he hadn't felt for a long time. He was standing again at the same noisy crossroads near the small green church resembling a bast basket full of mushrooms. He looked around boldly, and an old man in a long frock coat, pointing with obvious emotion, said to the young woman walking next to him, "That's the merchant Gavrilov. He used to be rolling in money, but now, look what's become of him—a cabby." And Timofey felt good that he'd been taken for a merchant. But suddenly, to the right of a man with a tray of *pirozhki* for sale, a woman in a blue dress stepped back. Her light hands disappeared under her kerchief with such a familiar, special motion; there was something special and melancholy about her walk. . . . Immediately, that clarity which had been fluttering about inside Timofey started to fly away like the petals of a wild rose are carried away by the wind. His eyes began to sting. He wanted to cry out, and he grabbed the reins; and the horse—it was always submissive—seemed to recognize her, too, and bolted into the crowd! They hit a little boy carrying a satchel, and his books went flying. The man selling *pirozhki* fell down, and someone in a long gray shawl suddenly appeared in front of them. . . . Timofey shouted, whipping his horse, "Stop her, stop!" A ruddy-cheeked policeman blew his whistle, himself enjoying the confusion, the sound of his whistle, and the incomprehensible thing that was going on.

Timofey was taken to the police station. He sat in jail for a week and was then let out: they decided he was sick. That week the horse grew thin, as if it, too, was ashamed. Timofey sold the horse, spent the money on drink, and returned to his village in his worn-down shoes. During that year his father had already contracted to build a fourth *izba*, but he was still the same intimidated man. Fat geese waddled around in the meadows where the grain had been harvested;

in the mornings, a thin layer of ice formed on the river, and the aspens had all turned solid yellow. The thought of going to town hadn't even entered Katerina's mind; she walked around the village in the same patched blue dress, and it seemed as if she had been given someone else's life to live and so she was living it.

Soon after Timofey's return, a wolf killed one of the colts out in the field. Timofey and his father skinned it, dragged the carcass to the ravine, and threw it into the bushes. His father gave him a shotgun loaded with buckshot and ordered him to sit in the bushes. Who knows? Wolves are vicious in the fall, hungry; they just might come for the meat. And in fact, at dawn, a pair of wolves appeared in the bushes of meadowsweet above the ravine. Timofey had never realized that they had such huge heads. He fired, the wolves jumped, and one of them began to limp. But Timofey was bored and wanted to sleep. "I'll find it tomorrow," he decided, and headed home.

People were still asleep in the village, but when he started walking down the street, smoke was already appearing in the chimneys, and the small windows began to glisten orange with reflection from the stoves. An orange flame also flashed in the window of Katerina's *izba*. Timofey looked in. Katerina was standing with her side to him and was taking a splinter of kindling wood from the top of the stove. The stove, apparently, was slow in heating up, and she wanted to add some kindling. And again, Timofey saw her hands: light, white, and downy, somehow reminding him of linen. When she touched her chest with them, it was as if they were flashes of summer lightning, not illuminating, but making her face as well as the other person's face tremble. Seeing her standing motionless with the kindling, Timofey even experienced some kind of tender feeling. But barely had she moved and dropped her hands, barely had the outline of her breasts appeared like a steep bank emerging in a fog, when Timofey began to feel rotten and ashamed—because he had thought of marrying her and didn't have the strength to talk of marriage both to his father and to her; and because he was waiting again for that word "enough"; and because he, a healthy man, and it would seem a daring fellow, was standing like a beggar under her window, not only not daring to walk in, but even afraid to think about it.

To rid himself of such thoughts, Timofey let fall a fat gob of spit, and after spitting, he felt the weight of the rifle on his shoulder. He took a cartridge and couldn't remember whether it was buckshot or small shot. "No matter—only three steps," he thought, and that same unusual clarity that had come to him once at the crossroads near the small green church welled up in him again.

He didn't kill her. The shot hit her in the shoulder. For a month and a half she lay on a bench under a sheepskin coat sent by Timofey's father; she didn't come to the trial. Timofey couldn't explain anything to the court; he was ashamed to speak of witchcraft, although he wanted to. "Like a piece of kindling wood sticking in the back of my heart," he said, and he threw up his hands. The court gave him one year. After serving his time, he never returned to his village. He had formed many friendships in prison: he had begun hanging around with his new friends at fairs and sitting around in taverns with gypsies. Life seemed easy, without any responsibilities. He kept thinking, "I've gotta go see my father, fall at his feet and say . . . ," but what he should say, he didn't know himself. He never did manage to find the time to go to his father and, moreover, his clothing had gotten all torn and tattered.

It was fall again; there were light frosts, and the sky looked as if it were covered with hoarfrost. Unusual argamaks[4] were brought from somewhere near Orenburg[5] to one of the fairs. Lately the peasants had fallen in love with purebred horses, and the gypsies had proposed some kind of business deal to Timofey. But those who had brought the argamaks were also experienced horse traders, more cunning than the gypsies. The argamaks were kept in a shed. One side of the shed faced a dark alley. The gypsies sawed away one of the boards. "Go on in," the youngest one said to him impatiently. Timofey jumped in; pain he had never known before struck him in the knees—the horse traders had placed wolf traps along the wall. He let out a scream. Lanterns began flashing and someone fired a shot. They beat Timofey for a long time with their fists and lashes, and tried to find out from him where the gypsies were. He told them. Then they hit him in the side with a chunk of wood and threw him into the ravine outside the village. He lost one eye, began to limp, and ill fame began to follow him. Now, even when he was drunk, he had no thought of returning to his father. The gypsies chased him away, he wore out all his clothing, went hungry, and then one day some fellows from a neighboring village suggested that he kill a man. For the murder they promised him some felt boots and a sheepskin coat, and agreed to take him to town.

"That's right, brothers, she did me in, that lousy woman! The deal's on, I agree absolutely!" he shouted. He heard his voice and ordered some vodka. He was brought half a glass. Lying in the middle of the men in the sled, he lied to them about his love for a priest's daughter: how the priest chased him away and tried to get the village to run him out of town. . . . The fellows, heaven knows why, roared with laughter until they reached the corner of a large five-walled *izba*. They suggested he knock on the window, call for Ignat, and stick a knife in his stomach when he comes out. Timofey did just that. Ignat came out—a tall, priestlike peasant in a long sheepskin coat. There was a large peaceful moon, Ignat's face was also peaceful, and his coat seemed blue and its collar looked like clouds.

"Don't get in people's way!" Timofey shouted, striking him with the knife.

However, the knife slipped and suddenly everything got mixed up in Timofey's body. He had a clear sensation of bitter snow in his mouth and of the snowdrift swaying; and the moon slipped between his hands. . . .

In the morning Timofey was found dead near the ice hole in the river behind the barns for drying crops. His head was smashed in three places, and his gums were completely bare, like a baby's. His native village was thirty versts away; people thought his father wouldn't come, but he did, with a pair of chestnut horses hitched to a sled. He took a look at his son's face, made the sign of the cross, and covering him with a cloth, asked that he be put on the sled.

And so Timofey lay in his own house for the last time. A bald-headed deacon was reading the Psalter, a cat was playing with the fringe of the tablecloth, and Timofey's sister was preparing the dinner for the wake. Everything was peaceful: no howling, no big preparations. In the hallway the carpenters were working on the coffin, and the sarcastic carpenter, who at one time had worked with Timofey on putting up Anfinogenov's *izba*, was teasing a recently married friend. A lot of people came to pay their last respects to the deceased. The carpenters swept all the sweet-smelling shavings scattered throughout the hallway into a corner so that it would be easier to walk. Katerina came, too. She crossed herself, straightened out the copper coins that were slipping off Timofey's eyes, and kissed his forehead. The copper coins gave his face a frightened and timid look. "Enough," Katerina said in a whisper, and crossed herself once more. In the hallway she looked at the coffin. The carpenters were resting and smoking. It smelled strongly of cheap tobacco. She wrapped her scarf around her and tied it tight on her chest so that it wouldn't fall off her shoulders, and bent low to the ground

And now no one would have stopped her from taking any wood for kindling.

1926

Night

Love and melancholy are founded on blood.

Afonka Petrov's older brother, Filipp, died. Died on the first day
of his married life, in his wedding bed. And for the wedding Filipp
had prepared a long time; his father-in-law was a prosperous miller,
he was taking his son-in-law into his own household, and demanding a lot of money for it. Filipp turned every which way he could,
but the region was poor, there was just no money to come by, and
moreover, Glafira, his bride-to-be, was close by—close to his very
heart; and so off he went to the city. He lived there a little more
than a year, and when he returned, he couldn't say anything except
that the signs there were black with gold letters—perhaps because
Glafira had eyes the color of rye which bloomed under her straw-
colored hair. That's probably it. For this reason, even during the
few hours he had for sleep in the city, his aching body kept seeing
those rye-colored eyes. And so, on the eve of his wedding, he
brought all his earthly goods to his father-in-law's in his own troika with a gilded shaft-bow and bells. People came running to see
Filipp; the miller embraced him on the porch, visibly moved, with
tears in his huge closely spaced eyes—and a bit drunk. Later Filipp's folks arrived in a *tarataika*:[1] Aleksandr Ilich and Marya
Yegorovna, also drunk and talkative; Afonka came too—their
younger pockmarked son with his uncertain gait, wearing a new

blue cap and thick down-filled gloves. They all sat at the table embracing each other and incessantly boasting. The old Petrovs kept saying that their son Filipp was a persistent fellow, and that he would get his place in life; and the miller kept bragging about his daughter, the beauty, shouting so that the whole five-walled *izba* resounded with his boast that Glafira's eyes were like a well and that in his youth he, too, had cast spells on dozens of females with his eyes. But Glafira's eyes really were like the deadly barrel of a gun, and she didn't raise them at the groom. As for Filipp, he sat next to her, straight, strong, a bit pale but calm; and only in his heart it felt as if a bee were buzzing around, and every little now and then a needlelike pain made itself felt.

They hitched the troika again and left for the soviet, even though it was just one street away. The registration went quickly, and the chairman, cheerful as well and not even wearing a hat, got in the troika next to the miller, and then the whole train of wagons headed for the church. It was the beginning of spring—the ribbons with which the horses had been decorated dangled damply in the wind, and through the horses' manes the coachman could see the bright sky—and he drove the troika through all the streets in the village. Sparrows, pulling out pieces of clean straw from the *zavalinki* of the *izbas*, enjoyed the sight of the train of wagons dashing past; little boys ran after the dark blue clumps of dirt flying like clouds from under the horses' hooves and wagon wheels. The boys got tired quickly, their faces became strained, but they couldn't fall behind the train and the ringing bells of spring—and the drunken eyes of both men and horses.

The wedding party, on returning to the mill, again began to drink, yell out songs, and boast. The chairman shouted that if he wanted to, he could outshout any village priest—and in fact his voice sounded unusually wild and piercing. Filipp continued to sit in the same straight and stern way, only he grabbed his bride's hand under the tablecloth and squeezed it as if he wanted to wring out all the strength he had accumulated in the past year and a half—and yet didn't know how. Glafira felt both pain and pleasure; her hand was growing numb, and the numbness was going to her heart—she just couldn't bring herself to raise her rye-colored eyes. After that, the newlyweds were escorted to their bed, and for a long time the miller danced clumsily in front of his daughter, constantly winking his huge and closely spaced eyes. The guests were on the point of leaving, but somehow lingered on around the table and then suddenly started to drink and dance again. The accordion player, who had just about fallen asleep, struck the accordion keys; and then the sun came out, too, and also struck the accordion player's fingers, and the guests passed out wherever they could. Filipp's mama, Marya Yegorovna, drank little but felt happier and more joyful than anyone else; and she, in particular, was pleased when the guests passed out; then, crossing herself, she checked on everyone and covered everyone she could with fur coats. Afonka had fallen asleep outside in the wagon: she covered him with two sheepskin coats as well as a bed curtain and, with joy in her heart, thought that her old age would be good and easy, and that they must choose for their younger son—and he did not have as much going for him as Filipp and was not as stern—a bride who was more cheerful, and arrange an even better wedding than Filipp's so that their love would be stronger. Then Marya Yegorovna went back into the *izba* but didn't feel like sleeping—and so she got the idea of milking the cows. She took the milk pail and was about to go out into the entranceway when joy again swept over her, and she went back. Quietly, so as not to make any noise, she put the milk pail among the scraps of food and broken plates on the floor, walked up to the door of the *gornitsa* where the newlyweds were sleeping and slowly made the sign of the cross over the door—and shed a few tears; and after shedding a few tears, she again made the sign of the cross. A dull moan was heard at that moment behind the door, and Marya Yegorovna, in the same voice she used with cows about to calve, said, "There, my dear one, there . . . just bear a bit longer," and slowly, grabbing the milk pail, she headed out. But on the porch she heard a primitive wail, and the milk pail fell clattering down the steps.

Glafira, disheveled, wearing only her nightshirt, ran out and collapsed on the old woman's shoulder.

"Things are bad with Filipp, bad!" she cried out.

The old woman took a quick look at Glafira and gently covered her hips with her shawl, and then she said tenderly, "It's all right, my dear, it will pass. He's got it from worry."

She took a dipper of water, made the sign of the cross over it, and went into the room. Filipp, as straight and stern as ever, was lying on the bed, and only his face looked as if he had been surprised that after all his suffering and patience he had still managed to receive his reward.

And then they buried him and walked back from the cemetery changed people. It all began when the miller seemed to think that the grave was not as deep as it should be, that even here they were trying to put something over him. He had climbed down and measured the grave himself. And walking from the cemetery through the muddiest places, he muttered, "It's like he's said awful things about the girl. . . . Now the whole *volost* will have something to laugh about. The girl's life is ruined. . . . "

Old man Petrov, who was walking beside him, wanted to comfort him but didn't know how—besides, it would have been shameful to lie that Filipp had not even touched his wife.

"Nowadays everything heals quickly," he said, frightened of his own words.

As for reading Glafira's face, it was difficult to imagine what she was thinking and if she even knew what Filipp had died of; and only

Afonka, who met her by chance in the front entranceway when they were bringing in the lid for the coffin, saw her eyes and her lusterless moist mouth. She stopped by the doorjamb and passed her hand over her eyes and mouth as if she were locking within her for the rest of her life the joy she had experienced that one night. A cold dew fell on Afonka's heart, and suddenly, running into the hut, he cried out with tearful envy, "I'd be better off dead!"

Marya Yegorovna looked right at him in amazement and said, as if to the whole world, "O Lord, life has sure taken a funny turn. And you, too."

At the funeral feast, as they were eating the *blini*,[2] Filipp's father turned the discussion to the need of returning the troika. Then the miller, as if expecting such talk, shouted and even banged the table with his spoon.

"So, the shame brought on my daughter is not worth three horses?! Now we'll be the laughingstock of the whole *volost*—the miller, they'll say, is a sorcerer, and so is his daughter. Who'll take her now? She'll die an old maid, or else the soldiers will drag her down to the gutter. . . . "

And suddenly Glafira shook her head and, casting a look at everyone with her huge rye-colored eyes, closely spaced like her father's, she said in a drawling voice, "Apparently it was God's will . . . ," but she did not finish saying what had been fated in her life, and no one asked her again.

Nevertheless, old man Petrov, after a bit of alcohol, got bolder and began to haggle, and in the end he managed to get back one of the three horses, with the harness thrown in, but the miller flatly refused to return the money Filipp had provided him. The horse won in the bargaining was tied to the shaft; it bucked to the side and wouldn't walk straight, but its eyes were as happy as on the day of the wedding.

In the past few days a lot had changed in the fields. Greenery appeared on the knolls, and the land smelled of grass; and only in the ravines snow, pockmarked and gnawed out by the wind, lay in patches. A barely noticeable fog hung over the ravines.

Immediately old man Petrov began to talk of sowing and said that the spring, in all likelihood, would be warm. His words were exactly the same as last spring, but now Afonka didn't believe them and it was hard for him to listen.

Two versts from the village the road forked—one road, the narrower, led to Afonka's native village, and the other, a bit wider and muddy, led to the station. Several carts, loaded with logs, were moving dolefully, the horses kept getting stuck to their bellies in the mud, and a gaunt, scrawny peasant, particularly skillful at making his whip sing, walked around the string of carts. A reddish-brown dog howled—at who knows what.

Afonka looked at them; he felt an even stronger twinge in his heart and again he remembered Filipp's death and Glafira's eyes, filled with strange joy and satisfaction. He jumped off the *tarataika* and said he would return home on the iron horse. And although it was about forty versts by train to his own village, and a full sixty, and even more, by country roads, people were always surprised if anyone took the iron horse. Old Petrov was even surprised now, but he didn't say anything; he simply tightened the reins and straightened out Filipp's bucking horse with his switch.

Afonka rushed to the station as if the train were waiting for him, but when he got there, it suddenly turned out that there was no need to hurry, and perhaps it was not even worth going on the iron horse. At the station peasants, who had brought logs, stood around smoking; two soldiers, returning from a short leave to their barracks, were reading the *Village Newspaper* out loud and constantly interrupting their reading with various bits of village news. Afonka had not been drafted; there was something not right with his chest, although to look at him, he even seemed like a sharp fellow—only his mouth was very puffy and long. Afonka envied the happy soldiers and asked them for a part of the paper, but he couldn't get into a conversation with them. The station windows, dirty and cold, barely let the light in—and soon it began to get dark; four hours remained to train time. The watchman, rattling the keys he held in one hand, began to sweep the floor.

"Pick up your feet!" he suddenly shouted angrily at Afonka.

And then Afonka, waving the newspaper, also began to shout and demanded that a report be filed. At first both the peasants and the Red Army men looked at him with curiosity: they thought, either he's drunk or he's picking a fight, but then they turned away with almost hurt looks and began to talk about their own matters. The argument raised his spirits a bit, but soon he felt bored again, and it began to seem to him that the watchman, standing by the stove in his dirty sheepskin coat and holding a dirty broom, was trying to invent the kind of mean trick that would let him disgrace Afonka for the rest of his life. And when the watchman suddenly yelled out at the top of his lungs—so loudly that the newspaper fell out of the Red Army fellow's hands—that the train would be three hours late, Afonka began to feel unbearably uneasy and walked out, slamming the door hard behind him.

A damp wind was blowing, splattering the crooked lantern by the station bell with drops of clumsily falling rain. A slippery slime, peculiar to stations and smelling of kerosene, glistened under his feet as if all the day's vileness were reflected in it—this whole hoarse sound of the rain, the wheezy snore of the ironwork on the roof, and the consumptive whistling of the electrical wires. Immediately beyond the station, on both sides of the roadbed, began a forest—a pine forest with tall trees—but now also kind of strange and without its hum and fragrance, as if enveloped by the slime.

Afonka turned back. And it was at this point that a freight train pulled slowly into the station, its wheels screeching. Heated cars were in the front, and two flatcars, loaded down with rock coal in the shape of a broad triangle, loomed darkly at the end. And the fact that the coal was being transported like sand, without any covering or sides on the flatcars, was a big surprise to Afonka. The same abusive watchman, now wearing a hood and gloves, walked past all the heated cars, lighting all the platforms between the cars with his lantern. He didn't bother with the flatcars loaded with coal. Afonka ran around to the other side of the locomotive; the bald-headed engineer was smoking one quick cigarette after another, as if he were stealing the flame. Afonka, grabbing the bulky plank placed on its end as a side support, jumped up on the pile of coal. The engineer's cigarette, which up to now had glimmered before his eyes, suddenly went out. He remembered that he was wearing a new quilted gray jacket covered with beaver, and that coal soils clothing. The train made his shoulders lurch forward. The coal under the plank onto which he was holding made a crunching noise. It turned out to be very awkward to sit this way; the plank was rocking, his body was sliding off, and the coal, fine and damp, was getting into his sleeves and boot tops; his nose itched, and he had no success whatsoever, no matter how much he tried, in finding a large lump of coal to hold onto. Soon the coal began to roll under him and it seemed that Afonka would now be able to sit above the plank, but the flatcar suddenly swayed in a very unusual way. . . . Afonka grabbed the plank with all his might.

A golden doll of sparks bobbed in the dark sky—it would bob up, and then go out. The wheels chased after the doll with a rumbling, hissing noise; the slopes answered with the whistling sound of suddenly awakened pines, and when Afonka at one point bent down, the rails suddenly glistened like horns. And the plank rocked more and more, and kept growing cold and slipping out of his hands. Afonka tried in vain to wrap his legs around the plank, but it leaned completely over and then, beside himself, he started to rake through the coal with his hands and feet. A jagged mound of coal, which reminded him of a block of ice, happened to come his way. But at this point a small junction brought the golden doll of sparks to an end—and the junction stationmaster asked the engineer for a cigarette. Afonka had considered jumping off but remembered his jacket soiled with coal—they'd hold him up to ridicule—and so it occurred to him that up above, on top of the coal, it would be easier for him to hold on. He clambered up. The engineer threw down his finished cigarette, the wheels picked it up, the buffers clanged in approval, and the heated cars again rushed on.

Soon Afonka made out another person sitting on the coal, an *arshin* away from him. When Afonka bent forward and looked at him, the person said something. Afonka couldn't make out what was said, but sensed some melancholy complaint. Cupping his hand, Afonka lit a match and brought it up to the poor person's face. He saw large kind eyes, a bony old-woman's face, and a mouth compressed in apprehension. With cheerful melancholy Afonka yelled out, "Old woman, where are you going?"

And because he had yelled out, the old woman apprehensively fixed the bag on her shoulders. She sat cuddling a large piece of coal with her felt boots. There wasn't much room up there and, moreover, the weight of two people made the smaller pieces of coal scatter; and soon Afonka had to sit with one shoulder pressing against the old woman. She touched his side gently—it must have been with her mitten—and then she got bolder and touched him even more forcefully. Afonka had wanted to curse her, but at that moment the locomotive whistled, and after the whistle he didn't feel like cursing, and besides, the old woman had quieted down, and soon thereafter was leaning lightly against Afonka with her bag against him. The bag was hard, as if made out of wood; it probably contained dried crusts of bread—and Afonka remembered that he'd probably seen this old woman at his brother's funeral feast. And again envy and an incomprehensible weariness enveloped him—and he asked, "Did you scrape together a lot of stuff at Filipp's funeral feast?"

Again the old woman mumbled something unintelligible and doleful.

Soon Afonka's back began to ache; it was very uncomfortable for the two of them to sit together like that, and when the train was held up at a junction, Afonka considered running over to the other flatcar, but then, people could have been sitting there as well. In the darkness the next flatcar resembled a haystack turned upside down. Moreover, conductors, discussing waterproof raincoats, passed by with their lanterns. One of them said something casually about the coal spilling off the platform,[3] and then an angry deep voice rang out suddenly from the darkness: "What a job of loading, those shirkers!" The voice carried such contempt and such power that long after the conductors had passed, and long after the train had started again, Afonka kept shivering and breathing heavily in displeasure.

"Isn't this where you get off, old woman?" he asked in a whisper.

The old woman's whole body swayed, and his temples suddenly grew cold. In this way, with his temples heavy and cold, he sat for a long time until he realized that the train was moving very quickly and that all this time he had been thinking of the old woman. "Now," thought Afonka, "if you were to nudge her lightly in the back, in her hard hump, and then land a blow on her neck, the old woman would go hurling down the slope[4] and her place would be freed up. Otherwise, she could just as easily land me one." But he knew very well that the old woman wouldn't touch him; all the same, it was nice to think about it, and that way there were no thoughts of Filipp's proud death. And the old woman, as if reading his thoughts, began to move, and her hand in a light mitten quietly touched Afonka's elbow. Afonka's pushed her away, and her hump began shaking next to his shoulder. Something began to torment his heart—and he started counting to ten. But the clatter of the wheels interrupted his counting, and weariness, and anger tormenting his heart, surged over him. A broad dark blue cloud suddenly appeared in the sky. Again he resumed his pointless counting. "Six, seven," he muttered, and began to feel for a place with his foot so that, by planting his legs against it, he could then strike the old woman with more dexterity. For a moment the clatter of wheels crushed his thoughts, but soon the warm murmur of anger made the clatter disappear again. His leg was almost all stretched out, his fist had tightened, but then he sensed that his legs, which were a bit frozen around the knees, were being gripped by mittens—and the old woman's hump came to rest right by his chest. Shrieking, the old woman rubbed her face on his beaver jacket.

"Old woman, have you gone berserk or something?" he said, and his voice was such that it even frightened him. He remembered that his jacket would get dirty, and so he tried to pull the old woman's hands away from him, but they gripped him with furious force; one of them caught hold of his pocket, and it was this hand that was very difficult to tear away; moreover, it did occur to him as an afterthought that the old woman would ruin his pocket. And so he began to swear, and then his anger quickly left him; but the old woman still would not let go of his pocket, and now he no longer thought about why it was necessary to hurl the old woman down the slope; he began thinking about how he could push her off without falling off himself. Moreover, the conviction that if he let go of the old woman, she would push him off—this conviction took hold of him more and more. And the old woman was becoming increasingly more adroit, and now her hands were working his body like a kneading trough. And at this very moment he remembered that he had gotten very little sleep the last few nights—he had comforted his mother, and he had to keep an eye on his father as well while he himself was tormented by incomprehensible thoughts. Both yesterday and today he'd eaten almost nothing—his head began to spin, his legs grew weak, and he fell with his whole body on the old woman. Now all of her came to rest under him; he lay with his chest on her hump but her hand gripped his pocket as tightly as before. And suddenly he was reminded of one village girl, Marfa; his insides burned with wild desire (only later did he figure out why this desire had arisen: in giving herself to him for the first time, the girl had tugged at his pocket in the same way), and the fact that this old woman could arouse desire in him angered him to the point of tears.

"Take your hand away, you hag!" he shouted.

"I won't let go," the old woman suddenly uttered hoarsely and distinctly.

And then using swearwords—bringing in God and mother—he began to spit at her hump and shawl; and the more he spat, the more his phlegm-filled spit stretched out—as if one continuous sweetly bitter piece of rhubarb was emerging out of his mouth. Finally his hands began to hurt, her shawl slipped down to his mouth, and it became more difficult to breathe. But at this point there was the flash of a signal light, the train approached the station, and there began the dim squeaking of doors opening. The old woman dropped her hands and rolled downward. Afonka rubbed his body, said something foul and insulting about the old woman, and jumped off. This was the station he needed to go to—about five more versts remained to his village. By the light of the station lamp he examined his jacket; the coal had not dirtied it as much as he had thought it would—he cleaned it off easily with some snow. So as not to meet the old woman again, Afonka didn't go into the station but walked around it and headed for his village.

The next day was Sunday—and another feast for the deceased.

Relatives gathered, spent a lot of time pitying Filipp and saying that all this ruination was due to the war, that all soldiers had pieces of their hearts broken off by shells. And no one said a single word about Glafira. And when everyone had left, the father, for some reason, took the bridle off the wooden hook, and holding it in his hand like a gift, said to Afonka, "How was your trip home?"

"Good," Afonka answered irritably.

Judging by his father's voice it was possible to think that he had gotten some clever idea and that by answering in an irritable way Afonka was thereby agreeing with his father. And so it was.

The father slapped Afonka's shoulder with the bridle and said, "And that's just what I say. We can settle things without going to court. We'll say that Filipp hadn't slept with the woman at all, that is, that he hadn't touched her. The laws nowadays are like a black radish—everyone holds on to the green top. So Filipp began to get undressed—and, well, that's when it happened. No one saw her, after all, undressed, except our old woman . . . so, what kind of a wife could she be to him? However, a rumor could spread throughout the *volost*—that she's a witch and all kinds of other things. . . . What disgrace for the miller. And so I say, he'll take you, Afonka, as his son-in-law. The old man doesn't have long to live, he keeps complaining about his legs, and he has a big house with five walls, and in addition, it comes with a mill with a number of millstones."

"It's quite a mill," the mother said in adulation. It seemed to her that perhaps their life could resume its previous form and that if Afonka went off to Glafira, it would be as if Filipp had returned. But Afonka silently took the bridle from his father's hands and hung it up on the hook.

The father waited, thinking that his son would say something, but Afonka kept quiet, and the father thought that even if Afonka was always reckless, he was obedient. With such thoughts in his head he decided that everything was settled in regard to Filipp's horses. He left. The mother went up to the window, to the bench there, and, running her fingers over the towel she found there and apparently trying to smooth over an offense that wasn't all that clear to her, began to talk about something. Afonka kept standing by the hook, not listening to what his mother was saying. He was offended that his father had left so soon, without any doubts about his son saying yes. Afonka knew very well himself that he wouldn't refuse and couldn't understand why. He knew that he'd get into bed next to the empty eyes drained by Filipp and that for his whole life he'd hang around her body like a hungry dog, and that his heart would last through a long life. Afonka's heart wasn't like his brother's. . . . "It'll hold out," the thought contemptuously flashed through his head. And Glafira has no place to go—with or without him—she'll put up with abuse and beatings, and dark autumn nights. . . .

"Who's that you're talking about?" he suddenly asked, listening attentively now.

"Well, now . . . my dear Afonushka, a beggar woman appeared in our parts; she's told us her whole life story, from the day she was born . . . such a life—we've spent the whole morning with her, and couldn't leave her side. Her eyes may be old, but they're large and kind. I'm suffering, says she, but then, wherever he comes from, a kind person appears and warms me with his good deed. And so you should warm Glafira with your deed. Today, she tells us, she's riding sitting on coal . . . you know, on the platform . . . but the conductor was passing by, called her down off the coal, took her to his quarters, offered her tea, and even gave her a fifty-kopeck piece for the road. She thought, she says, he was from her part of the world, but he was from completely different parts, just a kind soul."

"A kind soul, you say? Does she have a hump?"

"Who has a hump?"

"Oh, that old woman."

"Naturally she has a bag on her back, though who knows if there's anything in that bag. . . . "

Afonka burst out laughing; he immediately felt more cheerful, as if he had suddenly come to stand on his own two feet. Afonka patted the bridle with the palm of his hand and changed shoes—his walk seemed to have changed. At this point some fellows came by and started inviting Afonka for an evening out. Nightfall was still a long time off, but they still had to manage to get some vodka, and to make arrangements with the accordion player, and the girls. They got the vodka quickly and had a bit of it. The accordion player came with a new unusually sonorous accordion. Afonka felt like going out. The fellows, embracing and pushing one another for a long time in the front entranceway, walked out.

The day was bright and the visors of their caps were burning bright like mirrors. Their village stood on a small hill, and was so cheerful and bright that it seemed unable to get its fill of joy at having reached such a height where so much land was visible that if one tilled it for a lifetime, one couldn't retill it; and if one sowed it, one couldn't resow it.

Near the barns some small boys were playing *babki*,[5] and the knucklebones glistened in the air like fish jumping.

"I'm getting married, fellows, my treat!" Afonka suddenly shouted, and then they started having an even better time.

The fellows began to hoot, and sensing a drinking bout in the making, began to try to guess who the bride was, flattering him by picking out the best girls in the *volost*. And again no one said a single word about Glafira. And the fact that no one said a word about Glafira filled Afonka's heart with a frightening and inexpressibly cheerful anxiety. He waited until they named the most beautiful and the richest eligible girl—Annushka Bolenkova. Then he shouted, "And maybe it's her! . . . I'm paying for three liters!" and the fellows went to the local tavern keeper. Stepping over the threshold of the tavern, Afonka stumbled, and again he felt inexpressibly frightened and cheerful. Lyubka the tavernkeeper was not to be found at home; her nephew was there—gaunt Mitya, nicknamed Archangel. People said that the tavernkeeper lived with him, playing city-love tricks on him, which she had learned when she worked as a cook. Mitya had dry eyes as if they had been sucked dry of moisture, and he had a bad lisp. He gave the fellows only one bottle of vodka and like a peasant woman hid the money in his boot top, in the stocking. He didn't dare sell them a second bottle without the tavernkeeper present, and, in response to the fellows' questions, answered that Lyubka had gone to the woman who watched over the school, who had some beggar woman with her. "She's telling Afonian[6] stories," he added, and licked his lips rather wickedly. The fellows kept saying that they should wait, but Afonka's heart began to ache even more from the vodka he'd drunk, and he asked the fellows to go to the school watchwoman's place. And so the fellows, to the sounds of the accordion, followed Afonka, and the sun, it seemed, became even larger during this time and hung low over the houses, taking up almost the whole sky. The school watchwoman, Lyubka the barmaid, and the strange beggar woman had already moved to another house—to the widow Paraskeva's. Afonka knocked on the window and beckoned with his finger—and he knew who'd come out. And he was right—yesterday's beggar woman came out. She yawned and looked tenderly at the fellows. Her gums were rose-colored and coated with soft bread crumbs. Afonka thought she wouldn't look at him, but she did—and didn't recognize him.

"Give us Lyubka the tavernkeeper!" Afonka shouted. But even now the old woman didn't recognize his voice; continuing to smile in the same tender way as before, she turned the latch with a click and left.

Soon Lyubka the tavernkeeper appeared—chesty, with full

lips—and since no one there was a stranger to her, she started by saying that it was difficult to get vodka in town, and that she had gotten tired of such hard work; apparently, she wanted a bit more money or was simply playing games with the fellows.

And again Afonka shouted, "My treat, I'm paying, take all you want!"

And in response to his last words the beggar woman came out to the front entranceway. She took a sharp look at Afonka's feet planted wide apart—there was a generosity about his whole figure—and fixing a nonexistent bag on her shoulders, she came down the steps. She stood next to him and still couldn't recognize him. Then Afonka leaned over her and screamed right in her face, "What do you live on, old woman?!"

And suddenly the old woman's tender eyes clamped shut; she stumbled back and her hand made a gesture as if she were grabbing Afonka by his pocket. She had opened her thin shriveled lips, but Afonka, surprising even himself, hit her with full force in the mouth. The old woman's head rolled back slightly to the left, but Afonka hit her from the left, in the back of her head, and when she fell to the ground, he hit her in the temple with his heel and walked away. The fellow who was the most drunk in the group yelped, hit the old woman in the side with his fist, but then jumped away and fixed a vacant stare on Afonka. The fellows shouted, "That's just what she deserves!"—although no one knew why she deserved it; but a little bit later they took a closer look at the old woman. Her legs were writhing convulsively. The fellows threw themselves on Afonka. He didn't resist but only bellowed loud and long, and when they began to beat him, he defended his face with his hands. They beat him a long time, clumsily and mindlessly. A lot of village men came running, and no one wanted to come to Afonka's defense; but then no one goaded the fellows on, either. When old man Petrov came, they let Afonka go; he lay there bloody and dirty not far from the old woman, who had now somehow become cleansed—someone had already arranged her arms in a cross. Old man Petrov stood for a while, stroking his thin beard; he wanted to say something—and yet he couldn't. He tried to lift his son by the arms and also couldn't. Then the village men took Afonka slowly and silently, and led him to the cooler.

In the morning he was taken away to the city. There, until his trial, he sat in prison as long as it was necessary, and at the trial, when the judge, a glib and self-confident man, who decided immediately for some reason that Afonka was a horse thief, cardplayer, and drunkard, said, "Defendant, your last statement," Afonka did get up; he did want to tell them how he was riding on the coal from his brother's funeral, but he couldn't remember the name of the long cart on which the coal was being transported. He got all confused, and lots of words got all jumbled in his head. He began talking about some conductors and continued for a long time, and lied clumsily and in vain. Afonka kept looking around and shifting his feet. No one, except old Petrov, came to the trial, and the old man wanted to complain, too, that his old woman was not in good health, that his household was falling apart, that even Filipp's horse, which the miller had returned, was limping. The miller himself had taken to drink; Glafira was walking around thin, ragged, and prayerful. The old man looked at him with reproachful eyes. The judge frowned and thought that Afonka apparently had killed the old woman in order to cover up some sins she might have known.

"You don't have anything else to say?" the judge asked dispassionately and pleased with his own voice.

"Nothing," Afonka answered, and only then did it occur to him that he couldn't say anything that people would understand—and he burst out crying in a shrill and childlike manner. The father also started to cry, but the court went to deliberate. The court returned quickly. Afonka had dry and dull eyes again; he stared at his father a long time, bowed low to the judge, as he had not bowed to his father his whole life, gave a scowling smirk, and was taken away to prison to serve out his sentence.

1926

Fertility

For Fedya Bogomilsky

Chapter 1

His little son Alyoshka came running back home. Merrily swinging the horse's halter, he gleefully announced that Serko had torn his fetters on a rock and galloped off into the hills. This was no laughing matter. With a stern face, Martyn turned to his son and reluctantly gave him a lash with the halter across his sweaty back. And when he struck him, he felt such sorrow and pity that it was hard to tell if it was for his son or for the horse that had gotten lost in the hills. Looking at the cross of the chapel visible through the fence, he crossed himself and said meekly to his wife, "Now don't wait for me for supper. . . . If she had been smeared with pitch, she wouldn't have run off, but now the horseflies, probably, have made her run off to the glacier. Just look at these rotten fetters! No matter how strong a horsehair you use to make them, they still rot. Soon the whole herd will be lost. . . . You work and work."

His wife, a small, sickly, and emaciated woman who looked like a prematurely hatched baby chick, knew that her words and anger were pointless. With watery saliva spattering far out of her mouth, she shouted at him, "Sure, you're worn out, you devil! . . . Just look, you're as big as the church. . . . And now you have to go and beat a poor defenseless kid. . . . You should give yourself a whack in the mug for your laziness. Oh, if only I could end it all sooner. . . . "

To go up to the hills, you had to go through the whole village, the cemetery, and the pine grove; from there the birch grove began, after that the Holy Ravine, and, further on, the hills. Martyn took and put on his one new cotton shirt, the one with big flowers on it. Leaning hard against the storeroom door, Pelageya turned pale with anger; her mouth had grown dry, and she herself had become terrified of her anger. She jabbed her thin finger at him as though piercing something; she took a good look at her finger and started to wail in a thin voice, as if from a great height.

The road went along the shore of the lake, where boats, turned upside down, lay scattered in the unusually green grass. A light fog hovered sleepily over the shore and the lake. The distant mountains, which hung above the valley like a ring of snow, were also covered with a bluish-rose haze.

Only one boat, which belonged to Martyn, lay closest of all to the water, on its side; the bottom was cracked, the oakum had come out of it, and, to add insult to injury, someone had done something foul under it. Kids, probably.

Martyn wanted to curse, but he remembered that not only his boat but his nets, too, had rotted a long time ago. It was hot. The dogs, their flat pink tongues hanging out, looked at him lazily, as though inviting him to go on by and not disturb their sleep. Martyn gave his shoulder a quick jerk, and fixed his shirt.

"I'll fix it, I guess. Maybe I'll start on Monday or on Tuesday. . . . "

He didn't know why he began to feel good. He loved to go off into the bare hills. It was easy to think about treasure there; rarely did he meet there fellow villagers who would immediately accuse him of idleness. The villagers were Old Believers, called Kerzhaks in the language of the Altai region; they loved to help each other in their own pious way, and they loved for others to make frequent mention of such help. But Martyn would keep forgetting, and it was just as difficult to fill him with piety as it was to fill a barrel with spit.

As he started up the path to the cemetery, he ran into Yelena, the wife of Skorokhodov, the Scripture reader. She was tall and plump; her flaxen braids showed from under her long kerchief and fell to her old-fashioned blue *sarafan*.[1] Martyn liked the feeling of abandon that wafted from her. Her plump white hands were softly touching her little chin, when a sleepy crow flew low over her.

"Hello, Martyn Andreich," she drawled as she glided past him. And her white hands seemed to give him a reckless smile.

"Mmm, mmm . . . what a honey," Martyn said after her. "Boy, those priests' daughters are just like gray horses, they're either tame or really wild."

And suddenly, as if it were howling, his heart began to ache sharply. At first he seemed to control himself, but then his heart jerked like a pike on a hook, broke loose, and took off. Martyn looked at the windowpanes iridescent with age, with some small fish quivering in them. The sun was high; a rooster crowed in a bass voice like a bull's; a boy, holding the Psalter in both hands, ran past Martyn triumphantly.

In the cemetery, he noticed that the birches growing by the graves and old-fashioned grave markers were becoming covered with yellow pollen. For some reason he remembered that if the color green stands out in a rainbow, there'll be a good harvest, and he looked up at the sky. In the Holy Ravine he listened for Serko neighing, although he remembered that he had tied him up in the birch glade about three versts from the ravine. Near a stump, which for some reason looked like a whitefish, he picked some overripe, darkish red strawberries. The berries were dark and sickeningly sweet. He spat them out in disgust and continued his ascent through the birch grove. Then he thought of his wrecked boat and decided that Yelena was somehow at fault.

"That pot-bellied beauty," said Martyn mournfully, "she's asking for it. . . . "

And again his heart began to ache, and the grass under his feet seemed hard like hay.

"I'll fix your kisser for you! Just let me get my hands on you."

And he started shouting in a way that made even him tremble.

"Serko-o! . . . Serko-o! . . . Hey!"

His shout echoed clearly, without reverberation. Rocks began to tumble with a crumbling sound. Both the echo and the chink-chinking of the rocks indicated that the mountains were near. Martyn should have taken a right, but he headed left, up the steepest path. His knees got tangled in a buckthorn bush, and a huge spiderweb, with a fat spider in the middle, stuck to his face. It seemed to him that he understood his life, that he understood all his needs, that he understood everything he had to do . . . and yet, he ran uphill for a long time until sticky sweat began to roll down into the waist of his pants, almost binding his legs together.

Now he was surrounded by full-grown larches; here and there sheets of bark had been pulled off them (for covering cattle sheds), and the bright yellow sap resembled frozen icicles. Orange-capped mushrooms looked blue in the grass; the pecking of a woodpecker somewhere was revealing treasure. Martyn looked around and got mad again, either at the horse or at Yelena, it was hard to say which. The cool air overpowered him and he lay down—he had a weakness for sleeping—but again he seemed to feel a thorn sticking in his side. He hit the trunk of the larch so hard that the yellow dust from the tree settled on the halter.

"I'll fix your fat face! A beauty, big deal! Alyona,[2] thirty-three years old."

Chapter 2

Aspen leaves lay wrong side up. The aspen grove and the little ravine he had found were thickly overgrown with cow parsnip.[3] Martyn, just like a child, loved cow parsnip. He broke one off, couldn't eat it, and, without even thinking about it, turned to the left. At the very bottom of the ravine Martyn dropped the cow parsnip and slipped on it. After falling, he suddenly felt something damp and cold on his knee. He bent down: flowing right at his feet was a little stream, so clear that a spiderweb, which had fallen into it with the little branch it was on, could be seen on its bottom. The ravine felt unfamiliar to him. Bees were buzzing; someone must be keeping bees nearby. He caught a bee; it began to buzz affection-ately in the palm of his hand, as if hurrying him to release it—and didn't sting him. He watched it fly around a bit and then walked further along the brook.

That a brook was flowing here seemed a big violation of order to him, and this even stifled the feelings in his heart and made him forget he had gotten his pants dirty. Where was the brook coming from? The lake in the Kok-Tash Valley would fill up this spring with the melting snow from the mountains; in the fall it would grow very shallow, and then it would be easy to catch carp and tench.

"A spring must have started to flow. I'll have to see where it's coming from. And Serko, most likely, has come out by the water. Where else do you look for a horse if not by water?"

The ravine soon ended, and the brook was now flowing from the birch grove. Now it was no more than half an *arshin* wide; it was flow-ing slowly. The birch leaves that fell into it clung to one another, and then, playfully twisting and turning in the water, floated on. In places the water was so clear that you'd notice it only by its bubbling sound.

"It's a spring, all right." And suddenly, as he came out of the birch grove, he saw a swamp, an honest-to-goodness swamp with little mounds overgrown with pungent-smelling sedge. This was really strange: no one had ever heard of swamps on the mountain slopes surrounding the Kok-Tash Valley.

"Am I lost or something?" Martyn thought, and he anxiously climbed up a high barren cliff. And then suddenly, above the smell of the pines, he caught the smell of blossoming grain from the valley below. In his excitement he felt as if an ear of grain had gone down his throat. It seemed to him that through the bluish film of the fog covering the lake and the valley he could see fields densely covered with a pattern woven of stalks of grain. Tendrils are jingling, the playful oats are winking, and the millet looks shaggy, like Old Believers' beards. . . . A lot of carts are coming to look at the fields. People's voices are ringing clearly. That means there'll be good weather. The granaries will have to be supported with cedar beams so they don't burst. . . .

"I'll gather my grain, buy a rifle for sure, go hunting ermine in the boulders . . . and then we'll see."

He remembered Yelena again and rushed to the stream.

It was more difficult to walk through the swamp; the aspen grove was all rotten wood; his feet often got stuck in the bubbling mud, the swamp clay. Just before the swamp came to an end, a crane darted out of the aspen grove. Awkwardly, spreading its legs wide, it started running, looked around in fright, and then flew away slowly. Rising above the cliff on which Martyn had been standing, the crane screeched mournfully. And the crane, and the swamp, and the melancholy—all this was pointless, meaningless. Martyn rejoiced at the sight of the mountains, the extensive gray fields, the bare cliffs in the distance, and the steady wind carrying the stony smell of lichens.

The brook was almost a foot wide, and it met him with the rumbling of the pebbles it was carrying.

"I must be seeing things . . . and yet, I can't find Serko."

He had climbed really high; the horse would hardly have come this far. A fog now covered the swamp he had walked through way down below. Before him stretched cold-looking cliffs covered with rusty-colored lichens, which made them look as if they were covered with tattered rags. An icy wind lashed from above, inflating his shirt with cold air. Sticking his shirt in his pants, Martyn shook the bridle stubbornly.

"I'll get to the bottom of these crazy things."

The sun had risen high in the sky, but it was cold; each step got easier and easier, and he felt as though he were running, but in fact, like a watch, he wasn't going anywhere. Valley fatigue, familiar to everyone, began to make itself felt, but, Martyn still didn't turn back.

To the left of the mountains the dark brown ridge of the hills came into view. The brook was pushing into them. Standing on the highest hill, Martyn could make out below, even farther to the left, the beginning of the barren rocky valley called Talas, which lay adjacent to Kok-Tash. It was uninhabited and bare; cold streams of water from the glaciers rushed there, united into a river, and headed for Nor-Zaysan. On top of the mountain it was even colder; he went back down the mountain.

Finally he caught sight of the inaccessible Tilyashsky cliffs. They rose into the thick blue heaven as high as five of the tallest pines; their peaks resembled boats that had been stood on end. A huge golden eagle circled over them reluctantly and malevolently, like a sentry. Beyond the cliffs lay the glaciers: unexplored ice fields, eternal frosts, and death.

And now Martyn saw that a huge mass of rock, about the size of a chapel, had broken off from the cliff, and exposed something resembling a window or cellar. There, pieces of ice that looked like blue threads on a weaving loom shone dully, and it was from that spot that the undiscovered brook gushed toward freedom. Higher up and to the sides of the icy cellar, where small rock had fallen, were wide cracks the width of the palm of your hand.

"What wonders!" Martyn said with a chuckle. He was pleased he knew where the brook was coming from. From a rose-colored rock, which resembled a spider, he leaned over a tiny pool of water to drink his fill. He saw the reflection of a hawk in the water, and it looked like the hawk was circling right above him.

"Shoo!" he said cheerfully.

But the water was so cold; it felt as if a rock had hit him in the teeth. A calmness came over him; he whistled, winked at Lord knows who, and then started running downhill. In one of the meadows he ran into Serko, who was standing up to his neck in grass and furiously switching horseflies away with his scraggly tail. On seeing his master, the horse neighed; leaves of meadowsweet were stuck in his sparse teeth. Meadowsweet was in bloom, and that meant that the carp would swim right into their nets.

Chapter 3

In the morning he groomed Serko, and his wife couldn't get over it for a long time. Later on, he felt like going to the lake. He bailed out the boat and filled the cracks here and there with tow. Alyoshka sat down at the oars. In the *kurya,* a narrow stretch of lake overgrown with reeds, he ran into some village fishermen, well fed and healthy looking. In their boats they had large baskets full of fish: grayish-yellow carp and dark amber tench. The men encouraged Martyn.

"Good for you! Keep up the good work. They're jumping right into the boat!"

Martyn smeared the inside of the trap with unleavened bread; the water seemed to bend the twigs as he was lowering the trap and, for a long time after that, circles spread in the water. The morning was bright, like fresh canvas. Wisps of clouds floated across the sky in flocks. To live, oh to live and laugh a bit on a morning like this and in places like these. . . .

From the warmth his eyelashes stuck together like birch fibrils. Martyn began to smear the second trap, but suddenly he again felt a pang in his heart; he put aside the clay pot with the dough and looked at the mountains.

"It sure is sweltering, Alyoshka."

"So, it's sweltering," Alyoshka countered. "I see you want to go to the hayloft. Any time now the wind's gonna blow from the glaciers and the heat'll die down. I'll set the traps."

"I've gotta go to the field. Turn back, Alyoshka."

Alyoshka felt hurt.

"Can't I at least lower the trap?"

He lifted up the wide wicker trap, which resembled an earthenware pot, more adroitly and swiftly than his father. Martyn was pleased with his skill, but he was also annoyed that his son didn't respect him; just wait, in about eight years he'll force his father to the sleeping bench above the stove and take over the household himself. Martyn said this to him.

"And you better believe it," Alyoshka answered confidently. "And just lie there."

Martyn got angry and swore at him.

After they had pulled the boat onto the shore, Alyoshka took his knife and went into the birch grove to cut some branches, and Martyn went off to the plowed fields. The new stalks of grain, the ends of which formed an even plane with the earth, shone as if they had been polished; from time to time the taller and larger stalks, "the princelings," would jut up above the surface in the wind. Everything was as it should be: a light wind during the blossoming, clear weather, and good grain taking form in the stalks. There was the smell of warm straw and dry earth, sparrows played in the dust, and the quail were tapping out "bobwhite, bobwhite."

A swarm of gnats was circling in the air; there were a lot of cabbage butterflies. All this portended clear weather and a good harvest. Martyn's heart ached even more. It was the heat or he'd gotten tired from spending so much time on the water. He returned home and climbed into the hayloft; his wife had just brought some freshly cut hay. The hay was fine like hair and smelled of honey. He listened vacantly to the woman's grumbling and didn't even swear at her as usual. He sullenly looked at the dilapidated roof of the hayloft and shook his head as if the roof could collapse any second now and crush him. He lay like that until evening; then he ate some potatoes with onion, put the ax under the bench with its blade facing the wall, and went back to the hayloft.

And Martyn lay there the whole next day. His wife began to worry.

"Does it hurt anywhere, huh?"

"Maybe I should see the doctor," thought Martyn. But the doctor lived far away, more than twenty versts, and moreover, Martyn believed that doctors could treat only stomach problems; they hadn't learned to treat anything else.

"What are you lying here for, like a piece of ice!"

On hearing his wife's words, Martyn recalled the blue wall of ice that had forced out the bottom of the cliff, and the cold brook gushing with a roar from under the ice.

"Put some bread aside for me for tomorrow. I've need to go up into the boulders."

In the morning he left for the boulders.

"It wouldn't hurt to take a dip," he thought as he walked through the Holy Ravine toward the swamp.

The marshes in the swamp had already gotten rather deep; here and there in the open spaces the wind swayed the sedge on the water as it tore through the aspen grove. Ducks quacked, and a light layer of steam rose above the flooded tree stumps. Martyn feared that maybe the swamp had expanded to its full size and he would have to walk all the way around it. Beyond the swamp, the stream became even wider; it picked up and carried stones the size of a goose egg, and with a hissing sound dug its own lair in the mountains. The little rock on which Martyn had recently knelt when he took a drink of water from the current was submerged and seemed to have grown in size. It was as if the ice under the cliffs had receded, opening a wide cellar. Martyn stuck his hand in the current, which grabbed it like a noose and started to pull.

But a feeling of melancholy settled deeper and deeper in his soul, like those layers of ice. Martyn moved from under the shadow of the cliffs and immediately felt warmer, although the cold air from the glacier wafted through the cliffs.

"What heat! That glacier's melting there, probably. . . . Just look how it's eaten through the rock, just like a mole."

And the thought crossed his mind that now the real heat was beginning; the ice would really start to melt in a couple of weeks or so.

The sun fell into the cellar, and the ice bared its fang-shaped teeth. A big piece of ice, the size of a barrel, broke off with a metallic ring and, rocking back and forth, was carried off to the hills by the current.

"It's really gonna start to flow now. It really is. . . . "

He wanted to joke that now they wouldn't have to fill their cellars with ice for the summer, but suddenly a tormenting thought seared him from head to foot to such an extent that the calves of his legs began to ache.

"I'll bet there's gonna be a river in the valley."

He still couldn't figure out how a river could form and flow into the valley, through the big expanse of black earth, through those fields and meadows where an ear of grain was as heavy as a human hand and the hay on the pitchforks resembled a beaver hat.

Without looking back, he rushed down the mountain.

He ran through the pine forest, and then out onto the road. Here he caught up with Mikita Turukay-Tabun, a happy-go-lucky muzhik. Turukay was a useless good-for-nothing, a shallow type, and if it weren't for his father and father-in-law, he'd always be sitting by the lake with a fishing pole, telling stories and catching perch. He had a slovenly look, coughed constantly, and lied a lot. Turukay was sitting on a cart loaded with birch poles. On seeing Martyn, he started whooping and howling; his horse, used to his antics, merely twitched its ears.

"Martyn, my dearest friend, you cockroach, my sweet kitchen roach, where'd you come from? Would you believe: I'm carrying my hundredth load of poles this week, and I almost fell into this pit; a bear, the son of a bitch, comes crawling out of the darkness. . . . Good thing my horse is smart. Hop on, I'll give you a ride."

Martyn got on. The tender white bark on the poles had peeled off in many places revealing the green layer below. Martyn—who knows why—started feeling sorry for the birches, and he even felt sorry for the liar Turukay.

"A river is heading for the valley," he said quietly. "It's coming from the glacier. I just saw it myself."

"A river! You don't say! That means we'll float rafts on it. I'm a master at raft making, brother. Back before the Revolution, I was in great demand. All the merchants wanted me to make rafts. I was offered so many brides, with dowries. Thousands."

He propped his hands on his sides and chuckled for a long time.

"Or I'll open up a mill with sixteen pair of millstones, with 'lectric[+] light. I'll take a kopeck per *pud*, and that will be the end of all the millers in the district. They could even kill me, I suppose."

"Stop talking nonsense, Mikita. I'm serious—a river."

"Really? Look, the horse has gotten all sweaty from you. As soon as you got in, it started sweating all over. There's something going on in your heart. That's what it looks like."

"In my heart?" Martyn asked.

But Turukay had evidently gotten bored.

"A young girl came to see me recently, came for some eggs. I bought some new chickens, you know . . . Dutch. Ten rubles a pair. Each chicken, I dare say, weighs half a *pud*. So I say to this girl, 'Go to the coop, the chickens have laid some fresh eggs there, gather them yourself. . . . ' I was trimming the wagon shaft. 'Go more to the right, that's where they lay.' But to the right, a pile of poles had come undone. There was a big hole in the coop. And so she plopped right in . . . only waving her hands. . . . And she got stuck, would you believe it, among the poles, her skirt over her head, and shouting. As for me, I run to the shed quickly for a twig and start tickling her from below. She's waving her legs, writhing, twitching her rear end. . . . She wet herself all over. . . . I almost died laughing."

He rolled around on the poles for a long time, slapped himself on his thighs, and squealed.

"What a sourpuss you are, Martyn. You look like you just ate a toadstool. . . . How about the story of this priest's wife and their worker who are walking along and meet two dogs?"

But when Martyn didn't burst out laughing at this story either, Turukay felt hurt.

"You're all listened out or something, Martyn. You're no fun. It's like being stuck with you in a wicker basket."

He struck the horse, and the poles shook and made a snapping sound. Turukay started singing a song. Who could Martyn tell about his troubled heart?

Martyn couldn't sleep. When the moon rose above the lake and extinguished the stars lazily twinkling on the water, he began to feel so melancholy that his fingers ached. He started walking through the village. Like everywhere with the Siberians, out in the open next to their *izbas* lay all their treasures for everyone to see: plows, mowing and reaping machines. The weather was ruining them; the moon shone dull and blood-red on the rust covering them. The gates were high, like those of a fortress, with tin roofs over them. Cats, fat and satiated, sat on the log fences.

It was St. John's Eve. On this night, young girls gather twelve different kinds of grass, put them under their pillows, and divine their future. Boys and girls, their arms around each other and their fists full of grass, were walking quietly, not speaking, like cows returning from their watering places. Soft heartrending sighs could be heard here and there in the front gardens, and Martyn felt a heaviness in his stomach. In one *izba* a woman woke up and remembered that tomorrow was St. John's Day; naked, by the light of the moon, she went to the window and put empty earthenware pots on the windowsill for "St. John's dew": the top layer of sour cream on milk gets thicker from "St. John's dew." Her breasts wouldn't fit into even one of the earthenware pots; rocking sleepily, she didn't even notice Martyn standing under her window. The windows were wide open everywhere, and all the Kerzhak *izbas* seemed to be snoring in their everlasting sleep. The cattle in the yards were breathing calmly as well. If they don't go into the barns, it's to the good; it means clear weather. In one *izba* an oil lamp was flickering; the widow there was selling liquor, and the people were drinking quietly, too, as if to make themselves sleepy. In the window Martyn saw Yelena's husband, the Scripture reader Skorokhodov; he was trying to persuade a neighbor to go home. Martyn got the urge to have a drink, but who would give him the credit? Then he really got angry, let out a string of curses, and set off for Skorokhodov's *izba*.

He made his way through the front garden—a bird-cherry branch slashed his hot face—and climbed up onto the *zavalinka*. The blocks on the *zavalinka* rocked (the earth had been removed from the walls so that the logs of the *izba* wouldn't rot), the spaces between the logs of the *izba* smelled of moss, and the *izba*, filled with the light of the moon, smelled of bread and man. Yelena was lying on the bed, and her plump hands and arms hung down to the floor, as if she was trying to grasp her braids. Her child, making whistling sounds through his nose, was sleeping on the *golbets*.[5] The moon disappeared behind a cloud, and Martyn was thrilled to see the dark inside of the hut. An even stronger smell of man came from there.

"What wealth," said Martyn to himself dejectedly, and spitting into the pot put out for the dew, he headed back.

The boys and girls were heading for their homes. The girls were swinging their hips, and there was a heavy odor of sour bread coming from them, but the boys just seemed to be asleep.

Martyn stopped in front of the chapel; the straight Old Believer's cross was leaning from old age. Martyn didn't believe in God, and it seemed to him that all believers just pretended, but now he said in a hurt tone, "I see God is sleeping. I guess I'm the only one with a heart that must ache. . . . "

Summer lightning without the accompanying thunder flashed above the snow-covered mountains; the reeds swayed silently, and the fish jumping out of the water seemed to melt in the air.

Chapter 4

Martyn was sitting on the fence; he was winding a piece of rope around a joist so that he could try pulling it later with the horse and straighten out the rickety gate. Antip Skorokhodov walked by. He was a strong muzhik, with wide shoulders and a streak of gray in his hair; his hat sat low over his long ears, which looked like cucumbers. After a few more steps, Antip stopped, thought for a second, and, straightening out his jacket, returned to Martyn's gate.

"Martyn, you know I can flick you off this fence like a bird," he said, putting his strong hairy hands on the logs.

"Go ahead and do it," said Martyn reluctantly. "Maybe you'll straighten out the gate, too. You can't crush a mouse with a haystack."

Skorokhodov turned his back to him and, looking at the lake, said, "You keep practicing your witchcraft. . . . You keep promising to flood the village."

Martyn got angry and shouted, "If I knew how to read and had some schooling, I'd outdo all of you fat-bellied devils. You're a Scripture reader. You've learned the Scriptures by heart. Why can't you understand that the village will be flooded? The water will come up to your woman's belly, and then you'll weep and groan."

"Fine, Martyn, you just keep on trying."

He leaned toward him, looked in both directions, and sweat appeared on his temples.

"Now you've started traipsing through the mountains, and I understand you. . . . You're just using the water to divert people's attention, but your main thought is gold. I'm not playing any games. Take me with you to look for gold. We'll hire workers and I'll send my brother. I'll take care of all the details myself, to the last fine point."

There were mines all around in the mountains there. At one time there were mines even in the neighboring deserted Talas Valley, where glacial streams flowed. It was the more worthless, idle people from villages such as Ilinskoe, who had no luck farming, who'd go off prospecting. "He went to look for gold" was sort of a reproach. To tell the truth, for all their efforts, they didn't return rich men from the mines.

"You don't sleep for thinking of gold, and you don't understand, you devil, that soon, in a month or two or even sooner, the village will be flooded."

Antip shook his fat hairy finger at him.

"Don't play games, Martyn. I'm telling you, I'll go in with you."

Watching him walk away, it was hard to tell if he was a priest, a merchant, or a sorcerer. His jacket was long, and so was his hair. In one hand, he had a bunch of herbs and roots, and in the other, a whip.

Martyn got angry at his silly thoughts and for thinking, "It would be nice to go prospecting with him. You'd see Yelena every day." He threw the sun-warmed rope to the ground and shook his fist at the gate.

"A big thing like that is good only for hanging yourself."

He looked at the mountains.

"I'll float away myself, let all my junk sink, but I won't go."

But two days later, he took his shovel and went.

In the Holy Ravine, the cow parsnips had already dried out a bit; he felt like eating. He stopped and wondered if he should go back home for some bread. In the bushes next to him, a twig snapped and someone snorted. Martyn pushed the bushes apart and saw the face of Antip Skorokhodov covered with a cobweb. Skorokhodov also had a shovel; his hands were nervously playing with the handle, and his whole body looked severe. He held his head a bit to the side, as if reading prayers.

"I thought I'd have a look where you dig for your gold, Martyn."

And he sighed guardedly.

"Let's go. Why should you have to follow me?" Martyn said. "Did you grab any bread?"

Antip pointed at his protruding chest; Martyn nodded and went first.

The swamp was completely flooded with water. The water apparently did not have enough time to evaporate and, losing itself in the grass in several streams, it searched for a way to the valley.

"See?" pointed Martyn.

"So?"

Looking at his lips, Martyn understood that Antip was thinking of something completely different and that it was unlikely that he saw the water or even thought about it. A knife wrapped up in a rag stuck out of his pocket, and this knife got Martyn especially angry.

"Am I still going to have to mess with you fools much longer? Do you understand?"

Antip did not take offense at his abusiveness. Somehow, not in keeping with his character, he hitched up his pants and looked kindheartedly into Martyn's eyes.

"This should be dearer to you than gold, you narrow-minded blockhead. The stream flows into the valley, and the valley is like a saucer—no inflow, no outflow. You just try dripping water into a saucer . . . dripping and dripping. . . . "

"So, are the deposits here, Martynushka?"

Martyn spat fiercely. "You fool!"

"Where, then?"

"Higher up."

Martyn didn't bother taking him to the Tilyamsky cliffs: all the same—a dead piece of wood is a dead piece of wood, and not a man. On the lowest hill of the chain blocking off the channel into the Talas Valley, Martyn stuck his finger into the earth and said, "Dig here, but deeper."

He sat next to him on a rock and glumly watched the shovel moving in Antip's hands. Antip had not dug more than an *arshin* when his shovel clanged and broke.

"I've hit rock," Antip said in bewilderment. "Maybe we should dig in another place, because this layer of earth is very thin."

"No need to. You won't get past it."

The Talas Valley lay before them: barren, grayish-brown, and quiet. Just imagine how much water it could hold!

In the meantime, Antip grabbed a shovel full of earth and ran to the stream. There he sprinkled the earth onto his hat, brushed it against the nap for a long time, and, returning, shook the handle in front of Martyn's face.

"There's no gold, you know, none."

"And there never was," Martyn said getting up. "Let's go home. I thought I'd use my strength to divert the water, but now there's nothing else to do but blow it up. You should have a talk with the elders."

All of a sudden Antip shook and turned pale.

"Don't you dare get smart with me! Don't you try to distract me! . . . You show me, since you've agreed."

"I'll show you a place," Martyn said quietly, and he started to tremble, too. "Where'd you get this idea of yours? But then you probably know yourself. Go on. I'm not your worker or your wife's."

Skorokhodov suddenly began cursing out loud, using all sorts of obscenities; evidently he couldn't control himself, nor did he want to. He followed Martyn like that through the whole pine forest to the graded road; he kept on cursing until Martyn marveled, "Boy, are you greedy, Antip! Like a gopher. Cross yourself and draw a circle around yourself with a candle end."

Chapter 5

The plowed fields began after the common pasture. Turukay often liked to sit by the gates to the pasture. He could stop every cart coming into or going out of the village and talk and fib a bit. Everyone liked Turukay for his tales and for believing a lot of things. But the one thing he didn't believe in was death, and he wouldn't tell stories about how and where someone had died; he'd say such stories were the inventions of old women.

"I'm not gonna die," he'd say, fully believing it. "I'll spend my days blaspheming and then turn myself into a house spirit or water spirit—and then you just try and find me."

The little boys in the village always guarded the pasture. Turukay would tell them stories and egg them on to steal from other people's gardens and poppy fields. The boys would often get caught; who knows, maybe Turukay himself tattled on them. Then they'd get real whippings with wet stinging nettles. Turukay would laugh for a long time at those who got whipped.

When Martyn approached the pasture, Turukay opened the gates wide for him, bowed to his waist, and suddenly started roaring with laughter.

"Skorokhodov's wife was just beating him in the field. He just went by ahead of you, as if made of stone. And you, Martyn, keep looking for gold. Last year I happened to be in the Talas Valley. I look and see a gold nugget the size of an egg lying in the road. I grab it and plop it into my pocket, but my pocket had a hole in it. So I get home and find only a pocket full of air. So many tears shed, so much misery!"

After the incident in the mountains with Antip, Martyn's mood improved somewhat from Turukay's lies. The latter's eyes looked clear and happy; he looked as if he were ready to leap on the mountain.

"And you, Martyn, look for this one kind of grass. It will reveal all kinds of treasures to you, heal you of any illness, and charm any woman you want."

"There isn't any such grass that will charm a woman. Or else I'd have looked for it."

"I tell you there is. I saw one old man in town, this eunuch of a merchant. He gave me one tiny blade of it. He says you can find treasure, any woman you want, or cure any sickness. And at that time I had a terrible stomachache! I should have said something about the treasure, and then I could have gotten some doctors from Petersburg, but I blurted out, 'I want to heal my stomach, I have terrible diarrhea.' It was as if the blade of grass had never existed, and my illness disappeared as if a calf had licked it away with its tongue. Yeah. . . . "

Martyn grabbed him by the shoulder and said, "And you, Turukay, you wanna join the Party?"

Turukay even closed his eyes tight with joy.

"It'd be nice to join the Party, Martyn . . . to be a *volost* chairman. But that very same eunuch said to me, 'That isn't Lenin in the crypt. Some soldier is lying there in his place, and Lenin himself is now wandering throughout Russia, choosing reliable people so he can declare war on the entire world.' He says he needs to get a thousand officers, but he's only gotten five hundred. It's very simple. He could even come to our village and say, 'Why shouldn't Turukay be commander-in-chief, if he's in my Party? Put some medals on Turukay and give him an Arabian horse, and. . . . '"

"Hold on, commander-in-chief," Martyn interrupted him. "I'm talking for real. Let's form a Party in the village. We'll close their flies for them."

Turukay blinked, looked to the side, and flexed his elbows.

"Let's do it. Still, it's strange. We've lived for so many years without the Party, but today it turns out that you can't live without it. And what am I going to be in it? I may have learned to read and write, but it's all been Church Slavonic. Besides, it's all flown out of my head because of all my worries."

"You'll learn."

"That I can. I'm a great student. I'll get it all in three days."

He spat furiously and rolled up his sleeves.

"We'll show them, the SOBs. They'll soon be wearing silk shirts, but people over there are suffering. Yeah. . . . "

The evening was quiet and gray. Turukay ran through the whole village and lied that instructors were coming from the city in three carts, and that he, Turukay, had sent the main Party person a packet, and what he had written there, he added threateningly, they'd figure out for themselves. The elders, who had come out of the chapel, gathered in a group and began talking about the weather, saying it was time to turn the fallow land a second time and to plow the new lands—the so-called virgin lands with their acid soil—a third time for the wheat crop. They talked a bit about their old life as well and about how expensive cloth had gotten: twenty rubles per *arshin*. At that moment some women were passing by, trying to agree on going out the next day to pick strawberries and grasses for dye. Martyn's wife was also among them. A tall village elder with a dull and stubborn face, Mitry Savin, beckoned to her with his finger.

"Well, how's your Martyn?" he asked her sternly.

"I don't know, Mitry Vasilich. He keeps yearning, but for whom I don't know. And now he's cross. Why, I haven't a clue. That's for you village elders to figure out."

"He's giving you a hard time. Tell him we'll come see him."

To go see Martyn was pure torture for them. They talked some more about the weather and the harvest, and finally adjusted the old-fashioned caftans on their backs and left. Martyn heated up some tea in the cast-iron stove; the elders thanked him but asked him to pour some boiling water instead of the tea. But they didn't even touch the boiling water. They asked Martyn if he had put away much hay for the winter; his wife answered for him. Then the tall elder Mitry Savin said in a drawl, "Martyn Andreich, why don't you forget about this thing that Turukay is chattering about? It can only lead to no good, and thousands of people are hankering for our land. And our land is better and richer than all others. We've lived so many years without the Party, and now here you are. And over there in Artyomovka, the youngest Glafirov went off to the city, joined the Kamsamol,[6] and married a Jew girl. The second one went also and got done in by vodka. Only the third has found happiness: he has a quiet wife who's hardworking but, as for him, he stays at home. He's learned the craft of making deerskin boots. We've given you help, and we've given you grain, and we'll give you some more if you need it. We can get you some oxen for your work. And if you feel that you can't work, well, you should leave and go look for gold. We won't forget your family. . . . "

The village elders didn't want to speak to Martyn, but these were crazy times: if it weren't for the Party, he'd burn them down and then find such laws that the people who had suffered the fire would find themselves on trial.

"I don't want any gold!" Martyn shouted suddenly, putting his arms akimbo.

He didn't want to shout and he knew very well that it was ridiculous to put his arms akimbo, that it made him look like Turukay, but somehow he just got carried away.

"I don't want to. I want to have a talk with you."

He even began to sweat, but he raised his arms even higher.

"I wish to go with you, elders, into the mountains. The whole way. The glacier is heading for the valley."

"The glacier has been moving into the Talas Valley for centuries," carefully said Vasily Tyumenets, a portly elder with watery red eyes, "and now what would make it want to turn toward us?"

"Get up, please," shouted Martyn suddenly. "Alyoshka, get the cart ready for tomorrow."

The elders chewed their lips a bit and asked to leave earlier, before it got hot. When they had left, and his wife, with a long sigh, began cleaning off the table, Martyn felt ashamed that he had shouted at the elders who had never done anything bad to him, and that he had been so difficult, like a drunk, and proven himself a fool. "Tomorrow," he decided, "I'll be more sensible." But in the morning he started playing the fool again; he put on a new shirt, borrowed a belt with a shiny buckle from a neighbor, and rode through the village, shouting loudly and chiding the elders. He rode slowly and wanted Yelena to see him; he even stopped opposite her windows, pretending to fix the breast-band of the harness. The windows were wide open, but Yelena didn't turn around; she was putting bread in the oven, and a round bread shovel sprinkled with flour kept flashing in front of the dark mouth of the oven. At the sight of this, Martyn couldn't stand it anymore. Pointing to her backside, he poked the quietest elder in the group, the devout Sidor Labashkin.

"Boy what a butt, what a butt—just look! You should get hold of such a body. You wouldn't survive in one piece, old man."

"Knock it off, you evil one. You don't wear a cross," Mitry Savin said to him in a stern voice.

"And I never will," shouted Martyn. "I'll turn the whole village upside down, that's easier. To do that, I don't care about anyone. . . . My soul's on fire. I'm ready for anything."

But Yelena didn't turn around even at this.

After passing the common pasture, they drove faster. A huge tail of black dust trailed along after the cart like a shadow. The elders looked at the fields and said, "The flowers smell stronger every day, and that means the grain is becoming fuller, heavier. The buttercups are blooming early—that means the oats will be nourishing. When it's going to be warm, mice leave food outside and don't drag it into their holes. When the cats sleep soundly, that also means a warm winter." The crickets were chirping loudly and jumping high between the ruts in the road. The sky looked sultry, and although a morning sky, it was almost yellow.

But suddenly a huge puddle of water blocked their way.

"Should we drive around it, or what?!" Martyn suddenly shouted with elation. "Now you've got what you've been waiting for! Now choose a name for the river! You've got to christen it, you old devils!"

The elders gasped. A brook, bubbling and foaming, was racing directly through devout Sidor Labashkin's field.

Then Martyn pointed at the sky and began counting the signs on his fingers.

"The mountains can be seen clearly—hot weather; the cats are sleeping a lot—that's warm weather on the way; the mice are keeping straw outside their holes—that's warm weather. And the ice is melting, the glacier is coming, your end is approaching, and . . . Enough rolling around with your women, enough. . . . Give others a chance. How about it?"

The elders were silent, but the elder Labashkin climbed down from the cart and grabbed the ears of grain, crumpled over and growing in soil loosened around the roots by the water, and began to cry quietly, like a child.

Chapter 6

All the little boys gathered at the stream, and right away garbage appeared by it. So that the field wouldn't go entirely to waste, they quickly cut the wheat and began to dry it on the shed roofs for forage. The roaring stopped quickly, and no one could believe that the water would rise in the lake. Then Martyn stuck a sodden measuring rod into the water, and the water rose half a *vershok* in a day's time. No one believed him. And then the elder Mitry Savin himself stuck a pole in and sat next to it all day without taking his eyes off it. The water rose a *vershok* on his rod.

Turukay-Tabun, with his index finger bent, went running

through the village shouting, "Brothers, it's risen a *vershok*. And from tomorrow on it'll rise half an *arshin* a day. Some rocks have even tumbled down over there; I've seen them myself."

No one believed Turukay, but the elders did go to the mountains and take a look at the stream.

"What's the name going to be?" said Martyn to them spitefully. "Shall we name the stream Woman's, eh?"

Antip Skorokhodov shouted at him, "You sorcerer, you son-of-a-bitch! This is what your sorcery has brought, and now you're laughing! A rabbit costs two bits, but it'll take a hundred rubles to catch you."

"Harvest time is a special time of the year," sighed Mitry Savin. "We'll look in on you again in the evening, Martyn Andreeich."

"Come on by. We'll make sure you get enough to eat."

Martyn somehow ran into Yelena and tried to say something to her, but it turned out really badly. She straightened her kerchief, shrugged her shoulders, and said in disgust, "You're not half the stud you think you are," and went on her way.

Later on, Martyn found the right words, but the chance never presented itself and, moreover, he couldn't really decide if he should say anything to her.

Like the last time, the elders came and sat down according to height, with the shortest one closest to the icons.

"Maybe we should send you to the city. . . . "

And the quiet Labashkin finally said, "A *vershok* per day, that's going to be the end of man."

"Why go to town?!" Tyumenets objected in anger. "They'll say, 'You're kulaks, rich people, go ahead and drown, to hell with you.' People in the city have become poor. They want money so bad, they rob you a ruble twenty for chintz."

Then Mitry Savin jerked his large head and said in a sharp tone,

"Why torment and torture ourselves? We must act. Like you said before, Martyn, you'll have to form the Party in the village."

"Really, Martyn . . . the Party."

"They say everyone helps and believes a Party man."

At this moment someone knocked on the window, and Labashkin's little grandson shouted that the water had risen another half-*vershok*. All signs pointed to a prolonged drought—good for the crops, but as for the glaciers. . . .

"Maybe we should go to the *volost*, the committee. . . . "

"The *volost*. . . . They'll gather a council of people cut of the same cloth as us, the scribe will write a resalution,[7] and it will take a month to get to the city, but a month from now the water will be standing in our streets. And then they'll come from the city, God knows what in- terstructions[8] they'll have. They'll wear out the horses with hard work at harvest time, they'll eat us out of house and home, and then they'll just disappear."

"We'll have to do it by ourselves."

"By ourselves," said Labashkin with a long sigh.

Mitry Savin started speaking sharply again: "On the other hand, maybe it'd be possible to help out someone in the city with money or something. We should find some of our boys who've gone off after gold and barter a bag of gold from them. They won't get any more in China anyhow. It may not be money, but they'll be flat- tered. Who'd say no?"

"But what do they understand about glaciers? What can they ac- complish if even God himself can't. . . . We need a person who knows something about lerigion."[9]

And Labashkin fell silent again for a long time.

"Have Martyn form the Party," Savin said decisively. "We have to choose someone."

"I choose Turukay," said Martyn.

Fertility

"Turukay's good for a scarecrow, but not for the Party. Leave Turukay for our enjoyment. Yegor Okushkov is poorer than anyone else."

Tyumenets started waving his hands. "Yegor won't go. He loves his fishing and moonshine. He'd like more water. He'd even sleep in it."

"The *mir* will make him, he'll go."

"That's it, the *mir*."

Mitry Savin bent one finger toward his palm.[10] His fingers were long and dry like kindling wood.

"That means we have one. With Martyn, that's two. We should get the poorer ones from the gold fields."

"They won't leave the gold fields now. Right now the water is coming down from the mountains. It's the perfect time for panning for gold."

"Then Semyonov. He's always praising Soviet power."

"Semyonov speaks through his nose and he wheezes. They'll say he's a drunkard or something even worse. They won't let him in."

"They've started their own little monopoly."

"But that's not for getting people drunk but for increasing appetites."

"One thing's for certain," said Tyumenets. "He's got an appetite until he falls face first into a ditch."

Sidor Labashkin turned out unexpectedly to be a person easily amused. Holding his stomach, he laughed for a long time. Finally he burst out in a sweat and crossed himself.

"Forgive us, oh Lord, our sins. . . . We've got to send a tiligram[11] to Moscow—who's the main guy there?—and tell 'em what's happening; that's how we're drowning."

"By the time they check it all out, the whole glacier will be melted."

Martyn got tired of listening and banged his fist on the table.

"Why is it you don't believe anybody! Do you take my words for some dumb village woman's? Am I talking to you about women?"

Mitry Savin looked at him calmly and answered him just as calmly, "We believe in haystacks, in hayricks, and in God."

Nonetheless, they did decide later to send a delegation to the city. They chose four men, thinner and with longer beards than the others. They looked at Martyn for a long time and finally said that he, too, could go, but only if he'd behave himself. They put on jackets that were dirtier than usual; for a long time they practiced how at first they'd have to praise Soviet power, thank them for the all their good deeds, the agronomists, the schools, their freedom of religion, and only later add that the agronomists almost never visit, the harvests are a total loss, and a lot, you know, could be done with harvests. . . . And about tractors—well, they'd heard about them. And all this is hindered by our ignorance, and that glaciers from the snowcaps are moving in on us, flooding the village. We won't be able to pay our taxes, not to mention even for tractors. Couldn't they help blow up Deer Ridge and divert the stream into the bare Talas Valley?

The city inn was dirty and stank of cigarettes; the bedbugs didn't let people sleep, and in the daytime some strange blind people came round and sold cigarettes at twenty kopecks a pack. The blind people were a nuisance and called the peasants bourgeois. But then some gaunt fellow in a soldier's overcoat and a Tartar cap, wearing cracked glasses, latched onto them. He promised that if nothing came of their going to the soviet, he knew the right people. Nevertheless, they found the essential person in the soviet. They told him the story they had worked up in the village. The essential person thought a long time, sent them to another who thought just as long, and both of them, apparently, couldn't think of anything. The first one, rummaging in some papers, asked, "Do you have a lot of workers?"

"What do you mean workers? We're all relatives, we're the same family."

"But do you have any? We'll discuss it," and he ordered them to return in a week.

"We should offer him a bribe," thought the muzhiks, "but we're afraid."

They had to wait a week, and then another five days, five whole days. In the meantime, the gaunt man in the soldier's overcoat brought another gaunt man, who must have been an Armenian. For three rubles they wrote two petitions and then somehow produced two contractors who dealt in explosives. With pencils in hand, the contractors sat down at the table, took out of their breast pockets thin books with pages lined in red ink, and pondered for a long time. They chatted in the next room, did some more figuring, and asked three thousand for blowing up Deer Ridge and "regulating the whole question"—five hundred now, a thousand on the spot, and fifteen hundred after the successful completion of the work. The elders grunted and gave a hundred rubles. The contractors announced that the observatory forecast thunderstorms and heavy wind, and that outside there was already a big storm with rain, and that others wouldn't touch this job even for five thousand.

In the evening Yegor Okushkov came galloping in from Ilinskoe with two glass vials of the very best large-grained red gold panned near the swamp behind which the mountains began.

Chapter 7

In the soviet Yegor Okushkov, his fishy-smelling hat shaking in his hands, explained in detail to the two essential persons how his fellow villager, Antip Skorokhodov, had found a deposit near the swamp, how the two of them had begun panning, and how on the first day they'd collected two vials. They've decided to give these vials as a gift to the people's government and to tell it about the discovery of the new gold fields. The essential persons got all excited, and some short-haired young girls quickly ran out of the adjoining rooms. Shaking their curls, they touched the vials and squealed with delight. Because of this noise and because it was not he, but Antip Skorokhodov, who had found the gold, Martyn got a headache and heartburn. Then the photographers came running; at first they photographed Yegor Okushkov and then all the peasants from Ilinskoe. The peasants did their bowing and thanking, and returned that same day.

And in the city after their departure people began relating stories about the new gold fields: one priest, supposedly, panned forty thousand rubles worth of gold in just two days, and a village scribe discovered a nugget almost the size of a horse's head. An advertisement asking people not to believe these nonsensical rumors appeared in the newspaper, and consequently they believed them even more. Wagons began squeaking and heading for the village of Ilinskoe; with carefree abandon, dreamers packed their knapsacks, left their jobs, and set off for the mountains on foot. Campfires burned at night along the roads, and there were several forest fires.

Those who came to the gold fields stopped beside the common pasture, where Turukay would meet them. He told stories about extraordinary events and was drunk every day. In the village they began to sell bread and milk at triple the price, and the women all became owners of silk shawls from Moscow.

Then three young engineers arrived, who got drunk the very first day; they got girls from the whole village and danced Russian dances clumsily with them. The girls squealed, and boys in their exuberance tried to embrace the engineers. Skorokhodov's wife Yelena didn't leave the side of the oldest engineer in blue trousers and a white silk shirt. Martyn walked past the merry-making party a couple of times, but no one invited him to join in. Turukay vomited, cursing vilely; for some reason his hands were covered with sour cream. The engineer went home with Skorokhodov and his wife, who, Martyn thought, was swinging her hips spitefully.

At home Martyn found everything in order: apparently his wife could manage the household better without him. No one spoke to him about the Party, nor did anyone mention the gold; only his wife reproached him once: "How can it be, Martyn Andreich, that you kept going and looking so often, and yet the gold was found by others?"

"There is no gold," Martyn retorted despondently. "They're all lying! And they're lying to themselves. It's women's talk, lies. . . . "

And this was closer to the truth. No one from Ilinskoe worked in the gold fields; every now and then the elders would go to the city, claiming to sell the gold they had dug up, but in reality driving cattle to town. And no one took any interest in the water rising in the lake. Once Martyn tried to put in a measuring rod. Mitry Savin walked up to him and said quietly, "Don't make God angry, Martynka," and he pulled out the rod. Then he looked at him sternly and asked: "Your . . . this . . . what's it called, this . . . Party, is it forming?"

"It is!" Martyn wanted to shout, but he couldn't. He could only twitch his sparse eyebrows.

"We don't need a Party. You'd better stay away from us, Martynka, you and your ideas. 'The Party's forming.' Rubbish."

He took a few steps away from Martyn, turned his back to him, and began to unbutton his pants. The water in the lake was clear and cold. Martyn also wanted to take a dip, but it seemed that Mitry Savin had taken possession of all the water with his body, and that it was the lake, and not Mitry Savin, grunting.

He didn't feel like going up to the snowcaps and the glacier, to the gold fields, and even he had trouble believing in his luck anymore. He attempted to walk around the lake with his sweep-net, but all he got was a dead carp. The carp smelled bad, and the dirty scales stuck to the palm of his hand like a glove. Martyn held it in his hand for a long time and didn't even notice that he had gouged its eyes out. He threw it back into the lake . . . and started to cry.

Chapter 8

The harvesting and putting up of the grain was almost finished by the day of Saints Frol and Lavr;[12] fences had been put up around the piles of grain and hay. The glossy birch fence posts seemed to shake like the belt on the body of an obese person; the field mice ate so much that they crawled back into their holes sweating. The common pasture was partitioned off, and on the day of Saints Frol and Lavr the cattle lay around the whole day. The cattleyards had been cleaned up, and repairs made to the outbuildings. The men started checking their sleighs and sledges, and weaving different types of bast baskets for carting off the chaff. It was as if nothing in particular had happened in Ilinskoe. The water from the lake had almost flooded the streets; as in the spring mud season, people had to walk along the *zavalinki*. Here and there water reached up to the spokes of the wheels.

"It sure is warm," the muzhiks repeated reluctantly. "It sure is warm, even though it's coming from the glacier. . . . "

But Martyn didn't even bother to look at his own field. The muzhiks came reluctantly for the workday his wife had arranged, but, after doing their share of work, wouldn't stay for the small afternoon meal. When Martyn saw the muzhiks who had come, the way they walked, their quiet evil voices—even Turukay-Tabun, who turned away from him—he again felt the lure of the mountains. His wife coped with all the fieldwork almost by herself. Only once did Martyn cut her some wood from dead trees for drying out the sheaves in the barn. His wife sheared the sheep, combed out the wool, and began to make saddlecloths. The *izba* began to have a sour smell.

"You've tormented me to death," said Martyn, but his wife didn't say anything in response.

The wide drainage ditch on both sides of the high hill, blocking the flow of water into the Talas Valley, was ready; the people working the gold fields had scheduled Sunday for blasting the middle part of the hill, which kept the ditches from merging, for blasting those gold veins you work with a pick.

Just like the first time, when he had seen the stream flowing from the glacier, Martyn put on his best colored shirt, stuck a slice of bread under it, and headed for the mountains. He had to avoid the main street, which was flooded by the lake, but then he didn't run into anyone on the side street either. Since early morning, almost the entire village, except for the most decrepit old people, had left for the hills and mountains.

Just like before, the birch trees were rustling in the cemetery, a light haze hung over the mountains, and only the nameless icy stream rushed through the fields and through the Holy Ravine, like a silvery blue knife cutting the valley. And when Martyn had gone around the swamp and remembered that there wouldn't be any rush of water today, that tomorrow and the day after tomorrow the amount of water in the lake would start waning and the lake would recede to normal, that flails would begin resounding on the threshing floors, and huge wagons, reinforced with iron bands, would take the grain into town, he again felt a pang in his heart. And the stream seemed to sense its final hours and rushed down the mountain with a plaintive din, foaming and snorting like a horse and neighing loudly in the birch groves. Martyn stood a while and looked. A quick-moving titmouse trembled in the reeds. And then

Martyn, with painful clarity, remembered the past few months, his short fame and power, and the fact that he couldn't reap any benefit from all this—all he got was the muzhiks' hatred toward him and a totally ruined farm. A feeling of melancholy again grasped his heart and made him want to cry.

Why should he go into the hills? The muzhiks would just look at the icy stream flowing down into the Talas Valley, only exchange crafty glances, laugh at the stupid city folk, and then go their separate ways. Later the city folk would leave as well and only the inaccessible Tilyash cliffs would be left, and beyond them, the glaciers, preparing their snowstorms for the fall.

Martyn returned to the edge of the swamp. The leaves of the aspen trees quivered sleepily and the swamp smelled of drunken satiety. Martyn sat down on a fallen aspen tree and lowered his feet in the stream. A green lizard began to rush around dazedly on the pebbles between his feet. He maliciously broke off its tail with his heel. The tail was left behind, still quivering, but the lizard hid. And the trees in the swamp kept banging and banging against each other, like people leaving and entering a room and slamming the door each time. Martyn sat thinking about the same old thing. He screwed up his eyes; the water in the current gurgled as if being poured into a bottle. And Martyn remembered that in all this time he hadn't gotten drunk even once. . . . He should leave, maybe go home and sleep, but somewhere inside him was still the hope that the muzhiks coming down from the mountains would stop beside him, with one of them saying, "Well, thank you Martyn, you've done a lot for society."

The green shadows from the trees were at his feet, then they slowly moved across his face, then behind him, and finally disappeared completely. It was most likely long after the noon hour, time for dinner. At this moment an oily-sounding rumble reached him from the glaciers. The stream seemed to quiver and then began babbling even more loudly.

"You won't blow up a damn thing!" Martyn said maliciously. "It would be better if you were washed away, like wood chips! You're only smoking up the sky. . . . "

Something dark and tall flashed among the aspens. Martyn looked more closely. A person looking for a dryer spot was rushing toward him. Behind, moving his arms quickly, ran a little boy.

Martyn stuck out his neck, shook his head, and cursed vilely. It was Yelena. She probably hadn't been up in the mountains for a long time or perhaps she was happy that her five-year-old son could keep up with her like a grown-up. Her face shone with rosy pleasure, she held her kerchief in her hand, and her flaxen, *bylina*-like[13] braids were terrifying, like the glaciers. Like a thorny wild rose on a pitchfork, but dressed in crimson.

"What are you sitting there for?" she shouted to Martyn from afar. "I stayed to work around the house, but the village is quiet as a log. Motka calls me, 'Let's go, Mama, let's go.' Well, I took off. . . . Am I going the right way?"

"Yes," Martyn answered gloomily, turning away. "You'll get there, all right. They're waiting for you."

"What did you sit down on the log for? I thought you were a water or a mountain spirit. Are you still sorcering?"

"I've turned my ankle," Martyn lied. "They're not going to get anywhere anyway."

"What do you mean, they're not going to get anywhere? But they've wasted so much effort and gold."

"Gold?" Martyn asked in surprise.

Yelena realized that she must have said too much. All of a sudden she leaned down to his foot. "I know a thing or two, you know, about fixing bones. Let me feel it. It isn't broken, is it?"

Martyn caught sight of the nape of her neck–plump, pink, slightly damp—and of her strong shoulders. The folds of her *sarafan* appeared wet to him; her shoe, with its ridiculously stylish high heel, was lifted in the air. Everything inside Martyn seemed to calm down, and then he glanced at the stream. The water was babbling more quietly; about half an *arshin* of dark blue pebbles along the shore were still wet. The larger stones were already drying out.

That means the blasting was successful. That means the stream has been diverted into the Talas Valley.

And Martyn had the feeling that he had begun to shout, both in fright and in jest. He was about to cover his mouth—to stop this shouting—but his arm and the hair on his head seemed to be made out of metal. . . . And suddenly he remembered how the muzhiks had been whispering with some strangers, idlers from the gold fields, how once he had met three elders traveling to the mountains in a cart; the faces of these men were greedy and sweaty, and their hands tightly clutched a box, covered with a small floor rug.

The salty sweat of anger filled his eyes. He squinted.

"Have they diverted it? Because of the women they've diverted it, that bunch of weak-willed mares. And who told them to? Who?"

He felt thirsty. His legs were heavy. Her stern neck and its nape with the plump fold bending toward his feet seemed to call for pity, but what kind and for whom, he couldn't imagine. . . . And although he realized that to think so was wrong and stupid, nevertheless he thought that now only Yelena understood how much misery she had caused him, how she had ruined his life, what insults she had brought upon him; and he believed that now she was ready to make up for it in every way. Her feet, set wide apart, lazily and at the same time quickly moved about, searching for a softer spot. It seemed that if you touched her with your finger, she'd fall over, but he couldn't just touch her. It was simpler and easier to give her a shove and feel the frightened vile flesh of her thighs under his boot! Martyn looked at the palm of his hand, and the fact that it was dry and dirty even made him happy. He spit on his fingers, and shaking all over from fright and an incomprehensible joy, struck Yelena with full force on the rosy nape of her neck. His fist slid off her neck onto the embroidery of her *sarafan*. Yelena gasped and fell over. Her little boy started to howl "Mommy!" Martyn struck her face with the back of his left hand, and with his right, pushed the boy with full force behind the tree trunk onto the grass. Yelena was about to get up; her throat tightened up. Martyn grabbed one braid, wrapped it around her neck and pulled her braids toward a birch bough. Her eyes started to roll and she grew hoarse.

"So you will, will you!" screamed Martyn, winding her braids around the bough. "So you'll flirt with everyone? Am I just a block of wood in your eyes? Huh?"

A film of cold and heavy moisture formed on his chest, and a dry heat struck his legs; fumbling with her clothing and grabbing with his teeth the braids wound around the branch, Martyn pulled open her *sarafan*. The chintz seemed extraordinarily strong, but in his fingers it parted like water.

The little boy screamed in the bushes, "M-m-mommy!" Her clothing reeked of sweat, and it was strange to see on this attractive and strong woman's face fear, trembling, and his, Martyn's, saliva.

Later the woman, her legs spread unattractively, crawled around the birch tree for a long time, untangling her braids from its boughs. A large tuft of hair, darkened with saliva, remained on the bark. Grabbing her torn *sarafan*, the woman tucked her large white breasts into her shirt as if into a sack. With the back of her hand she slowly wiped the saliva off her face and then started howling, "Oh, Mother of God, oh! . . . What's happened to me? Oh!"

The little boy's screams became deeper and somehow more pitiful. The tip of his nose was red, and only now did Martyn notice how much he resembled his mother.

"Scum, he's asking for it too," said Martyn and went to the stream to wash up.

Only sparse puddles were left in the deeper spots of the stream's channel. The water felt surprisingly warm to him.

The woman, getting caught up in her skirts and with her rear end shaking ridiculously, ran uphill. Her little boy, bending over comically, hurried after her.

Martyn sat down on the log again. His fingers were still hot. He had no thoughts but, for some reason or other, was sorry that he had washed up. His mind was still working, and he had the feeling that he had wasted the last bit of water. Moreover, he was thirsty, and now a weakness and trembling overwhelmed him, such as he had never experienced before.

A vast silence hung over the empty bed of the stream. A crimson aspen leaf appeared to be slipping along the pebbles that weren't dry yet; it was hopping about, moving along, babbling, but everything was without sound, and everything was in vain. Martyn closed his eyes, and a lot of things in this world reeled past him.

An oriole let out a long cry and Martyn thought, "It looks like the muzhiks are coming down."

The muzhiks, in fact, were descending silently from the mountains, with their hands behind their backs.

They stopped in a tight group a few feet away from Martyn. One of them was breathing heavily, wheezing, and spitting a lot. Martyn opened his vacant eyes and, for some reason, put his right hand in his pocket. Skorokhodov stepped out in front, and removed his caftan, which was bordered with triangles on the collar and chest.

"Well, go ahead, hit me," Martyn mumbled. "Sorry for your woman? Come on, hit me."

Skorokhodov turned pale, raised his hand as if for a greeting, and said unwillingly, "Why hit you? . . . Hit you for what? . . . "

Martyn squinted and reeled. And with his hand still raised, Skorokhodov walked past him almost reluctantly and, suddenly turning around, he struck Martyn on the bridge of his nose. A yellow light, the color of resin, flashed in the back of Martyn's head; he grabbed his chest.

"Don't," said an elder, eaten up by smallpox.

Someone in the crowd said calmly, "It wouldn't hurt to teach him a lesson. Just think how much gold we've lost because of him. Give him one, Semyon, for the gold. . . . "

"Yeah, for the gold!" Skorokhodov shouted suddenly. "You sorcerer. How much money on account of you! . . . How much livestock has perished!"

Martyn could only move his mouth greedily, as if he couldn't get enough to drink. Skorokhodov bent over and grabbed a rock in his hand. Blood came gushing out of Martyn's cheek like water.

"That's the way!" shouted the bald old man and, jumping up and taking a running start, he struck Martyn in the chest.

Martyn began to bellow like a calf and didn't stop bellowing while they were beating him, at first with their fists. Then they took him and tossed him up in the air and threw him down on his back. His head plopped to the ground; his arms, white and much too dry, flailed about. The bald old man began stomping on Martyn's arms and then wheezed and jumped on his stomach. Martyn's stomach made a cracking noise, a muddy liquid flowed out of his mouth, and he kept on bellowing absurdly, like a calf. The bald old man was now stomping on his head and slipping off of it, as if it were a wet rock, and the bellowing still didn't stop. At this point a young curly-headed lad, who up to now had been standing on the side and shouting louder than anyone, "Get him in the mug, in his ugly mug," took an oblong stone, pushed the elder aside and, screwing up his eyes, struck Martyn with the stone in the temple.

When Martyn had grown quiet and even stopped twitching, the bald old man wiped off his sweat, straightened out his shirt, and crossed himself.

"We've sinned all together, we'll answer all together."

"All together," nodded the curly-headed lad.

Yelena sat the whole time on the log where Martyn had recently been sitting. Her little boy was hiding his weeping face in her skirts. Her hair was pulled back tight under her kerchief; her eyes were dry and expectant, and she was looking somewhere over the heads of the muzhiks. When Martyn's body had stretched out and the curly-headed lad had taken Martyn's fingers, which he had bitten raw, out of his mouth and placed his arms in a cross, Skorokhodov walked over to her, shook his head, and suddenly struck her between the eyes with all his might. She fell back over the log and lay there for a long time, until the muzhiks had left and her little boy had lost his voice sobbing. Then she straightened out her kerchief, took her little boy by the hand, and began to make her descent into the valley.

The valley filled again with a fertile silence; satiated geese honked again in the harvested fields, and the moon's reflection in the lake was warm again and resembled a round loaf of bread fresh from the oven.

1926

»»»» ««««

The Dinner Service

The watchman had barely appeared in the church's doorway, intentionally rattling his keys to shake off his drowsiness, when Katerina Alekseevna was already standing by the church porch. It was some kind of a minor church holiday; the bell ringer took a long time deciding which bell to ring; the priest, white-haired and deaf, and suffering from shortness of breath, was late; the old woman was displeased with a lot of things and made the sign of the cross with firm sweeping motions of the hand; and she seemed to think that everyone in church understood and feared her displeasure. And she also thought that there she was in church, standing stern and straight and all in black, but in reality, her quilted jacket, soiled and patched over ineptly, added to her already stooping posture. Her flabby cheeks were covered with hair of an unappealing gray color, and her sharp nose seemed puffy and sweaty to everyone, and all because she rarely washed with soap.*

Whenever she got down on her knees, she would turn around to look at Anfiska, a small girl who had been assigned to look after her; the girl would rush to help her and make the kind of face everyone in the house made, that is, to indicate that they feared the wrath of

---

*This story first appeared in the journal *Red Virgin Soil* 5 (1927) without any division into paragraphs. In subsequent editions the format was changed to make it more readable.

Katerina Alekseevna. But in fact Anfiska thought the old woman was pretending, that she was not devout and went to church only because . . . well, how else could she pay back the kindness of her masters whom she had served as a cook for almost fifty years and who gave her a tiny room behind the kitchen, food and clothing till her dying day, and the services of Anfiska as well. Who really finds it interesting to stand in a stuffy little church smelling of putrid incense and cheap wax when it's August outside; slightly yellow leaves, full grown and tired of their joyful life, are lazily falling off the trees and coming to rest on the iron prongs of the fences; these leaves smell of fruit and this fruit is flooding the bazaars.

A stupendous and sunny fall is approaching the city; the city is thundering with activity, and birds are thunderously noisy in the sky, and there is also so much turmoil in man's soul! But the old woman is cold and she's wearing several pairs of stockings, all woolen, one stocking on top of the other. Her slipperlike shoes are made of thick felt, with the backs missing; and when they leave the church and when they reach the threshold of the church, Anfiska always hurries the old woman, pulling her hand and shrieking, "Come on, come on!" (from the church porch fruit gardens and tree branches glistening in the sun and wind are immediately visible) and the old woman trips on the string mat; Anfiska always forgets to look at the old woman's feet, and each time the old woman leaves her shoes here and walks outside in her stocking feet.

Once outside, Anfiska has no desire to watch over the old woman. Here, business-minded and cheerful peasants with scarlet-red fingers were selling raspberries bursting with juice; the customers watched and laughed as the raspberries, which had soaked the paper with their juice, spilled from the basket onto the ground and lay there, still the same happy juicy berries. Grapes shone light blue on the stands. The grapes kept their aroma to themselves, and Anfiska thought that her mouth would never discover this aroma;

and the small boys standing near the dealer thought the same thing, although there were times, people said, when the dealer would give a grape or two to a boy. But Anfiska couldn't stay here; she had to take the old woman home—and then, Anfiska didn't really envy the boys but was pleased at their happiness in which, by the way, she had little faith. And today, as always, the old woman walked up to the porch and stopped at the door to wipe her feet so as not to leave any dirty footprints, even though the day was dry and dusty; but it was impossible to argue with her. The old woman grabbed the door handle for support—and then it turned out that she had again forgotten her slippers on the mat in the church. Anfiska's fingers were always widely spaced (as if there were other fingers between these fingers, not given to others to see, and even Anfiska seemed to think so); Katerina Alekseevna looked at these fingers, which were straining intensely in different directions, and slowly said, "Go." Anfiska went as asked, although she didn't really feel like it.

Now it's very damp inside the church; the watchman is roaming around and grumbling; he doesn't like to see children in church; it always seems to him that children come to church to steal candles (the watchman is a shoemaker; he had two daughters, but they had abandoned their father, left him for the happy life of big city streets; perhaps they even found that life, only they didn't inform their father). The apartment of Katerina Alekseevna's employers was empty—this one had gone to work, that one on a date, and still another, simply out to enjoy the sun—and Katerina Alekseevna, as always in such instances, walked all around the apartment before she went to her own tiny room. The cook always opened the door for her; she was now clattering dishes in the kitchen. The cook was large and stout, with a big behind, and couldn't bear any children; and her husband, who had lived in the country, threatened to find another wife for himself. The cook would say that she didn't have children because of the lack of fresh air; she would constantly open the *fortochka*[1] to let in fresh air, although her employers forbade her to do so; they would say that the cold air would go from the kitchen to Katerina Alekseevna's little room, and she could catch a cold. They kept repeating this not because they were afraid that, so to say, Katerina Alekseevna would die, but because they didn't like sick people who, it seemed to them, constantly spread infection; and the master of the house, Fedor Sergeich, rotund and with hair combed over his bald spot, even rushed to kiss a lady's hand first so that he wouldn't pick up an infection from the saliva of those who had kissed the hand before him.

As for Katerina Alekseevna, she thought the cook wanted to eliminate her from this world in order to take the little room for herself, and for this reason she wouldn't tell the cook about a remedy which, she knew, helped women bear children. And the cook understood this, and for many years they were on the point of talking things over, and yet they both lacked the gumption to do so. The rooms were bright and spacious but wallpapered, for some reason, with dark paper with large unnatural flowers at the top; and all the guests were complimentary and delighted, for some reason, with this darkness and these flowers that resembled wood chips.

The best and most cheerful piece in the room was the sideboard. This sideboard was left over from those times when people were not ashamed (as they are now) that they ate a lot and ate well, while others went hungry. This sideboard was built by people who ate a lot—and when Katerina Alekseevna stopped before it, the sun was streaming through the whole window and striking the dark oak, striking the carved leaves that decorated the side doors; dark wooden grapes adorned these doors and they, too, glistened in the sun and seemed translucent. The main part of the sideboard, reaching down almost to the floor, was held up by happy little children carved out of oak; their tummies were round and strong, and on their hard little cheeks exulted the grease that they had preserved for centuries. The shelf that united the two parts of the sideboard was a thick solid piece of oak. From this huge block you could have built a boat or, let's say, you could have put a whole roasted steer on it. Then the smell of meat would have filled the whole house; the man of the house would have drawn near with a knife, and the guests, glancing confidently at the steer, would have moved their shot glasses closer. . . . On this board stood a forgotten French porcelain sauceboat with pale roses that almost seemed to be fading away. This sauceboat was part of the dinner service that the whole family, many families, many of Katerina Alekseevna's employers took pride in.

Oh, that dinner service! Katerina Alekseevna was its servant for fifty years, more than fifty, for seventy years! She first came to it as a small village girl, and the cook, gray-haired and gentle, gave her strict lessons about the need to wash this service carefully; she taught her with the same words that Katerina Alekseevna now uses with the little girl Anfiska. Many wars, bank failures, and even revolutions (which removed from this apartment Persian rugs and Kerman shawls radiant with white circles and cashmere hearts)—a lot had passed before this service, and its pale flowers reminded their thin and fat owners that there are rose bushes that bloom even in winter and don't lose their petals and leaves even during heavy storms. Such words bring pleasure to many people—and the sideboard held the pale thoughtful-looking roses in its stomach tenaciously and joyfully. . . .

Katerina Alekseevna wanted to remove the sauceboat so that no one would hit it accidentally; she wanted to put it in the sideboard and had already extended her hand and was about to feel the cold smooth surface next to her skin when, at that very instant, she sensed a small and disturbing pain in her side. This pain passed quickly and was replaced by a sleepy weariness, which also passed very quickly. But her feelings of anxiety remained, and she didn't dare face this anxiety; she went on to her little room. The way to this little room was through the front room and down a small dark corridor, one door of which led to the kitchen and the other to Katerina Alekseevna's room. The door was so low that you always had to bend down, and Katerina Alekseevna, a step away, would always bend her head; but now she hit herself and, what's more important, felt the pain only when she came to a stop by her bed. The pain didn't surprise her; what surprised her was that she couldn't understand where this pain had come from and, moreover, she didn't believe that the pain was the result of hitting herself against the doorjamb. She began to feel sleepier and sleepier, and had the feeling, particularly in her hands, that she had performed some long and monotonous, rather than exhausting, work. Her fingers, it seemed to her, were beginning to stick together, and although her eyes had already been stuck together for a long time, she saw everything clearly and distinctly. The window was poorly washed; it had lines left by the water. She felt like opening the window. She even told Anfiska, who had just walked in, about this window.

The trees in the garden were already bare because the garden was in a windy place; and through the tree trunks the cupolas of a monastery were visible in the distance, and those cupolas had a dull shine like ripened fruit. When Anfiska turned away from the window, the old woman was already lying stretched out, and she had such a stern face that it was only now that Anfiska felt truly frightened of it. Both of the old woman's hands were clasped together: the skin on her fingers was rough and puffy, and covered with wrinkles and dirt. The old woman told Anfiska clearly and distinctly, "Go bring pla . . . , but not from the kitchen, the sideboard."

Katerina Alekseevna felt like speaking, and she thought she was speaking in a whisper because she wanted to cry out not from joy or grief but from some unknown feeling she had never experienced before. She tried to purse her lips but they wouldn't move, and she saw that Anfiska was bustling and hurrying so clumsily that her bustling was only interfering with her movements; and when Anfiska appeared in the door with a plate in her hand and the door frame cut off part of the pale rose, for the first time Katerina Alekseevna felt offended that she had been given a person who didn't understand simple words and simple wishes. As for Anfiska, she saw in this motionless face which had turned crimson a bold malice, and this malice was so obvious and intense that Anfiska, knowing that she should run and tell about Katerina Alekssevna in the kitchen, nevertheless did not have the strength to run; and when the old woman said to her angrily, "What did you bring? Should've brought two!" Anfiska went and brought a second plate.

The old woman tried to sit up; Anfiska placed a pillow behind her back, but this didn't seem to be enough, and so she added the quilted jacket and then even the felt boots. And the old woman, overcoming her unbearable sleepiness and seemingly trying to control her face, which was seized with a convulsion and, thinking she was succeeding, unclasped her hands, took a plate in each hand and, when she took these plates, she had the clear feeling that now she had no one to fear; she waved her hands violently, and a light happy feeling of boldness took possession of her, and sleep blew like a dry wind into her eyes. She could no longer hear the dishes bang against each other and break in her hands, and she didn't feel her thumb come down on a sharp piece of porcelain or sense the sharp edge. Her face was deep red, and a paleness gradually began to leave the tip of her nose and spread to her cheeks. This white spot kept getting wider, covering her whole face, and her body kept straightening out and straightening out. Anfiska stood by the stool near the bed, and she wasn't afraid to see this intense, deep-red face turning pale, but a puzzling thought did frighten her to the point of shivering: why did the old woman break the plates? And only when it occurred to her that they might decide that she, Anfiska, and not the old woman, had broken the plates did she feel better; and the old woman's immobile face seemed frightening and yet dear to her, and she started to weep bitterly.

1927

»»» ««««

The Mansion

Chapter 1

It all began when Ye. S. Chizhov brought a batch of *krendels*[1] from a town in the northern Urals to sell in Petrograd. Although the thick *krendels* kept getting moldy and Yefim Sidorych kept cleaning the mold off in his hotel room, he sold this batch, just like the other batches, for a good profit. When he was bargaining with a customer, a fat and gloomy fellow wearing a quilted khaki jacket, they heard some shooting on the square by the train station. But political meetings and all kinds of elections and even the overthrow of the tsar did not prevent him from selling his *baranki,*[2] and Yefim Sidorych soon forgot about the Revolution, since other thoughts, unexpected and more terrifying, filled his heart and mind. One day, on waking up in the morning, he suddenly felt a need that couldn't be denied: a need to have a house, a wife, and cattle, cows, horses, a lot of equipment and harnesses—that is, everything he had thought about rarely before, since he considered himself a care-free fellow, capable of living out his years without superfluous cares, worries, and vodka. He roomed with his mother, Varvara Petrovna, and his aunt, Katerina Petrovna, in a large room with a kitchen, which he rented from the bookbinder Smirnov for four rubles a month; in addition, Yefim Sidorych lived with the book-binder's wife, a shrill and restless woman. The bookbinder's wife was not demanding; she was as affectionate as her character would permit. On Sundays she baked good *shangi*[3] and bought unusually sweet sour cream somewhere. Life was comfortable and easy, and the unexpected abundance of desires, which awakened in him in the room in Petrograd, greatly distressed Yefim Sidorych. And in order to detach himself from these desires, he tried to fulfill them immediately and acted as people usually act in these circumstances: he fulfilled, if it can be put this way, the shadows of his desires. He wrote a letter to his old acquaintance, Staff Captain S. M. Zhilenkov, who lived in the town of N., and in this letter, among other bits of news, he mentioned his dream of buying a house. Then he picked up a ruddy-faced girl on Nevsky Boulevard (her cheeks had that caustic glow of the city), took a carriage ride with her, and, after lying in bed with her for the few minutes allotted to him by nature, he ordered some fried eggs and milk. And neither he nor the girl was surprised that he ordered fried eggs and milk, and that the milk was watery and tasted like whitewash. In appearance Yefim Sidorych was well-proportioned, with a wedge-shaped beard and empty but at the same time insistent eyes. He was often mistaken for a teacher, and it never occurred to anyone that Yefim Sidorych Chizhov was a former shoemaker and harness-maker, and that the skin on his fingers was saturated with an indelible dark-yellow color and his fingernails were dark blue and unusually hard. And the girl from Nevsky asked him if he, Yefim Sidorych, was perhaps a teacher, because now a lot of teachers were participating in political meetings. Yefim Sidorych gave the girl a hostile look and thought: "Time to go, it's time to go."

And that very day he left for the town of N.

But even in the town of N. those nagging and tormenting desires that had seized Yefim Sidorych in Petrograd did not abate, but assumed a kind of incomprehensibly mocking character. For example, on the very first day of his arrival Yefim Sidorych met Zhilenkov, the staff captain, the one to whom he had written. Zhilenkov had been drafted into the army and before that had occupied himself, as he used to say to himself, with "a system of land use," but as he said to everyone else, "I'm trying to locate pastureland"; and he always had a habit of directing people's thoughts about him in the opposite direction from the truth. And his "system of land use" consisted of dealing in real estate, mainly timber. Ye. S. Chizhov's letter seemed suspicious to the staff captain and, therefore, he tried to meet Yefim Sidorych the very first day of his arrival. Fixing his gaze on Yefim Sidorych, with his eyes constantly changing color, and fluttering his whitish and unusually long eyelashes that seemed to extend to his forehead, the staff captain asked tensely, "Are you going into the Orenburg steppes? What for? Come on, you're going to Orenburg, don't deny it!"

"But why should I go to the Orenburg steppes?" Yefim Sidorych asked, perplexed.

Zhilenkov, looking as if he was being insulted and made a fool of by this conversation, walked a few steps away and shouted, "I'll find you a little house! Go, make your fortune, and I'll find you one in the meantime."

Yefim Sidorych immediately came to understand how one could make a fortune in the Orenburg steppes. Many traders tried to drive herds of cattle from there to the center, but the roads were poor and the cattle kept dying. . . . But to take *baranki* to Petrograd was just as dangerous, and fortune, like all things in life, depends on luck. Yefim Sidorych did head for the Orenburg steppes; he quickly and successfully drove a herd of fat and rumbling-hoofed cattle to the city. And again Ye. S.'s money grew, but the Revolution grew along with the money as well. The cattle, brought in a drive from the Orenburg steppes, were already being eaten by discontented soldiers at the front. Yefim Sidorych was already being hurried to make the next trip in order to persuade the rebelling soldiers with rich meat, but at this point Staff Captain Zhilenkov came to see him, and at the same time the Grand Duke B., a pretender to the Russian throne, as rumors had it, was brought to town.

Zhilenkov declared that in the center of town was a mansion, fully within Chizhov's financial means, two stories of stone with wooden additions in the form of a dove.

"What do you mean?" Yefim Sidorych asked dumbstruck.

And that's how it was: when Yefim Sidorych was looking the mansion over, the wooden sheds reminded him of a dove with its wings outstretched. And behind the sheds a neighboring estate was visible: a gloomy three-story house with narrow windows that resembled a prison. A sparse birch grove pitifully spread out from it. And how could two such different houses stand side by side? The small mansion, recommended by Zhilenkov, was planted all around with fir trees; the sand-covered paths resembled strips of ripe rye waving in the wind. Yefim Sidorych bought the mansion and painted it green. Immediately Zhilenkov appeared and reacted with suspicion to the green paint. Zhilenkov said that in the *uyezd*, on the estate of Prince Khavansky, despondent because of the Revolution, furniture was being sold quickly for next to nothing. They bought the furniture, upholstered it in silk, and the upholsterers declared that the furniture was antique and valuable. Yefim Sidorych's ridiculous success pursued him; he immediately believed the upholsterers when at another time he never would have, and he asked his aunt, Katerina Petrovna, to call Staff Captain Zhilenkov.

Chapter 2

Zhilenkov, taking offense, said that Yefim Sidorych undoubtedly knew the true value of the furniture, but nevertheless promised to get some catalogues. According to French catalogues of antiques, it turned out that the furniture belonged to Napoleon the First's brother and that it was brought to Russia in 1815, and it cost——. Zhilenkov even screwed up his eyes with hurt and envy.

Katerina Petrovna found a bride for Ye. S.—the daughter of a local lawyer, Markell Markellych Yepich. Manichka Yepich was the kind of bride Yefim Sidorych had wanted: seventeen years old, sedate, and conscientious. Katerina Petrovna had suffered her whole life in shame because she lived on her nephew's support; often, looking at Yefim Sidorych's neat little beard, she wanted to say in a hurt tone, "I'm leaving," but she would say something completely different. Now it seemed to Katerina Petrovna that she had paid him back for her daily bread. Markell Markellych did all the talking, and the whole time convincingly at that, and his daughter Manichka kept silent the whole time, and this was no less convincing. The whole town respected the Yepich family, and the family respected everyone. The lawyer's affairs were not in good shape; he was pleased to be marrying off his daughter, the more so since Yefim Sidorych was not demanding any dowry. Yefim Sidorych should have felt comforted! But anxiety and a new desire possessed him, and this anxiety seized him on Cathedral Square. And this is how he wound up on Cathedral Square.

Grand Duke B. was at first housed in the Stroganov Palace, a huge building decorated with a colonnade, which stood on Cathedral Square. A multitude of guards and sailors protected Grand Duke B. In town, and most often on Cathedral Square, some strange lanky officers with frightened and at the same time insolent faces began to appear. The locals strolled the square proudly. And Varvara Petrovna invited her son and sister to take a stroll on Cathedral Square. From the day that her son had become a young man, Varvara Petrovna always wanted to listen to her son, but it always turned out to be impossible to do so. And even in the matter—in the most important matter in one's whole life—of building or buying a house, she believed her son had done the wrong thing. If there's a rebellion in town, then you must buy a house in the country! The old woman was a head taller than her son, with the firm step of a soldier and with the same gray, insistent eyes as her son. Yefim Sidorych despised politics and headed for the square with reluctance. The windows seemingly dipped in red wine; the flat tin-colored roof resembling a gray cloud; the square, overgrown with sparse and seemingly cast-iron grass, and the air of the kind in which you could hear a soldier grunting in the courtyard, throwing his belt on the cobblestones, with the buckle suddenly ringing; and the wire that sheathed the palace facade—barbed wire resembling grass—all this for some incomprehensible reason enlivened Yefim Sidorych. Yepich, strolling with his daughter on the square, walked up to him. Yepich introduced Yefim Sidorych to an officer whom they hadn't noticed immediately for some reason, although he was both tall and broad-shouldered. The officer's name was Golofeev, Sergey Sergeevich; he had served in the guards at one time; he was a monarchist who understood that the monarchy was perishing, but didn't know where he should go, and he was a man who didn't believe in the people. His reproachful yet expressionless face twisted so that it was difficult and unpleasant to look into his eyes, and to some people who conversed with him, it seemed as if they were talking to a dead person. Markell Markellych began to speak about the monarchy and the Jews. He was even writing a book about the rhythm of Egypt in which he was trying to prove that Jews had brought rhythmical Egypt to ruin, for they were antirhythm. Officer Golofeev was looking into the windows of the Stroganov Palace with hopeless boredom. It was getting dark. Yefim Sidorych squeezed his bride's hand. She responded. Yefim Sidorych began talking about his mansion. Everyone looked at him perplexed, and he unexpectedly offered the officer an apartment in his house. The officer agreed.

"You're a real hero!" Markell Markellych exclaimed, embracing Yefim Sidorych.

"I'm not a hero," Yefim Sidorych answered, "but I do admit that actions must be immediate."

And everyone agreed with him, understanding and not questioning what actions are immediate and after what thoughts they follow.

Chapter 3

A new Bolshevik commissar was appointed for Grand Duke B. The name of this commissar was Petrov, Ivan Grigorich, and he had a brother, Semyon Grigorich, the chairman of the provincial soviet. Commissar Ivan Petrov kept insisting at a plenum of the soviet that it was shameful and bad from standpoint of agitation to keep the grand duke in the Stroganov Palace. The grand duke was now an ordinary person, no greater than the rest, and a harmful person at that. The plenum agreed with the conclusions of the freckle-faced and short-armed commissar, and resolved to move the grand duke to a smaller dwelling, which called for less money being spent by the proletarian government. And so they moved Grand Duke B., a corpulent old man with a woman's voice, to the three-story house next to Yefim Sidorych's mansion. It insulted Yefim Sidorych to see from the window of his mansion the grand duke entering the house and talking with the Bolshevik Commissar Petrov condescendingly, and perhaps even ingratiatingly. In the evening Yefim Sidorych, Officer Golefeev, and Yefim Sidorych's future father-in-law, Markell Markellych, were standing by the door of the balcony, from where they could see windows covered with barbed wire, windows in which the swaying silhouette of the grand duke often floated by. Yefim Sidorych was the first to feel sorry that the balcony was covered with snow and that it was impossible to walk out and wave a white handkerchief to the grand duke and, moreover, that a white handkerchief would not be seen against snow.

"You're a rabid monarchist!" Markell Markellych said condescendingly. "I never expected it! It's time for the grand duke to think about a change, too."

"It's time, it's time," repeated Yefim Sidorych, and a cold shiver of excitement passed through his body. Officer Golofeev glanced at him with his expressionless, yet malevolent, eyes and turned away.

Because of the bustle, rations, and orders posted on fences, Yefim Sidorych agreed (and Markell Markellych, too, it seemed, because he had placed his hopes on Golofeev's love for his daughter) to postpone the wedding. Moreover, he had no particular hope that the anxiety which possessed him would disappear. Now he greatly mourned the passing of the monarchy. Markell Markellych was even put in the position of trying to suppress Yefim Sidorych's grief. Commissar Ivan Petrov, shaking his hair, still long from his prison days, was again arguing at a plenary session of the soviet that an officers' organization was noticeably present in the region; that prisoners of the imperialistic war were becoming agitated; that a counterrevolution was brewing while Grand Duke B. was living in a huge house consisting of thirty rooms at a time when the proletariat of the factories. . . . Shaking an empty and grimy carafe, the commissar began to lament. . . . A hum of approval passed through the hall of the governor's house. The plenum agreed with the words of Commissar Ivan Grigorevich.

And so, on a warm, pre-spring evening, when a snowstorm, more like rain than snow, played outside and the fir trees seemed to have passed through ice floes, leaving frozen drops of water on their needles, Yefim Sidorych was drinking tea with his family and friends and listening to Markell Markellych outline his plan: sailors could be used to get a large shipment of flour through to Petrograd. They heard a timid and short ringing of the doorbell: such a ring often announced Golofeev and his friends, the same kind of people as he, dead-faced, obsequious, and ill-dressed. Yefim Sidorych opened the door without asking who it was. Before Yefim Sidorych stood Commissar Ivan Grigorevich; behind him could be seen Red Guards and sailors with revolvers and bombs. The commissar, not without some satisfaction, in a cheerfully businesslike voice read a resolution of the plenum of the local soviet, from which it was obvious that the soviet recognized the living space occupied by Grand Duke B. as huge and extremely costly to the proletarian government. It is giving over this living space to a children's home, and the grand duke is moving to the mansion belonging to citizen Ye. S. Chizhov.

"How can you evict me?" Yefim Sidorych asked quietly. "You shouldn't evict me, and besides, I have lodgers!"

"Together with the lodgers," the commissar answered. "Take your pillow and get the hell out of here, together with your questionable lodgers!"

"But what about my furniture?" Yefim Sidorych asked.

"The furniture stays with the commune!" the commissar answered.

And Yefim Sidorych took his pillow and blanket and went to Smirnov, the bookbinder, who still lived near the cemetery. On parting, Markell Markellych kissed him sympathetically, but didn't invite him to his own apartment.

"Life near the grand duke has placed certain obligations on you, and certain suspicions," Markell Markellych said, "and I have a family and a marriageable daughter."

"I understand your position," Yefim Sidorych said, and he truly understood Markell Markellych's position, and for a minute was even sorry for him.

Chapter 4

Yefim Sidorych woke up from the stench and hiss of burnt potatoes. The women were quietly talking in the kitchen. His old mother was grumbling: "Should have bought a house out of town. . . . At least if they had taken it away for debts!" The smell of burnt potatoes even made Yefim Sidorych feel happy for a moment; he remembered the beginning of his love for the bookbinder's wife. But now she's gotten fat, her body is spreading out, and she smells bad. Yefim Sidorych got angry. "Somebody reported to the authorities, somebody got envious! The whole town envied my Napoleon furniture! How often they talked about it!" Conversations about the grand duke and feelings of sympathy toward him, and the fact that he pitied this corpulent old man who was being tortured by being moved from place to place, and whom they might possibly even put on trial—all this seemed ridiculous and unnecessary to Yefim Sidorych. But he immediately repented his thoughts and went to eat the potatoes. The potatoes were the same as those he ate in his mansion, but here they seemed watery and not as tasty. He thought that the bookbinder's wife would come soon and begin flirting with him, and his mother and aunt would discreetly leave. Afterward the bookbinder's wife would start wheezing, opening wide her wet onionlike mouth. He looked at his mother angrily and shouted, "Everything! You contradict everything I do! I wish you'd hurry up and leave this world!" His mother began weeping loud and long, and his aunt Katerina Petrovna, remembering the food she felt guilty eating, put the fork aside and began to cry, too. "No, in vain has Yefim Sidorych spoken about the monarchy!" He even spit at the thought of such ideas.

Yefim Sidorych met Officer Golofeev on the street. Golofeev was heading in the direction where Yefim Sidorych's fiancée lived. "He's gone to win her away from me. He's feeling happy!" Yefim Sidorych thought, and didn't bow to Golofeev. The latter made such a face, as if he had known for five years that Yefim Sidorych would betray him, and straightened his back. Yefim Sidorych quickly went to the post office, asked for some paper and an envelope, and with a trembling, sweaty hand wrote a denunciation to the Cheka.[4] After he had dropped the letter in a mailbox, Yefim Sidorych felt incredible shame and weariness (of the kind he had suffered in Petrograd). He rushed to write a statement to the *ispolkom* so that they would let him have his Napoleon furniture because of its tremendous "spiritual" value to him. He seemed to feel a bit better, and, strolling through the town, he kept trying to convince himself that he had done the right thing: Golofeev had nothing to lose, he'd start a rebellion, and there were more than enough dead without this. And the friends who come to see him probably have dynamite in their pockets. The next day he went to the *ispolkom* to get an answer about his furniture. A resolution, written with a badly sharpened blue pencil, lay on his long note: "No act. tak. on cit. Chizhov's request." And at this very moment he heard about Golofeev's arrest, and only when he had heard the details of the arrest did he notice that the one telling about it was Staff Captain Zhilenkov, now in a soldier's tunic without any epaulets. "Does my furniture have any spiritual value?" he asked Zhilenkov. The latter stepped back suspiciously and agreed right away. Yefim Sidorych felt very sad. He went to the bluff, to the pond. From here he could see Cathedral Square and the Stroganov Palace. Bolshevik military courses were already being given in the palace. Manichka Yepich was walking across the square arm-in-arm with a neatly dressed soldier. Yefim Sidorych realized that he trusted Manichka and that she trusted him, although as a suitor he was both elderly and not that handsome. And she immediately left her admirer, walked up to Yefim Sidorych, and gently shook his hand. Yefim Sidorych walked over under the shade of a poplar tree with her and squeezed her little elbow, although he wanted to squeeze her little breasts; and she sensed that he was squeezing her breasts, because she said in a bashful whisper, "What are you doing, Yefim Sidorych?" Manichka Yepich knew how to sympathize with people expertly and silently, and they understood that she was sympathizing with them. For example, Yefim Sidorych told her about the furniture that was taken away, and she added sympathetically what Yefim Sidorych had forgotten: "Right now it's impossible to take the furniture abroad but, you know, the time will come." And this addition to his thoughts greatly moved Yefim Sidorych. And moreover, from their conversations he realized that she really could be faithful because she didn't like any kind of worry.

At night Yefim Sidorych wrote a letter to the *ispolkom* in which he contended that there was no point in moving the grand duke from place to place, and that he should be ripped out by his roots, that is, shot and shot immediately, for bands of officers and English spies were organizing in town, and an upheaval was possible. . . . He wrote with sincerity; sometimes in the moving parts, where he was defending the rights of the poor, tears would appear in his eyes. He recalled his childhood; there wasn't even a crust of black bread, and when he wandered around the flea markets, he saw people eating tripe and entrails at seven kopecks a portion; dinner like that he considered good fortune; he spent the night on a sailboat by the pond . . . his masters beat his hands with boot trees . . . inside the building it stank of wet leather. And now he's been thrown into the same situation! . . . And the grand duke is partially guilty here as well! . . . He wanted to sign his name but changed his mind and

wrote: "In the name of fifty shoemakers and saddlemakers. . . . "
And then illegible scribbles. Yefim Sidorych took the statement to
the *ispolkom* himself. On the staircase of the *ispolkom* he again met
Zhilenkov with a star on his soldier's cap. "They're giving me a
company," he said loudly to Yefim Sidorych's face. "Denunciations of me won't help—they trust me." And Yefim Sidorych answered, "And I trust you, too." Out of spite Zhilenkov shook his
thin and long finger at him. For three days Yefim Sidorych was
filled with expectation. Although he hadn't added an address, it
seemed to him that any minute now some important commissars
would come and thank him for his splendid thoughts. His face was
burning, and he was terribly thirsty. He slept badly, and the third
night of his insomnia he tried to write poetry: the three-hundred-
year yoke must be cast off, destroyed! But the verses didn't come
out the way he wanted them, although inside he felt quiverings unlike all his other quiverings, and he felt increasing pity for himself
and his hapless life. He took his verses to a newspaper. The pink-
cheeked secretary looked them over quickly and said, "There are
thousands like these," and gave him an issue of the newspaper. In
boldface letters the newspaper reported that Yefim Sidorych's request to execute the grand duke had been fulfilled and that the sentence had been carried out. "But, you know, that's me! That was
my wish!" Yefim Sidorych shouted to the calm secretary. Ye. S.
Chizhov, waving the paper around, flew down the stairs. On the
porch of the governor's house he folded the paper twice in a way
that the announcement about the execution could be read immediately; he carefully adjusted the newspaper in his pocket and
thought of his pillow. But the thought of his pillow was funny to
him, and he went quickly to his mansion. A long-legged Red Guard
in patent leather boots stood by a heap of barbed wire. Barbed wire
had already been put around the fence of the mansion; telephone
wires were strung through the fir trees; the Red Guard, it seemed,

looked at all this with sadness. "Back," he said mournfully. "Who are you looking for?"

"This is my house and my furniture," answered Yefim Sidorych, taking the newspaper from his pocket. The Red Guard glanced at the paper and yawned—his eyes were sleepy and hungry—and with unexpected gentleness said to Yefim Sidorych that the grand duke had been here, that's true, and that the day before yesterday he had been executed, and now Commissar Petrov would move into this mansion with his secretaries and staff. "Is that the one who was so insistent?" Yefim Sidorych asked spitefully. The Red Guard answered, "No, brother. The one who kept silent. Semyon Grigorich." Yefim Sidorych didn't believe the Red Guard and sat down next to the house on a rock. Soon Commissar Petrov arrived in a car—happy, broad-shouldered, with a hunting dog on his lap. Both the guards and the commandant of the house looked at the red-brown dog with special affection. The Red Guard on watch duty said something to the commissar, who looked in Yefim Sidorych's direction and even headed toward him with a joyful and kind look, but then turned back halfway, and, whistling, disappeared into the house. The dog jumped around him, and its happy yelps and capers could even be heard inside the house. Yefim Sidorych said indignantly to the Red Guard, "I'm not even asking for the house. Give me back my furniture! I was the one who made possible the elimination of the grand duke. I was the one who proposed it to them." All of a sudden the Red Guard lazily took his rifle in his hand, "And I'm sick and tired of looking at you, old boy! You're sitting here, and I'll fire at you even if you're sitting!" Yefim Sidorych crossed himself and slowly walked away from his house. In the soviet he was told that the question about his furniture, as before, was still open. That evening Yefim Sidorych drank tea with Markell Markellych.

"I supported this power!" Yefim Sidorych exclaimed. "I supported it in spite of all the objections of friends and relatives. And what have I gotten?"

Markell Markellych wanted to speak; he opened his mouth but Yefim Sidorych brought a cup of tea close to his face and shouted, "You've even poured me weak tea out of hate! I approved of Zhilenkov's action. I approved the execution of the grand duke. . . . "

"He kept a stiff upper lip, they say," Markell Markellych said pensively, glancing at Yefim Sidorych's tea.

"Zhilenkov is an officer and a patriot, but in the Red Army . . . what use is he?"

"He kept a stiff upper lip as he was about to be shot," the lawyer said suddenly in a loud voice, looking into Yefim Sidorych's face. Yefim Sidorych smiled in dismay.

"God is his judge."

"God?" the lawyer cried out, and his forehead turned crimson and sweaty.

Yefim Sidorych got up, pushed his cup away, and said sharply, "I'm guilty, I repent. The old man was killed for nothing. But I can't forgive your shouting, Markell Markellych."

And Yefim Sidorych left both his bride-to-be and his father-in-law, and, crossing the yard, now empty but at one time filled with fowl, grain, and manure, he felt great shame and confusion within himself.

Chapter 5

Yefim Sidorych often went to the *ispolkom* for information on new laws. He spent a long time familiarizing himself with the laws, copying them out on a piece of paper and then putting them into his petitions for the return of his furniture. No sooner would he submit his petition than he would remember that the Red Guards were lying on his furniture with their boots on, and that the commissar was boldly flicking the ashes of his cigarette onto the silk of his, Yefim Sidorych's, sofas—and he would write a new petition. And each time the arguments he brought forth seemed more and more convincing to him. Spring and summer and fall came; mutinies, uprisings, and food rationings spread throughout the province; Commissar Petrov got himself a new car, made a trip to the Polish front, and brought back a cheerful and big-bosomed wife; the wife soon gave him a daughter. Yefim Sidorych was passing by the mansion; they were celebrating a child's birth there, laughing and drinking. Yefim Sidorych had already forgotten the color of the silk on the sofas and chairs; only the raspberry color of the morocco leather in the study still lingered in his memory, and that was only because the watchman at the *ispolkom* had suddenly appeared in shoes made of raspberry morocco leather. Both the smell and the design of the leather were familiar to Yefim Sidorych. "Did they rip it off the sofa?" he asked the watchman. "I don't know where they got it from," answered the watchman. "The chairman just gave me the shoes."

Famine came, and during the famine Varvara Petrovna, for the first time in her life, fulfilled her son's desire—she departed. She was buried in the fall. Yefim Sidorych dug the grave himself, and when it came time to fill it, his hands suddenly grew weak! He looked at his hands: they had become so wrinkled that they were unrecognizable, and the yellow dye of the shoemaker's trade had now even spread over to the back of his hands. Yefim Sidorych felt sorry not for himself but for his mother's years and death, and then he began to feel sorry, too, for his aunt, Katerina Petrovna, and her years, and then for some reason, he suddenly recalled Golofeev, who'd been shot, and Zhilenkov, who'd recently come back from the war, still as suspicious and frightened as ever, although now a decorated Red officer. Zhilenkov worked in the field of art: he was setting up the city museum. . . . When he returned from the funeral, Yefim Sidorych spent a long time writing a denunciation—as he had done tens of times before, and as he would do tens of times later—about the activities and idleness of the provincial commissar, Semyon Petrov. After sending his denunciation—this was true for many years now—he was unshaken in his belief that he was "right" (that's what he thought to himself, "right," no longer understanding what he was right about: monarchism, the bourgeois republic or power in general, or perhaps the triumph of spite), and then he went to see Markell Markellych. They had settled their differences long ago. Manichka Yepich was true to Yefim Sidorych as before—possibly because there weren't any other suitors. There was this one commissar-suitor, but an incomprehensibly disgraceful rumor about Manichka spread about—and the suitors disappeared. She lost some weight but quickly gained it back and began to wait for Yefim Sidorych again. Markell Markellych became a defender of human rights and in important moments loved to say, as he turned to the judges: "Your proletarian self-awareness should move with the rhythm of the epoch. Now look: Egypt. . . . " Zhilenkov was already the director-curator of the museum and an expert in confiscated valuables. Winking and sniggering, he brought Yefim Sidorych a small document that clearly proved that Ye. S. Chizhov had bought the "Napoleon" furniture with his hard-earned money, that it did not present any special value, and that, it would appear, people who knew art would not object to the return of this "Napoleon" furniture to its rightful owner. Markell Markellych obtained a similar piece of paper from the trade union; and later, when Yefim Sidorych joined the cooperative, even the cooperative confirmed the petitions on Yefim Sidorych's behalf by people both in the world of art and in trade union work. Yefim Sidorych kept an eye on the life of Commissar S. G. Petrov—his life was not a happy one! The commissar, apparently, was bored: he drank a lot, played cards from time to time, and sang military songs in the morning. His voice got more and more hoarse, and his body grew corpulent, and he no longer had the same nimbleness when, slamming the gate shut, he would run to his wife. And his wife, too, had aged noticeably: her cheeks now drooped, and she had begun to wear dressing gowns and had stopped reminiscing about Poland.

And so it happened once that the commissar shouted profanities at some workers who were drunk and installing a water main during the night. Yefim Sidorych informed on him. Before, a few years back, he would inform on only what he knew for sure about the commissar, but now he would write a denunciation on any rumor! His respect for power and his fear of it were disappearing; he saw that it was possible to dupe this power just as easily as he had previously duped state institutions or merchants. The commissar was called to a Party trial (it's not known whether it was because of the workers or because people were chattering about his involvement in an opposition group), and the commissar was sent off to the North! He left ingloriously, and his secretaries and many drinking buddies abandoned him. The watchman from the *ispolkom*, in his worn-out morocco leather shoes, came to say good-bye to Commissar Petrov. The mansion stood empty for two days, and on the third day two carts drove up to its iron fence; Yefim Sidorych and his bride-to-be were sitting in them! An official from the *ispolkom* opened the doors: "Yes, of course, it's vital to reupholster the furniture, but the furniture itself doesn't demand any particularly major restoration." Zhilenkov silently congratulated Yefim Sidorych and silently stood by the *zags*[5] where Ye. S. Chizhov and M. Yepich had gone to record their triumph. Then the newlyweds, after inving him to a wedding celebration at their place in the *volost*, drove out on the main road to the country. Markell Markellych, with tears in his eyes, watched them leave, and when the wagons and the gig with the young couple had disappeared from view, he turned to Zhilenkov. "We're getting old," said Markell Markellych, sighing. Zhilenkov looked at him angrily and suspiciously, and then gave a frightened and amiable smile.

In the morning Yefim Sidorych woke up before anyone else. He opened the window wide. Before him stretched the *volost* square, and the huge yellow sign of the cooperative where he worked glistened with dew in the bright sunshine. He turned around: splendid furniture—decorated with bronze, flourishes, and wood from foreign lands, its silks and braids rustling, filled all the rooms. Behind the partition slept his faithful wife; her even breathing was strong and managerial; she had a right to sleep like that because throughout the many trials she had to bear she had preserved her loyalty. Yefim Sidorych took some raspberry preserves from the cupboard. On the porch Katerina Petrovna was setting up the samovar. Yefim Sidorych drank his tea, cup after cup, and looked at the splendid road that led to the *volost*. The dark dust resembled silk, which is so essential for furniture and for happiness! Yefim Sidorych's heart was filled with a peaceful, triumphant expectation. Outside the window a tree sang a song with a lisp and birds flew silently among the branches, inaudibly flapping their warm and fluffy wings.

1928

1

Tannery owner Mikhail Denisovich Lobanov had many plants in Moscow as well as in other cities. He had a long and low-built house, with such a huge number of rooms that people constantly got lost in them, and yet Mikhail Denisovich's wife, whom he nicknamed Sophia the Wise, always complained that they needed one more room. He had a lot of business connections and had earned a good credit rating, but for some reason he had little faith in the power his business brought him, although there weren't, and couldn't be, any reasons for doubt. His relations with his wife were amicable; they had quarreled only once, when his wife, with her large crystal eyes in which newspaper truths invariably glistened and were reflected, after reading an article by some eminent professor striving to prove that it was time for Russia to enter the American market, got all inspired and demanded that Lobanov immediately enter the American market and, since they had been planning for a long time to go abroad, that he invest appropriate sums of money in foreign enterprises. Lobanov refused to put his money into foreign business, but so as not to continue the argument with his wife, he proposed a mutually convenient solution to her: he would deposit a set sum of money in a running account in one of the American banks, a sum that would appear to indicate the possibility of his playing a part in a number of American enterprises. His wife agreed. Right away there appeared a Mr. Rister, a representative of an American bank, a man already on in years with bushy and short eyebrows that somehow resembled pills. Mr. Rister turned out to be a very obliging and a very well-informed man, who, with his flowing speech, argued that people's salvation lay only in depositing in the Express Bank sums of money in keeping with their social position, and Lobanov agreed to participate in this salvation not without some satisfaction. Nevertheless, he didn't risk a large sum!

He was constantly gnawed by worry; he was even afraid of being sick because then no one could make any sense out of what was going on in the house and the frightening truth was becoming clear to the whole household staff—that in the matter of the leather business no one except Mikhail Denisovich understood anything or even dared to understand. And so he was afraid to lie in bed and imagine what would happen to his tanneries without him and where his money would go, and those thoughts weren't made any easier by the joy he derived from work, when bundles of dirty and foul-smelling hides were brought to the warehouses, still carrying bits of earth from Mongolia, Turkestan, or the Urals, lands he kept intending to visit but never had enough time for. And these dirty and repugnant hides were quickly converted into pieces of his fame, heavy and gleaming like bronze, and his factory's name resounded through half the world!

Sometimes, finding it unbearably difficult to suppress his worries, Lobanov would take to drink, and then his pallid face, the color of blotting paper, with unhealthy-looking sagging red cheeks, and his terribly thin and long body, for which the shop assistants dubbed him "the candle holder," filled with clarity. Sophia the Wise, with her crystal eyes sparkling and shaking her finger—the most memorable detail in her whole figure was this neat little index finger resembling a stalk of wheat—would come to scold him. She would look mournfully at the package of letters left unanswered, and at the litter and dirt, which, for some reason, she hadn't noticed till just now! . . . But his system didn't tolerate vodka very well and the hardest thing for him was "to down a drink the following morning for his hangover." He'd stare a long time at the vodka, which he'd pour into a glass so he could down it in one gulp, and only when he'd hear his wife's guarded steps, and remember her excited crystal eyes with reflections of newspaper truths reflected in them, would he hold his nose with his fingers to block the smell and then take long gulps until everything again became clear and simple for him. Then he would sit down by the window of his tiny workroom and again think it strange that his huge and low-built house, with its endless number of tastelessly decorated rooms, could be occupied by people who were virtual strangers to him, the owner, and that he lived and worked in the tiniest room of all and rarely felt the desire to go into the so-called "front" rooms. Here come his children, his son and daughter—who knows why and what they're studying—entering the gates on horseback. They have poor riding posture, but the caretaker, using a miserable broom to sweep autumn linden-tree leaves of an extraordinary color into a metal dustpan, and not understanding that these people are riding horseback very ungracefully and lethargically, bows humbly and low to them. The children have galloped through the gate, and the caretaker continues to gather the unusually beautiful leaves, thinking like everyone else that these leaves are trash and rubbish.

2

During the Revolution Lobanov lost everything: his factories, his house, his wife and children. But after a while—it is difficult to specify more precisely, because some people suffer a year and others a month or a day—Lobanov began to sort through what had happened. This process of sorting was hindered the longest time and most of all by thoughts of his deceased wife, Sophia the Wise, with her little raised finger. His son was killed at the front, and his daughter left for Ukraine with a pilot and lived there so happily, apparently, that she had no interest in her father. He was evicted a long time ago from his long house, which he left mournfully and couldn't forget for a long time; he kept confusing the side streets and walking out on Pyatnitskaya Street. His factories were taken over a long time ago, and his money safe and his "famous" checkbook from the Express Bank, because of which he'd had the only quarrel with his wife, were taken away. Little by little Lobanov recovered. One of his former shopmen gave him a recommendation, and he began to work in his former field of specialization in the appropriate trust. He married the widow Maria Ivanovna, who had at one time worked for his late wife, Sophia the Wise. Maria Ivanovna was a simple woman with a broad back, which led everyone to call her a freight handler; one didn't have to argue with her about newspaper truths; she held to one truth to which it was not difficult to adjust: man, above all, must have a full stomach and be clothed so that he's warm, and the rest will take care of itself. Lobanov got used to and even grew to love the communal apartment with its constant quarrels and opportunity to observe children growing up, adults changing and people gradually mastering the art of maintaining one's own dignity, that art which is so characteristic of the people of our country.

Lobanov got very involved in his new business and quickly became an important specialist. He attended a lot of different meetings, wrote reports, expressed his opinions, and quickly began to notice that now much that had hindered his work before was discarded, and that first of all it was money that was discarded, because his salary sufficed only for clothing and keeping himself warm; you couldn't possibly consider it money, when earlier, for example, he could give his children toys like a railroad running through eight rooms with rails and signals and a real locomotive. He understood to what extent his thinking had been muddled by his earlier wealth, which, moreover, the people surrounding him used and used unwisely; and it was this lack of wisdom, as he understood it now, that had both angered and preoccupied him most of all. It was for this reason that he would start drinking before, and this was why his business deals, which he had intended to complete in the near future, often fell through. Now he gradually lost his habit for vodka, and should he get sick, he could be sick in peace and not go through his illness with drinking bouts and sighs.

He was lying down. The room was quiet. He had found peace. From all his former riches and opulence there survived only the bamboo screen behind which his wife, Maria Ivanovna, was in fact sleeping. Herons with very long necks are guarding her sleep, herons on rose silk, sold to him sometime in the past as a piece of ancient Japanese art, but on which he had recently found a German label; and that which would have angered him earlier now only made him laugh. . . . Children are playing in the hallway, and children are also playing outside, and under the window, as soon as you open one of the panes wide, the caretaker is complaining that everywhere you look and at every step twins are being born, and he said this in such a hurt voice as if these twins were being born to him. Through the window Lobanov saw the sky, which looked like a tree that had lain a long time in water. His thinking was that whether things were going well or poorly in the trust, the thing was that people were replacing him and not complaining about his illnesses, and it was amusing to remember to what extent there, in his former life, people had been afraid of his illness and to what extent now young specialists were even glad when he was ill and glad to try their hand at running a complex and responsibly filled venture.

Only one thing somewhat disconcerted Lobanov: now, just as before, he believed that the most wonderful accomplishment of man was the opportunity he had of moving from place to place and seeing oceans, unknown islands, people, forests and steppes, but to travel—which he had wanted to do a long time ago and which, he rationalized, he had never quite managed for lack of time—was still as impossible for him now as before. But even this disconcerting thought suddenly found a positive resolution: he was told that the trust wanted to send him, Lobanov, to Paris to hold talks with French firms that wanted to place an order, worth a huge sum of money, for a consignment of calf hides, which were just coming into fashion. Out of those hides they made coats and purses for Parisian ladies, which is to say, for the ladies of the entire so-called civilized world. Lobanov, after listening to the proposal and agreeing to go, for the first time after many years walked up to the mirror in the trust's front office, where he could see his whole figure (at home he saw himself only when he shaved, and then he saw only his beard and his somewhat bulging eyes), and here, examining himself, he had to admit that he looked younger and that his skin, with that unhealthy color resembling blotting paper, now had smoothed out and taken on a fresher look.

3

In Paris his friends took him, like all visitors, to the Place de l'Etoile, where the ashes of the Unknown Soldier are buried and into which twelve streets continuously pour twelve streams of cars. These twelve streets appeared motionless to him, all strangely resembling one another, and cars similar to each other moved motionlessly in the smell of gasoline fumes. These streets reminded him of the faces of company owners he had met immediately after his arrival and with whom he, conscious of his superiority over them, had talked today about hides and trade. He sensed in their faces that same anxiety that had possessed him previously, and he understood that these people, as had also been true of himself earlier, saw little of life, and that they had little appreciation of it, be it only of its physical aspect. They all have disgustingly good digestion, their glossy faces are carefully shaved and powdered, but spiritually they are closed and lonely. Lobanov knew very few truths, but those he did know he now knew with certainty; he could enjoy his knowledge with assurance and confidence, but they knew even less than he did. . . .

He bought a brightly colored postcard with the Tomb of the Unknown Soldier and decided to send the postcard to his wife. And on the postcard a crowd of brightly colored cars stood out in a motionless and strange way, and the Arc de Triomphe resembled a horseshoe. Lobanov bid good-bye to his friends, who were somewhat surprised that he had not expressed his wonder and excitement at the sight of the Place de l'Etoile, and went into a café. He wanted to buy neckties, since all his co-workers in Moscow had asked him to bring as many ties as possible from Paris, but in the shop windows he passed there were such unappealing and gaily colored materials that it seemed strange and funny to him to think that in Moscow you would put such bright and tasteless rags around your neck. And in the café much seemed funny and strange to him, and he remembered with pleasure that Maria Ivanovna had not asked him to bring her anything from Paris, and that in general Paris didn't even exist for her, and that in her understanding of things, Mikhail Denisovich had gone off on some long business trip a bit farther away than the Volga. Lobanov drank a glass of bad strong coffee, which he was no longer used to drinking, and decided that he must buy the ties in stores located somewhere on the outskirts of the city. He got up, intending to head for the subway, when he caught sight of a building in front of him, not far from the Opera, with the sign "Express Bank."

At first he had an unpleasant sensation, but then he began to cheer up. He remembered that funny Mr. Rister, with the strange eyebrows that looked like pills separately wrapped in paper; he remembered with what a knife-sharp crease his trousers had been pressed and how proud he'd been of his America. He wanted to find out: is that Mr. Rister still alive and will he recognize his former client? He walked in. Immediately and with unusual courtesy he was informed that Rister was well and thriving, that he had received an important post, and that if it were convenient he could receive Mr. Lobanov in three minutes. And in precisely three minutes he was asked to go on in and doors were opened wide for him with the utmost courtesy. Mr. Rister received him politely, but now the politeness was more restrained and more appropriate than that of the office employees who had received Lobanov downstairs. Rister's amusing eyebrows now completely resembled pills separately wrapped in paper, and what's more, if such a comparison can be made, pills that had grown thoroughly moldy from the passing of time and neglect. He was dressed casually in a standard American suit, which Americans are so proud of, but he was even more proud of his country across the Atlantic, of his well-being, and the fact that he didn't understand a damn thing about what was going on in Russia and was not obligated to understand. Mr. Rister immediately said, "You see, Mr. Lobanov, how good it is that you listened to your wife and deposited your money in our bank."

It was unpleasant for Lobanov to acknowledge to himself that the American would change his tone and conversation about the money as soon as he found out that his client was a Soviet citizen, and so Lobanov said as simply as he could, "What's so good about it—it's gone, all the same."

And then Rister said what he had decided to say the minute he found out who had come to see him, "Even if a flood were to cover the earth, even then your money would be safe with us. Of course, I know your papers were confiscated and perhaps even your name is different now, but I know and remember your face, and that's enough for you to receive the seventy-five thousand in your running account with us."

He looked around with pleasure at the furniture in his office and repeated, "Yes, seventy-five thousand plus the interest due you."

4

"Seventy-five thousand dollars?"

"Yes."

Mr. Rister was astounded that Lobanov didn't know how much money he had in his running account, but he attributed his ignorance to those spiritual difficulties Lobanov had experienced and was still experiencing. Mr. Rister felt a respect for those imaginary patches with which Lobanov's suit was covered. Rister in agitation walked the length of his narrow office, furnished with the big and uncomfortable furniture, which is so standard for all large firms and banks, and which everyone knows is both unattractive and uncomfortable but nevertheless continues to be used in furnishing offices. Rister was left with his opinion and impression even when Lobanov tugged at his jacket that fit him well anyway and said that he'd drop by the bank in the next few days.

Lobanov sat bored and tired in the metro. The world no longer seemed to him as clear and simple as it had been recently; it was already branching out into several small streams and each stream was slowly widening; and Lobanov remembered the faces of the firm owners he was supposed to meet this evening and those faces, it occurred to him, were, of course, more human and less estranged than he had thought. His own weariness and the stuffiness in the metro were beginning to affect him; the world was not growing smaller in size because of this, but was somehow becoming painfully more precise. His world was filling up again with worries, and with those conversations Lobanov had conducted with the firm owners to whom he could sell his hides for a good price but to whom now he wouldn't sell because he couldn't conduct talks with the same casual spirit, and, most importantly, contempt, which the firm owners had clearly noticed. It seemed to him that he must put a stop to repeating senselessly, "Seventy-five thousand, seventy-five thousand," although he really wasn't repeating anything but thinking of something else the whole time, mainly about buyers of calf hides. He stopped at the entrance to the hotel and an amusing thought occurred to him, that now with the seventy-five thousand he could demand anything he could possibly want; but what he could possibly want, he didn't even know himself! He's already an old and sufficiently worn-out man, but like a little boy he's standing on the street and wondering what he could demand for seventy-five thousand dollars. He began to feel uncomfortable and ashamed.

The street was passing by him, motley and brash: people were kissing and weeping—from happiness or unhappiness—and no one paid attention to them or at least people pretended not to, because almost all the people in this city constantly and each day repeated to themselves, "We're in Paris"; and it continually seemed to them or appeared to seem that they were all different from what, in fact, they were. And it occurred to Lobanov that here he was standing out on the street and reflecting about himself only because he was in Paris, but were he in Moscow he never would have stopped like this.

He walked into his room, which was papered in unbelievably bright French wallpaper of a canary-yellow color with mauve spots. But in the room as well it occurred to him again that he could buy anything he wanted; and since he was experiencing some difficulty in breathing, worrisome at that, he decided that the easiest way of getting rid of that feeling was to order something. A hotel servant with his upper lip pulled up so far that the lower lip reached all the way to his nose, walked in noisily. Lobanov stood thinking a long time. The servant was used to everything; he stood with his head bent, examining Lobanov's boots, which the latter kept meaning to polish from the moment he crossed the border station but which were still left unpolished. He finally asked for water. Lobanov took out the postcard with the Tomb of the Unknown Soldier. The servant brought him the water. Lobanov rested the postcard against the glass containing the water, and for some reason it occurred to him that he must take better care of things. He took off his boots. A feeling of suffocation, sweet and light, again traveled through his whole body; he lay down as he was, in his clothes, on the bed. The Arc de Triomphe was reflected motionless and at an angle in the glass of water, and the brightly colored cars looked both motionless and unreal. Lobanov listened closely and here's what alarmed him: he no longer heard the wary rushing sound of the Paris streets; it was as if the whole city was wearing galoshes. He wondered if he shouldn't walk up to the window, but suddenly he understood what had particularly bothered him that evening, and why: now once again he wouldn't be able to allow himself to get sick! But as soon as this thought crossed his mind, one thing became clear to him right away: he wouldn't be able to stay here, abroad, far from his native land and the job he had today; and another thing—now he was working harder and with greater love than before, in his former life. And finally, no matter how much he tried in his mind to belittle and lower the significance of the work he was doing now in order to find justification for his former life through this process of belittling, there wasn't, and couldn't be, any justification for it! And because of this overpowering clarity, and because of the decision he had accepted in his heart—to return home as soon as possible—he felt a sense of relief, and he sighed deeply and freely, and then suddenly felt a sharp and crystal-clear, ever-widening numbness around his heart.

He rejoiced at this numbness. He lay down and stretched out fully. With complete satisfaction he took a breath and reached for the glass. Unbearable thirst overpowered him; he brushed his hand against something that felt strange. Suddenly everything became clear and simple to him as if a dam had burst and he had been carried off, rising easily and high in the water. . . .

From his last motion in life the water in the glass swayed back and forth, and the cars, now acquiring their true essential colors, poured around the Arc, and the Arc de Triomphe sailed on, too, gradually losing its color. . . . Official medical science, represented in the figure of the old and gouty hotel doctor, acknowledged "that Soviet citizen M. D. Lobanov died from what is known as a heart attack."

1929

The Drummers
and the Magician Mattsukami

When I heard the voice of the beggar, I suddenly understood why his greasy, dirty hand and his turned-up mustache irritated me so much. A slight fear, similar to the one you get when you find in a book the same thoughts that were disturbing you even before you started reading and that you can't put into words—that kind of fear took hold of me. The beggar noticed and understood the pity in my face. This pity was bound more with me than with the beggar and, for this reason, was more noticeable and more exploitable! The beggar's thoughts were more or less as follows: "Suffering over the past—whether his own or someone else's—is not important; because he feels sorry for himself, this fellow, walking by the sooty blacksmith's shop that used to be a tavern in tsarist times, is dying to be left alone! He has faith in his abilities, and it seems to him that he'll be able to tear apart the icy ring that binds his chest day and night. Every minute it seems to this fellow that he has or is about to get an idea or that he'll do something that will destroy his cold sufferings. And if I start talking to him, no matter how stingy he is, he'll buy my silence!" With wearied dread I kept an eye on the beggar. And he, for his part, watched my eyes to see where they would come to rest. "Let him tell me about the deceased," I thought. "Then I won't have to get tired and wait for the denouement of the story. If I'm standing next to a grave, the denouement is obvious."

The beggar walked toward the mound, which was decorated by two brown crosses and a black slab, around which wound a long string of white hieroglyphs. The grass next to the mound was all trampled; a lot of curious people must have visited this place. Many of them had pondered death here. Perhaps I was destined to hear some sort of local story about revenge or rage or a revolutionary feat. But the greasy beggar with the red curled mustache told me about the love of two drummers and the magician Mattsukami— wonderful and happy-go-lucky people—who at one time had worked with me in the Azgartz Brothers Circus.

"Your excellency, your excellency, comrade knight. First, take a look over there, beyond the ravine. There, beyond the ravine, there's a fog, and there, in the fog, believe me, lies the village of Vyazemy, and in this village there lived an old peasant by the name of Nikolay Osipych,[1] who wielded the needle of the cobbler's craft. And this old peasant raised a daughter who was, in a word, beautiful, healthy, and tall like a priest. I don't know what she was really like, but anyhow, she brought only happiness. So he'd do his work, and let's say his work wasn't any better than that of any other cobblers, but Varvara Nikolavna[2] could take a shoe in her hand, run her fingernail along the nails, and immediately people would pay twice as much for the shoe. He'd sew and sew, three pairs a day, only there wasn't as much leather then, and things took a lot longer: it was a half day's ride from Vyazemy to Moscow—as for our forest, a cat couldn't get lost in it—but in reality it was a five-day ride to Moscow, and if you took the highway, then at every step five black bandits would jump out without fail from behind every bush! As long as these bandits roamed in groups without *atamans*,[3] you could put up with it, but they didn't see any advantage in this, and so three leaders appeared among them: the drummers Mitya and Sasha, and this Japanese fellow, with such gentle eyes. He had an Orthodox[4] name . . . his name was Vol."[5]

"You've forgotten, old man. His name was Mattsukami! He was Mattsukami."

"No, you've been told some other story about some other Japanese, but I saw this one myself, and I'm saying his name right: Vol. That was it. These bandits are fighting among themselves and with the Soviet power, and the leaders of these bandits get bored. They're killing a lot of people, but there's no respect, no money. . . . "

One day the cobbler Nikolay Osipych was twisting a special type of waxed thread since, you see, he was putting a sole on a policeman's boot. His daughter Varvara Nikolavna was fanning the samovar, and, like now, there wasn't any karaseen,[6] and in the window and through the fence you could see the moon and the sparks from the samovar. Nikolay Osipych looked at this moon—it sort of sloped gently, like a cast-iron pan—and the cobbler began to feel uneasy. He turned around to admire his daughter's beauty, and her eyebrows were thinner and darker than waxed thread. His entire soul began to ache. Nikolay Osipych looked at the boot, and the boot was awful. It looked like almost an *arshin* of leather would be needed for the sole. It seemed to be the kind of boot that could take you across swamps and seas safe and sound. And the policeman himself, people said, worked for the bandits. "What's this?" thought Nikolay Osipych. "We've lived and broken bread, and now even this boot has an uneasy look." And he was just thinking this when the bandits' *telegas* were already singing on the other side of the fence.

The bandits' *telegas* at that time made a special light sound—the bandits didn't spare the grease—but the peasants' *telegas* in those days howled hungrily. Nikolay Osipych runs out to the gate to pay them his respects. In the telega sat Mitya the Drummer in a pink soldier's shirt, Sasha the Drummer in a light blue one, and the Russian Orthodox Japanese Vol, whose face was kinder than all of the Russian faces, in jacket and tie. Vol the Japanese speaks gently to Nikolay Osipych, "Get a big bottle of moonshine on the table this instant, you old crow!"

In the old days, no one in the village would have lent Nikolay Osipych any moonshine—vodka doesn't like credit—but now the whole village understood: the bandit *atamans* had come for something serious, and the old man received three bottles right away.

The dark blue holiday tablecloth was already on the table, and above it stared three ugly faces: two of them red like raspberries and one gentle and yellow. And below their faces shone the glassware, and in front of it lay their revolvers. "Well," the old man thinks, "my only hope is Varvara, the kind of person she'll prove to be in such circumstances and the way the robbers will react to her." And Varvara walks around each one the same way and says nice things to each of them. The old man's heart sank and stopped when the yellow face began speaking gently and pushing the moonshine away from himself and moving the revolver closer.

"We haven't come for moonshine, old man! There are barrels of moonshine waiting for us in every village and in every field. We've come for glory."

"What kind of glory does a cobbler have, Mr. Bandits? Kill an old man, if that prepares you for glory."

"Your daughter has been prepared for glory and happiness. We've fought and fought, we've killed and killed, but suddenly it occurred to us: Mitka kills because he envies everybody, Sasha because he enjoys being so strong and brave and being able to hack people to bits, but I feel sorry for people. People live badly. Why should they suffer too much? Once they've been born, they'll have to die anyhow."

"You're right about that," Nikolay Osipych answered the gentle Japanese.

"Of course I am. And such thoughts made us feel happier immediately. And then we began to think: with our character, we have little to console ourselves with; we need to pick a wife with the same character. One man said to us as he lay dying, 'I feel sorry for you. Go to the cobbler Nikolay Osipych, he has a daughter, and you will find glory and happiness with her.' And here we are."

"Right." the old man says to them. "Here's my daughter walking around before you. Let her choose who she wants."

Varvara squinted, her face calm, and out of her foolish mouth come the following words: "Your choice is my choice, Nikolay Osipych. You're my father, I'm used to obeying you."

Well, now the old man really got scared. There sit the wide-shouldered bandits: Mitya is envious of who knows what, Sasha is happy about who knows what, and Vol the Japanese is looking at the whole world gently and frighteningly. Choose Mitya the drummer, and Sasha will kill you; choose Sasha, and Mitya will kill you; and better not think about the Japanese fellow. Nikolay Osipych is overcome by a feeling of loss. He sits there and weeps, and the bandits look at him with sympathy, without even a smile. They just wait. The old man gets up and heads for the door, and the Japanese says after him, "Don't you run too far, old man. The policeman is guarding our *telegas* outside. And he's also been ordered to keep an eye on you. Besides, you're kind of deaf, and the policeman doesn't like to shout loudly. What if you don't hear the soldier's warning and our faithful guard takes a shot at you?"

And the old man explains to them that he's also had, so to say, an unfortunate incident with the policeman: the policeman's second boot isn't in any of the rooms. And now even the bandits were surprised at the size of the policeman's boot! But the old man doesn't need the policeman's boot as much as he needs to pray before dying, not that he believed in God so much, but if he's going to die, he should die according to tradition, otherwise they'll strike you down like a dog and you won't be able to show your human side. Nikolay Osipych is standing in the yard, the moon is shining even more brightly, all damp, in tears; and the old man feels sorry for the moon and himself. The policeman's boot is lying by the porch, and on the other side of the gate the policeman himself is pacing barefooted with his rifle. The nails in his boot are like tears, and the sole is like silk, and the old man thinks, "To my sorrow now, I've made boots for people. Without boots they'd have walked about the earth less; they'd have stayed in one place and thought and worried about their own happiness and not someone else's." Such are his thoughts, and he looks at the boot with reproach.

Suddenly the boot moves and speaks to him in a bass voice: "Don't be angry at yourself for fixing me, old man. I can give you some grateful advice for your good repair work."

The old man is embarrassed to listen to advice from a boot, but nevertheless says quietly, "Speak, if you have anything sensible to say."

"Take your daughter and lock her up for the night in the barn," the boot said to him quickly.

"How can I lock my daughter in the barn if there's a sow and a mare in there?"

"Lock them up all together," the boot answered the old man.

The old man went back to the bandits and asked them to be so kind as to let him have until morning to decide which one of the three Varvara would marry. The bandits were tired of arguing; they were sleepy and lay down on the featherbeds; and the old man took his daughter to the barn. This didn't surprise Varvara at all; she figured that he needed time to think, that he was saving her from a fight. She spread out her sheepskin coat and lay down to sleep on the hay beside the mare. And the mare was really young, she kept prancing around; and the sow was the dirtiest of pigs, she kept spattering mud all over; and it was smelly and noisy in the barn. Varvara fell asleep as soon as she lay down; the old man didn't even have a chance to give her any advice or commiserate with her.

In the morning the bandits wake up the old man, shove their revolvers right under his mustache.

"Where did you take your daughter?"

The old man heads for the barn with the bandits and thinks to himself, "I'll open the door, and whichever bandit is standing closest to my daughter, he's the one I'll give her to. Besides, it's morning, it's not so frightening to die!" The old man undoes the lock, pulls the door open, and there emerge, your excellency, comrade knight, three Varvaras at the same time, each one just like an exact copy of the same icon. All three are wearing the same shagreen leather boots, the same sheepskin coat with a patch on the elbows is thrown over their shoulders, and even the same piece of straw is caught in each one's eyebrows.

The old man felt scared and glad at the same time: he'd satisfied the bandits, but he'd suffered a total loss himself, because there was no mare and there was no sow in the barn, and what's even sadder, you couldn't tell who was Varvara and who was the sow Khavronikha. At this moment it began to rain, and the bandits had no time for surprises. They seized the three Varvaras and, without saying a single word, joyfully galloped off in the rain. The policeman took his boots, and Nikolay Osipych was left alone.

At first he was treated with great respect in the town. How could it be otherwise—three sons-in-law and all bandits—but later, when the bandits' fame had retreated beyond the forests and mountains and had begun to rumble more quietly and later ceased altogether, people began to dicker with the old man about the cost of repairs, and they didn't elect him to the governing board of the cooperative; and when his new fifteen-ruble samovar lost its luster, old man Nikolay Osipych grew melancholy and began to think about his daughter Varvara more and more often. And his thoughts were somber and dark. He'd wonder what Varvara's life was like—even if Varvara didn't have a good life, and the mare or sow did—and the old man would wind up getting angry as his thoughts would come to an end. Once he got so angry that he climbed down off his bench, grabbed his money bag, and set out.

A lot of time had passed, but there was still just as much mud on the high road, and there even seemed to be more. Near every village, no matter where you'd stop, everyone would be telling about the shepherd Yermila or Afanasy who'd drowned in the mud.

After some time the old man reaches the outskirts of R, a big, beautiful town, but its inhabitants are all sort of sickly and troubled, and it was awful how they loved to bury each other. A man lives a normal life, nobody pays any attention to him, but as soon as he dies, then they begin. They write music and booklets, and when they bear him to his grave, they weep at every crossroad, and they promise to erect a monument at every crossroad. And they immediately rename in the deceased's honor every street along which they've carried him. A sullen and emaciated man with a briefcase passes Nikolay Osipych. He's wearing a faded soldier's tunic, and there's something drummerlike in his face. The old man asks him, "Aren't you Mitya the Drummer?"

"I am Mitya the Drummer," he answers.

The old man asks him, "Don't you remember, didn't I give you my daughter Varvara in marriage?"

Mitya answers him in a weak voice, "I reckon you did, and there's your daughter having a good time in the meadow in front of my house."

And the old man takes a look. A new house has been built, and there's a meadow with little pine trees laid out in front of it. The house has windows so wide that it seems that people don't have time to sit out in the sun. And his daughter Varvara is galloping around the meadow, her skirt pulled up around her waist, her eyes crazed, her mane trimmed. A ball is rolling in front of her, and the ball also has a crazed look. Varvara just gallops and gallops, and oh, how she laughs! She's surrounded by young lads, each one fleshier and more broad-shouldered than the other. They look at her and then they, too, roar with laughter. And the emaciated Mitya the Drummer stares at her and is envious of the fleshiness, and of the laughter, and of himself for not being able to tear himself away from Varvara. And the inhabitants of R walk around Mitya, looking at him to see if they'll bury him soon, and they recall the feats he's performed. Mitya the Drummer asks, "Well, Nikolay Osipych, has your daughter Varvara changed?"

"That's not my daughter Varvara," answers the old fellow. "That's the mare from my barn. As for me, I'm going on to S. You can all perish alone by her side."

And the old fellow set out straight for S.

S is a large and beautiful town, but its inhabitants are worried and busy. Each one has a pencil in hand, and each is hurrying to a meeting; and at those meetings they see a bourgeois in each other and immediately denounce each other. If someone doesn't work, he's a bourgeois. They show surprise and sit in meetings. And if someone works, they also show surprise and sit in meetings. And there's a square in the center of the town, and in the square there sits a beggar, dirtiest and happiest of all. That beggar can barely move his legs because no one gives him anything. But then who feels like giving anything to such a happy fellow! He sits in his own meetings and denounces himself.

The beggar was overjoyed to see Nikolay Osipych, immediately wrote a denunciation of him, and shouted gleefully, "Hello, my dear cobbler father-in-law. My wife is good and faithful, unlike my fellow workers. They've all gotten jobs. I come to see them, barely make it, and I tell them: 'Vanka Kain was being lead to his execution by his former brigand friends who had become policemen. They take him past a grove, and in the bushes a nightingale is singing. Vanka Kain asks them: 'Shouldn't we go to the woods to listen to the nightingale, robber-policemen?' And they ripped off their policeman's uniforms and went off with Vanka Kain to the woods. And my associates say: 'Why should we go off into the woods when we have a gramophone that can reproduce the sounds of a nightingale much more naturally?' Call for a cart, dear father-in-law, because I can't move about on my own two legs."

"How come you can't move around on your legs?" asks the old man. "Have you lost the use of your legs because of your sins or something?"

"What sins of mine?" asks Sasha the Drummer. "I don't get around so that I won't be considered a bourgeois and my neighbors won't call a meeting about me. My neighbors are bored. They say heroic pictures are playing at the movies and they, too, want to do heroic deeds, but what kind of heroic deeds can you do in S? Is going to court or having a meeting about your friends a heroic deed?"

The old man hurries to his daughter; he doesn't feel anything, but nevertheless it suddenly becomes difficult for him to walk, and Sasha the Drummer says joyfully, "Don't worry, go on, that's my house you smell. My wife is neat and tidy, and that stench, my neighbors have thrown it all in my yard, out of spite. . . . "

The old man takes a look: Varvara has gotten obese and big breasted and her eyes are swollen. There's filth and stench in the *izba*. She leaps at her husband and gives him a swat in the face.

"When are they going to give you alms? Do you want me to work?"

And Sasha the Drummer looks cheerfully and says to the old man, "You have a rare daughter, you have an affectionate daughter. I'm happy for human flesh and warmth. I thank you, my dear cobbler."

Nikolay Osipych answers him, "May you die, Sasha the Drummer, next to your sow, you deserve it. As for me, I'm going to go to A."

And the old man set out straight for A.

A is a large and beautiful town, and its inhabitants stand erect and have proud voices. The people there love to organize holidays! There's a flood, and they organize a holiday. The tenth such flood, they say. About fifty persons sit at the table and sign papers. They're organizing a holiday, making speeches and weaving wreaths; it's such a rare event. In the middle of the town the buildings have been made ready for the celebrations, and a garden with monuments has been laid out. And there's a swarm of people in the garden. The old man asks: "What's the occasion for this celebration?"

"Well, the Japanese guy Vol," they answer him, "has gone and died, and it turns out that the fiftieth Japanese has died in our town and the five-hundredth visitor has gone up to the coffin of that Japanese man, and now we've arranged a public fête. And besides that, his wife has denounced him for being a bandit and a traitor. And that's our millionth denunciation!"

The cobbler Nikolay Osipych answers, "His wife couldn't have denounced him. His wife is my daughter Varvara, and I've come rushing with great joy to see her. Unlike the other Varvara, she hasn't slept with anyone but her husband."

The person next to him replies, "I believe that, although she did something with me."

"And with me, too!" said someone else nearby.

And more voices resounded. Now the old man began to shout, "She was a husky broad, why shouldn't she sleep with a man? Besides she's clean, neat. . . . "

Everybody started laughing maliciously and, for the old man's benefit, pointed their fingers at Varvara and at the face of Vol the Japanese. And the Japanese's face seemed to be saying, "Excuse me, but I've gone; I'm fond of all of you, but I won't take my wife with me—and this is my last magic trick." And he had such gentleness on his face that the inhabitants of A, after peering at it, decided to arrange a holiday in honor of Vol the Japanese. They're looking for a reason to begin making preholiday speeches, and they got so carried away talking that they forgot about the Japanese guy who's lying there and smiling gently. He lies there one day, a second day, and his wife Varvara has already found a new husband and has picked out a new lover as well, and she doesn't like her husband anymore and has written a denunciation of him, and there's filth and grease throughout the house. . . . At this point the old man Nikolay Osipych said, "My daughter's turned out to be lower than a sow and stupider than a mare. I'm going to go, brothers-comrades, to the town of. . . . "

And the old man remembered that he didn't have any more sons-in-law and that there weren't any more towns he could go to. He felt sorry for the bandits, and he took Vol the Japanese and set out for the town of S, and there, above the Volga, there were shouts and unrest.

"Sasha the Beggar," they shout, "has died without coming to a single meeting. He's died and couldn't receive his punishment."

The old man took Sasha the Beggar and set out for the town of R.

I raised my head. The road and cemetery were empty. My drunk and greasy storyteller had left long ago.

Where did I interrupt him? At what point did I replace the storyteller? Where is the old fellow Nikolay Osipych now? Wasn't he the one who had approached me and gotten offended because I interrupted him (why else wouldn't a beggar ask me for alms)? Nikolay Osipych left the cemetery and me without finishing his story about the two drummers and the magician Mattsukami.

1929

Yegor Yegorych's Dream*

(Excerpt from the Novel *Y*)

My almost daylong dream can only be explained as a case of nerves. I, if you will recall, went to bed early in the morning and woke up in the dead of the night, about 3 A.M—woke up with the phrase "So, that's what you intend to do!" firmly fixed in my mind. And this phrase referred to the doctor. He was prowling around the room and bending so much that he appeared to be down on all fours, testing his fitness. His eyes had an unbelievable sparkle; they sparkled so much you almost got the feeling that they could be turned off. I sat up in bed, feeling terribly light and carefree. "Stay there, stay there. I'll be gone just a moment, to get a knife," he said. "Got hold of a rooster for a very good price. We'll cook it, and thanks to it, we'll have a dinner like no one has ever seen." And, in fact, just now I could discern the rooster under his arm. However you might interpret the importance of this bird, one thing was indisputable for the moment: before us was an extremely large specimen with splendid delicate gray plumage like cigarette smoke; it had a little head decorated with a dark blue, almost black, comb and a fiery red tail. Its feet were tied with a handkerchief. It sat quietly, and its gaze expressed something unusually wise, the source of which had something to do with apes, if not man. I felt confused for a moment, as I gazed into its eyes that tried to make you listen to

*Title chosen by translators.

reason; for a moment I even wondered: "Am I sleeping?" And I averted my gaze. The rooster found me again. Its eyes conveyed a contempt with which no man had ever looked at me, and I thought: "No, I must be sleeping. How can a rooster look like that?" Stirred to action, by this anxiety most likely, I climbed off the straw mattress and with my bare foot began fumbling for a slipper on the floor, all the while gazing into the rooster's remarkable eyes, which, I would have to say, projected a commanding look. A splinter dug under the nail of my big toe. I pulled it out right and burst out laughing. "What's with you?" asked the doctor. "Oh, I thought I was sleeping," I answered. "When it's dawn and you're getting up, it always seems you're still asleep," the doctor answered in a happy mood, rummaging in the bag where we kept the food. "Need iodine?" "It doesn't hurt," I answered, putting on my shoes hurriedly and at the same time glancing sideways at the rooster. The rooster was watching the doctor from under its dark blue comb. Soon the doctor got the knife, the kind they call a cobbler's—where did he get it?—tested its blade with his finger, and, honestly, I got the impression that the rooster was smirking. "Are you going to kill it yourself?" "Others will," the doctor answered evasively. And then, trying to catch the rooster's gaze, I said, "Allow me to kill it!" And again, the doctor answered with uncharacteristic evasiveness, "We'll see later." "You don't have an experiment in mind, do you?" "We'll see later," the doctor responded again. The rooster was now sitting on the doctor's arm, its gaze directed somewhere above my head, and it appeared to be asking with its strikingly wise look: "Don't you, doctor, have a better cutthroat than this one?" Incited to action by this unusual contempt, I quickly threw on some clothing. The doctor, impatiently tapping his heel, was waiting for me. The rooster sat motionless, and if it hadn't been for its eyes, you'd have thought a stuffed bird was sitting on the doctor's arm. Hastily leaving our room, we—even more hastily, almost running—dashed down the hallway. Zhavoronkov, with his deathly flaccid face, came slowly down the staircase, peering at the street door. Old women and his wife trudged along behind him; suddenly, emaciated children came charging down together. Then Teresha Troshin, with a multitude of guests with sleepy faces and cards in their hands, ran past us, leaving us behind. They smelled of wine; they were chewing on something, and all of them were staring at the door as if they wanted to empty it just as they had been emptying bottles a short while earlier. Nasel, surrounded by lots of relatives, made his appearance in smoothly ironed trousers. Then there appeared Larvin, with a bicycle and a bared Finnish knife; his brother Osip, with a Finnish knife as well and a cake in his hand; their mother, Stepanida Konstantinovna, smelling of iodine and carrying jars of medicine; Liudmilla, winking and keeping an eye on the people—with the lips of a procuress and a real bitch—oats were pouring out of her pockets; Susanna, cold, weak-willed, with shoes on her bare feet and a coat thrown over her shoulders; old man Murfin, crimson-faced and breathless; Savely Lvovich plunged into the crowd and disappeared; and bringing up the rear, I saw Mazursky, followed by four well-proportioned fellows wearing sports outfits and displaying fists as big as a good-sized sitting stool. "The Lebedevs," I thought, "and Mazursky as well—apparently he's fooled everyone and stayed in Moscow." Not only were those just enumerated moving in the crowd but around each one, crowding on three or four sides of each person, moved a lot of other unfamiliar people who nevertheless were somehow familiar, undoubtedly some of those who came here at night with bundles that came rolling in on trucks at night—the ineradicable element!—and filled cellars and attics with them, and brought drunken drivers and greedy peasants with their empty eyes. It was getting light. Where in the world is Cherpanov? For a long time the human flood had been pouring out in a wide stream into the street but the hallway was still full. The fresh air, rosy-blue with a kind of porcelain shine to it, was filled with too-insistent pride in itself; the wide-open door revealed a court-yard with cobblestones. Suddenly we stopped. A trumpetlike rumbling went through the crowd. Doctor Andreishin appeared in the blue square. "Please!" he exclaimed in a magnificent drawl. When did he slip away from me? And why is there still no sign of Cherpanov? And I wondered again: "Could I be dreaming all this?" And although I had matches, I nonetheless asked my neighbor for some. He thrust them into my hands, not looking at me, but examining the rosy-blue square where Dr. Andreishin was standing with his back to the cobblestones and shaking the rooster on his arm. I lit a cigarette and intentionally held the match until I could feel my finger burning. The disgusting tobacco and the blister from the burn made me shed my illusions completely, and the thought that this might be a dream disappeared; but from deep within me, my state of consciousness weakening, it suddenly occurred to me: "Could it be the head of some mystical sect? Not some ordinary one but one with ancient rituals. A rooster? What does a gray rooster have to do with all of this?" Since I've gotten to know the doctor well, he always shows a rare hatred of everything mysterious and metaphysical, but you can always find more than a few people who say one thing and think another: we'll fool them, everything will be fine and there'll be the fine smell of incense.[1] I began to look for Cherpanov. After a bad night's sleep, he was standing in the doorway of the bathroom, spitting and scratching his back on the doorjamb. I headed toward him. One step, two. Another one: an empty bath-room, and steam rising from the water. How could you make any sense out of all this? "Please!" the doctor shouted again in his drawl and disappeared. The crowd came rushing out, carrying me with it. I couldn't find Cherpanov anywhere: not close by, not near or in-side the house. The wide courtyard, cleaned up and decorated with heavy autumn dew and at the same time somehow shameless and brazen, instantly filled up with the crowd. The crowd was particularly thick around the doctor. "Yegor Yegorych, come closer!" he shouted to me. I made my way through the crowd. The doctor raised his knife (an ardent curiosity registered on everyone's face), the rooster bent its head, and, I contend, it frowned and most unwillingly closed its eyes. The doctor made a waving motion with the knife. A sigh—quiet, suffering, and somehow dislocated—flowed through the crowd. But the doctor—I admit I had a poor view—apparently missed and struck the rooster between its legs.

The rooster flapped one wing, shamelessly and insolently stamped its feet, jerked its shoulder, and gave a snort; I assure you, a snort. Two small white pieces of rope—the halves of the handkerchief slit into two—fell to the floor. The rooster climbed up onto the doctor's shoulder, gave another snort, and—over the heads of the crowd—flew to the open gates, where the doctor once had attempted to rip off Leon Cherpanov's handlebar mustache. The crowd of people rushed silently toward the gate—each person in step with the other—toward the rooster. The rooster started marching forward! The crowd stumbled. The rooster crouched down. Then it straightened up and began to strut ceremoniously down a side street. "Catch it!" someone's voice trumpeted. I started running. I heard the soft tramping of many feet behind me. Without turning around, I kept on running. I remember I had a terrible desire to catch the rooster. But Nasel's relatives, trying to cut off the rooster's path, had already managed to run way ahead. "Let it run," I thought, nonetheless moving ahead of everyone else, my hand already extended to catch the rooster by its fiery tail. The rooster stopped for a split second and gave me such a wise human look that my hands dropped to my sides and I stopped, and the crowd left me far behind. Slowing down my steps—besides, I was terribly out of breath—I now had a chance to look around. We were already on Ostozhenka Street. Kicking their feet and decorating their running with swearwords, the Troshin family ran out, shoving playing cards into their pockets on the run. The rooster was running far ahead of us, shaking its fiery tail and taking broad steps. The Troshins were all red in the face and drops of sweat were rolling down their temples. "Catch it!" Lightly pushing me aside, the Troshins darted past, adding, "It's a routine matter. You're falling behind. What will they say in the countryside?" This stupid reproach worked on me in a strangely positive way. No longer feeling tired, I started running again, at first repeating to myself that the most important thing in any matter is to get used to things, the rest depends on your talent, and then the most important thing is to sleep it off. But what's the use of pondering over all this? My reflections won't be of any help at all; they'll just tangle my legs. Now and then people would get ahead of me, and then I would get ahead of this one or that one. Troshin and his Troshins had fallen behind back there; now they were jogging beside me, looking dust-covered and pitiful; at this point Stepanida Konstantinovna ran out front, Susanna's alabaster face and lock of hair the color of Karelian birch flashed past, and then the thin lips of Liudmilla—but they became exhausted and fell behind; now, in front of the Cathedral of Christ the Savior,[2] Zhavoronkov overtook everyone; I saw a penknife in his hands, and a cry of exorcism escaped from his throat! "That one will certainly catch it and kill it," I thought, but the amazing thing was that even Zhavoronkov was not any closer to the gray rooster than the rest. The rooster! If it lets us come three steps closer, it'll be all over—but what kind of a chance do we have when it's fifteen steps away and still quickening its pace and swishing the sparks of its tail so much that the most chronic sweat exuded from deep within us and streamed incessantly, from head to foot. And at the same time we still have all kinds of junk to carry; we'll fall behind whether we want to or not. We kept getting very angry at each other and insulted by each other's behavior; if someone tried to get ahead—why does he, the fool, want to get ahead of the rest?—and if he did, our general anxiety and swearing were replaced with good wishes and even ingratiating behavior: we hastened to pass him the knife. In town the tram cars had already begun to run; I think it was a little after four; I can't establish the exact time because the clock on Prechistenskaya Square was covered over with an issue of *Izvestiya* for some reason or other; already the last line of trucks was carrying out "ennobled" pieces done in old Russian style from behind the wooden fence that surrounded the Cathedral of Christ the Savior; peasants from Ryazan[3] and Penza[4] were already nesting on the classical forms of the cupola, sorting through the scrap; totally exhausted shouts from the tram windows rang out, directed at us: "I understand when you have to let a deceased go by, or a car, but we're sick and tired of this running!" It must have been so crowded in the tram car that the rooster—by the way, much better looking from the running—did not arouse either indignation or the least bit of attention; perhaps there weren't many swearwords you could hurl at a rooster. You'd think we were running like madmen! We were running, I would say, in a businesslike way, which may have seemed like a planned run and then, on closer look, maybe not. But then, there are a lot of things in life you should take a closer look at; there are a lot of places where you can make yourself a nest; and there are a lot of people you can show affection to!

We're not arguing, Yegor Yegorych, no, we're not arguing with you—take a closer look! Moscow, it's still of average size, but it's supported by its thousand-year greatness; it has already furnished many future centuries with Soviet benches, and it has erected tribunals! Moscow! One is already gone, another one exists now, and there will be still another. Moscow! It's already too late to see it, to greet it and shake its hand before its neglect and disintegration, and before the dustiness of its streets is covered up with asphalt. Here comes Yegor Yegorych running out into the square where Trade Row[5] used to be; he still remembers the Church of Paraskeva Pyatnitsa with its incredibly well-matched bells; he would like to admire the scene a bit longer, but feeling a remarkable lightness today, he has already leapt out onto Theater Square after the gray rooster, then in the direction of the Trade Union House,[6] where, in the Hall of Columns—with the columns resembling stearin candles, and with the chandeliers resembling Bengal lights about to flicker out—there is a regular session of the congress; the person giving a report is already standing in front of the microphone, behind him are diagrams, and up above a portrait of the Leader. The delegates are taking notes; the report is either about a strike somewhere in Silesia, the exploitation of colored labor in Guinea, or the construction of an electric station on the Voksha River in the heart of the Pamirs,[7] where two hundred kilometers beyond the mountains lies India, listening intently to the rustle of red flags. You remember the year when Moscow was suddenly covered with a mesh of scaffolding like a yellowish veil; when at night carts, wagons, and trucks loaded with bricks, cement, and wood poured into this veil; what picturesque drivers in peasant coats, orange from brick, sat on the carts; how the tram tracks made their way out into all the side streets, how blue welding fire hissed over them! . . . Let all these machines, digging up and moving soil, seem naive hundreds of years hence (just like these lines); those factories hurling metal at us and wringing out of man the repulsive patronage of the past; those planes, those weapons, those tanks, and that cavalry; let it be so, but never shall mankind see such skill and thirst to harness all its strength, and such touching sources of heroism!

The rooster has turned down Tverskaya Street!

The rooster has turned onto Tverskaya Street!!

Tverskaya!!!

Excuse me, dear author, that I have so brazenly interrupted your reflections. Apart from the fact that you have forced your way into the novel, appropriating the best piece, which I had intended to keep for myself (we may be close, but not that close!), you're exhausting us as well with your censures, while the rooster has truly turned onto Tverskaya! Wonderful! All the better to catch you on Tverskaya. Stop taking such broad steps! Bury yourself in the post office building; its silhouette was cut out before the revolution decided to finish painting the distant image of the Five-Year Plan. Ruins had stood here for many long years, waifs and bandits huddled in them, and it is precisely in regard to these ruins that B. Pilnyak[8] had maintained to the author that on this very spot bandits had attacked him, B. Pilnyak, the writer, but had returned his gold watch upon learning he was a writer, and, what's more important, they apparently considered him a wonderful writer. How sensitive our bandits are! However, after hearing the story about B. Pilnyak, the rooster jumped over my head and dashed into Kamergerskaya Street, where stopping before the Moscow Art Theater, it shouted: "Cock-a-doodle-doo!" But they're still asleep, those great actors: Stanislavsky, Kachalov, Moskvin, Khmelyov, Batalov, Livanov,[9] and others; otherwise they would have come out for sure; they would have admired for sure this strange crowd and this unusual rooster with its human look; they would have known not only how to get something educational and useful from all this, but also they would have discovered something a little bit bold in the rooster's look: something of animal subterfuge and human cunning, in a word, some new proof, a new opportunity to stuff as much as they wanted into their new system. Empty excuses! The rooster runs on. An excavation: the crimson building of the Moscow Soviet, the Statue of Liberty. It is here demonstrators begin their cries; it is here they test their voices; it's nice and warm here for shouting

"Long live!" so that afterward you can rush across Red Square with stupefying speed and not remember anything, but after seeing the photograph of the leaders looking at you from the top of the mausoleum, waving their caps, to voice the reproach: why didn't you see that cap, that hat, those eyebrows, that hand with the sword, those orchestra trumpets scorching the sun! I love Strastnaya Square,[10] and the monument to the poet[11] whom the naive sculptor turned into a giant; I love, as I walk by it, to glance at the wrought-iron fence around the Museum of the Revolution, and then to walk out on the B Ring[12] . . .

"You know, it's tough being a secretary. . . . "

The rooster is racing along irrepressibly. From here, from the B Ring, the Moscow of factories, industry, and daring opens wide in all directions with no apologies. Electricity, automobiles, airplanes, textiles, steel, books, unconcluded projects, laboratories: from the lightening depicted on the All-Union Power Company to the smallest laboratory flasks of the amateurs; the Empire-style mansions; poor-looking wooden houses with front gardens. . . . But you, whose steel heart beats unceasingly, where are you leading us, O rooster? But it twists and turns, moves back and rushes onward, through the alleys, boulevards, and streets; we have just rushed past Sukharev Tower,[13] and our acquaintances have rushed out from the market. "Where are you heading? Where?" they shout at us, falling silent in astonishment because we're running past. "You won't be able to deceive us," they think. "We'll find something to reap a profit from!" And they dash after us. Without stopping, we pass trucks and tram cars; bricks are being carted past, homes are being built, train stations flash by, trains roll on, loaded with railroad ties, iron, timber, and nails; grain, hay, and meat are being transported; thousands of whistles, thousands of rails, roads, and bridges; all around and everywhere, everything is being built, concrete and steel are being poured, textiles are being produced endlessly . . . I'm lost in thought. Where is he running? Sparrow Hills are already in front of us and Neskuchny Garden[14] has settled into changing shadows. Here, among the birches, this is where we'll catch it, our little rooster! It's already past noon. The river has been warmed by the bathers; boats are colliding, a hydroplane is droning, cruise ships appear now and then in the distance—and boy do I want to gobble something down! The more so since even the river resembles a knife with which, before anything else, bread is cut. The damned rooster keeps rushing and rushing along. What if it doesn't stop? Collective farmers are riding into town on the highway; we are already intertwined in the countless ribbons of kitchen gardens; the gray heads of cabbage are already filling out; they resemble tattered parcels coming from Kamchatka[15] to Tbilisi,[16] where they encounter the liquidation committee by which they are sent to Moscow to play it safe, and the latter city, without giving it much thought, tosses them at Tashkent,[17] and the latter, squinting its narrow eyes, casts them quickly to Leningrad, and from Leningrad they travel with spread-out sides, many-eyed and round-eyed, back to Kamchatka, having nevertheless attained a weak resemblance to a head of cabbage. Behind the heads of cabbage appear the golden heads of the Novodevichy Monastery.[18] Phew! What a thing. This would be the place to grow a little sad; it would be enough to think about the unrequited love for a curly-haired pupil of an artist who came from Tbilisi and settled near the Novodevichy; I had such a thing happen to me, but why think of such failures, just pick up your heels, for the rooster is turning left, Fili[19] looms before us; the rooster takes a left turn again. It's over, I can't run anymore—let the author run if he wants to! This way, devil knows where it'll wind up, be it Kuntsevo,[20] Zvenigorod,[21] or even Smolensk![22] So! It's tired! Yawning!!! Sniffing the air! Exhausted and with steam rising in swirls from it, the rooster has stopped on Poklonnaya Hill. Near it a decrepit old woman with a

hook nose and yellow temples is digging up potatoes with a wood-
en shovel. Perhaps it's from exhaustion, but even more than the
rooster's fate, I want to know: Why is the old woman digging with
a wooden shovel and why doesn't she glance at the huge crowd that
has come running here? And the rooster? Oh, it's repelling to even
think that someone will now make one swishing swoosh of the knife
on its delicate thin throat, and its gray wings will fall convulsively
to the ground. I turned my attention entirely to the old woman.
"Huma-a-nita-rians," came the very respectful whisper of Savely
Lvovich carried from somewhere nearby. "To hell with you—I
hate the rooster, truly—kill it yourselves!" It's better to make your
way into the open spaces and stroll through the fields—and for this
reason I started to leave the crowd. I was stopped; someone tenderly turned my head from the old woman to the rooster. All around it
had gotten quiet. To its very death the rooster will now be surrounded by a wide and tight circle as in a round dance. My shoulder is being forced downward. Aha! We squat down so that the
rooster doesn't slip away between our legs, since it doesn't have the
strength to fly over us. This is as clear as clear can be! It has spread
out its gray feathers, its beak is open, its breathing is hard, and, by
the way, its eyes are wise as before and, perhaps, even wiser. I gather my strength, but an irrepressible desire begins to take hold of me
more and more: it's time to slice off that little head. Good riddance!
And we're moving at a half-crawling pace, as if we're dancing
squatting down. The circle grows smaller—and just when someone
should have lain down and made that sawing motion with his hand,
this strange circle of many people suddenly broke apart as people
let go of each other's hands, and the people in the circle formation
bent their necks low and touched the ground with their foreheads,
spewing out most loathsome deference. "And if I, too, am to show
respect," I think with malice, "then before I lose my last shred of
self-respect, shouldn't I see for whose sake I must lose it?" And so

I raised my almost-bowed head. "And so this is the secretary of a great man!" I whisper dumbfounded, only in order to whisper . . .

The rooster stands bold, happy, and erect, with its head raised. One wing it has put behind its back, the other behind the gray breast of its jacket, in the opening of which are visible the specks of a white vest. Its comb has shifted, it lists to the side and has assumed the clear outline of a black cocked hat, that is, in its contemporary outline.

"Yegor Yegorych," I heard, "enough sleep." Because long dreams are like the utterances of a poor man whose house has been invaded by thieves at night: "What are you looking for, you idiots, here at night when even during the day it's impossible to find anything here?" Besides, the rooster needs to be cooked.

"The rooster!" I exclaimed, jumping up and rubbing my eyes. "What an incredibly strange dream! And who killed the gray rooster?"

The doctor said that to his great regret he did not take the time to find out the rooster's color and who had killed it, for he had bought the rooster at a market both already killed and plucked as well.

1929–32

Introduction

1. Parts 1 and 2 (but not Part 3) appeared in a somewhat edited form in 1935 (New York: Vanguard Press).

2. "The Child" (Dite, 1922) was included in *Great Soviet Short Stories*, ed. and trans. F. D. Reeve (New York: Dell, 1962), and in *Fifty Years of Russian Prose*, vol. 1, ed. Krystyna Pomorska, trans. Helen Colachides (Cambridge, Mass: MIT Press, 1971). "Hollow Arabia" (Polaia Arapia, 1921) was anthologized in *The Serapion Brothers/A Critical Anthology*, ed. Gary Kern and Christopher Collins (Ann Arbor: Ardis, 1975). "The Desert of Tuub-Koy" (Pustynia Tuub-Koia, 1925) was translated by George Reavey and published in *Modern Soviet Short Stories* (New York: Grosset and Dunlap, 1961), and in *Fourteen Great Short Stories by Soviet Authors* (New York: Avon, 1959). "How Burial Mounds Are Made" (Kak sozdaiutsia kurgany, 1924) was translated by Maurice Friedberg and Robert Maguire and published in *Russian Short Stories*, vol. 2 (New York: Random House, 1965). In addition, a small paperback volume of Ivanov's prose (*Vsevolod Ivanov. Selected Stories*) was published in the USSR (Raduga Press, 1983) in a limited edition of 7360 copies. The translations vary in quality from story to story; some contain awkward English syntax, poor punctuation, and literal renderings of idioms.

3. *Y* (Lausanne: Editions l'Age d'Homme, 1982); *Y. Roman. Dikie liudi. Rasskazy* (Moscow: Kniga, 1988). *The Kremlin* was published in a censored edition in the USSR in 1981 under the title *Uzhginskii kreml'*, and under Ivanov's original title, *Kreml'*, in a 1990 edition (Moscow: Sovetskii pisatel'), in which several pages of deleted text had been restored.

4. See, for example, the volume devoted to Ivanov's prose in the series "Klassiki i sovremenniki" (Moscow: Khudozhestvennaia literatura, 1987).

5. Two critical studies already direct the reader to look beyond the partisan cycle of works, although both authors were constrained by the times

in which they wrote their books: E. A. Krasnoshchekova, *Khudozhestvennyi mir Vs. Ivanova* (Moscow: Sovetskii pisatel', 1980); and L. A. Gladkovskaia, *Zhizneliubivyi talant* (Leningrad: Khudozhestvennaia literatura, 1988).

6. This is generally the year given for Ivanov's birth in both Soviet and Western sources. Tamara Ivanova, in *Moi sovremmeniki, kakimi ia ikh znala* (Moscow: Sovetskii pisatel', 1984), provides some evidence that it might be 1892.

7. Ivanov admits in one of his autobiographies that he immediately joined both the Socialist Revolutionary Party (the chief competitors to the Bolsheviks) and the Russian Social Democratic Workers' Party (Bolshevik as of 1918). Gladkovskaia, *Zhizneliubivyi talant*, 16.

8. I am grateful to Vyacheslav Ivanov for sharing this information with me.

9. Mikhail Slonimskii, "Sibirskii mamont," in *Vsevolod Ivanov—pisatel' i chelovek*, ed. T. V. Ivanova, 2d ed., enl. (Moscow: Sovetskii pisatel', 1975), 90.

10. Elizaveta Polonskaia, "Kak i tridtsat' piat let nazad," in *Vsevolod Ivanov—pisatel' i chelovek*, 97.

11. It is interesting to note that Ivanov's contemporaries remember the story, "Glinianaia shuba," opening with the phrase: "V Sibiri pal'my ne rastut."

12. A. Z. Lezhnev, "Put' k cheloveku (o poslednikh proizvedeniiakh Vsev. Ivanova)," *Prozhektor* 3 (1927): 22.

13. Aleksandr Voronskii, *Mister Britling p'et chashu do dna* (Moscow: Krug, 1927), 160.

14. Vladislav Evgen'ev-Maksimov, *Ockerk istorii noveishei russkoi literatury* (Moscow: Gosizdat., 1927), 270–71.

15. Solomon Pakentreiger, "Po sledam zveria," *Pechat' i revoliutsiia* 3 (1927): 69.

16. Leopol'd Averbakh, *Kul'turnaia revoliutsiia i voprosy sovremennoi literatury* (Moscow: Gosizdat., 1928), 130–32.

17. I. S. Grossman-Roshchin, "Napostovskii dnevnik," *Na literaturnom postu* 20–21 (1928): 43–48.

18. Ivanova, *Moi sovremenniki*, 220.

19. Ibid., 77.

20. Edward J. Brown, *Russian Literature since the Revolution* (Cambridge, Mass.: Harvard University Press, 1982), 75.

21. Vsevolod Ivanov, *Perepiska s A.M. Gor'kim. Iz dnevnikov i zapisnykh knizhek,* comp. T. V. Ivanova and K. G. Paustovskii (Moscow: Sovetskii pisatel', 1969), 70.

22. E. A. Krasnoshchekova, "Kommentarii," *Sobranie sochinenii v vos'mi tomakh,* vol. 4 (Moscow: Khudozhestvennaia literatura, 1975), 714.

23. See John Snelling, *Buddhism in Russia: The Story of Agvan Dorzhiev, Lhasa's Emissary to the Tzar* (Shaftesbury, Dorset, and Rockport, Mass.: Element, 1993), especially 213–35.

24. For a fuller analysis of this novella as well as some stories from *Mystery of Mysteries,* see V. G. Brougher, "The Occult in the Prose of Vs. Ivanov," *The Occult in Russian and Soviet Culture,* ed. Bernice G. Rosenthal (Ithaca, N.Y.: Cornell University Press, 1997).

25. Ivanov's footnote explains that the *gyghen* is "the head of a Lamaistic order, the incarnation of the Buddha or one of the Buddhist saints."

26. See V. G. Brougher, "Myth in Vsevolod Ivanov's *The Kremlin,*" *Canadian Slavonic Papers* 35, nos. 3–4 (1993), and "Ivanov's *Y* and the Rooster Metaphor," *Slavic Review* 53, no. 1 (Spring 1994).

27. *Perepiska s A. M. Gor'kim,* 367.

28. W. F. Ryan, "Alchemy, Magic, Poisons and the Virtues of Stones in the Old Russian *Secretum Secretorum,*" *Ambix* 37, pt. 1 (March 1990): 46.

29. Ibid., 46–47.

30. Voronskii, *Mister Britling,* 157.

31. Maria Carlson, "A Historical Survey of Occult Interests," in her *"No Religion Higher than Truth": A History of the Theosophical Movement in Russia, 1875–1922* (Princeton, N.J.: Princeton University Press, 1993), 15–37.

32. In *skaz,* the narrator is usually provincial, semiliterate, or uneducated, and his language reflects the peculiarities, local and individual, of the spoken language, thus making his "voice" stand apart from the author's own.

33. E. A. Krasnoshchekova, "Kommentarii," in Ivanov, *Sobranie sochinenii v vos'mi tomakh,* vol. 3 (Moscow: Khudozhestvennaia literatura, 1974), 33.

34. Georgii Iakubovskii, "Literaturnye bluzhdaniia," *Zhurnal dlia vsekh* 3 (1929): 120.

Empty Arapia

1. In Russian, *Vcherashny Glaz:* the name of a village.

2. *zhamka:* a pacifier made out of chewed-up bread wrapped in a piece of cloth.

3. An area of the Syr-Daria region in present-day Kazakhstan.

4. Sarta: land of the Sarts, natives of the Syr-Daria River region.

The Child

1. Irtysh River: a Siberian river, one of the longest in the world.

2. Whitsunday: the seventh Sunday (fiftieth day) after Easter, observed in certain Christian churches to commemorate the descent of the Holy Spirit upon the apostles.

3. Corruption of "expedition."

4. Lebiazhe: a small village in the Semipalatinsk oblast of modern Kazkhstan; Ivanov's birthplace.

5. *stanitsas:* large Cossack villages.

6. Corruption of "telescope."

7. Semipalatinsk: a large city in today's Kazakhstan.

8. *telega:* a four-wheeled cart without springs.

9. *beshmet:* a type of quilted coat.

10. *auls:* Muslim villages.

11. Refers to Red Russians. In order to inject an ethnic flavor into the speech of his characters, Ivanov at times employs approximations of words from Kazakh, Kirghiz, and other languages of Central Asia and Siberia (he had "his own mixture and version" of these langues, Viacheslav Vs. Ivanov pointed out at a conference in Saint Petersburg, 1995). Since such "approximations" play an important stylistic role in Ivanov's text, we leave them in English transcription and suggest possible meanings in our notes whenever we can.

12. *chuvluk:* possibly derived from *chuluk,* a woven Turkish bag or sack that resembles a small rug.

The Return of the Buddha

1. *aymak:* the Tatar term for district or region.

2. Corruption of the Russian *sazhen* (2.13 meters).

3. *uvariki:* the Mongolian term for recluses.

4. *burkhan:* image, idol.

5. The freezing point is 0 degrees and the boiling point is 80 degrees on the Reamur scale.

6. Head of the Peoples Commissariat for Enlightenment, Lunacharsky was in charge of education and culture after the Revolution.

7. Narkomnats: People's Commissariat of Nationalities.

8. *Dvortsovy most:* the bridge across the Neva by the Winter Palace.

9. *byliny:* Russian epic songs from the Middle Ages.

10. commune: a workers-revolutionary government.

11. *teplushka:* a boxcar with a wood stove in it.

12. Nevsky Prospekt: the main street of Saint Petersburg.

13. The Socialist-Revolutionary Party, formed in 1901; the chief competitor to the Bolsheviks for political power in 1917.

14. *Tengyur:* the part of the Tibetan Buddhist canon in which commentaries on the main sutras are collected (John Snelling, *Buddhism in Russia: The Story of Agvan Dorzhiev, Lhasa's Emissary to the Tsar* [Shaftesbury, Dorset, and Rockport, Mass.: Element, 1993]).

15. *Politruk,* i.e., *politicheskii rukovoditel* (political instructor).

16. A prior of a monastery of the Lamaistic order; the reincarnation of the Buddha (author's note). Although the English transliteration of the Russian would call for *gygen,* we have chosen the English version used by anthropologists because *gyghen* comes closer to the Mongolian pronunciation of the word.

17. Chrezvychainy Komitet, the state security organization, created in 1917 by the new revolutionary state; precursor of the NKVD and KGB.

18. Greens: another group of revolutionaries led by the Ukrainian general Makhno.

19. *kalaches:* small white loaves of bread shaped like padlocks.

20. The first Russian vernacular translation of the Gospel.

21. *beshmet:* a type of quilted coat.

22. *koshma* (pl. *koshmy*): a rug made out of felt material, usually long and narrow like a runner.

23. Judging by the context, *kutukht* is an approximation of the Mongolian *kutukhtu,* meaning "holy one" or "noble one" (Snelling, *Buddhism in Russia*).

24. Samoyed: a Uralic people living in Siberia.

25. *Kirsection:* Kirghiz Section.

26. *patra:* a bowl for collecting alms.

27. *suburgan:* Mongolian for *Stupa,* Buddhist reliquary or monument symbolic of the cosmic order (Snelling, *Buddhism in Russia*).

28. *padm:* lotus flowers.

29. In Uzbek, *bodiya* means desert or wide steppe area. Therefore, *mama-bodiin* would mean "the mother of deserts."

30. A *shanga* is a round sweet pastry filled with cheese and sour cream.

31. Saint Petersburg.

32. Perun: the ancient Slavic god of thunder.

33. A professor from Uzbekistan has suggested to us that Ivanov's mixture of improper Russian and Uzbek means something like, "Oh, God, how nice, how things are prospering!"

34. *Gubprodkom = Gubernsky prodovolstvenny komitet:* Provincial Food Committee.

35. *kurmysh:* a type of grain.

36. In Kazakh, *solai* means "thus, so."

37. *sharovary:* wide trousers.

38. *kiter:* as one of Ivanov's approximations of Uzbek speech, it may mean "Let him be."

The Field

1. Maksim locomotive: an old fashioned type of locomotive, with a large funnel-shaped smokestack.

2. Corruption of "commune."

3. Provmiltrib: contraction for "Provincial Military Tribune."

The Life of Smokotinin

1. Zlatoust: a brand of ax.

2. At this time, tea was more often sold in solid, or brick, form.

3. Peasants wore strips of cloth around their feet and legs instead of stockings.

4. argamak: a special breed of Central Asian racing horses.

5. Orenburg: an area located in the southern spur of the Urals.

Night

1. *tarataika:* a two-wheeled carriage.

2. *blini:* thick pancakes made with a yeast dough.

3. That is, of a railway car.

4. I.e., the slope of the railroad embankment.

5. *babki:* an old game played with the knucklebones of sheep.

6. Could be interpreted as a reference to the New Athos Monastery (Novy Afon) in the Caucasus, which sent people to wander around the country, relating the lives of the saints. It is possible that Afonka's confused mind reads this as some allusion to him.

Fertility

1. *sarafan:* a sleeveless peasant woman's dress.

2. Dialect for Yelena.

3. cow parsnip: *Heracleum sibiricum,* a plant of the parsley family.

4. Common peasant mispronunciation for "electric."

5. *golbets:* a structure alongside the stove for lying on.

6. Incorrect pronunciation for "Komsomol."

7. Corruption of "resolution."

8. Corruption of "instructions."

9. Corruption of "religion."

10. In counting, Russians bend their fingers inward, toward the palm.

11. Corruption of "telegram."

12. Frol and Lavr: the saints of agriculture in the Russian Orthodox Church.

13. Allusion to heroines (warriorlike women) of the *byliny.*

The Dinner Service

1. *fortochka:* a small ventilation pane in a window.

The Mansion

1. *krendel:* a figure-eight shaped pretzel or bread in the same shape. Peddlers would sell them strung on string.

2. *baranki:* made of the same dough as *krendels* but round in the shape of bagels.

3. *shangi:* round sweet pastries filled with cheese and sour cream.

4. Chrezvychainy Komitet: the Extraordinary Committee, later on the NKVD, and then the KGB.

5. *zags* (*zapisi aktov grazhdanskogo sostoyaniya*): register office, where people go to record marriages and report births and deaths.

The Drummers and the Magician Mattsukami

1. Usual pronunciation of the patronymic Osipovich.

2. Usual pronunciation of the patronymic Nikolaevna.

3. *ataman:* originally a Cossack chief, later the leader of any gang of brigands.

4. That is to say, Christian.

5. Vol: literally "ox."

6. Mispronunciation of "kerosene."

Yegor Yegorych's Dream

1. In Russian, a play on words: *vse ladno i budet ladan.* Literally, "Everything's fine and there will be incense."

2. The Cathedral of Christ the Savior (Khram Khrista Spasitelya) was built in 1837–83 as a memorial to the 1812 victory over Napoleon. On Stalin's orders it was demolished in early 1930s to make room for the never completed Palace of Soviets planned in honor of the First Five-Year Plan. It was rebuilt in the 1990s.

3. Ryazan: a city on the right bank of the Oka River in Russia. Its existence dates back to pre-Mongol times. It is mentioned in the chronicles under the year 1096.

4. Penza: a city located on a tributary of the Volga River in the southeastern part of Russia, and whose origins date back to the seventeenth century.

5. Trade Row (Okhotny ryad): located in the center of Moscow. In the nineteenth century and in the first several decades of the twentieth, an area filled with hotels, food and drinking establishments, and small shops. In 1924 the wooden shops were taken down, and in 1930 all trade was moved to another location.

6. Trade Union House (Dom Soyuzov): built in the 1770s for Prince Dolgorukov, this mansion was taken over by the Soviet government after the October Revolution for trade-union needs.

7. Pamir-Altai: a mountain region in southeastern Middle Asia.

8. Ivanov was one of the few people to defend B. Pilnyak when the latter came under strong attack after the publication of his short novel *Mahogany*.

9. Some of them performed in Ivanov's play *Armored-Train 14–69* (*Bronepoezd 14–69*), which he wrote in 1927 based on his novella of the same name.

10. Strastnaya ploshchad: today's Pushkin Square.

11. Pushkin.

12. B Ring: one of the circular roads ringing Moscow.

13. Sukhareva Bashnya: Built in 1692–95 and located on the Ring Road around Moscow, it was one of the strongholds of the Red Guards during the October Revolution. From 1925 to 1934 it housed the Moscow Commune Museum. In 1934 it was demolished.

14. Neskuchnyi Sad: In the eighteenth century, a beautiful green area of Moscow, formed by the convergence of three estates, belonging to Prince Golitsyn, P. A. Demidov (a millionaire factory owner), and Prince N. Yu. Trubetskoi. The terraced gardens descended to the Moscow River. After the Revolution the area became Gorky Public Park.

15. Kamchatka: a peninsula in the Russian Far East.

16. Tbilisi: the capital of Georgia in the Caucasus.

17. Tashkent: the capital of Uzbekistan.

18. Novodevichy monastyr: A convent founded in 1524. In the sixteenth and seventeenth centuries women from tsarist families as well as the nobility entered it, at times against their will. In 1922 it was turned into a museum. Today it is particularly well known for its cemetery, where many famous writers, artists, and politicians are buried.

19. Fili: An area in the western part of Moscow, on the right bank of the Moscow River. In 1927 the site of apartments buildings being built for workers.

20. Kuntsevo: a suburb of Moscow.

21. Zvenigorod: a city located on the Moscow River, thirty-two miles west of Moscow. Its existence has been traced to pre-Mongol times.

22. Smolensk: a city on the Dnieper River approximately 225 miles southwest of Moscow. The city is known to have existed since 863; it served as a major trade and artisan settlement on the route "from the Varangians to the Greeks."

European Classics

Jerzy Andrzejewski
Ashes and Diamonds

Honoré de Balzac
The Bureaucrats

Heinrich Böll
Absent without Leave
And Never Said a Word
And Where Were You, Adam?
The Bread of Those Early Years
End of a Mission
Irish Journal
Missing Persons and Other Essays
The Safety Net
A Soldier's Legacy
The Stories of Heinrich Böll
Tomorrow and Yesterday
The Train Was on Time
What's to Become of the Boy?
Women in a River Landscape

Madeleine Bourdouxhe
La Femme de Gilles

Karel Čapek
Nine Fairy Tales
War with the Newts

Lydia Chukovskaya
Sofia Petrovna

Grazia Deledda
After the Divorce
Elias Portolu

Yury Dombrovsky
The Keeper of Antiquities

Aleksandr Druzhinin
Polinka Saks • The Story
of Aleksei Dmitrich

Venedikt Erofeev
Moscow to the End of the Line

Konstantin Fedin
Cities and Years

Fyodor Vasilievich Gladkov
Cement

I. Grekova
The Ship of Widows

Vasily Grossman
Forever Flowing

Stefan Heym
The King David Report

Marek Hlasko
The Eighth Day of the Week

Bohumil Hrabal
Closely Watched Trains

Ilf and Petrov
The Twelve Chairs

Vsevolod Ivanov
Fertility and Other Stories

Erich Kästner
Fabian: The Story of a Moralist

Valentine Kataev
Time, Forward!

Kharms and Vvedensky
The Man with the Black Coat: Russia's
Literature of the Absurd

Danilo Kiš
The Encyclopedia of the Dead
Hourglass